Praise for *Brave Enemies*

"Readers of Morgan's *Brave Enemies* . . . are unlikely ever to take their eyes off the page—or even take a breath."

—*The Christian Science Monitor*

"Morgan . . . writes terrifically well of battle, portraying the tactics, equipment and close-range terror of 18th-century fighting."

—*The New York Times Book Review*

"A vivid, sometimes brutal, portrait of life in the Southern states during the war."

—*The Atlanta Journal-Constitution*

"With a plot that tears through the Carolina underbrush like a spooked rabbit, Morgan's novel of the American Revolution traces the gender-switching drama of Josie Summers, a pioneer girl raised in the same hardscrabble landscape of his 1999 bestseller, *Gap Creek*."

—*Entertainment Weekly*

"Powerful tale of American rebellion. . . . The novel starts with a bang and never stalls in its narrative pace. . . . Morgan has once again delivered a powerful and compelling novel that is certain to gain him more readers than ever."

—*Greensboro (NC) News and Record*

"Scenes fly off the printed page, burning themselves into a willing imagination to 'dominate memory.'"

—*The Orlando Sentinel*

"With tremendous narrative pace, a meticulous eye for colorful detail and a tight grasp of historical setting and military action, poet and novelist Morgan delivers a rousing and affecting tale of the American Revolution. [A] gripping story of love and desperation."

—*Publishers Weekly*, starred review

"Morgan brings the past to life. . . . [His] eye for detail makes compelling reading whether he is describing working on a farm or fighting with muskets and bayonets."　　　　　—*Richmond Times-Dispatch*

"Resonant. . . . Military history buffs will appreciate the first-person account of the Battle of Cowpens. Romantics will enjoy reading John and Josie's love story and their continual faith that the other is alive and that they will someday be reunited."　　　　—*Winston-Salem Journal*

"Gripping. . . . A riveting story of romance and a testament to the notion that in any honorable conflict, both sides can be hailed by the term 'brave enemies.'"　　　　　—*BookPage*

"A colorful, historically realistic novel. It is a story of desperation, love and shocking events that occurred during the Revolution."
　　　　　—*Daily Somerset (PA) American*

"An important and deeply original novel, ambitious in its sweep, a love story set against a gritty and gripping backdrop of history that gives us a better understanding of ourselves."　　　　—*Creative Loafing*

"While the historical context of this story is stirring, the principal characters make it compelling. We have such an emotional investment in them because they are vulnerable yet courageous, resilient, and complex."
　　　　　—*Our State* (NC)

BRAVE ENEMIES

BRAVE ENEMIES

a novel by

ROBERT MORGAN

A Shannon Ravenel Book

ALGONQUIN BOOKS OF CHAPEL HILL

2007

A SHANNON RAVENEL BOOK

Published by
ALGONQUIN BOOKS OF CHAPEL HILL
Post Office Box 2225
Chapel Hill, North Carolina 27515-2225

a division of
Workman Publishing
225 Varick Street
New York, New York 10014

First paperback edition, Algonquin Books of Chapel Hill, October 2007.
Originally published by Algonquin Books of Chapel Hill in 2003.
Printed in the United States of America.
Published simultaneously in Canada by Thomas Allen & Son Limited.
Design by Anne Winslow.

This is a work of fiction. While, as in all fiction, the literary perceptions and insights
are based on experience, all names, characters, places, and incidents either are
products of the author's imagination or are used fictitiously.

Library of Congress Cataloging-in-Publication Data
Morgan, Robert, 1944–
    Brave enemies: a novel / by Robert Morgan.—1st ed.
      p. cm.
    "A Shannon Ravenel book."
    ISBN-13 978-1-56512-356-4 (HC)
      1. South Carolina—History—Revolution, 1775–1783—Fiction.
2. Cowpens, Battle of, Cowpens, S.C., 1781—Fiction.   3. Passing (Identity)—
Fiction.   4. Spouses of clergy—Fiction.   5. Women soldiers—Fiction.
I. Title.
PS3563.O87147B73 2003
813'.54—dc21   2003050240

    ISBN-13 978-1-56512-578-0 (PB)

10 9 8 7 6 5 4 3 2 1
First Paperback Edition

For my grandson, Evan

Whensoever hostile aggressions . . . require a resort to war, we must meet our duty and convince the world that we are just friends and brave enemies.

—THOMAS JEFFERSON

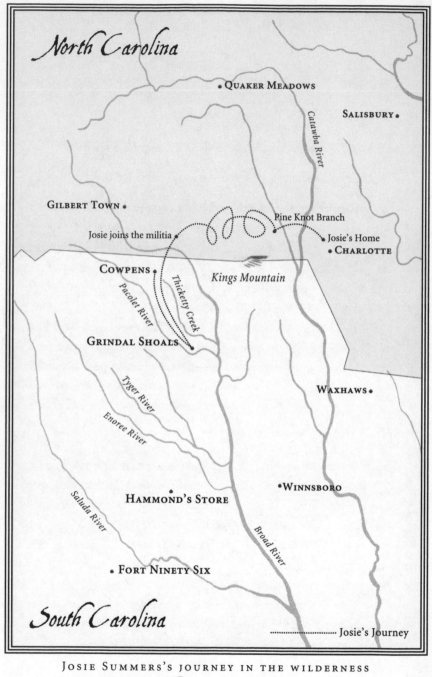

North Carolina

• QUAKER MEADOWS

SALISBURY •

Catawba River

GILBERT TOWN •

Josie joins the militia •

Pine Knot Branch

• Josie's Home
• CHARLOTTE

COWPENS •

Kings Mountain

Pacolet River

Thicketty Creek

GRINDAL SHOALS •

WAXHAWS •

Tyger River

Enoree River

• WINNSBORO

HAMMOND'S STORE

Saluda River

Broad River

• FORT NINETY SIX

South Carolina

•••••••••• Josie's Journey

JOSIE SUMMERS'S JOURNEY IN THE WILDERNESS
OF THE CAROLINA FRONTIER
1780—81

Prologue

Spartan District, South Carolina
January 17, 1781

I WAS THE ONLY one nearby who wasn't running around. The redcoat
threw down his musket and held his hands up. I thought he was hoping
to surrender. The cavalry was coming toward him, and I stepped forward
to protect him from the sabers. Col. William Washington's men were
hallooing and chopping at every Tory still standing. A man's head went
flying and rolled on the ground like a musk melon.

It seemed impossible I could be there. I felt like somebody else. I had
no business being there. I raised my rifle at the Tory, and he never took
his eyes off me. He looked as if he might be eighteen or nineteen. I
stepped closer, holding the gun on him. His face was black with smoke
and dirt, and when I got closer I saw his cheeks were wet. He was crying
and trembling.

"Give me quarter," he said.

Somebody ran between us, and then somebody else. I stepped closer,
wondering what I was supposed to do with him. In the smoke and confusion I couldn't think of anything. Tears streamed down the redcoat's
dirty face. A few minutes before, he had thought we were fleeing and he
was the victor. And here he was with his hands raised. I aimed my gun
at his chest and stepped closer.

"Give me quarter," he said, and swallowed.

I was going to have to protect him. If somebody tried to shoot him
or take him away, I had to protect him. It was my duty to see he didn't
get sabered by Colonel Washington's South Carolina cavalry.

"I'll give you quarter," I said, trying to sound loud and firm.

But even as I said it I saw the pistol in his belt. He patted down his red coat and reached for the pistol. "Give me quarter," he said again, his voice shaking. But while he said it he reached for the pistol, like he meant, Give me quarter or I'll shoot you.

It happened so fast I didn't know what to do. He held one hand raised over his head and with the other grabbed for the pistol. His face was wet with tears.

"Give me that pistol," I said. But he'd already gotten the pistol out of his belt and was pointing it at me.

"We'll give you quarter," I said. But he was cocking the pistol. You never saw such a strange look as the boy had. Half his face was crying with grief and half was determined to fight on. He was so confused he was crazy.

"You rebel turd," he spat between his teeth.

I still had my rifle aimed at his chest, and when I saw the pistol hammer bang and smoke spurt out I pulled my trigger. Rifle smoke covered the face and chest of the redcoat. He was knocked back like he'd been hit by a bull. Blood jumped from the hole in his chest, blood almost black compared to the cloth of the tunic. The boy fell with one hand raised and the other clutching the pistol. He never took his eyes off me. I'd never seen a face like that.

When he fell, I was going to make sure he didn't get back up. But then I felt something wrong with my foot. It was like I'd been kicked and my foot had gone to sleep. I looked at the rags wrapped around my right foot. They had been torn open and blood was running out. His pistol shot had hit my foot.

The strangest thing was I didn't feel anything but a twitch down there. There was so much mud and dirt on the rags it was hard to see anything. I took a step and my foot felt cold.

Just then I saw Col. John Howard of the Maryland regulars riding through the field. As he got closer the Highlanders fired at him. They still stood in a line and hadn't surrendered. Their bayonets stuck out in front of them and their tartan caps were bright in the early sun.

"Will you surrender?" Colonel Howard hollered to the Highlanders.

"We'll nae surrender to rebels," the Highlander officer hollered back.

"Then give them one more fire," Col. Andrew Pickens yelled to the South Carolina volunteers. Several fired into the Highlander ranks and a half-dozen men fell.

Colonel Washington and his South Carolina cavalry were all over the field. They rode down any redcoat that still carried his musket or sword. They carried sabers long as muskets, and some held lances and some wore pistols on their belts. They had gold patches on their shoulders, and they rode easy, like they lived on their horses. Some had sheepskin capes thrown over their shoulders. No foot soldiers could stand up to dragoons. I didn't see Col. Banastre Tarleton and his dragoons anymore. There was so much smoke you couldn't see far anyway.

A British officer took hold of Colonel Howard's stirrup and ran alongside as the colonel tried to ride away. "We'll give you quarter," Colonel Howard said.

But the redcoat wouldn't let go of the stirrup. I reckon the officer wasn't at himself in all the panic and suddenness of what had happened. The colonel looked around and saw me a few yards away. "Young man," he hollered at me, "take this man prisoner and see he's not harmed."

My rifle was not loaded and I had no way to guard the officer. But I couldn't disobey Colonel Howard. I took a step in his direction, and suddenly pain like a scalding hot needle drove into the bones of my foot. Pain washed through me in a hundred bolts of lightning. I knew I was falling in the broom sedge but couldn't stop myself.

I DON'T EVEN REMEMBER hitting the ground, but I do recall the smell of cow manure in the broom sedge. I reckon the Cowpens were just covered with cow piles and we'd been too busy that morning to notice them. Last thing I remember was the smell of broom sedge and frost down under the stink of smoke and blood. It was like I was sinking and there was nothing to hold me up, and the cow piles were turning gold.

But while I was drifting under the field I could hear what was going on above. Surely I was told about it later. But I seem to remember like I'd seen it myself, the horses galloping over where I lay, chasing each other in the field. And Colonel Washington riding way down the Green River Road chasing some dragoons. He rode so hard he got ahead of his other men.

They said later that Colonel Tarleton saw Colonel Washington coming after him all by himself, and Tarleton and two lieutenants turned and faced the American. "There's the blackguard by himself and I will kill him," Tarleton spat out.

They cut Washington off at the far end of the field from where the British were fleeing and surrendering. Colonel Washington saw what trouble he was in and raised his saber as Tarleton lunged forward. But Washington's blade broke across Tarleton's sword and he had nothing to defend himself with but the stump. It looked as if Colonel Washington was going to be hacked to pieces, and he started backing away. Tarleton and the two other men came after him. But just then Washington's black bugle boy rode up and fired his pistol at the attackers. Tarleton drew his two pistols and shot Washington's horse.

The rest of Washington's bunch arrived then and Tarleton and the other English turned their horses and galloped away. "You blackguard traitors," Tarleton called over his shoulder.

They say Washington's horse stumbled backward. A horse makes an awful whinny when it's in pain. It backed away a few steps and fell.

The Green River Road stretched south like a red string across the woods and through the pine thicket. I was told how Tarleton rode down it hard as he could make his horse go with whip and spurs. Colonel Washington had taken another man's horse and rode after Tarleton like he was in a race to the finish.

All along the road there were dozens of baggage wagons and little groups of slaves watching over the supplies. A cluster of slaves stood around a fire on the side of the road warming their hands. It was a cold morning and they were trying to keep warm after traveling most of the night behind Tarleton's army. They were cooking potatoes in the coals. Tarleton and his men galloped past them on the long road going south.

IT WAS LIKE I was deep under the Cowpens and heard the Tories all around asking for quarter. Sgt. Harold Gudger of my North Carolina company kicked one in the face where he lay on the ground with his hands up. Sergeant Gudger kicked him in the side of the head and in the face, and then kicked him again. "Let's hear the British halloo," Gudger said.

With his mouth full of blood the Highlander spat on Gudger's boot and the sergeant kicked him again. And then a shot rang out behind the sergeant and he fell down. I think it was my friend T. R. Heatherly that had fired at Gudger. T. R. had finally gotten his chance.

Nearly everybody in a British uniform on the field who wasn't dead or wounded had given up. The little group of Highlanders over to the right were still reloading and firing at the militia. But the field was in such confusion I guess it wasn't easy to pick a target. The bagpipes kept playing and the men in tartan caps fired again.

"Kill the Scottish polecats," somebody said.

Colonel Pickens ordered a group of men to march with him toward the Highlanders. When they got close enough he yelled to the major to surrender.

"We'll nae be slaughtered like cattle," the major of the Highlanders shouted.

"We'll give you good quarter," Pickens said.

The pipes kept playing their tune. It was strange, like everything else that day. The sound of the music made it hard to hear what was being said. A patriot stabbed the bag of the pipe with a hunting knife and the music ended in a sour wheeze. The Highlanders dropped their muskets and raised their hands.

The cannon on the left had not been surrendered. The artillerymen were trying to reload again. In their blue-and-red coats they worked furiously ramming in a charge. They worked as the soldiers around them fled or gave up. The man with the burning match stood ready to light the vent, but I don't think they knew where to aim the three-pounder. Prisoners were so mixed up with Continentals and volunteers they couldn't fire in any direction without hitting redcoats.

"Halt!" one of Washington's cavalry called to the crew of the cannon. They wheeled the grasshopper around at him and the fuse man touched the powder vent. But I reckon the barrel was set too high, for after the cannon jumped back and smoke punched out of the mouth, the shot whined across the field, but the horseman kept riding toward them.

The artillerymen started reloading again just like they were behind their own lines. From where I lay I heard the cavalryman yell "Halt!" again. The fuse man reached his burning linstock toward the vent of the cannon and the cavalryman shot him.

Other volunteers had seen what was happening and they shot the artillerymen one by one as they tried to fire the cannon. The last artilleryman pulled out his sword and thrust at a volunteer, and the patriot shot him in the face. From where I lay under the field I could see it all.

It felt like I was rising under the battlefield toward the surface of the ground. I was floating to the surface. As I rose higher the voices got louder. I rose past layers of rock and veins of water, past roots and bands of clay and old bones, past groundhog dens and nests in rocks where hundreds of rattlesnakes were sleeping through the winter all tangled together.

When I broke through the top to daylight, it was like a gun was fired in my face. The air was so bright I could hardly open my eyes. And when I did look around, my eyes hurt as if they were scalded. The sun flared in the clouds like a torch a few inches away. I looked way up in the air where crows were circling and there was just a break in the clouds. I looked so deep into the sky it was as if I was falling away from it forever. The air was damp and cold and there was nothing beyond the crows but blinding clouds. There was nothing out there to hold on to. I was scared and I looked over at the light above Thicketty Mountain, and the light drove me back against the ground.

A man bent over me and said, "Let me look at your wound, laddie. I'm a doctor." He wore a tartan cap and epaulets on his jacket. He was a Highlander officer.

Men lay all over the field, and prisoners were gathered in bunches huddled in the broom sedge. Flags lay in the weeds and peavines. Here and there men had started fires and warmed their hands over the flames. The air was damp and cold, now that the smoke had blown away, and the sun was so coppery it was obvious not much time had passed since the battle had started. It was still early morning, but it felt like hours and maybe days had passed.

"Hold still, lad," the officer said. I must have jerked without knowing it. He cut away the lacings and rags of canvas and they were all wet with blood. "Steady does it," he said.

He pulled out a blue bottle and spoon and poured the spoon full. "Drink this," he said.

I could tell from the scent it was laudanum. I took the stuff on my tongue and it tasted like mold from deep in a cellar, mixed with old ink and juice of metal. Soon as I drank it, something warm went down through my belly, and then it turned cool, and a cool flame reached out through my arms and legs, soothing the terrible pain in my foot.

The officer picked the bloody bits of rag and thread out of my foot, but I didn't seem to care. It didn't matter that he was taking all the wrappings off and making the wound bleed more. I'd been hit on the ankle, and he picked out threads and pieces of leather and bone. The cold air made the wound bleed worse.

"Look away," the officer said.

I looked over to the left and saw Gen. Daniel Morgan ride up and get off his horse. He walked between the groups of prisoners, shaking hands and slapping boys on the back. "Benny Tarleton is running for tall timber," he said. The general's face was red in the morning air. He had a big scar on his cheek that twisted his face a little sideways.

Old Morgan patted a Maryland private on the back and shook hands with a lieutenant. "We kicked his arse all the way to the Broad River," the general said.

There was the little drummer boy that had been with the Maryland regulars. He still carried his drum and I don't reckon he was more than nine or ten years old. He stood by the fire warming his hands, and when Old Morgan saw him the general rushed over and picked him up and kissed him on both cheeks. "We done it, honey," he said, "and you helped us too."

He set the boy down and turned around. "What you did here this day will never be forgotten," he said. "I take my hat off to you all. The people will honor you and the girls will love you."

The general walked across the field roaring his thanks to the wounded and to men standing by fires. He stopped at a fire and held out his hands to the flames. Old Morgan was taller than the other men. The shoulders of his blue coat looked wide as an ox yoke. He turned and looked at me on the ground and stepped over and knelt beside me.

"Give me your hand, son," he said. The general's eyes blazed in the light. I reached out and he took my dirty hand in his huge paw. He had the hand of a woodchopper, with hard calluses on the palm. I saw the awful scar on his cheek, like half his mouth had been torn away and then healed up.

"I will never forget what you have done," he said. When he stood up I saw pain on the general's face. He winced and turned white like he'd been wounded. "This old rheumatism has gotten me," he said and limped away.

A cheer went up across the field. Everybody except the prisoners was cheering him. He walked down the field stepping around bodies. Wagons were coming up the Green River Road from the south. It was Tarleton's baggage wagons that hadn't been burned. Slaves walked along behind driving cattle. There was a wagon with a chimney on it, the blacksmith's forge I'd heard about. A cheer went up when a wagon with two big grog barrels on it creaked by.

Where the cannons had been taken on the field, men stood around admiring them. The brass shone like gold. Something jerked my leg and I looked down and saw the officer picking at the wound with a knife and a kind of pin. "Hold still, laddie," he said, "and be so kind as not to look." He picked out pieces of bone red as painted splinters. I jerked again.

"You must hold steady," the officer said. He looked at my wound like a man studying fine print. His army had been defeated and yet the Scotsman was doctoring me. He picked out more bits of skin and cloth and slivers of bone.

"Your foot may have to come off," the officer said.

"No," I yelled and tried to jerk away. But my arms didn't move the way they were supposed to. They were too little and weak. My hands felt far away.

"You'll not help yourself that way," the officer said. He wiped his hands on a rag and stood up. I decided I'd not let him touch my leg again. I would slip away into the woods. I would find a spring in a thicket. My mouth was so dry my tongue stuck to the roof of my mouth and my teeth felt stuck in glue.

"Do you want a drink?" a soldier said. He bent down holding a canteen. When he pressed it to my lips I could taste the damp cedar wood. The water was sweet as white honey as he poured it through my lips. Living water, I thought, remembering the Bible.

"You'll live," the soldier said.

I drank more from the cedar canteen. My body was all dried out and I was parched to my fingertips. The man holding the canteen had a blackened face, and I noticed the strangest thing. I was looking at him and the clouds beyond him. And it felt like the world started tilting up. The ground beyond my feet rose toward the sun so steep I was about to slide backward. I could hardly hold on to the ground.

Then it was like I was upside down and all this hot water and sand filled my mouth, and I was about to choke.

"Turn your head over," somebody said. I tried to turn my head and hot water came scalding through my nose and down my chin. My throat gushed again and my nose burned and my mouth was full.

"Hold his head," somebody said.

The ground spun around and somebody put a hand on my forehead the way Mama used to when I was sick. His hand was cool and my forehead wet as grass on a July morning.

"Where's Mama?" I said, and somebody laughed as if he were way off at the top of the world. I was so tired I couldn't move a finger. I couldn't blink an eyelid. I was washed out and limp as a rag. And then I felt this storm coming from somewhere, like the wind behind trees on the other side of a hill. There was a grumble and a low roar, and gusts breaking through. But the spate was in my throat, boiling and flooding.

"Turn your head," somebody said.

But I couldn't move at all. The swill gushed into my mouth and rushed down my chin and on my neck. Somebody wiped it off with a piece of rag. I spat and spat.

When my mouth was finally empty I got cold. A chill came over me all at once and my bones started aching and rattling. The shiver went down to my toes and my teeth were clacking. I shook and couldn't stop. I shuddered and jerked.

"Get him a blanket," somebody said.

They wrapped me in something, but it felt thin and cold as a table-cloth. I jerked so hard it seemed my bones were pulling apart. The air was blowing through my bones.

"Take this," somebody said. He put a bottle to my mouth and poured in some more oily ink. I tried to spit it out but swallowed a mouthful anyway. It went down like a trickle of warm oil, filling cracks and running along veins and pooling up in corners. I started to warm up around my belly and the heat spread to my ribs and groin. Warmth spread to my shoulders and elbows.

They lifted me up. I reached out and felt all the arms holding me up. They were trotting and we moved faster and faster.

"Hold still," somebody said.

It was as if I were floating in a warm swamp. There were flowers on the banks and a bird singing in the trees. It was a mockingbird that knew all the songs. There was grass way back under the trees and beyond the hayfields, and beyond that the haze of the mountains.

"Hold his shoulders," somebody said. They gripped me harder. A purple moon circled somewhere above my head. I remembered what it was I was afraid of.

"You can't cut off my foot," I yelled as loud as I could.

"Steady on there," the officer said.

It took all my strength and all my will to say it. I had to pull strength from my toes and my fingertips and from behind my ears. The air was on fire and the crows were laughing high in the sky. Men were laughing too.

"Oh Lord," the doctor said.

Hands were touching me, hands on my hips and on my belly. Hands on my chest and on my throat.

"I never saw the like," somebody said.

I tasted the flower of fever, a taste thick as porridge on my tongue. I had sleep in my mouth and thick batter drying on my tongue.

"I never would have thought it possible," somebody said.

I knew I had to find my rifle. I'd dropped my rifle. But I couldn't recall anymore. Mama would ask me what happened to the rifle. I stayed in the swamp, sinking deeper and deeper into the warm mud. There was silt and salt and rotten leaves, and leeches in the mud. I settled until my eyes were level with the water. There were lizards and crawfish on the bottom.

I tasted the dry fever flames and the crust on my tongue. It was fever water, swamp water I sank into. Things floated in the pool, scums and slimes, crusts that shone like metal, skims and spiders. Bugs and water dogs crawled up my britches leg. Mud squeezed between my toes.

I was pushed back and down, and the breath got sucked out of me. And then I raised up and the light hit my face. My nose stung inside and my eyes burned. My ears gurgled as I was thrown back and the water streamed off me. I tasted hot mud and couldn't get my breath. My eyes were full of mud.

"Is my baby all right?" I said.

Everybody all around me laughed.

ONE

DID YOU EVER SEE somebody stamp a terrapin, just stand over it and come down with a boot heel on its shell? Mr. Griffin would do that. Now a terrapin never hurt a thing, except a strawberry or tomato that was lying on the ground. A terrapin is the quietest creature. Even when it moves through the leaves or sticks you don't hear a thing. They say a terrapin will bite you and won't let go till it thunders. But I never did see a terrapin bite anybody. You come close and they pull their wrinkled neck and beak into the shell, and even their legs. They act like Mama did when something bad happened, they pull all into themselves.

But my stepdaddy, Mr. Griffin, would find a terrapin in the yard or on the road, or eating a dewberry at the edge of the woods, and he'd say to me, "Josie, this young fellow thinks he's safe, all closed up in his armor."

I never would answer, because I knew what was coming. Since Mr. Griffin married Mama when I was twelve, I'd been keeping away from him all I could.

"Thinks he's safe because he can't see nothing," Mr. Griffin said, and kicked the terrapin onto hard ground. And then he stood over the wrinkled shell and brought his foot down like a hammer. You would have thought the terrapin was a big walnut the way it cracked into pieces. Mr. Griffin raised his boot again and squashed the pieces so blood ran out and guts, and the feet looked like little wings mashed into the dirt.

"Let that be a lesson, Josie," Mr. Griffin said. "Can't nothing hide in this world."

And then he would tell me to clean up the mess he'd made. He'd grind his heel in the dirt to get the blood off, slap his pants, and walk away.

I would take a spade and scoop up the bloody pieces and throw them out back where the chickens would peck them clean. The backyard was littered with pieces of bleached terrapin shell.

When Mama married Mr. Griffin I was just a girl without any bosoms. I fed the chickens and ran in the woods till I was out of breath. I was a silly girl that wanted a daddy in the house almost as much as Mama wanted a husband. My real daddy had died of the fever when I was nine and Mama and I had been alone in the house in the woods north of Charlotte until Mr. Griffin came.

A woman and a girl can't keep a place, even if they work like Trojans. There's too much chopping and sawing and lifting that has to be done. Somebody has to hitch up the horse and plow, and somebody has to pull out stumps, and somebody has to kill hogs. Mama was afraid of strangers, but she hired a man when she could, though he always left. She couldn't afford a servant.

It seemed the most wonderful thing when Mr. Griffin came. He showed up as a peddler, and he stayed to dinner, and he stayed the evening to fix Mama's clock that had stopped. And after that he came back several times, and then Mama married him.

"Josie, we're going to be a true good family," he said, and took me on his knee. I hadn't sat on a man's knee since Daddy died, and I felt happy and safe to be held by big strong arms and hands that brushed across my chest.

"Josie, you're going to be me own true love," Mr. Griffin said, and kissed me on the forehead.

But Mr. Griffin made me work harder than Mama had. He said a young lady should not be spoiled. A country lass could not be dainty. He made me milk the cow and strain the milk. He made me carry corn and water for the horse. He made me clear out the stall with the wooden fork and tote water from the spring.

"We must all do our share to help your darling mother," Mr. Griffin said. He said it while he sat on the porch smoking his pipe. Or he said it while he sat on the bank watching the cow graze in the weeds by the branch. He said it while he leaned on the milk gap and I carried leaves to spread in the cow stall.

"The Lord has put us here to earn our keep by the sweat of our brow," Mr. Griffin said.

Mama was so happy to have a man in the house and in her bed she would not disagree with him about a thing. She was afraid, and she believed her duty was to obey. She believed a woman just had to keep her mouth shut. When I argued with Mr. Griffin and he raised his voice, she pulled herself into a shell just like a terrapin. She hunkered down in a corner and wouldn't say a thing. Even if she didn't take his side in a quarrel, she never took mine either.

My first bad quarrel with Mr. Griffin came when I was fifteen. I was beginning to have a woman's shape by then and Mr. Griffin fastened his eyes on me when I was alone. He followed me with his eyes and ran his eyes up and down my bosoms in a way that scared me. When I was bathing he came into the room and then lingered as he excused himself.

"Me and you don't have to fuss," he said one day when he caught me in the corner of the bedroom where I was making their bed. I tried to turn away and duck under his arm.

"I'm the best friend you'll ever find," he said. He smelled like tobacco smoke gone sour. Before I thought, before I could stop myself, I kicked him hard in the ankle. It just happened that Mama walked into the bedroom at that instant and saw me do it.

I kicked Mr. Griffin so hard he yelled and jumped back.

"Josie!" Mama said, and I saw the terror on her face.

"The devil has got her in his power," Mr. Griffin said. He told Mama I must be punished, if I was to be saved from the gallows and hellfire. He said my soul was in danger unless I learned to behave and was punished for my pride and wicked temper. Mama only nodded her head. All she had seen was me kicking Mr. Griffin.

"Are you sorry?" Mama said. "Tell Mr. Griffin you're sorry." Mama wiped her eyes and pleaded with me.

"Next time I will kick you in the straddle," I hissed at Mr. Griffin.

Mama's face turned white and Mr. Griffin slapped me hard. Mama started to pray.

"You will go out to the crib and shuck corn," Mr. Griffin said. "You will shuck three bushels of corn and you will shell it to take to mill."

Mr. Griffin grabbed my left arm and put his paw on the back of my neck and pushed me out of the bedroom and out of the house. He pushed me across the yard, scattering chickens, to the corncrib.

"You will work until your heart is calm and you have time to repent," he said. He pushed me up the steps of the crib and closed the door behind me.

But shucking corn until my hands were raw was not the only punishment Mr. Griffin had in mind. As soon as I was inside the crib he latched the door behind me. The door had a simple latch with a peg that held it in place. I was locked in, and the slats of the crib were too close together for me to reach through.

"Help!" I yelled to Mama. But she just stood on the porch watching me.

"The Lord will hold us responsible for teaching that child," Mr. Griffin said. His shirt had come loose from his pants and the tail hung almost to the top of his boots.

"Let me out!" I yelled.

The corn had just been gathered and I looked at the heap of un-shucked ears. At first I thought I wouldn't shuck one single ear. And then I thought, No, I'll work hard until he lets me out. For I've got to get out. And then I'll think of my revenge.

First I tried reaching through the cracks to touch the peg, but it was too far away. I looked around for a stick or wire. There was nothing but corn shucks and cobs. A cob wouldn't fit through the slot, but a stiff shuck would. The problem was to find a shuck stiff enough to push the peg out of its hole in the latch.

It began to get dark and started turning cold. It was October and the days were warm, but the nights chilly. I shivered and looked for the stiffest shuck I could find. But every time I pushed a shuck through the crack it bent on the peg and wouldn't push it up. I reckon the damp of the evening made the shucks softer.

I sat down on the shucking stool and cried because Mama let Mr. Griffin treat me that way. I hated it she was so afraid of Mr. Griffin, so afraid of losing him. Since she married Mr. Griffin Mama had acted stranger and stranger. I knew she was afraid of being left alone as she got older, there way out in the woods of Carolina, east of the Catawba River. And if I didn't have Mama to help me I didn't have anybody.

I cried so long I shivered and felt dizzy. I reached back to the floor to steady myself and felt this strip of leather. It was a ring of leather on a peg, and I knew it was the shucking stick Mr. Griffin had made for himself.

I grabbed up the shucking stick to see if it was long enough to reach the latch pin. In the dark I had to feel my way to the door and find the crack closest to the latch. Squeezing the leather band flat, I worked the stick through the opening. In the house the candles had been lit, but out-side the only light was starlight.

I pushed the stick hard against the wall and felt the peg come loose in its hole. I was sweating I was trying so hard. I pushed a little more and a little more, and the wooden pin raised out of the hole. I eased the stick up with all my strength and all my patience and heard it clatter loose and drop to the steps and ground. I'd been holding my breath till I almost smothered.

The door of the crib creaked as I pushed it open. What was I going to do now that I was out? Was I going to march back into the house and announce to Mr. Griffin I was free? Was I going to take a piece of stove wood and hit him on the side of the head? Or should I run away into the woods and never come back? A little farther west were the mountains and the Cherokee Indians. But there were also bears and panthers and wolves in the mountains. I stepped out on the ground wet with sweat and shivered, trying to think what to do.

Then I heard horses' hooves and voices. It sounded like there were lots of horses. And I saw lanterns.

A jolt of scare shot through my bones, for I knew these were either outlaws or rebels, gangs of men that had fought in the militia or that hated loyalists and rode in the night and burned the houses of Tories, those still loyal to the Crown. Mr. Griffin was known to be a loyalist, but so far they'd left him alone. He was too cowardly to argue his views and sympathies in public once the royal soldiers left the district.

"Halt!" somebody yelled, and all the horses stopped in front of our house. Someone with a lantern got down and walked to the front door. I kept to the shadows, edging behind the crib.

The man with the lantern knocked on the front door, and I saw another man with a lantern coming right toward me. Another with a musket followed him and I thought they must see me in the dark. But they walked right by me to the back of the house.

"We'll rub the polecat's nose in his own shite," one said. It was Mr. Pritchard, the miller from over on Bethel Creek. I cringed behind the crib.

Mama opened the front door. She had a shawl wrapped around her shoulders, and she held a candle.

"Mr. Griffin, we have aught with you," the man at the front door called. I don't know what Mama answered, but the man yelled again, through the door, "Mr. Griffin, our business is with you."

The man with the lantern pushed Mama aside and started into the house. But there was a yell from the back of the house. I held my breath, and Mama ran out into the front yard. Mr. Pritchard and the other man, who I saw was Lonnie Sims from Fair Meadow, came around the house leading Mr. Griffin between them. Mr. Griffin had blood on his eye and cheek. I reckon they had caught him as he tried to run out the back door.

"You have seized an innocent man," Mr. Griffin said. There were tears in his eyes.

Mama ran up to Mr. Pritchard and pulled at his elbow. "Mr. Griffin is a poor man, staying on his own property," she said. "He's done nothing for the Crown."

"Surely you have the wrong man," Mr. Griffin said, his voice trembling so badly it was scratchy.

Mr. Pritchard took a letter out of his pocket and held it in the lantern light. "He's only wrote to the Tories a list of the militia members in the district," he said.

Mama gasped and grabbed at the letter, but Mr. Pritchard slid it back into his pocket.

They tore Mr. Griffin's shirt off, and his skin looked white as chalk in the lantern light.

"Surely you have the wrong fellow," Mr. Griffin said, but a man with a musket hit him across the face with the stock and Mr. Griffin sank to his knees.

There was a rail in front of the porch for hitching horses, and they tied Mr. Griffin over the rail with his hands spread wide and his backside up in the air. Mr. Pritchard took a stick like a broom handle from his saddle and hit Mr. Griffin across the buttocks and back. He hit him until the skin broke in several places. "This is what we will do to the king when we catch him," Mr. Pritchard said. "And we'll do it to Tarleton when we catch him too."

"No!" Mama screamed, but somebody grabbed her and pulled her away. A man slapped her hard across the mouth, and I saw blood mixing with tears on her lips.

"You leave Mama be," I yelled, and ran out into the lantern light before I thought. The men were surprised to see me. I ran to Mama but was pulled away by strong hands.

"Next time your womenfolks won't be able to save you," Mr. Pritchard said. "Next time we'll burn you out and kill all your household. Tonight we give you a stick, but next time it will be the rope."

He hit Mr. Griffin on the legs, and he hit him on the small of his back. He hit him on the backside and on his thighs, and Mr. Griffin screamed. Mr. Pritchard hit him a dozen times on the back and Mr. Griffin howled and pissed on himself.

Mama sobbed. Her shawl had slid off her shoulders and been trampled by the men.

Mr. Pritchard leaned over and shouted in Mr. Griffin's ear, "Have you heard our message?"

Mr. Griffin cried like a baby. He was sobbing so hard he jerked and couldn't talk.

"Cat got your tongue?" Mr. Pritchard said, and hit him several times on the back so it bled even worse. Blood ran over Mr. Griffin's shoulders and over his neck.

"Are you going to scribble any more to the Tories?" Mr. Pritchard said. But Mr. Griffin was jerking so badly he couldn't talk. All he did was shake his head.

"Are you going to betray your neighbors again to the Crown?" Mr. Pritchard yelled.

Mr. Griffin jerked his head but couldn't speak. His legs and buttocks were covered with whelks and blood. Mr. Pritchard and the other men got on their horses and rode away, leaving us standing there.

MUCH AS I HATED Mr. Griffin, my heart was softened after he was beaten so badly. Even if he had done such a thing, such a stupid thing as writing to the loyalists and giving the names and whereabouts of leaders of the militia, it still softened my heart to see a man hurt so badly he sobbed and shited on himself.

Mama untied one of Mr. Griffin's arms and I untied the other. Mr. Griffin's back was a sight you didn't want to look at. The stick had broken the skin in so many places it appeared raspberry jam had been smeared over his back and backside. His legs and thighs were swollen so much they looked broken. Mama and I had to drag him into the house for he could hardly walk. We dragged him to the bed in the corner of the front room, and he whimpered and mumbled as though he was out of his head. "Blackguard fools," he whispered. We laid him on his belly on the bed.

"Idiots, traitors, idiots," he whimpered.

Mama wasn't at herself she was so scared and confused. She had forgotten all about Mr. Griffin locking me in the corncrib that evening. She stood with her face in her hands looking at Mr. Griffin's awful back.

"Will you do something, Josie?" she said. "Will you do something for Mr. Griffin?"

"We're lucky they didn't burn the house and kill us all," I said.

"Will you do something, Josie?" Mama said again.

There was naught to do but get some salve we kept for sores and colds and rub it over Mr. Griffin's wounds as best I could. He groaned and hollered out. I tore an old sheet and tried to bind the worst places, but his back and backside were all raw and open.

I gave Mr. Griffin a drink of the medicine whiskey, and that was the best I could do. And then I remembered Mama had a little laudanum in a bottle from when she had the grippe. I mixed some drops of laudanum with the liquor, and after he drank that he slept. Mama sat up with Mr. Griffin the rest of the night.

• • •

YOU NEVER SAW ANYBODY who felt as sorry for themselves as Mr. Griffin did. While he lay in bed he'd holler out and ask me to bring him tea or whiskey. He especially liked whiskey with a drop or two of laudanum in it. And he liked sweet things, sweet cordials and cakes, biscuits and honey, cakes and jelly.

When he was lying in the bed he'd weep to himself and call himself "poor Charlie." That was his name, Charles Griffin, and he talked about bad things that had happened to him in Maryland before he came to the Carolina upcountry, when he was a peddler. I couldn't stand to hear him weep and talk to himself. But Mama hovered over him and petted him like a baby. "You know, Mr. Griffin, you must forget all that," she said. "You have a family now and Josie and I will take care of you."

I expected Mr. Pritchard and the other riders to come back. I expected them to burn down our house. I heard them riding by several nights later and saw their lanterns on the Charlotte Road. But they never stopped. I guess they had other, more pressing business. I guess they knew other Royalists and loyalists that needed to be beaten or hanged.

Much as I tried to stay away from Mr. Griffin, Mama made me dress his wounds every day. Somebody had to rub oil and salve on them and tie on fresh bandages. His back was so badly hurt it took days for all the blood to dry up. The worst places were so deep they kept bleeding. At the edges the cuts dried up and got scabs. The scabs grew hard as amber and crumbled like pine resin. But the deep sores were still runny and they festered with pus in them. I rubbed salve on the bad places and black blood and yellow pus ran out. I shuddered, looking at the stuff that ran on my hands. And soon as I finished I washed my hands.

"What are we going to do?" Mama said.

I had to help Mr. Griffin to the chamber pot, and then I had to help him to the outdoor closet. I had to stand by and smell his stink and listen to him grunt and breathe hard. And when he went to the outdoor closet I had to listen to him weep. When he was doing his business he got sad and cried.

Because I had to nurse Mr. Griffin, he grew even more familiar with me. He leaned on me and he put his arm around my shoulder, and he hollered out when something touched his back or backside. He leaned his head on my shoulder and called me his lass. His arms were strong, even though his back had sores all over.

"The blackguards near killed me," he liked to say.

I guess my feelings about Mr. Griffin changed a little while I took care of him. You can't feel hate for somebody you're caring for. You can't feel hate for somebody that needs you, and if you're doing for somebody you have to have sympathy for them.

I found that I liked to help somebody in pain and need, even Mr. Griffin. I liked to nurse the hurt and sick. To nurse somebody makes you feel more hopeful about yourself, and stronger. A sweetness came into me as I did for Mr. Griffin. I told myself I was doing it for Mama, and I *was* doing it for Mama. Mama herself just stood and looked out the window a lot of the time. She couldn't seem to decide what she wanted to do. She was more and more distracted. But a sweetness flowed through me because I was helping a body in need.

I brought Mr. Griffin things to eat, and I brought him tea. I emptied his chamber pot and I brought him drops of laudanum in water and in whiskey.

Mama continued to act stranger and stranger after Mr. Griffin was beaten by the rebels. She would ask me to do every little thing, and she just stood by the window looking down the road.

"They are coming," she would say.

"Who is coming?" I said.

But she wouldn't say who it was she expected. I guessed it was Mr. Pritchard and his band, but they rode mostly at night. Mama stood at the window in broad daylight watching the road while I carried water from the spring and heated it in the pot in the backyard and did the washing. I dusted inside the house and scrubbed the floor.

"Gather the eggs and scatter chicken corn," Mama said. But she never took her eyes off the road.

"Nobody is coming," I said.

"They will be here," Mama said. Billy Saunders drove by in his cart loaded with hay, and then there was nobody.

ONE DAY MAMA LOOKED down at the floor and saw a big spider. It was not a wolf spider, but it was a big brown ugly thing. She jerked away and pulled up her skirts and her face grew white. I took a broom and hit the spider, and I'm sure I killed it. But we couldn't find the body on the broom or on the floor.

"It jumped away," Mama said.

"I'm sure I killed it," I said.

"A spider can jump a long way," Mama said.

She shook her skirts and she made me shake my skirts. She was sure the spider was on her legs or under her petticoats. She shook her skirts again and again and told me to sweep every corner and crack of the room and to sweep the ceiling. If she saw a bit of lint move, or a piece of leaf tracked into the house, she jumped back in horror, as if she had seen a black widow.

Our house had always had spiders. There were spiders in boxes and between cracks. Spiders built wide webs in the cellar over the potato bin and stretched their webs in the attic. Mama had got more and more afraid of spiders.

When I brought the washing in from the line she looked at the linen to make sure no spiders or other bugs were hidden in the folds. She looked in the meal bin and in the salt gourd. She would not go up into the attic for dried beans, but made me go. I had been bitten by a brown spider when I was five or six. The spot had swelled up and I was a little sick. But I soon got well and had almost forgotten about it. But Mama started saying I had almost died.

"I remember feeling bad for a little while," I said.

"We thought you were gone," Mama said. "We had to keep you awake all night, afraid that if you went to sleep you would never wake."

I thought she would get better as time passed and Mr. Griffin began to heal. I did most of the work and I helped Mr. Griffin to the porch and back. I hoped Mr. Pritchard and the rebels wouldn't return. I wanted things to be normal, and I wished I had some friends. I'd always lived too far out in the country to have any friends.

Mama had a fine sugar bowl which she used when we had white sugar. It was a piece of china her grandmother had in the old country. She kept it on the shelf to look pretty, because we almost never had white sugar. One day I noticed it on the board beside the fireplace in the kitchen. I thought maybe Mama had decided to use it again, and planned to buy some white sugar. I was too busy taking care of Mr. Griffin and looking after the house to notice anything I didn't have to.

The sugar bowl stayed on the sideboard day after day, and once while I was dusting I decided to put it back on the shelf where it would be safe. For some reason I looked into the bowl. I lifted the lid and saw what appeared to be moss or knots of black thread inside. Looking closer, I saw some of the threads moving. The bowl was filled with spiders, some still alive. I put the lid back on and carried the bowl into the backyard and dumped it. Some of the spiders crawled away and some were dead. I stamped the running ones. I stamped them the way Mr. Griffin stamped the terrapins, and when I stopped they were all smeared on the ground.

The sugar bowl had spots and specks inside it, like fly specks on a ceiling. I washed it out on the back porch until it was shiny inside. When I finished cleaning the bowl I saw Mama watching me at the back door. Because she was so worried about spiders I decided not to tell her what I had found. But later, when I thought about it, I saw the spiders couldn't have gotten into the sugar bowl with the lid on. Someone had put the spiders in there. Someone had gathered up the spiders still alive and put them in the sugar bowl. And it had to have been Mama that did it.

THE EDGES OF MR. GRIFFIN'S back healed up. The scabs got hard and started crumbling off like brown sugar. And where the scabs came off the skin was red, tight and red, but it wasn't broken. And after a few days the redness started going away and it got white and began to turn slick and puckered a little in scars.

The little places were all healed up, but the deep places in the middle of his back were still runny. I rubbed salve on the sores where the skin was red. I'd heard of letting maggots eat the corruption from a wound, but didn't have any maggots. I kept the places covered so the flies couldn't blow them. I guess flies might have blown their maggots in the wounds if I'd let them.

IT WAS SOME MONTHS after the beating when Mr. Griffin was up and around again. He was more familiar than ever with me. He told me to finish shucking the corn. I hated to go back in that crib, and I looked at him hard.

"Let bygones be bygones," he said.

I didn't even answer him. I didn't know what to say to answer him.

"Don't be a stubborn lass," he said and pulled me to him.

"I'll be whatever lass I choose," I said.

"You'll break me poor heart with your stubborn ways," he said.

No sooner was he up and about than Mr. Griffin tried to fondle me. When Mama wasn't looking he grabbed my shoulders and tried to touch my breasts. I slipped away and ignored him. Sometimes I tried to tease him, to make it all seem just a silly game. After all, he'd been beaten. And he was my stepdaddy. Mama didn't seem to notice a thing. I knew she didn't want to notice anything.

IT WAS THE NEXT YEAR, in October of 1780, just after the great battle at Kings Mountain a few miles to the south and west. We heard rumors of the awful fighting, how John Sevier and the Overmountain men killed Maj. Patrick Ferguson and all his soldiers. We heard Mr. Pritchard was there, and the other men that came with lanterns and whipped Mr. Griffin. We heard it was a great victory for Colonel Sevier and the patriots.

"They'll pay for it," Mr. Griffin hissed between his teeth. "The blackguard traitors will pay for it."

I had grown as tall as Mr. Griffin and I was almost as strong. I looked at myself in the piece of mirror in my room. One day, to get off by myself, I walked in the pine woods beyond the field. I had to get away from Mama, and I had to get away from Mr. Griffin's eyes on my bosoms. I had to get away and think what I was going to do. Mama acted so strange it scared me. I didn't want to be strange that way. We lived in terrible times and in murderous times. It was only a matter of time before they came and burnt us out.

The pine woods were cool and damp. I liked the musty smell of the rotting needles and the sweet smell of the resin. There was a place where the needles were thick as a pillow on the ground. I could sit there and listen to the wind in the tops of the pines. It sounded like an ocean up in the sky. I shivered and listened to the moan and wondered what was going to happen to me. When the wind stopped and the woods were quiet, I could hear needles dripping off the trees, hitting limbs and twigs like little splinters, sprinkling on the ground.

I knew I had to get away from Mama's house, because something awful was going to happen. One way or another, because of the war, because of Mr. Griffin, because of Mama's blindness, something terrible was about to happen. I sat on the pine needles until one of my legs was almost asleep. And when I finally stood up I had to wait while my leg itched and buzzed and got its feeling back.

"So this is where you hide?" somebody said. I whirled around and saw Mr. Griffin. He was standing partly hidden by a sweet shrub bush. He must have been watching me for a long time. His face was flushed a little. I took a step toward the field.

"Don't be afraid, lass," he said. "You know I'm sorely fond of ye."

"You ought not to have followed me," I said. My mouth was dry and there was a catch in my throat.

"I thought you might be lost," he said, a little short of breath. My heart jumped, for I'd never been alone with him in the woods before. I took another step back. I turned and pushed a limb aside. My leg was still mostly asleep.

"There's something I wanted to tell you," Mr. Griffin said.

"You can tell my mama," I said.

"Don't concern your mama," Mr. Griffin said.

As I stepped through the pine trees he followed. I didn't want to look back. As I stepped faster he speeded up. "I wanted just a word with you," he said.

I figured if I could get to the edge of the field, to the open field, I'd be safe. If I could get close enough to the house, Mama would see me and hear me if I hollered out. Limbs slapped my face and twigs hit me in the eye. Mr. Griffin touched my shoulder and I ducked down. He was a little bigger than me and stronger than me.

"Just a word," he said.

I crashed against limbs and slammed into a tree when I looked back. I stumbled and Mr. Griffin grabbed me by the waist. I twisted as hard as I could and lunged in the direction of the field. He stumbled and lost his grip and I began running again, limping as the feeling came back into my leg.

But as I reached the edge of the woods I saw I'd gotten lost in my panic. Instead of the field right behind the house, I came out near the branch, down where the hogpen was. We had two shoats in a log pen down there, far enough from the house so you didn't smell them.

Mr. Griffin came crashing after me. I figured once I got to the open I'd run fast as I could before Mr. Griffin caught me, and then I'd scream.

But the instant I stepped out into the open Mr. Griffin grabbed me. And when I tried to twist out of his grip I saw the look on his face. His cheeks were flushed and his eyes looked drunk. I reckon the running had roused him up. I'd never seen a man so roused up. He was trembling he was so excited. Seeing such excitement, I wanted to run, and I wanted to give up. I'd never felt like that before. I was out of breath and confused.

Mr. Griffin grabbed at my dress and tore it so one of my bosoms was exposed. He held me by the waist and tore the dress more.

"No!" I said, and hit him with my elbows. I wrenched around and my dress tore worse, and we both fell to the ground.

The dirt around the hogpen was a mess because the filth inside the pen spilled out between the logs and spread in the weeds and grass. The mud was thick as jelly.

The filth that squeezed out of the hogpen had dried and soaked into the weeds. Rain had spread the stink farther but washed it thin. The dirt near the trees smelled like manure and rancid cobs. I fell back in the mud from the pen, and my hair got stuck in the muck and tangles of weeds and cobs.

Mr. Griffin was so excited he didn't even notice the mud and the stink. He ripped my dress off and put his hand between my legs. He untied his pants and pushed himself on top of me.

I screamed but the side of my mouth was pushed in the muck. It was an awful taste.

I kicked at Mr. Griffin. I knew if I could kick him between the legs I could hurt him. But he was on top of me and my legs were spread. I could only roll a little, I couldn't kick.

Mr. Griffin huffed like he was in pain. He strained till his eyes bulged out, gulping air and holding my arm down. I tried to hit his face and he laughed. He groaned and sighed.

After a few seconds Mr. Griffin grunted and rolled off me. He sighed again and pushed himself up. "You're a sweet girl, Josie," he said as he pulled up his dirty pants and buttoned them.

I didn't say anything. What was the use to say anything now that he'd had his way? I lifted myself out of the muck. Straw stuck to the muddy dress and was tangled in my hair. I was weak from running and fighting and sore between my legs. I had to wash the filth off me, and I had to tell Mama what had happened. I had to make her understand what her Mr. Griffin had done. Troubled and afflicted as her mind was, surely she could see what an evil man he was.

As I got to my feet and turned toward the house, I was startled to see Mama standing under the poplar tree at the edge of the yard looking toward us. I didn't know how long she had been there. She might have just come out of the house and seen me getting up from the grass, or she might have watched the whole thing.

I felt so ashamed for what had happened, and I felt ashamed that Mama might have seen it. She was not well and I didn't know what she might do. Mr. Griffin lurched away from me toward the barn, brushing his clothes and patting his hair in place.

As I walked toward Mama I began to cry. It was like the worst thing in the world had happened and I was afraid to look Mama in the face. Everything was twisted. The air was twisted and the day was wrenched around. I sobbed as I got closer to Mama. I wanted her to take me in her arms. As I reached out to her she hissed, "You hussy! You shameless girl!"

"No," I said, and tried to take her elbows in my hands. But Mama flung my hands away and slapped me hard, and then she raked my cheeks with her fingers, cutting the skin.

TWO

AFTER MAMA TURNED AWAY from me and ran toward the house, I
stood under the poplar tree sobbing. My cheeks were bleeding and my
tears stung the cuts Mama's nails had made. Mr. Griffin had disappeared
into the barn and I was alone in the yard between the house and hogpen.

I was soiled and disgusting. I had to wash myself off and I had to get
away. I wanted to die. I stumbled toward the pine woods and fought my
way through the brush and limbs. I knocked briars and vines out of the
way like they were hands reaching for me. When I got to the creek I
knelt on rocks and began to wash myself with the cold water.

Maybe it was the surprise of the creek water on my face that made me
stop crying. It felt like I had been blinded and the cold water made me
see again. And I saw that things had gotten so bad and desperate that I
had to think clearly. I had to be cunning if I was to survive. Mr. Griffin
was evil and Mama was insane.

I washed my face and my arms and legs. I washed between my legs
with the cold creek water. I tried to get the mud off my torn dress and I

picked mud out of my hair. I cleaned myself as best I could and looked at my swollen, streaked face in the water, and then I sat on a rock and planned what I would do.

It was impossible to ever go back and live as we had before. Mama had attacked me. Mr. Griffin had violated me. I had no choice but to leave. I shivered as it got dark and cold, and I saw what I must do.

First I crept back to the shed at the edge of the yard and took a pair of shears Mama used to snip flowers. While there was still a little light, I knelt over a pool in the creek and cut my hair shorter. Hair fell in hanks into the water, floated for a while, and then sank. I tried to make my hair look like a boy's.

After it was dark I crawled and crept back through the thicket to the edge of the yard. I was cold and sore but no longer crying.

There was a light in the kitchen where Mama and Mr. Griffin must be eating supper. I stood at the edge of the woods and watched the lighted window, and I watched the stars get brighter in the wide sky over the house. It was scary to be outside.

When the light in the kitchen disappeared I knew Mama and Mr. Griffin had gone to the parlor. Mr. Griffin would smoke his pipe and have a glass of sweetened rum, and Mama would sew. I shivered in the chilly air and crossed the yard to the woodpile.

The ax we used to chop wood and split kindling and kill chickens was stuck in the chopping block. I worked the ax loose and rested the head on the ground while holding the handle. I waited in the cold air.

Before he went to bed, Mr. Griffin would come out into the backyard to relieve himself. It was impossible to know when he would—it depended on how much rum he had drunk, or how soon he got sleepy.

I moved to the edge of the house and stood in the shadow of the porch. The moon had risen over the oak trees and threw eerie light across the fields and yard. It did not seem possible I was standing outside my own house holding an ax, but there I was.

Mr. Griffin must have drunk more rum than usual that evening, for soon I heard steps in the house. The back door creaked open and there were steps across the porch. Sometimes Mr. Griffin pissed from the edge of the porch, but in good weather he usually stepped out into the yard. I was relieved to see him walk down the steps into the moonlight. He moved almost to the woodpile before he stopped. I heard the hiss and tinkle of piss on the chips and saw the flash of his arc.

Quietly as I could I stepped up behind him and raised the ax. I brought the ax down hard as I could but must have missed his head and hit his neck or shoulder, for he called out and spun around. I raised the ax again and hit him in the face as he turned toward me. He moaned as I hit him on the head, and the skull popped like a terrapin shell he had stomped. As he sank to his knees I thought of him pushing me down in the muck of the hogpen and tearing my dress, and I hit him again.

When Mr. Griffin lay still in the moonlight, I listened to see if Mama had heard the commotion and come to the door. The house was still. I walked on tiptoes up the steps to the back door. I hoped Mama had not gone to bed but was still sewing in the parlor.

The only light was in the parlor and I slipped down the hall to their bedroom. Feeling my way into the room I opened the door of the wardrobe where Mr. Griffin kept his clothes. Quick as I could in the dark I ripped off my dress and put on one of Mr. Griffin's shirts and a pair of his pants. If I could look like a man or boy I might be able to survive while traveling in the hills. I got Mr. Griffin's winter coat and slipped it on, and I took his spare Sunday hat.

I knew Mama kept her coins tied in a handkerchief in the top bureau drawer. I fished around in the drawer until I found the handkerchief and slipped it into a coat pocket.

My plan was to hurry back into the night without Mama seeing me. I needed to get far away from the house by daylight. But as I tiptoed down the hall I hit a broom and knocked it over. The crash seemed to shake the house.

"Is that you, Charlie?" Mama said. She turned and saw me in the lamplight in the parlor door. Because I was wearing Mr. Griffin's clothes she started screaming. I stepped toward the light to quiet her and saw the blood on my fingers. Mr. Griffin's blood had splashed on my hands and wrists and on my face. Mama screamed again when she saw the blood, and I ran out of the house and into the night, taking care to avoid Mr. Griffin's body by the woodpile.

IT WAS COMPLETELY dark in the woods, and I plunged into the pines and ducked and pushed limbs aside until I found the trail. The hat kept getting knocked off. Where are you going? I said to myself. Do you know what you're doing?

When I found the river trail I walked faster. The trail was wide enough for a horse and rider, and there were puddles and boggy places along it. I stepped in mud holes and hurried. I didn't want to be seen by anybody I knew. I didn't know where I was going, but I wanted to get there as fast as I could.

The trail ran down to the Catawba River and along the river. There was a ferry there and a low ford where you could drive a wagon across. But I wanted to cross the river secretly in the dark. There was wilder country west of the river and nobody knew me there. I ran along the trail and jumped over rocks.

It was so dark I couldn't tell exactly where the ford was. I found a wide place where the river was shallow and the bottom was rocky. I took off my shoes and pulled off Mr. Griffin's pants and held my bundle to my chest. As I started wading, the water was so cold it bit and burned. My feet ached as I stepped over rocks into deeper water. The river smelled of mud and sour leaves, but it smelled clean compared to the hogpen.

The glow in the clouds glistened on the rippling water. The river dimpled and swooped over rocks. I was about halfway across when I stepped into a deeper place and the water came up to my groin. The river pushed me and I almost fell. The cold water stung where I was so sore. I braced myself and took short steps. Water splashed up on my bundle, on my face. I worked my way step by step over the rocks to the mud of the western bank.

I didn't have a lantern and I didn't even have a flint for starting a fire. I was only sixteen and I'd never been across the river. It was October and getting cold. I dried myself off with the pants and put them on and pulled the shoes on.

Josie, you are lost, I said. You are plumb lost in the dark woods. I knew there were wolves and panthers in the mountains, in the woods to the west. I knew there were bears and rattlesnakes, though the snakes quit crawling after the first frost. I had Mr. Griffin's coat to keep me warm, but I needed a roof over me and a wall to keep out wind. I needed a scrap of fire to warm by.

The river slurped and whispered. I wasn't hungry. I was too tired to be hungry. But I would be hungry the next day. The little handkerchief of coins wasn't worth anything in the woods.

A shooting star flung off sparks above me and I shivered, wondering if it was a portent for me. I saw Mr. Griffin lying in the yard with his head mashed in.

I looked for the trail up the bank of the river. I picked my way around a birch tree and some hazelnut trees. It looked like there was a kind of trail. But was it just a rabbit trail or a deer trail? There were settlements on the west side of the river, but I didn't know where they were. I knew Gilbert Town was farther west. I climbed up to the level ground and looked around.

In the dim light I saw a steep hill way off and some tall trees against the sky. A bird screeched in the woods not too far off. When you're confused it's better to go slow and calm yourself, I told myself. Maybe if I thought hard and was careful I'd see what to do.

As I climbed up the hill trying to find the trail, it got so dark I couldn't see my feet. Limbs slapped my face and briars raked my pants legs. I strained to see what was ahead, looking right into the shadows. When I looked sideways out of the corner of my eyes I could see a little better.

I could at least see the dim shapes of trees and avoid hitting them. I turned my head and stepped to the side, then stopped and listened. But all I heard was a bird squawking down toward the river. There was no light except a few stars.

Stumbling and feeling my way between limbs and bushes, I climbed till it felt like I was on level ground. But there was no light of window or campfire in sight in any direction. I took a few more steps and turned around, and wasn't even sure where the river was anymore. The dark looked the same on every side.

I held out my hands and touched a big limb. Following the limb I came to a big tree that felt like an oak. The tree was wide as a wall and the ground under it was thick with leaves. I thought I would sit down and lean against the tree for a while and think about what I could do.

Wrapping Mr. Griffin's coat tight around me, I pushed myself against the big oak so it could protect me from the damp breeze. The tree was like a big friend comforting me in the dark, with its roots deep in the hill and the limbs high above. A current seemed to be flowing in the tree and from the tree. It was rooted deep in its place and was calm. I wanted to be calm and certain as the tree.

I thought of Mama alone in the house with her mind so confused and troubled. And I thought of what I'd done that day. Tears squeezed into my eyes and they wouldn't stop coming. My throat got stiff and sore and wrenched with a sob. I put my face against my knees and cried.

After I sat there a long time the dampness seeped through my clothes. The cold began to sneak between the threads and fibers of Mr. Griffin's coat. I must have gone to sleep and dreamed, for I thought the river flew by me two or three times like a big bird. And when I woke it seemed I'd just heard a scream. I listened and heard only the breeze stirring limbs, and a flutter off in the leaves. A dog barked so far away I wasn't even sure it was a dog.

When you are out in the cold your body burns like its own stove. I could smell my warmth against the cold dampness. I shuddered as the warmth of my blood and the smell of my sweat fought the cold soaking in through the clothes. My skin tried to seal itself off from the cold as I huddled in the little house of myself.

I hunkered down in Mr. Griffin's coat and tried not to breathe. I sat still and hoped to hold in all my smells. When you stay awake the night stretches out longer and longer. I sat there listening to all the rustles and flutters, the chirps and barks. I listened for snakes crawling and bats flying. I must have gone to sleep again, for when I opened my eyes again there was light and I could see the trees around me.

What a relief that day was coming. I'd made it through the night. I was comforted to know I had lasted through the night. Without shelter or fire I'd stayed the whole night in the strange woods. But I had to find something to eat. And I had to find a place to stay for the next night. I felt the handkerchief with the coins in my pocket.

As the sky got brighter it was clear which way the east was, and which way the river was. I needed to go farther away from the river. I needed to keep going to the west. I stretched myself and felt how stiff and sore I was where Mr. Griffin had hurt me. I'd have to walk slowly until I felt better.

The oak woods that had appeared closed in in the dark looked open in daylight. I picked my way through trees; there was no sign of a path or trace. I was hungry and cold. I had to find a farm or camp. But there was no clearing in the woods. I couldn't even find a rabbit trail.

I must have walked a mile when I heard a shout. I froze and listened, and there was another shout. Something banged like a stick on a log. The sound came from far down the long hill. I heard a cry and then laughter.

Where there were people there might be something to eat. I started running toward the shouts, but as I got closer I slowed down to tiptoe steady and quiet. I was so short of breath I thought I would smother.

I came to a creek among laurel bushes, and the shouts seemed to be on the other side. I waded through the gravel and mossy rocks and climbed into the thicket. When I pushed a limb aside I saw a kind of road through the woods. A party of men was coming and I slipped back out of sight.

Through the laurel leaves I saw the men were carrying something on a pole. It was big enough to be a bear or panther. There were at least a dozen men shouting and laughing. And someone was crying. As they got closer I saw the thing slung on the pole was not an animal but a woman, an old woman. They reached an opening in the trees and stopped, and they cut the woman's feet loose so she could stand with her hands still tied to the pole.

"Long live the king," she cried. I saw she didn't have any teeth. All her clothes had been torn off. Her face looked old but her breasts appeared surprisingly young.

"If we cut your eyes out, granny, you can't be no Tory spy," a man carrying a pistol said. He had long brown hair and a big belly that pushed through his vest. He seemed to be the leader. Another man had started a fire, and they hung a bucket over the flames. The bucket had a stick in it and I could smell tar. "We're going to dress you up, granny," the man with the pistol said.

"You'll burn in hell," the woman spat out.

A man with a razor caught her head in the crook of his arm and started to shave her head. The gray hair came off in hanks and bunches. When all the hair was gone her scalp looked raw and was bloody in places. The man with the pistol took a gourd and dipped tar out of the bucket. With a rag he smeared hot tar on the woman's face and head. The hot tar must have scalded her, for she screamed and kicked at him. He wiped tar all over her shoulders and back, over her breasts and thighs and legs.

Another man opened a sack of feathers and shook feathers on the tar. Feathers fluttered across the clearing and men ran to pick them up. They covered the woman's face and body until she looked more like a snowman than a person.

"We don't want you to get cold," the man with the pistol said, and threw a handful of feathers in her face. As soon as she was covered they cut the woman loose and she fell to the ground. But then she picked herself up and started stumbling away. She limped and tripped, caught herself, and started running.

"Squawk, squawk, squawk," the men shouted, and flapped their arms like wings. They cackled and laughed as the old woman ran down the road shedding feathers like a broken pillow. Soon she was out of sight.

"This calls for a drink," the man with the pistol said. Someone passed a jug to him and he hooked his thumb through the handle and took a long swig. The jug was passed from hand to hand and they all took a long drink.

"I think we ought to go to McIver's next," one of the men said.

"No, we promised to settle with Brattle first," another said.

"Why don't we go to Brattle's and then to McIver's," the man with the pistol said.

"What if somebody warns them?" a man with spectacles said.

"That's why we have to hurry," the man with the pistol said.

I wished they would leave so I could go to their fire and warm up. If I had fire I could have a light in the dark, and I could cook a fish if I caught one in the creek. The men didn't seem to have anything to eat, but at least there was the fire. I held my breath and stayed still.

They took their time and passed the jug around again. And then the man with the pistol took the bucket off the fire and opened his pants. He pissed on the smoldering sticks and when he finished there wasn't even a wisp of smoke.

They finally started walking down the road, and when they were out of sight I ran to the charred sticks and found only ashes and the smell of urine. Feathers were scattered all over the clearing and tar was dripped on the sand.

I started walking again. I was so hungry I felt I was dreaming. I walked away from the road toward the west, away from the river. My legs and feet were numb. I kept thinking I heard somebody walking behind me, or to the side of me, but when I turned to look nobody was there. A hawk floated far overhead. A ground squirrel scurried away in the leaves. I hoped my mind wasn't going strange the way Mama's had.

I walked all day through the woods, and near dark came to a little river. Without taking my shoes off I stepped across the rocks and shallow places. Then I climbed up the far bank and sat down to rest. I didn't want to spend another night alone in the woods. I had to find something to eat, and I had to find shelter. I had to find somebody to help me. As the sun disappeared the air got colder. I couldn't sit against a tree for another night. I looked around at the darkening woods.

And then I saw a lantern way off up the hill between the trees. It was a weak light, but where there was a light must be people. I had to find people. I couldn't stay by myself out in the cold woods any longer. I started walking faster toward the light, dodging limbs and stumbling around bushes and big trees. But the light didn't get any closer. Whoever held the light was moving too. The yellow of the light was mellow as melting butter. I followed the lantern as it swayed and bobbed along through the trees. I heard voices too but couldn't tell what they were saying. I just followed the lantern as quietly as I could. Maybe they were outlaws, or maybe rebels like Mr. Pritchard's gang.

Now the strangest thing was I saw this other light coming through the woods on my right. It got closer and closer, and I heard the people carrying the second light greet those with the first lantern. It was good to hear somebody speak in the dark woods.

"Are you going to the meeting, brother?" a voice said.

"Aye, sir, to the meeting at Zion Hill," a second voice said.

I followed both lights on the trail, walking quietly, trying not to break a stick or rustle the new-fallen leaves. Were they going to a rebel meeting? Was I following outlaws starting on a raid? The country was full of robbers and deserters. And then I heard a woman's voice too and figured they would not be outlaws. You didn't hear of outlaws traveling with women. In the dark I got as close behind as I dared. The trail ran through some pine woods and then came out in a clearing. And way ahead I saw a lighted window.

As we got closer I saw other people around the glowing window. There were people gathered there. And when we got closer still I saw it was a little building with a steeple on it. It was a little church sitting on a hill surrounded by woods. A tide of relief washed through me. Mama and I had never gone to church that much, but I'd been baptized when I was a baby. I'd gone to church on Easter and Christmas. A church house seemed like a safe place.

I set Mr. Griffin's hat straight on my head and marched right up to the door of the log church like that's where I'd meant to go all along. As I came into the little building people turned to look at me and a few nodded. Some women stared and a few smiled. There were maybe ten or twelve benches in the room, and two lanterns hung up front above a table. I shivered and sat down on a bench at the back. Now that I was inside, I saw how cold I'd gotten. There was no fireplace in the building, but it was warmer inside than out.

A tall skinny man in a black coat stood up at the table in front. He didn't look to be more than twenty-four, maybe twenty-five, years old.

"My friends, you are all welcome," he said. A white scarf was tied around his throat, but all his other clothes were black. His voice was plain but pleasing. He said he welcomed us there to a place of worship, in these troubled and desperate times. He said he welcomed us to the fellowship with each other, with song and prayer, and to fellowship with the Lord in Heaven.

"Without are wolves and thieves and whoremongers," he said in a quiet voice. "But in here we are gathered to praise the Lord. In here we are gathered to rejoice and praise the Maker with prayers of Thanksgiving. We are gathered to uphold the light in darkness. We are gathered to ask the Lord's blessings on our lives in these days of great peril."

"We will lead in song," the preacher said. "We will raise our voices in a hymn."

The song he started singing I'd heard before. It was "Jesus Shall Reign" I found out later. He started singing and the others joined in, and I found myself singing too.

> *Jesus shall reign wher-e'er the sun*
> *Does his successive journeys run;*
> *His kingdom spread from shore to shore,*
> *Till moons shall wax and wane no more.*

When everybody was singing these words it felt as if the church was a different place. The log church was lifted up to a new level. The lanterns got brighter and sweeter. Everybody was singing together. A few minutes before I'd been out in the dark of the creek bank, trembling with fear, and now I was with other people singing sweet music. It seemed impossible a little log church and a few words set to music would make such a difference.

When the hymn was over the preacher bowed his head and prayed. I bowed my head but didn't close my eyes. I was still too afraid to close my eyes. The preacher prayed that the Lord would bless us and guide us. He asked the Lord to hear our voices, and to show us the way in these dark times.

When the prayer was over the young minister looked out over the gathering. There were old men and women, and people in good clothes, and there were people in rags or nearly in rags. There were big old boys that smelled like liquor, and there was a blind man holding on to a stick.

"My friends, I don't know what burdens you carry in your hearts tonight," the young preacher said. "I don't know what sins of omission or commission you carry on your conscience. I don't know what deeds of charity or deeds of selfishness are on your minds. But I know that in our hearts we are all troubled. In these perilous times we are all fearful. I know that we must comfort one another."

After he had talked for several minutes the preacher asked if anyone had a testimony to share with the congregation.

A woman who held a baby to her breast stood up. The baby was asleep and the woman talked in such a low voice I had to lean forward to hear her. "I'm here to witness the Lord's mercy," she said, not in a whisper but like she was talking to just one person, the preacher. "I was a woman barren like Sarah and I prayed the Lord would give me a child. It looked like I would live to old age and have no one to care for me and comfort me.

"One night I had a dream and in the dream I seen this herb garden on the mountaintop. And a voice in the dream said if I picked the herb and drunk a tea from it I would have a child. I told nobody about the dream, but the next day I walked toward Chilton Mountain and found the herb there. It was unlike any herb I'd ever seen. My friends, the leaves was gold and shaped like guineas. I brought the leaves home and dried them and made a tea.

"Within months I was with child. And last year was born this beautiful daughter. The Lord gave me this Rebecca. I'm here tonight to thank him."

When the woman sat down I saw the tears on her face. In the lantern light the tears shone like sparks.

"You have honored us, Sister Wensley, with your witness," the preacher said.

The old man with the cane stood up. His eyes were cloudy and turned the wrong way. He had a week's beard and his hair pointed every which way. He turned away from the preacher to the crowd, as if he was going to preach himself. He leaned on his stick and faced us, but you could tell he didn't see anything.

"The Lord has sent me a vision," he said in a trembling voice. His voice sounded like a saw scratching on a nail. "The Lord troubled me until I couldn't sleep and I got up and walked outdoors. With my stick I climbed up on the hill behind my house and turned my face to the stars. Lord, show me your message, I said.

"The Lord opened these blind eyes and I seen the valley before me with a river running through it. I seen the houses and barns, and this church on Zion Hill. A light come down out of the sky and shone on the church, and a voice out of the sky said, 'Go to Zion Hill and say I have somewhat to tell them.' 'What do you want me to say?' I said.

"'Say to the people if they will be true and faithful in these perilous times, if they live by faith and the Word, in this time of infidels and harlots, of wars and rumors of wars, in these last days before the judgment, then I will send my special blessing. And them of that fellowship shall not taste death, but shall be took up when I bust through the eastern sky in all my glory.'"

When the old man sat down there was nodding and the men said "Amen," and the women said, "Thank you, brother" and "Thank you, Jesus." While the old man talked, I had forgotten where I was. I had forgotten running through the woods from Mr. Griffin and what had happened at the hog pen. I had forgotten the awfulness of what I'd done later and the fear in my heart.

The preacher looked right at me as if he knew what I was thinking. He looked at me like he expected me to speak next. He looked at me like he could see into my heart and see the burden there. I knew I had to stand up and say something. I stood up wearing Mr. Griffin's coat and pants.

All the faces in the little church turned to me. All ears were listening. I'd never testified before. I looked around at the faces and my jaw trembled.

"What is on your heart, boy?" the preacher said. "Say what is on your heart."

I opened my mouth but no words came out. I looked at the preacher and I looked at the congregation.

"The Lord will put words on your tongue," the preacher said.

I saw there was nothing to do but say what I felt. I had to tell how troubled I was.

"I have done wrong and I want you all to pray for me," I said. The words locked in my throat and I had to swallow. "A wrong was done to me," I said, "and I was tempted by the devil and brought low."

When I tried to go on the words set in my throat. The preacher looked at me and everybody was looking at me. The light in the room was twisting around and swimming. The air in the church swung around and I was skidding down and there was nothing to grab on to. Everybody was looking at me.

And then the air washed back the other way, and the church was a river of air running backward. I was swirled around and away, knocked backward. I reeled with arms out to catch myself. Hands reached to help me. Arms came from all directions and caught me.

I closed my eyes because the air was churning, and I felt myself lifted up and carried forward. My knee hit the corner of a bench and I was dragged forward.

"Bring him to the altar," the preacher said. Strong arms laid me down at the altar, and I smelled boots around me and felt the cold floor.

"We will pray with this our brother," the preacher said.

In my mind I saw the filth behind the hogpen and felt Mr. Griffin pushing me down in the filth. And I heard the grunt of pigs. I was so tired I lay there with my head on the altar. My legs were sore and my back was sore and I still hurt between my legs. I needed to rest and I needed to put down the great burden on my back and on my mind. Two days before I had been just myself, and now my life was ruined.

"Lord, help our brother to repent and forgive," the preacher prayed beside me. "For only when we forgive can we be forgiven. It is hardest of all to accept your love, knowing in our hearts we are unworthy, knowing we are weak and uncertain."

As the preacher prayed I thought what a wonderful thing it was that people could gather and pray and comfort one another. I'd gone to church from time to time, but had never been at a service so friendly, where others were concerned for my feelings. I had wondered why church was so important to some people.

"Help us to accept your comfort and your promise of joy," the preacher said.

Others prayed too, in a chain around the room. They knelt with me around the altar and every voice was different. I'd never felt such a fellowship, and such a connection. They were all strangers, and yet I felt the strength of connection. I was glad they didn't know what I had done. When the last one had prayed, then the preacher prayed again, and he asked what my name was.

"Joseph Summers," I said and felt tears running into my mouth.

"Let's welcome Joseph to our fellowship," the preacher said.

After I stood up hands reached out to me. I shook them as firm and fast as I could. I wanted to shake like a man would. My hand was rough from work, but I wished it was stronger. I had calluses from all the work I'd done. I tried to make my shoulders seem broader and my chest flatter. In the lantern light I hoped they wouldn't notice how thin my neck was.

"Let's give Joseph the right hand of fellowship," the preacher said.

Those that had not come forward before came now to shake my hand. There were only a few young people, a girl my age, maybe younger, a boy wearing a hunting shirt and a big knife in his belt. Most were older people, women wearing widow's black with shawls over their shoulders and scarves tied over their heads. Men with hands rough from holding ax handles and saws and scythes shook my hand.

What have I done to be treated so well? I thought. I'd hit Mr. Griffin over the head with the ax and dressed up like a man and run away. And I'd found this little chapel in the woods. Mr. Griffin had treated me like I was bad, and yet the preacher and the others treated me like I was worthy, like I was a man.

"We will sing 'Am I a Soldier of the Cross?'" the preacher called out. "We will sing the song of victory. Hell is short one soul tonight. We have cheated the devil, for Satan and all his angels are not as powerful as our prayer." The preacher hummed a note and raised his hand. As we sang I felt the firmness of the song, the strength of the music. It was a song of confidence, of victory. I didn't feel like myself, standing there singing. I was used to being quarreled at and accused of laziness. I had stepped out of myself and put on different clothes. A few days before I'd been Josie that was fondled by Mr. Griffin and pushed to the ground in the mud. And here I was shaking hands with people and singing. And they thought I was Joseph, come in out of the night.

After the song the preacher prayed again and then everybody shook hands with me again. Men patted me on the shoulder and women hugged me. And then they took their lanterns and left one by one, disappearing into the night. Soon there was only myself and the preacher at the door of the little church.

"You are welcome to our fellowship, Joseph," the young minister said. He took his wide-brimmed hat from a peg by the door and lifted a lantern from another peg. I didn't know what to do. I should have slipped out into the dark before anybody else. I should not have lingered. Yet there I was. I didn't have any place to sleep except in the woods. Maybe I could slip back and sleep in the church.

"Where do you live, Joseph?" the preacher said. He waited for me to go out and then followed, closing the door.

"I'm traveling," I said.

"You are a traveler and a pilgrim like me," the preacher said.

"Where do you travel?" I asked.

"I go from place to place in this valley," the preacher said. "Some communities have churches, and some don't. I preach in barns and tents, in brush arbors and in the open. I'll be back here at Zion Hill in two weeks."

As we walked into the darkness, I kept meaning to say good night and walk away into the woods. But I didn't. I kept walking with him.

"Do you have a place to rest?" the preacher said.

"No," I said. I couldn't think of anything to say but the truth.

"You're welcome to stay with me in my cabin on Pine Knot Branch," the preacher said.

A chill went through my belly. I didn't know a thing about the tall young preacher. I didn't even know his name.

"I'm John Trethman," the preacher said.

"I'm Joseph Summers," I said.

We shook hands and I told John Trethman I would accept his hospitality. Scared as I was, I couldn't think of anything else to do. I'd have to be careful. The least little thing could give me away.

"Just a moment," the preacher said. He stopped and handed me the lantern. I wondered what he meant and then he turned aside and unbuttoned his trousers. He faced the dark and I heard water sprinkling the leaves and bushes beside the trail. He broke wind.

"A service leaves me full of gas and water," he said.

I knew I was supposed to hand him the lantern when he finished and turn to the dark and make water myself. But that would have to wait until I was alone. That was the kind of thing I'd have to be most careful about.

When I handed him the lantern and his Bible we walked on. I wondered how far it was to Pine Knot Branch, but was afraid to ask. I was so tired I could have lain down on the trail and gone to sleep. As we came over a rise I saw a glow ahead. The sky was lit up and I could see flames beyond the trees.

"Oh not again," John Trethman said.

The fire was red and ugly. A shudder passed through me down to my toes. I was going to ask what it was, but I already knew. It was not a barn on fire and it was not a lightning strike.

"It's the home of a loyalist," John said.

We hurried up the trail, but there was dread in my feet and fear in my heart. What if we were taken for loyalists too? I didn't know what John Trethman's sympathies were. Was he a Moravian or a Baptist? Was he a Methodist or a Regulator?

It was farther to the fire than I expected. It must have been two miles or even three. As we got closer we heard whoops and hollers. And in the light of the great blaze we saw men dressed like Indians running back and forth and shouting. They were carrying jugs and throwing flaming sticks into the barn and haystacks. They were white men.

When the men dressed as Indians saw us they hollered louder, then got on their horses and rode off into the night. By the time we reached the yard they were all gone, and the house was nearly gone too. It was all in flames and the fire was so hot and bright it burned your face just to look at it. I held my hand in front of my face.

"Lord help us in our iniquity," John said, and I saw the horror on his face. When I looked where he was staring, I saw bodies hanging from the limb of a big oak tree beyond the corncrib. In the light from the awful fire, I saw they were hanging by the necks, a man and woman and little boy. There was blood on the woman's dress like she'd been wounded before they hung her. And the man's shirt had been torn off and his back was bloody.

John Trethman

I ALWAYS LOVED to watch clouds. Even as a boy in Virginia I could lie in the grass for hours and watch the luminous shapes of mist and vapor drifting far above. Some clouds were so thin I could look through them, and some were stacked so thick and high they appeared as alps that touched the sun, blinding as new snow and so tall they threatened to topple over.

Like all boys, I imagined forms in the clouds, sheep and puffs of cannon smoke, smoke signals from Indians, ghostly faces. I thought I saw prophets and apostles from the Bible and my ancestors beyond the blue staring at me.

Once after service our pastor, Reverend Wilson, a friend of Reverend Wesley, looked up at the steep and shining clouds and said, "Such a sight shows the presence and glory of God. How could anyone doubt it?"

I never forgot what he said, for his words gave me a shiver so strong it hurt. And after that I couldn't look up at the clouds without thinking of the face of God up there, a ghostly beard staring at me. Pastor Wilson said when Jesus returned and split the east in all his glory the clouds would part and he would appear to be standing on the clouds. When I looked up I expected to see Jesus soaring up there.

When I was at school at the College of William and Mary I would leave my studies from time to time to rest my eyes. I studied Latin and Greek and Hebrew until the letters swam before my eyes. To refresh myself I walked in the fields and lay down in the grass and watched the clouds over apple trees and hickory trees. I found that the farther away I looked the more refreshed I felt.

Later when I was walking on my circuit there in North Carolina, from church to church and congregation to congregation, I sometimes rested by the road or by a spring to ease my weary feet, and I watched the flocks and armies of clouds appear from the north and float to the south, in even formation. I watched the clouds drift as though grazing on the blue, and felt the wholeness and peacefulness of God's handiwork. It was a privilege to be alive with such beauty, as it was a privilege to serve the people of those hinterlands and settlements. Lift up your eyes unto the hills, I said, from whence cometh your help. And then I took out my flute and played to the trees and meadows, to the sunlight and breeze, or I opened my songbook and sang a carol for the foxes and deer in the thickets.

To see the new churches there on the frontier growing and strengthening would bring tears to my eyes. For I was blessed to have that chance, to begin at each place with a few, maybe four or five, sitting on a log or beneath a shade tree, on Briar Fork and Crowfoot, at Zion Hill and Beulah, and in a year or so each place had built a little church, a meeting place, and held regular services.

It was the least I could do to honor all the preachers who had gone before me for almost eighteen centuries, to carry song and word into the wilderness, to make each place more real by placing a chapel there, even a log chapel, to show where eternity connected with time in this world, and the presence of God was everywhere and anywhere we opened our hearts.

I had been blessed beyond my wildest plans to find so many there beyond the canebrakes and thickets willing to listen, thirsty for the word, happy to sing and testify and be baptized. I had come to the wilderness to witness and to pray, and my message was one of song and praise. I thought a service and a sermon were to give hope and strength in a troubled time. I almost never talked of hell, for people in those desperate days lived in their own hells. No need to warn them of suffering, for they were already suffering. I was called, if I was called at all, to bring joy and confidence to frightened and uncertain people. I could not countenance hate and killing. I would preach only love and praise. Our lives were too short for hatred and revenge.

When I was weary from all the burning and looting and hanging of the rebellion, the tarring and feathering and raping I saw almost every day, I would sometimes look up at the clouds to see beyond our time. Looking into the clouds was like looking off into eternity. And the clouds were going about their business of beauty and silence beyond the human depredations. To look into the clouds was to see into the larger scope and scale of things, the long time passing, to everlasting things. And I shuddered to think how little connected that world was to this. And I thought how little relation that vastness and steadiness had to this. It was a mystery beyond my understanding. I looked at the meadows and sun on the hills, and the lushness of ferns in a glade, and I thought how ugliness came from men, and how it was men that chose evil.

Sometimes a song would help wash away the ugliness, and sometimes it wouldn't. Sometimes only work and time would clear away the hideousness of what people did. Again and again I had noticed that just when we were ready to give up on our fellow men because they seemed hopeless and wicked, someone would surprise us with goodness and kindness, humility or sacrifice, and then we would want to start anew, building a community and fellowship. For we gave each other strength, and most of what we learned we learned from other people.

. . .

FROM THE FIRST TIME I saw Joseph I thought there was something different about him. In the lantern light at Zion Hill he looked so troubled and lonely, so pale on the back bench, cold and frightened. I had never seen a more sensitive face, a more alert face, or sadder countenance. Something terrible burdened his mind, something too awful for him to utter. I was struck by the hurt in his eyes even as I spoke and sang. I never saw anyone more in need of comfort and fellowship. I never saw anyone more in need of friendship. When he fainted in the church I saw he must not have eaten for days, and that some terrible secret weighed on his mind.

I saw it was my duty to invite him home with me. For what is our testimony worth if we cannot extend a hand to the homeless and hungry? What is a sermon worth if it cannot be applied? I never saw anyone more weary, or more grateful for a kindly word.

WHEN I KNEW I had the call, my goal was to become a priest in the Church of England. I hoped I might study at Oxford and be ordained an Anglican. I was in Richmond teaching music and letters to the sons of planters when I met the missionary sent by Reverend John Wesley. Never had I seen such power in preaching, such eloquence and sincerity, combined with learning and joy. The missionary, Reynolds Williams, told the story of Reverend Wesley's journey to the New World in his youth, of his work in Georgia and his meeting the Moravians. He told the story of Reverend Wesley's conversion by simple faith, his true acceptance of justification, even after he was ordained.

"We do not need ministers of vast learning," Reverend Williams said. "We need men of faith and joy to bring the Good News to this vast continent. We need men with confidence in themselves and courage in their hearts to bring a message of love and peace to these troubled colonies."

The war had just broken out the year before. The Congress had met in Philadelphia to declare independence. Whatever hopes I had of going to Oxford were no longer practicable anyway. But the missionary had shown me another way to serve. It seemed his words were directed especially to me.

"We need young men to go into the backcountry of Carolina," he said. "We need men not afraid of the howling wilderness, where Indians and bears and panthers lurk. We need ministers to carry hope and comfort to those caught up in bloody conflict, to those isolated, to victims of hate and anger. We need ministers who can soothe the fury of these times with hymnody and prayer and the spirit of forgiveness."

Reverend Williams accepted me as his student and he tutored me throughout the summer and autumn of 1776. Before winter came he ordained me in the church at Richmond. He ordained me because I promised to carry song and Scripture into the farthest settlements of North Carolina.

"We can give you only a small salary," Reynolds Williams said. "We cannot even provide you with a horse for your travels. The war has interrupted our supply from England. I'm afraid you must find much of your own subsistence. We will send you a pound every month, when we can. And you must write a letter each month informing me of your whereabouts and your progress. As long as letters can get through in these times of rebellion I need to receive your reports. And when these troubles are over perhaps we can provide a larger stipend. For now you are the evangelist, establishing services and churches on ground where no Christian worship was ever heard."

The missionary Williams gave me a prayer book and a hymnbook to carry with my Bible. He gave me his blessings and his commission. "You are another John going into the wilderness with song and prayer," he said. "Go with Christ's blessing to witness and inspire."

With my few belongings in a sack slung over my shoulder I made my way west from Richmond to the Great Wagon Road down the Valley of Virginia. The road was the main route of immigration from Philadelphia to the Carolinas. Families traveled south and west along its track. They traveled in wagons and carts and on foot, and on horseback and mule back. They drove cattle and sheep and hogs and slept in tents or thickets, or in their wagons. Oxen labored along the red-clay ruts.

It took a month for me to walk to the Piedmont of Carolina. On rainy days I slipped and stumbled through mud like red grease. In dry spells I walked through dust that rose like smoke from hooves and feet and wheels. Along the way I sang and prayed by campfires. I read from the prayer book and I read from the Scriptures. Often those around the campfires joined in the singing and prayer. I baptized several babies born on the way. I performed a marriage ceremony in western Virginia. I said the burial service for some who died.

I was pleased to be going away from the war, into the lush valleys of the South. I was a shy preacher at first, but the very roughness of the people and the road inspired me. Compared to the labor of travel and the rude folk and danger and vexation of the elements, I was the soul of wit and eloquence. The Reverend Williams had seen something in me, and he had been right. I had found my place and my people. And sometimes I was paid to teach music and letters to the children, and often I was given provisions as well as coins after services.

In the news I got from other travelers and from newspapers that circulated through the camps, I saw the rebellion was spreading, not dying out. There had been more fighting in New York and New England. A patriot army had been defeated at Montreal. Every colony was raising militias and sending soldiers to the Continental army. Those loyal to the Crown were beaten and tarred and hanged in some districts. Those joining the rebellion had their houses burned; their lives threatened, in other communities.

The Reverend Williams had warned me to stay above the fray. "You are not to take sides in this rebellion," he said. "You are a minister of peace and love. You cannot witness while supporting killing and hatred for your fellow men. The message of the Gospels is clear: love one another even as I have loved you. If you compromise yourself by taking sides in this civil war your ministry will be destroyed."

On the road south I passed militias drilling in fields and meadows, houses that had been burned by loyalists or patriots, bodies hanged from trees with signs around the necks saying DEATH TO TYRANNY or DEATH TO TRAITORS. I grew accustomed to cutting bodies down and digging graves and praying over burials. The section of the prayer book I used most often was "The Burial of the Dead."

By the time I reached the foothills of Carolina, near the Catawba River, the rebellion had spread into South Carolina and Georgia. The whole continent was in turmoil. Charlotte just down the river had declared its independence and was known as a patriot town. I chose to stop at the Catawba River and begin my work. I could have gone on into South Carolina or maybe even Georgia. How did I know when to pause and begin my witness?

It was winter, after Christmas, and one night I stood beside a campfire on the banks of the Catawba River and sang hymns with the travelers who had stopped there. Some were drovers, rougher men than most I met. A jug of spirits was passed from man to man in the firelight, even as I prayed and sang with them.

"Reverend," a man with a long beard and ragged coat called out to me. "Reverend, you can't do no good here," he said.

"I will do what good I can," I said.

The man took another drink from the jug and laughed. "There ain't no god here," he said. "This is Indian country. God don't come this far into the woods." He and his companions laughed again.

"God is everywhere," I said. "We only need to call on him and he will hear us."

The man looked up into the night sky and said, "I don't see no god up there."

"The spirit of the Lord is all around you," I said. "And the spirit of the Lord is within you."

The man with the long beard belched a long belch and grunted with relief. "Now I feel better," he said.

I saw that I had been given a sign. I had been sent a message by the most unlikely messenger. A voice told me that I had come to the place where I must begin my work. There on the banks of the river north of Charlotte a drunken man had said God did not come to this forbidding forest. I had found the place I was needed. I saw I had been guided by an unexpected hand. Where there was no song or prayer, no thought of the presence of the Comforter, I must begin.

I soon found there were churches scattered among the settlements east of the river. The villages and larger settlements had a few ministers. But west of the river, in the hills that repeated themselves forever across the distant valleys to the mountains, there were no congregations, no word or song. It was a world of briars and thickets, swampy valleys and rough trails, scattered cabins and tiny fields along branches. There was the town of Quaker Meadows to the north, later called Morganton, and Gilbert Town to the southwest. But most of the country between was wild. Families had settled in a few valleys and along ridge tops where the woods were thinner. Cherokees claimed much of the land and some-times made hunting forays into the river valley.

I began by walking from cabin to cabin and praying with each family. I sang and read from Scripture. I agreed to hold services in the cabins on Sundays. I sent word to all the neighbors there would be a service on Sun-day afternoon. And I began to build a cabin for myself with the help of one Curtis Satterfield on Pine Knot Branch, a few miles west of the river.

My fear was that no one would gather at the Satterfield home on that first Sunday. But eleven people assembled. They came out of the woods on horses and on foot, and they sat on benches by the fireplace, filling the little room. An exhilaration seized me. I knew this was the test. If I could draw people from the forest and ridges just once I had made a first step. I was so relieved to see the congregation in the little house I was inspired in my singing and in my reading from the prayer book, in my brief ser-mon. The air I breathed was richer as I stood before them. The light was brighter in that dim cabin as I sang a second hymn. This is what you must do and what you will do, I said to myself. I promised that when spring came to the foothills I would build a log church on the ridge and call it Zion Hill. And I knew that I would swing farther west and begin services there too. My back was strong and my hands were ready. I stood at the far edge of Christendom, pushing a way into the dark forest.

But even as I found my congregations and built my little churches on branches and distant hillsides, the war of rebellion raged all around. I read the newspapers that were available and listened to those I met and ministered to. Sometimes it seemed the war was a foreign thing, with battles in New England, a great victory of the patriots at Saratoga in New York won by Col. Daniel Morgan of Virginia, George Washington's victories at Trenton and Princeton, his defeat at the Brandywine, and the terrible winter of 1778 at Valley Forge. Those events were talked about like rumors.

But everything changed when the British landed in Georgia and took Savannah that same year. I heard it was Gen. Archibald Campbell who drove the rebel militias out of the city and into the back country. But the big loss was Charleston. Lord Charles Cornwallis sailed to that city and took it from Gen. Benjamin Lincoln. They said many patriots were killed or routed. That's when the war got closer. Charleston was the port, the trading center where people of the Carolina hills took their furs and stock to sell.

People said they figured it was Lord Cornwallis's plan to conquer the Carolinas and march on to Virginia where he would link up with the rest of the British army. And that turned out to be true, because he began to move his huge army up the river to the wilderness of South Carolina in the summer of 1780. We heard great stories about how militias led by Francis Marion and Thomas Sumter harried the royal army. The patriots lived in swamps and thickets, ambushed patrols, stole horses and supply wagons.

Pretty soon everybody knew about Cornwallis's cavalry commander,

Lt. Col. Banastre Tarleton. He was only twenty-six but already famous as a fierce fighter that never lost a battle. They said Tarleton was bold to the point of recklessness. He led his Green Dragoons across South Carolina, riding down on militias and chopping rebels to pieces with razor-sharp sabers.

The worst story was of the Waxhaws south of Charlotte in May 1780 when he won a battle, then ordered all the prisoners killed. That's when the phrase "Tarleton's quarter" became known. Tarleton's quarter was no quarter at all. He never took prisoners, and he became known as "Bloody Tarleton," as he won victories all over South Carolina. I read about it in a newspaper I got from Charlotte. Newspapers were passed from hand to hand, but you had to be careful who saw you had a rebel newspaper or a loyalist newspaper. Just reading the enemy's newspaper could get you whipped or your house burned.

As I traveled on my circuit in the summer of 1780, preaching and praying, baptizing and singing, I heard about the terrible battle of Camden in central South Carolina on August 16. Gen. Horatio Gates who commanded the southern Continental army was defeated by Cornwallis. Word spread fast about how Gates fled on his horse and never stopped until he reached Hillsborough, North Carolina. He was relieved of command by George Washington and replaced by Nathanael Greene of Rhode Island, who everybody seemed to admire.

People said a militia had been organized in the upcountry of South Carolina by Andrew Pickens of the Long Canes. But Pickens had been defeated and forced to swear an oath that he would never fight the Crown again. I heard story after story about how Tarleton and his dragoons and legion swept all over the interior of South Carolina, from Fort Ninety Six to the foothills of the Spartan District, burning the houses of patriots, hanging rebels and those suspected of being rebels in their own front yards, raping womenfolk, stealing whatever livestock and provender they found.

I was told that Cornwallis sent Maj. Patrick Ferguson into the Piedmont with a loyalist militia to cow the population along the North Carolina border. But a group of mountain men, the Overmountain men, as they were called, from the Watauga and Holston Valleys, led by Col. John Sevier, assembled an army to confront Ferguson. They said that if they did not stop him he would invade the mountains and destroy their settlements, or urge their allies, the Cherokees, to attack them. The Cherokees were their neighbors in towns along the Tuckasegee River.

People said Sevier and his men first gathered near Quaker Meadows up the Catawba River north of my churches. I was told they marched south to Gilbert Town and on to the pastures in the Spartan District of South Carolina known as the Cowpens. The Cowpens were open woods where cattle had been grazed for decades. It was known that people in the region pastured their livestock at the Cowpens and met there for hunting trips and even camp meetings.

The story was bragged all over the Piedmont that Sevier and his men made contact with Ferguson's forces in early October of 1780, and cornered the loyalists on Kings Mountain near the North Carolina line. Surrounding the mountain, the patriots planned to starve out the British. There was no water source on the steep mountain. It was told how the Overmountain men had long rifles that shot farther and more accurately than the British Brown Bess muskets. The patriots picked off British officers and sergeants at great distances, one at a time.

One man who was there told me it was like shooting turkeys. "Every time I seed a Tory I just touched him off," he said.

On October 7, 1780, Ferguson himself was killed and his men, those still alive, surrendered. People talked about the several fancy women in Ferguson's camp when the British finally surrendered.

I KNEW THAT TO be an effective minister there in the woods of Carolina I had to be a part of the life of the communities. An evangelist might sweep through and hold a meeting and exhort and save souls, then move on, but a pastor had to live with his flock and share their lives and hardships. I ate with the members who invited me to their simple homes, and I attended infare celebrations after weddings and wakes after funerals. I played games with the children and sang at corn shuckings and quilting bees.

Most of my members were farmers. They grew corn in little patches recently cleared along creeks, and they grew flax and vegetables. Some already had fruit trees on their acres in the forest. Some were hunters and trappers, and some traded with the Cherokee Indians. Some peeled tanbark and one was a blacksmith. Some were drovers and some made gristmills. A few were masons and many stilled spirits from corn.

The women worked even harder than the men there. They helped the men in the fields and in the woods. They sheared sheep and carded and spun the wool, dyed the yarn and wove cloth. They gathered herbs and roots in the forest, picked berries and dried fruit for winter. They sewed and quilted, made ale and apple butter. And of course they bore many children and raised them. They carried water from the springs for washing and made soap from fat and lye. Many women chopped with an ax same as the men did. Women hoed the corn and pulled weeds. I saw women driving oxen, though I rarely saw one driving a mule.

One day Curtis Satterfield, who was a carpenter, said they were raising a barn for his neighbor, Redmon, on Alphabet Creek Thursday next. "You're welcome to come, Reverend," Satterfield said with a wink, "if you're not afraid of mashing your nice fingers." It was not the first time I had been teased in the backcountry about my hands. Most men there had hands rough and calloused from work, joints swollen by weather and bruises, scarred and cracked. Most women had rough hands too. I heard the challenge in Satterfield's voice and I told him I would attend the raising and bring my ax.

"And bring your songbook for the ladies," Satterfield laughed.

It was a day in late summer, after the corn was laid by from hoeing and before the harvest began. The Redmon house was on a hill above Alphabet Creek. When I arrived there were already thirty people there, including women and children. It was the biggest gathering I'd seen since arriving in Carolina. Everyone was excited, as though a ceremony was to be celebrated.

Women had brought baskets of bread and cakes and pies. Mrs. Redmon was plucking chickens killed that morning for dinner. Children chased each other around the yard playing tag and hide-and-seek, and some bigger boys were damming a pond in the branch. But the men had arrived at daylight and had already dug out a level site for the barn, shoveling dirt out of the hill and raking it level, tamping it smooth. Several cheered me as I approached. They had already been working for hours. Curtis Satterfield wore his carpenter's smock and he seemed to be in charge.

"Do you know what timber-frame building is?" Satterfield said. He said it was different from building a log cabin.

"I can learn," I said and held the ax up to show I was prepared.

A great pile of logs had been cut and dragged into the yard on the side of the hill. Men with axes were hewing the logs into timbers eight or ten inches square. Others with hammers and chisels were cutting holes in the timbers already hewed.

"The timber frames will be mortised and tenoned together," Satterfield said. "When a side is ready it will be raised into place."

The wood they hewed was pine and poplar. The fresh pine smelled sweet as incense and the poplar smelled faintly bitter.

"Hey, parson, give us a hand here," Brother Gibson from Zion Hill called to me. I knew I was going to be teased that day, and I was determined to take it in good humor. Gibson asked me to help lift a heavy timber to join it to a crossbeam. The protruding tenon on the beam had to be mated to the mortise on the heavy timber.

We all lifted on the count of three and there were grunts and groans as the pieces joined. But I held on to the timber too long, for as the other men let go my fingers were mashed as the heavy piece sank to the ground. I must have cried out and then stood up wringing my hand.

"It's awfully sorry I am," Brother Gibson said.

There was a little blood where my fingernails were bruised. Satterfield looked at my hand and said I should go to the house and Mrs. Redmon would bind it up.

"It's nothing," I said. "Nothing at all." All eyes were on me, and I knew whatever I said and did would be reported around the countryside. I took up the ax and began to hew a timber.

By midmorning my hands were blistered and numb. My fingers would not let go of the ax handle when I tried to lay it down. But I was determined to persist and share in their labor, however much they teased me, however tired I got.

At dinner time I was happy to take a break and say grace before we ate. We sang a hymn, and then the women uncovered the feast they had assembled that morning. Young girls gave me things they had prepared themselves, pieces of pie and cake, puddings and jellies. Platters of chicken and ham loaded the table in the yard, along with bowls of boiled eggs and new potatoes. The men passed a jug around among themselves and I took a sip of the powerful corn spirits.

"I've never seen a warmer sense of community," I said as I looked at the crowd eating together.

"It's the August heat," Satterfield said, and the men laughed.

My fingers were sore and my back was sore, but it thrilled me to see such fellowship among my flock.

"How do you like real work, parson?" Mr. Redmon said. There was laughter all around, and I was going to say something about the pleasure of working together, but suddenly all grew quiet and turned toward the woods beyond the clearing. I leaned to see what they were looking at.

A column of royal soldiers on horseback had emerged from the trees and was riding directly toward us. When the officer in front stopped his horse beside the well he called out, "You know perfectly well such meetings are forbidden. Gatherings of more than eight persons are not permitted, except for holy services."

"This ain't a meeting, sir," Curtis Satterfield said. "We are just raising a barn."

"What better ruse to conceal a meeting," the officer said. "You will disband at once."

Sighs and groans swept through the crowd.

"I am the pastor here," I said, and stepped closer to the horseman. "We are raising a barn for Brother Redmon."

"Are you defying me?" the lieutenant said.

"We are just carpenters and farmers," Brother Satterfield said.

The officer pulled out his sword and pointed it at the gathering. "You will disperse," he said.

"I am Rev. John Trethman," I said. "I have worked with these people today and sang and prayed, and I give you my word they are only here to raise a barn for Brother Redmon."

I had taken off my collar and my coat that morning because I was sweating. The officer stared at me as though I was a tramp. "You will disband," he shouted again.

As the crowd backed away muttering the lieutenant dismounted and walked to the loaded table. The other soldiers dismounted also and helped themselves to the chicken and ham, the pies and puddings.

"This is an outrage," I said to the officer. "You have no right."

"I have every right, padre," the lieutenant said. "It is the duty of every loyal citizen to quarter and board the king's soldiers."

"What is your name?" I said.

"You don't need to know my name," the lieutenant said. "But I know yours. I will have my eye on you, John Trethman. Be warned, I have my eye on you."

As the soldiers ate the feast and drank from the jug, the members of the congregation dispersed. They took their tools and children, their baskets and horses, and slipped away into the forest.

. . .

I HAD SWORN I would have no part in the war, and I had avoided any word or deed that would suggest I was loyal to one side or the other. My supervisor had said I must be a messenger of love and peace. It was hard to remain calm and confident when houses burned nearby and farms were looted. Neighbors were hanged, as bands on both sides roved the country accusing and whipping, torturing and killing. They shaved women's heads and scraped their tongues with sharp knives. They raped young girls and then strangled them and left their bodies in swamps. Some bands seemed to be plain marauders and criminals, using the war as an excuse to rob and rape and go on rampage.

Because I was literate and from Virginia, many local patriots assumed I was loyal to the Crown. Because I read from the Book of Common Prayer and spoke proper English, I was suspect to some of the rebels. I was often threatened and had a church burned at Solomon's Branch. I was told repeatedly I should carry a pistol or a sword, but I knew it was far more dangerous to go armed. If my only weapons were my songbook and prayer book, it was easier to persuade a foe I was harmless, a mere parson and hymnodist.

But I believed the loyalists and royal troops were far more dangerous to me. The reason was I never made any effort to support the Crown. To royal troops and officials my very neutrality was an act of treason. In their view there could be no such thing as neutrality. You either supported the king, or you were his enemy.

A number of times while walking to my churches I'd been stopped and threatened by soldiers wearing the red uniform. One day a company on horseback came to the little cabin Curtis Satterfield had helped me build on Pine Knot Branch. The officer dismounted and strode to my door, sword in hand.

"And who might you be?" he said, and tapped me on the chest with his sword. I was not wearing my collar, only my linen shirt. I had been splitting firewood. I told him I was John Trethman, psalmodist and minister.

"I'm Lieutenant Withnail," the officer said. "And I'm here to stamp out sedition in these wretched hills."

I told the lieutenant I was a simple parson and singer of hymns.

"What better guise for a spy or courier than a circuit rider," the lieutenant said.

I saw the impossibility of proving my innocence by argument. I told the officer I would be happy to pray with him or sing for him. I tried to sound plain and simple. He placed the tip of his sword against my throat and said, "You may be as fond as you seem, but then again you may be playing a ruse."

I stood as still and calm as I could with the blade at my throat.

"If I find you are a messenger or spy I will return and castrate you," Lieutenant Withnail said. He drew his sword away and swung it, slashing the front of my trousers. When I looked down I saw the cloth had fallen away revealing my private parts. I covered myself with my hands as the lieutenant mounted his horse. As I watched them ride away I thought how sharp his sword must have been, and how close it had come to my person.

WHEN I WAS TEMPTED to feel sorry for myself and pity myself, because of the violent and uncertain times in which I lived, I often thought of Archbishop Cranmer, founder of the Church of England and author of the Book of Common Prayer. Cranmer had lived in the reign of Henry VIII and taken part in the Reformation. When I needed a hero I thought of Cranmer.

Thomas Cranmer was born in 1489 and became a brilliant student at Cambridge. But when he married secretly and was found out he lost his fellowship. After his young wife died in childbirth he was reinstated by his college. I was thrilled to read that one of Cranmer's favorite ideas was that Rome should not have so much control over the English church. He wrote a paper arguing that nothing in the New Testament gave the pope such authority over all churches.

When Henry VIII decided he wanted to divorce Catherine of Aragon and marry Anne Boleyn, and the pope would not grant him a divorce, the king became very interested in the idea of an independent English church. Hearing about the young scholar at Cambridge, he brought Cranmer to court. Cranmer impressed the king so much that in a short time he was promoted from a mere deacon to be archbishop of Canterbury.

It moved me that Cranmer was a great poet as well as minister. He translated the services of the church and the calendar into English and added words of his own to make the Book of Common Prayer. But like Peter, that other founder of a church, Cranmer was also very human. Sent to Germany, he met the theologian Andreas Osiander in Nuremburg. And Osiander had a beautiful niece named Margaret whom Cranmer married secretly and brought back to England.

In the terrible times of Henry VIII and Edward and Mary Tudor, Cranmer worked and argued, confronted, and survived, until Bloody Mary demanded he return the English church to Rome. I had wept when I read in *Foxe's Book of Martyrs* how when he refused he was tortured. An old man by then, he was eventually forced to recant his faith.

But soon as he regained his health a little he denied his recantation. No threats or tortures could make him budge. Condemned to burn at the stake in Oxford, he held his right hand in the flames, "the hand that hath offended," until it burned, and then he stepped into the center of the fire.

I admired Cranmer for his humanness, his fallibility, and the way he could rise above his weaknesses. If there was hope for me it was that I might rise above my failures and my weaknesses. For I too had the human stink and human frailty, even as I aspired to carry peace and hope to the broken world.

THREE

IT WAS A PITIFUL SIGHT, the three bodies hanging from an oak tree in the light of their burning house. You couldn't have dreamed anything more awful. The fire lit up the woods all around, like the door to hell had been opened and the world was burned by eternal torment. I smelled burning meat too but didn't know if it was stock in the burning barn or meat in the smokehouse. Smoke drifted across the clearing, making everything hard to see.

I'd never understood how men could hate each other and hurt each other so badly over politics.

"These are terrible times," I said.

"We must cut the bodies down," John Trethman said. I looked up at the oak limb and saw it was too tall to reach unless you were on a horse, and maybe not even then.

"We need a horse," I said.

"I'm afraid I'm a circuit rider that travels on shank's mare," the preacher said.

We looked around for a ladder or pole to climb on. Maybe there was a table we could drag under the bodies to reach the ropes. Everything in the house was burning up, and I didn't see anything to stand on in the yard. Preacher Trethman looked at the tree and he looked at me. "You'll have to stand on my shoulders," he said.

I'd not climbed trees since I was a girl. I was afraid if I climbed onto his shoulders he might feel my breasts or my thighs and see I was not a boy.

"Could we leave them till morning?" I said.

"These are the Fielders," Preacher Trethman said. "It's not Christian to leave them hanging here like common criminals to be a spectacle. The crows will come and peck their faces."

He knelt down beneath the tree and I stepped up on his shoulders. I was trembling and weak and my knees shook. I put my hands on the oak and John stood up. He was a tall man and I was just able to reach the big limb the ropes were tied to.

"Here," John said, and pulled a knife from his pocket and handed it to me. I nearly fell when I reached for the knife. I put the blade between my teeth, for I needed both hands to climb out the limb.

I was shaky and tired. But you don't know what you can do till you have to do it. More than anything, I didn't want the preacher to know I was a girl. For if he knew that, he'd find out I'd killed Mr. Griffin and that Mr. Griffin had shamed me. For some reason the most important thing in the world at that moment seemed to be climbing that limb and cutting down the bodies so he wouldn't know I'd been shamed.

The hardest thing was to pull myself up far enough to wrap my legs around the limb. My arms were weak and I strained till I thought my eyes would pop out. I tried to hook my legs over the limb twice and slipped back, but finally made it. Hand over hand, I cooned out the limb, not looking down. When I got to the boy's body I held on to the limb with my left hand and cut through the rope with the right. I had to saw the knife back and forth. When I got most of the way through, the last fibers tore and the boy hit the ground like a sack of corn.

I crawled out farther and cut the second rope. But the limb bounced and the rope swayed and it took me even longer to cut the woman down. But I finally made it and inched out to the last rope. My arms trembled so badly I could hardly hold on.

"I'm going to fall," I yelled.

"You're almost through," the preacher called back.

The rope swayed when I cut at it, as if the knife had gotten dull. I sawed at the rope and hacked at the twisted strands. I was so tired my arms felt frozen. The world was upside down and backward, and I tried to look only at the rope. The knife felt like it had no edge or that I was trying to cut with the wrong side. I stopped and just hung there. The glare from the burning house was hot on my face

"Just a little more," the preacher shouted.

I pulled all the strength from my toes and from deep in my guts. Smoke drifted in my eyes and burned my nose. I strained so hard tears came to my eyes. I rubbed the knife back and forth on the strings of the rope and sweat and tears made everything blur. With a crackle the rope gave way and the man hit the ground with a thud.

But as I put the knife in my teeth and reached for the limb with my right hand, my left gave way. I guess I had a cramp in my hand and couldn't grip any longer. My fingers slid off the bark and I fell backward. But my legs were still locked around the big limb. There I was, hanging upside down with the knife in my teeth. I let the knife go so I could holler out, and then my legs lost their grip on the limb and I hit the ground with a smack.

But what I hit was softer than the ground. It was the body of the man that had just fallen. My head hit his head with a bump, and there I was, face to face with his eyes bulging out and blood on his mouth and the rope around his neck. My lips touched his cold bloody lips and I jerked away.

I rolled aside and Reverend Trethman helped me to my feet. I was nearly too dizzy to stand. I bent over with my hands on my knees to catch my breath.

"They must be given a Christian burial," John said. "We will do it tomorrow."

The only building on the place that wasn't burning was the springhouse, and in the springhouse we found some old tow sacks. We took all the sacks and covered the bodies on the ground. And we carried rocks and poles and laid them on the sacks to hold them down. By then the fires were burning lower, but there was still plenty of light to see by.

THE TRUTH IS I WAS so tired I don't remember much of the walk to the cabin on Pine Knot Branch. It must not have been that far, but I stumbled in a daze, numb from all the effort and all the terrible things that had happened. I felt I was dreaming a long nightmare as I stumbled along behind John Trethman.

When we got to the cabin and stepped inside I saw it was just one room with a fireplace and a cot in one corner. There was a table opposite the bed all covered with books and papers. But it was a cabin with a loft. John held the lantern up and I saw the shelf built over one-half of the cabin. There were logs reaching out from the wall in a kind of ladder going up to the loft.

"You can sleep up there," John said. He gave me a blanket, a thin gray blanket, and I pulled myself up the logs to the loft. On the puncheons up there lay a tick stuffed with leaves or corn shucks. There was no fire in the fireplace below and the cabin was cold. I took off Mr. Griffin's coat and wrapped it over me, and I pulled the blanket over that. The bed was thin and rumpled and had lumps in it, but that didn't make any difference. I heard John say good night below, or maybe I dreamed it.

When I woke in the morning it took a minute to figure out where I was. And then I remembered that I was supposed to be a boy named Joseph Summers, and a pain cut through the center of my bones.

I'd always wondered what it was like to be a boy. Since I was an only child, I'd just seen boys at church and at school. We didn't have any close neighbors, but I'd played with boys while Mama was at quilting bees and spinning bees. Sometimes I wanted to be like a boy and climb trees and catch rabbits and possums. But boys were dirty. They caught toads and carried them in their pockets, and they didn't clean their fingernails. They wiped snot on their sleeves or the back of their hands. Boys could piss while standing up and they laughed when they farted.

I always wondered what it was like to have a thing hanging between your legs. I'd seen the thing on horses and on dogs. I wondered how it felt to have something sticking out there. I wondered how it felt to stick it in somebody. I shuddered and heard John Trethman stirring below. I looked over the edge of the loft and saw he'd started a fire in the fireplace. The cabin began to smell like smoke and burning cobs.

"Are you awake, Joseph?" he said.

"Yes, sir," I said. But when I stirred I felt the soreness and stiffness in my arms and legs. My groin was sore and my back was sore. In three days my body had taken a lot of punishment.

"Fetch me some water for coffee and I'll make us some hoecakes," the preacher said.

I threw the blanket aside and ran my fingers through my short hair and climbed down the logs to the puncheon floor. I put my shoes on and took the bucket he handed me.

"The spring's behind the cabin," he said.

There was frost on the ground outside. The sun was a red spot through the trees. I relieved myself in the woods and then crunched over grass to the spring. When I returned with the bucket of water the cabin was warmer.

"Here, let me do that," I said to John, and took the mixing bowl from his hands.

"Can you cook, Joseph?" he said.

"I can make hoecakes," I said.

He had measured out the cornmeal and shaken salt from the salt gourd into the bowl. He handed me a gourd of soda and I sprinkled some of that in too.

"Where did you learn to cook, boy?" he said as he poured water into the pot for coffee.

"On hunting trips to the mountains," I said.

When the coffee was ready and the hoecakes were ready, John cleared some of the papers from the little table and we ate there. The hoecakes were good and John got a jug of syrup to pour on the cakes. The steaming coffee warmed me.

"Now I must preach a funeral," John said, "much as I dread to."

I kept eating and didn't answer.

"I'm a song leader and a prayer leader," John said. "I like services of praise and prayer. I like testimonials and hymns."

"Could a funeral be a testimonial?" I said. I thought of the testimonies of the night before.

"It ought to be," John said. "It ought to be a celebration. But we're too human for that. We mourn our loss. We look at the dead body, and we exhort, as Reverend Wesley tells us we must. We warn and we scold."

I was surprised that Preacher Trethman was telling me how he felt. I'd never heard a preacher talk that way before. I poured syrup on another hoecake and ate it.

"The funeral of somebody murdered is sad," he said. "There is no moral, except that life is short and evil afoot in the land. In these desperate times a preacher can be hanged for what he says in the pulpit. People are all torn apart and confused, and hatred and revenge rule the land."

I couldn't think of a thing to say, for what he said was true. John Trethman was a handsome and eloquent man, but he was a worried man. Though he acted calm and spoke calmly, I could tell he was troubled. The death of the Fielders and the prospect of the funeral had shaken him more than I'd thought at first.

"It's easier to preach the funeral of those you don't know well," John said. "But when they are victims of murder, what is there to say, but fear God and love thy neighbor. The world is harsh and getting sadder."

He was so worried I wanted to reach out and touch his hand. I saw he was a good man and a grieved man. He was different from Mr. Griffin, and he was different from Mr. Pritchard. I wished I could think of some way to comfort him. He had welcomed me to the little church and he had comforted me. I couldn't think of anything to say to make him feel better. I wanted to touch his hand, but I didn't.

"We have work to do," he said.

I swept the crumbs off the table into my hand and tossed them into the fire. I rinsed out the cups and threw the water out the door. As the sun rose over the trees, the frost started melting on the grass.

That morning we walked from house to house in the country west of the river to tell what had happened to the Fielders. Some already knew, and maybe some helped kill them. John asked the carpenter named Satterfield to make coffins out of pine wood, and he asked somebody with a horse and wagon to bring the bodies to the church.

"There's something we'll have to do ourselves," John said as we approached the little church on the hill. The log building looked different in daytime. It appeared to have shrunk in sunlight. The steeple was the size of a chicken coop with a pointed top and I saw there were graves on the knoll out beyond the church.

"We will have to dig the graves," John said.

A spade and a pick leaned in the corner at the back of the church. John took the pick and handed me the spade, and we walked out to a high place above the other graves. From there you could see the creek through a break in the yellow hickory trees.

John took off his coat and began loosening the ground with the pick. I shoveled aside the sod he'd broken loose and dug down under the topsoil into the red clay. We dug three holes by moving back and forth between them. He loosened the hard clay and rocks in one and moved on to another while I shoveled out the clods.

"Why are graves always on high ground?" I said.

"Maybe the dead can see farther and clearer than the living," John said. "And their ground is set aside forever and shouldn't take up good farmland."

I soon had blisters on my hands. By the time we got the holes dug my hands were sore as my back.

WHEN HE PREACHED the funeral, John talked so quietly I had to strain to hear what he said. I sat on the back row as I had the night before. The three coffins lay in the floor at the front of the church. There was hardly room for them, for the little building was full. Word had gotten around and it appeared people had come for miles. I hoped nobody from across the river was there.

"A sad occasion brings us together here," John said. "It is an ugly time, a time that tries faith and tries hope. It is a time of testing. I didn't know the Fielders well, but I know they were people just like us. They worked the land and raised their cattle and sheep. And they were raising their son. We know they have gone to a better place, away from the trials and tribulations of this valley."

John paused and looked out over the gathering in the little church. "But what can we learn from their deaths?" he finally said. "What is the lesson, my friends, of these lives cut short?"

John paused again, as if he could hardly go on. And then he opened his black book, the one he carried in his coat pocket, and he read, "'In the midst of life we are in death: of whom may we seek for succor, but of thee O Lord?' The death of the Fielders can teach us that death is always with us, that death comes like a thief in the night in such an hour as ye think not. And the death of the Fielders teaches us that we must love one another. That is the new commandment."

In all the times I'd gone to church as a girl, I'd never paid much attention to the sermons. They all sounded alike. They were about heaven and hell and how awful people were. But when John talked, everything he said made sense. Everything he said seemed to come from the heart. When he spoke it was like he was speaking to me, and answering questions I'd thought about.

"Even the oldest among us live only a few years," John said. "Young

Phillip's life was still at its beginning. My prayer is that he knew the joys of childhood, that he ran and played and swam in the creek, and that he gave his mother and father joy."

John looked out over the congregation in the dim light. He was so tall he almost touched the beams of the roof. I'd never seen a man so pretty, a man whose words meant so much. What he said seemed to be what I wanted to hear, what I needed to hear. His words comforted me like nothing else had.

John paused again and gazed out over the congregation. He looked right at me on the back row. Then he bowed his head and closed his eyes and prayed.

"Death is not the end but the beginning," he said. "Death is the doorway to the long ages and the ageless days. Guide us through the dangers. Help us to see the sunlight and the far mountains, and the welcome path ahead."

When the service was over we carried the coffins out to the graveyard on the knoll. We had to make three trips, for it took six to carry each coffin. A breeze rattled the leaves on the oak trees above the graves, and purple-colored leaves soared out across the sky. As we assembled beside the holes and got ready to sing, a man on horseback rode out of the woods. He rode right up to the graves, and he had a handkerchief tied over his nose.

People stepped back a little from the graves to give the horseman room. And they stepped back a little from John. Some of the men had brought guns, but the rifle guns were leaning in the corner in the back of the church.

The rider didn't say anything for a minute. He just looked at the graves, and he looked at the little congregation. I wondered if he was there to rob us, or was he there to claim the bodies.

"You are welcome to join us, friend," John said finally.

"Reverend Trethman," the horseman hollered. "Them that give comfort to the Tories and aid the Tories will be treated the same as traitors. Don't matter what kind of collar they wear."

The man turned his horse and rode away. We watched the horse and rider disappear into the woods as if we had been slapped in the face. All the good feeling of the sermon was smashed by his hateful voice. John watched the masked man ride away, and I thought he was going to call after him. But he never did. Instead, he said we would sing "Jesus, Lover of My Soul."

It was a song of dignity and peacefulness. It was the perfect answer to the threat and anger of the man's warning. A song brought people together in harmony. It's hard to be angry while you're singing. After the hymn John prayed again, and then we filled in the graves.

As the crowd was breaking up Mr. Satterfield told John he was afraid for him. "You go unarmed from church to church in these fearful times," he said.

But John said it would not help him to be armed. For though he carried a weapon he might still be ambushed or waylaid. "My message is my only armor. A weapon would only invite violence," he said.

"You must at least not travel by night," Mr. Satterfield said.

"Brother Satterfield, if the devil would find me he will find me," John said.

By the time the graves were filled it was afternoon. John and I were left to finish the job ourselves. I had blisters on my hands, so I wrapped pieces of a sack around my right palm as I shoveled the clods into the last hole and heaped the turf in a mound. John put a cross made of hickory sticks on each grave.

"Why were the Fielders killed?" I said.

"I'm not sure," John said. "The rumor was they gave a horse to the redcoats and let them bivouac on their property. They may have given corn or hams to the royal soldiers."

"And for that they were hanged?"

"As scores of others have been," John said. "Many have been killed for less."

"And now they are gone," I said.

"Perhaps a stonecutter will one day makes stones for these graves," John said.

We placed the pick and spade back in the corner of the log church. I knew it was time for me to announce I was moving on. It was time for Reverend Trethman to dismiss me and go on to the next church on his circuit.

"Brother Joseph, what are your plans?" he said as he washed his hands in the branch and dried them on his coat. I washed my hands and dried them on Mr. Griffin's coat.

"I've thought about going to the mountains," I said, and paused. I couldn't tell the preacher what had happened to me. I couldn't tell him that I'd murdered Mr. Griffin.

"Do you have family there?" John said. "Do you have business farther west?" He looked into my eyes and put a hand on my shoulder.

"I don't know," I said, and hot tears came into my eyes. I didn't mean to cry, but my eyes got damp and light swelled in them. If I cried he would see I was a girl and send me away.

"You are sorely troubled," John said. "You are welcome to travel with me if that will lighten your burden."

"It will," I said.

"I have no horse and no cart. I hoof it from congregation to congregation. But you are welcome to walk with me and pray with me. It's better not to walk alone in the world."

More tears came to my eyes, but I turned away so he couldn't see them. I followed him on the path past the Fielders' burned house.

THE NEXT DAY WE walked from the cabin on Pine Knot Branch to the settlement at Crowfoot. Crowfoot was at the edge of the mountains, farther west than I'd ever been. It was at the edge of the Cherokee country, half a day's walk from the cabin.

"The Cherokees don't come into the valley," John said, "but they claim all the mountains."

John said the Cherokees had sided with the Crown and killed any patriots that came among them. Tories hid out on Cherokee land, in remote valleys in the mountains.

"Why would the Cherokees side with the Crown?" I asked.

"They have signed many treaties with the British," John said. "Perhaps they feel they have to honor those treaties. And they hope the king will prevent settlers from taking their land."

The road was just two ruts of cartway across the hills, what people called a topsoil road. There were puddles and rocks in the way and logs had fallen across the ruts in places. The road led down through muddy swamps and sinkholes along creeks. My shoes got dirty and I skipped to keep up with John's long strides.

"Why don't your churches give you a horse?" I said.

"My flocks are small and just getting started," John said. "They have no treasuries. A flock must grow before it can provide for a minister. A preacher must give before he is given to. Besides, I have nowhere to keep a horse and nothing to feed a horse."

I'd never met anybody like John Trethman. He gave himself to working for others, to encouraging and spiriting up others. He was tall and strong as any man, yet he thought more of songs and sermons than of profit from his work. He stepped forward with strength I found hard to follow. Yet I was happy to follow him.

"How many live at Crowfoot?" I said.

"Sometimes eight gather there for the service," John said. "And in good weather sometimes ten or twelve."

Where the road forded a creek we took off our shoes and rolled up our pants and waded across. John carried his Bible and songbook and prayer book, and I carried the lantern we'd need for the service and the walk back at night. The creek was so cold it stung the bones of my feet and shins. We sat on the other side and put our stockings and shoes on.

"We are like Paul and Silas," John said, and laughed.

"Who was Silas?" I said.

"Silas was Paul's friend," John said. "They traveled together and sang together."

We stood up and started walking again on the rocky ground. Briars picked at my pants and Spanish needles stuck to my coat. I tried to step around puddles. There were hills ahead of us and white clouds floated so bright you could hardly look at them. John looked up at the clouds and started to sing. His voice echoed off the trees on both sides of the road and I joined him.

IT WAS NEAR DARK when we got to Crowfoot. The church there was little more than a shed on the bank of the creek. It was made of rough logs with no windows. The benches were planks laid over stumps. There was no fireplace.

"Someday there will be a real church here," John said. "But now the settlement is only scattered cabins along the branches."

John made a fire outside the church and we baked some potatoes we'd carried in our pockets. That was our meal before the service. The hot potatoes warmed me, and I washed my hands later in the branch.

We lit the lantern and hung it in the building, and soon after the sun went down members of the congregation began to arrive. They walked out of the woods from both directions on the road. Women in bonnets and men in rough jumpers and hunting shirts came in and sat down on the benches. Some men brought their rifles and leaned them in the corner. John welcomed each one and introduced me as his helper. Folks nodded at me.

Just as John was about to begin, a short man came to the door and looked in. His face was red and his eyes wet. When he took a step inside I thought he was lame, but then I smelled his breath and saw he was drunk.

"You are welcome, Brother Albert," John called. The short man stumbled to the back bench and sat down beside me. He smelled like rotten peaches and unwashed clothes. John announced that the first song would be "When I Survey the Wondrous Cross."

The short man beside me sang, but in broken notes and to his own tune. He sang in a loud voice, like he was deaf and couldn't hear the others. He swayed as he sang and closed his eyes and hiccupped. John kept singing more verses, and everybody joined in as if the drunk man wasn't there.

When the song was over John led in prayer, but as he prayed the drunk man mumbled and belched and tried to pray along with him. "Amen," the short man said, and jerked his head. And then he said "Amen" again. Every time he said "Amen," he jerked his whole body.

When the prayer was over John began to talk about grace in our troubled times. He talked about the joys of gathering together.

"The Lord means for his own to fellowship together," John said. "For together we inspire and encourage each other. Together we comfort and teach each other. The Lord's work is done through fellowship and community. Alone we are weak, but together we are strong. Together we step forward to the future."

"Preacher," the drunk man hollered. All turned to look at him.

"Yes, Brother Albert?" John said in a calm and kindly voice.

"Want to testify," the short man said.

"We will have testimonials presently," John said.

"Want to testify now," the drunk man said, and stared hard at John.

"Then you shall testify now," John said, and grinned. There were chuckles in the room.

The drunk man stood up, and swayed forward and back. "Seen a vision," he said, and paused like he'd forgotten what he was going to say.

"Tell us your vision," John said.

The drunk man raised his finger like he had just remembered. "Woke up on Dogleg Mountain and seen a light over all the valley," he said.

He swayed like he was about to fall and then caught himself. "I seen the light shining on Crowfoot," he said, "and the Lord said out of the sky, Albert, you go to the Crowfoot church and tell the Crowfoot pastor I have somewhat against him." He stopped again and looked like he couldn't recall where he was.

"And what did the Lord say?" John asked.

"Lord said tell Crowfoot congregation they ain't treated Albert right. Ain't treated Albert square."

The church members looked at Albert like he was about to reveal a secret.

"How have you been wronged?" John said. "Tell us and we will pray with you."

"Ain't made Albert a deacon," the short man said. "Ain't recognized him at all."

"And now you have told us," John said. "Now you've brought the message to us."

"Ain't all," the drunk man said. "Lord said take up a collection for old Albert."

"Thank you for bringing the message to us," John said. There were titters and snickers in the church. "We will vote on deacons next year when there are more members," John said.

The drunk man sat back down. I figured he would keep interrupting John and disturbing the service. But he was quiet, and when I looked over at him again he was asleep, slumped in his old clothes, snoring like a bear.

FOUR

WHEN I BATHED or took care of nature's calls, I always made sure John was out of sight. When we camped on the circuit I bathed in thickets or in the dark hours before dawn or after sunset. I slipped away into the thickets or laurels for nature's business.

John just thought I was shy and modest. I wanted him to think that. And besides, it was true, I was shy, though maybe not for the reasons he thought. I kept my person hidden as much as possible. That was hardest when I had my monthly, for I had to wash the rags I made from an old towel and dry them in secret. I thought if he caught me I'd pretend they were pocket handkerchiefs and I'd had a nosebleed.

We traveled up and down the great river valley and into the foothills and mountains. To my relief we never crossed the river eastward because there were already many churches there and John was needed in the west, in the hinterlands, in back coves and far branches. He preached in tents and sheds, in people's houses and log chapels. He preached in an open meadow by a creek one sunny afternoon near Gilbert Town. He performed weddings and christenings. He preached at funerals and camp meetings, and gave singing lessons and Bible lessons. He conducted morning and afternoon services. He exhorted and got people saved. He visited the sick and the crippled, and he sat with the bereaved.

And sometimes a letter came for John. He picked up the letter at the store on Solomon's Branch. It was a letter from his boss in the north, and with the letter was a pound note. With that note John bought more salt and coffee and cornmeal and bacon at the store.

In the rolling countryside west of the river, John had seven churches scattered among the hills and valleys. They were about a day's walk apart and roughly in a half circle beyond his cabin at Pine Knot Branch. Some like Zion Hill and Crowfoot were on hilltops, and others such as Solomon's Branch and Beulah were down in valleys. Briar Fork was beside a swamp. Salem Ridge was on a rise of ground between two creeks. John wanted to visit each of his congregations once every two weeks. Some churches were solid log buildings with little steeples, and some were just sheds made of brush. But John also held meetings in tents and in people's houses, and out in the open. Once he held a service in the woods where there were just logs and stumps to sit on.

It was pretty country, with fields cleared on tops of ridges and along branches. Corn had been planted in many deadened acres where bare, girdled trees stood above the stalks. As we walked from church to church we passed men killing hogs and women boiling soap from fat. We passed a liquor still in a hollow, and mills where corn was ground into meal between grunting stones. We passed a forge where long mountain rifles were made for the militia, and a gold mine where men had dug into the hillside and muddied the creek.

Everybody we met seemed to know John and most waved to him and spoke cordially. "Would you pray for my sister?" a woman said, rushing to the trail and drawing John to her house.

More than once we met riders who were not friendly. We stood aside on the trail to let them pass. Sometimes they wore blue uniforms and sometimes red uniforms. They looked at John in his black suit and black hat with suspicion.

"What do you carry in that book?" an officer in a red coat called to John one day.

"Only the Scripture, sir," John said.

"Are you sure they are not coded messages?" the officer said, and stopped his horse.

"My only code is the Great Commission," John said.

"And which side gave you a commission?" the officer said. His buckles sparkled in the sun.

"A higher authority," John said.

The officer swung his riding whip as he spurred his horse forward. The tip of the quirt touched John's hat and knocked it into the brush. I picked the hat up for him.

It was such an odd way to live, going to a different community almost every day. I'd always lived in one place before. It was like every day of John's life was a Sunday, a holiday. Instead of working in the field or at a trade, he walked and he sang, he prayed and he preached. It was serious, and yet it was a frolic too.

Everywhere we went I helped him. I carried water for foot-washing services, and I lit the lantern when it got dark. I carried his change of linen and his Bible. When there was a funeral I helped dig the grave. At a christening I held the dry towel.

"Joseph, you are a good lieutenant," John said one day. "But if you will accompany me you must study the Bible also. You must know the Scripture."

I'd read only a little of the Bible in school, and I'd heard it read at church. But mostly I was ignorant of the Bible. However I had had a wonderful teacher in school, a man named Mr. Pickett who taught a school in our district. Mama paid for me to attend, and Mr. Pickett taught us grammar and proper English. He had come from over the water, from Oxford, and he had lived with the Cherokee Indians before he became a teacher. But he made us write proper and talk proper. Mama said that even though I was a girl I must know the king's English.

John said I must read the Bible every day. He said I should read it aloud to him. I asked if I should read it straight through from the beginning. He said no, he would tell me every day what passage to read, and each morning I would read a chapter or two to him. He didn't start me off reading Genesis or even Matthew. He said I should read poetry, and something hard to understand at first. He said I should read Ecclesiastes which I'd never read before.

> *Vanity of vanities, saith the Preacher, vanity of vanities; all is vanity.*
> *What profit hath a man of all his labor which he taketh under the sun?*
> *One generation passeth away, and another generation cometh: but*
>   *the earth abideth forever.*

John made me read it to him and I stumbled over some of the long words. I'd never read anything so hard and sad. The words didn't offer much hope, but they were beautiful. I hesitated and tried to deepen my voice. I said some lines again to get them right. John listened while he was shaving himself or wiping his boots with a rag. He smiled while he was washing his linen. John was the cleanest man I'd ever seen and his linen was always fresh and his collar tabs white as snow. He nodded and listened to the words of the Bible the way somebody might listen to a pupil play music.

> *To every thing there is a season, and a time to every purpose under*
>   *the heaven:*
> *A time to be born, and a time to die; a time to plant, and a time to*
>   *pluck up that which is planted.*
> *A time to kill, and a time to heal; a time to break down, and a time*
>   *to build up.*

I said the verses and sometimes he made me say them again. He never got angry the way most teachers do.

"Joseph, you must make the words of the Scripture your own words," he said.

I read from Ecclesiastes and I read from Daniel. I read from John and I read from Revelation about a new heaven and a new earth after the great battle of Armageddon. As I practiced I got better, so I could say the words with feeling, and with confidence. And reading the passages seemed to lift me up, make me feel older and wiser. When I read from the Bible the world seemed to make more sense.

To get to the church at Beulah we had to walk through a long canebrake. The stalks of cane grew so tall over the trail that they swayed and rustled as we passed beneath, whispering in dry rasps. Sometimes they hissed like snakes. If it had been summer I would have been afraid of rattlesnakes, for rattlers big as your leg lived in swamps and canebrakes. The cane was just grass, but it was hard to believe that grass could grow that high.

The cane was full of spiders, and I was afraid a black widow would jump out onto my face. I brushed cobwebs out of my way and told myself not to worry about spiders. I would not let my mind get strange the way Mama's had.

But I'd heard bears and panthers hid in canebrakes also. Panthers would crouch in the cane and pounce on their prey as it passed on the trail. With the breeze stirring the tall canes and making them sigh we wouldn't be able to hear a panther until it sank its claws in our backs. When I told John I was afraid of bears and panthers he said we were more likely to be attacked by animals wearing red coats or hunting shirts.

"It's the two-legged predators we need to look out for," he said.

"You don't even carry a hunting knife," I said.

"What good would that do me?" he said.

John was so goodwilled and peaceful it surprised me to find there was another side to him. It happened on the way to Beulah after we had passed the long canebrake. I reckon I was nervous from worrying about spiders and panthers and bears in the tall whispering grass. You couldn't see anything but the stalks in front of you when the cane was swaying and rasping.

The trail came out of the cane and crossed a swampy place and then a little hill. Beyond the hill the path reached a rushing creek. I think it was called Alphabet Creek. The water flashed and swooped through rocks and you had to be careful crossing it.

In fast water on tricky rocks you don't step right across the stream. If you do that the current will sweep your feet right out from under you, and the rocks will act like rollers. Instead you face upstream and work your way across sideways in little steps. Alphabet Creek was so fast I had to brace myself against it.

When we stopped to take off our shoes and roll up our pants John said he would carry the lantern across, but I would carry his songbook. He suggested I tuck the book inside my shirt to be safe while I carried my coat and shoes across. For some reason I decided to just hold the hymn-book under my arm and not bother to put it inside my shirt.

"No!" John yelled when he saw me crossing with my coat in my left hand and my shoes in my right and the hymnbook under my right arm. But it was too late for I was already in the creek balancing myself against the current. I inched sideways, feeling my way with my feet among the rocks. I kept my right arm tight against the book. But when almost across I started losing my balance, and before I thought I raised my arms. The songbook fell into the plunging water and floated away.

In an instant John jumped into the creek and dashed through the rocks to save the book. He climbed dripping onto the far bank at the same time I did. He wiped the book carefully on his shirt and held it up to the light. The binding was damp but the pages seemed dry except at the edges.

As soon as he saw the book was not ruined John turned to me. I'd never seen a fury so awful. "I told you!" he shouted, and shoved me with the songbook in his hand. He didn't hit me with the book, but he shoved so hard it felt like he hit me. "Are you entirely stupid?" he said. "I could have lost the only songbook I have."

I thought he was going to hit me across the face as he waved the book, but he stopped his hand. His eyes were terrible, and tears blurred and messed up my own sight.

"The book is not ruined," I said.

"No thanks to you," John snapped. He was like a different person. Even his face looked different.

But after we sat down on the moss and dried our feet and put on our shoes John calmed down. His pants had gotten wet and his shirt and coat also. But the Bible and prayer book were dry. He brushed his clothes carefully.

"I will be dry before we get to Beulah," he said.

I told him I was terribly sorry. I twisted my face to hold back tears.

"We are fortunate the book was saved," John said. He took a deep breath and added, "I'm sorry for my outburst." He put his arm around my shoulders.

I saw that he was embarrassed because I had seen a side of him he almost never revealed. He was kind and gentle and didn't want anyone to know the fury that lurked in him ready to spring out when he was surprised. I could see that he had worked to conceal and subdue his anger.

As we traveled to the different churches, to Crowfoot and Salem Ridge, to Beulah and Briar Fork in the hills west of the river, members gave us chickens and potatoes and loaves of bread. They gave us tenderloin after hogs were killed and honey when they found a bee tree. One woman at Beulah knitted John a scarf. The church at Briar Fork was really just a shed made of poles with brush nailed to the frame. But the folks at Beulah had built a church of logs, like the meeting house at Zion Hill. John said the churches were all about a day's walk apart. I know it took us most of a day to walk to any of them from Pine Knot Branch. They were scattered miles beyond the west bank of the Catawba River and in the hill country beyond.

John had a silver flute which he did not take to services. But he played it at the cabin. On a warm day he sat outside the cabin and played, and the notes of the flute seemed to answer the splash of the branch and the chirp of crickets. The notes of the flute seemed to float out in a stream long as the branch.

"Will you teach me to play?" I said.

"Whenever you're ready," John said. He kept the flute in a velvet-lined box.

Everywhere we went there was talk of Lord Cornwallis and Colonel Tarleton. Cornwallis was marching up the Broad River from Charleston. John told me about him and about Tarleton and his dragoons that were sweeping across the land west of the Broad River, killing anybody that opposed them. Tarleton burned the houses of patriots and hanged patriots. His soldiers raped whatever women they caught. Tarleton killed everybody, and he gave no quarter. Gen. Nathanael Greene had been appointed by Congress to command the Southern army. General Greene was camped somewhere near Charlotte, but everybody was scared.

"If Tarleton comes this far there ain't nothing to do but run to the mountains," people said.

Men joined the militia and got killed, and if they didn't get killed they fled into the woods and swamps and came home. "Nobody can stand up to Tarleton's dragoons," they said.

I KNEW THINGS could not go on as they had between the Reverend John Trethman and me. I had been lucky and I had been careful. But some day he was bound to find me out. It was certain as daylight that he'd discover my secret. I knew I should just leave, but I couldn't run away, and I couldn't tell him the truth. I couldn't tell him I'd lied to him. His tall figure and his kind face had become dear to me. I couldn't bear to disappoint him, and I couldn't bear to leave him. He'd taught me things and showed me important things. I had changed from being with him. I couldn't stand for him to find out I was a liar and an impostor, and a murderer. I was supposed to be saved. I was supposed to be a Christian and his assistant. I was supposed to be a student of the Scripture. And here I was deceiving him in a shameful way. I wanted to confess and tell him who I was. I wanted to ask for his forgiveness, but I couldn't leave him.

One cold night not too far into November, I'd climbed up in the loft and was half asleep. John must have stepped outside to relieve himself before going to bed. Suddenly he ran back in and climbed up on the logs and was shaking me.

"It's the northern lights, Joseph," he said. "Come see; the sky looks like the end of time."

He reached under the coat and under the blanket by accident. I reckon he was just trying to shake me. His hand reached right under my shirt and touched my breast. His fingers rested there for a second and then pulled away. "Why Joseph," he said, and climbed back down the logs.

I was awake in an instant and looked down at him standing in the firelight. He stood like he'd lost his breath. My heart had stopped, for this was the moment I'd been dreading.

"I meant to tell you," I said.

"Who are you?" John shouted.

I climbed out of the loft wearing only my shirt and got down on my knees before John. I was trembling so I couldn't stop myself. I had come to the end of everything. I hugged his knees and put my face against his legs to keep from shaking.

"I'm sorry," I gasped.

"Get up from there!" John shouted.

It's hard to describe what all happened next. John pulled me off the floor and I put my arms around his waist and my cheek against his heart. Would he hit me? Throw me out in the cold yard? He told me to hush my crying and my begging. He shoved me toward the fireplace and he stood there swinging his arms and shaking his head. I knelt beside him. I wanted to pray to him. I wanted to plead with him. I touched him on the shoulder.

John pushed me away, and he turned away from me.

"I didn't mean to fool you," I said.

"You have made a fool of me!" he cried. His face was white.

I had thought about what I would say if this happened, but I couldn't remember what I'd planned to say. Everything was crumbling, the way it did the day Mr. Griffin followed me into the pine woods. Everything I cared about was breaking to pieces.

"I'll go away," I said. "You won't ever see me again."

John just stood there and wouldn't say anything else. He drove his fist into the palm of his left hand. He acted like somebody that had been hit on the head and was in a daze. "I won't be made a laughingstock to my own congregations," he snarled, and stepped to the door. Before I could answer he disappeared into the night.

I didn't have on anything except the long shirt, but I followed him out into the dark. I tried to see into the woods and shadows of bushes. I called his name, but heard nothing except the whispering of the branch nearby.

But I saw this glow above the trees. It was red as a sunset, but the color was in the top of the sky. And then I saw waves and curtains in the light, and streamers sweep and tremble. Was it the end of time I was seeing? Was Jesus coming in all his glory? Was it a hell glow from the other side of the world, or the hate of the times burning up the world?

I saw greens and blues in the light and shapes weaving and dancing all across the northern sky. It was pretty and it was awful. I wanted to hide behind something. I turned away and looked at the dark woods.

And then I remembered what John had said when he came running into the house and reached under my blanket. He had seen the northern lights, and he was so excited he'd reached under my shirt without thinking. It was the northern lights sweeping all across the sky like some ceremony in a dream.

Some people said the northern lights were portents, telling of things to come. They were sent as warnings. We lived in awful times. I didn't want to think they were a sign to me.

"John," I called into the woods. I wanted him to come back and for-give me. Even if he slapped me and beat me, I wanted him to come back and tell me what the lights meant and what was going to happen to me. I had nothing to depend on but his advice and his wisdom.

A bird flapped away in the trees, but there was nothing else moving.

I'd forgotten I was wearing only the long shirt. I was shivering and covered with goose bumps. My teeth chattered when I called out, "I will be inside!"

The fire was low and I threw on some sticks and pinecones to build it up. I was shaking so I could hardly hold anything. I got the blanket from the bed and wrapped it around my shoulders. But as I held my feet and hands close to the flames and started to warm up, I felt how empty the cabin was. The cabin was just one room of logs, but without John it felt big as a cavern.

I listened for footsteps outside. I hoped he would open the door and I would hear his voice. I tried to think what I'd say when he came back. I put on my pants and coat, so I could leave if he ordered me to leave. I still had the coins I'd taken from Mama's bureau. But I didn't have any-thing else to call my own.

The seconds dragged slow as stone boats while I waited. I threw another stick on the fire and turned my side to the blaze. Something squalled in the trees outside. I ran to the door and looked out. The woods were dark and the sky was dark too except for a few stars. The northern lights had faded to a pink glow in the north. I looked out into the cold woods for a few minutes and then went back to the fire.

I MUST HAVE DRIFTED off to sleep, for when I woke I was slumped and stiff and the fire had burned down to coals. It must have been near morning. I got up to throw some kindling on the coals and maybe start heating water for grits and coffee. I was sure I'd have to take my things and leave when John came back. I might as well have some grits before starting out.

I was stirring the pot when the door opened, and there stood John looking cold and stunned. I could see he'd been walking in the woods all night without his coat. He looked nearly frozen and worn out. I reckon he had been so confused he didn't know where he had been.

"Come to the fire," I said. "I have some grits ready." I led him to the chair and poured him a mug of smoking coffee. It was my fault he was so worried and almost frozen. He was so cold he was numb. I wrapped a blanket around his shoulders.

"We cannot go on this way, Joseph," he said.

"Josie," I said.

"What an example I have set for my flock," he said, "living openly with a young woman."

"I will go away," I said. "They'll never know."

"I will know," John said. "And the Lord will know."

I put a hand on his shoulder but he pulled away. "I will gather my things and be gone," I said.

John coughed and then he coughed again. He had caught a terrible chill in the long night. As he sipped coffee he began to tremble. He shook so badly he could hardly hold the mug. He coughed again and I took the mug and helped him toward the bed.

"I will stay until you are well," I said.

"Keep away from me," John said. "Don't touch me." He coughed again and again. I wrapped him in the blanket and finally he slept.

I LOOKED AFTER John for almost a week, until his cold was gone. Every hour I worried about where I would go when I left him. I grieved that I couldn't stay with him. I asked him where he thought I should go.

"You must follow the path you have chosen," he said, and turned away.

But after a few days he looked at me, and the tone of his voice changed. I caught him watching me as I worked, and as I climbed into the loft to sleep. It was as though he was just beginning to see me. He talked no more about Paul and Silas, and he didn't ask me to read anymore from the Bible or *The Pilgrim's Progress*. But I read to him anyway.

One afternoon, when he was better, John sat at the table and wrote. He wrote with his head down close to the pages and the feather moved like a fern worried by wind. I thought he must be writing a sermon or a letter to his superior. I stayed away from the table and tried not to bother him. There seemed to be something sacred about writing.

When John finally stopped he stood up and took his coat from the peg beside the door. He gathered the sheets and folded them like a letter and then handed them to me.

"Do you want me to mail these?" I said.

"Read them," he snapped, and stepped out the door.

I felt weak in my chest and smothered, for I knew there couldn't be any good tidings in the letter. He must want me to read it because the letter said things he couldn't bear to say to my face. He was probably telling me to leave before he returned. I sat by the fire and read the trembling pages by the light of the flames.

> Pine Knot Branch Nov. 1780
>
> Dear Josie,
>
> I am writing this because I must make my thoughts clear to you and clear to myself. I don't trust myself to speak to you, for I am confused and troubled. I have never had such feelings as I have had in the past week.
>
> The truth is you have startled me and disturbed me.
>
> When I discovered you are not Joseph but a woman, I ran off into the woods confused as any schoolboy. Instead of acting like a shepherd to his flock, I acted only dashed and disappointed and frightened. For I saw how my ministry was threatened, maybe ruined. Any rumors that I had a young woman not my wife living in the cabin with me could destroy my testimony among these people.
>
> I can't believe it was the devil's work that sent you to me, much as it may seem that way. I must believe there is some purpose to your entry into

my life in these vexed times. For I have felt with you a kinship and connection from the first. Could I have been mistaken?

Josie, I invite you to be forthright with me, for we must decide what course to follow. I cannot part with you, and I cannot yet talk face to face with you. For I am embarrassed and humbled by my mistakes and weakness. I am unsure of my next step, and sometimes I doubt my purpose. In this broken world I am wondering where my true calling lies.

While others burn and punish and kill, I am certain I will not fight and I will not kill. I will preach peace and hope and I will preach turning the other cheek, or I will preach nothing. My testimony is of love, and my message is of faith and charity, if I have any message. Though surrounded by hate and carnage, I will preach love and peace, and the Gospel shall be my only sword. And compassion will be my only shield. I will not study war.

And I still believe you were sent to me for help and comfort.

Yours faithfully, John Trethman

I felt out of breath when I finished the letter. My cheeks were hot. I wondered what I could say to John when he returned. Should I take my coat and leave before he came back to the cabin? Should I get on my knees and beg him to take me to Georgia or the Cherokee country? Should I tell him all about Mr. Griffin?

Suddenly John slipped into the cabin, and I was going to speak to him. I held up the pages of the letter and opened my mouth, but he shook his head. He put his finger to his lips and shook his head. "We will talk of it later," he said.

That afternoon was the prettiest fall day you've ever seen. The sky was clear and the sun warm on fallen leaves. A few yellow leaves still floated out across the woods. John took his flute out to the branch and sat on a bank of moss. I followed and sat behind him as he played. He played a melody that wandered slow as a cow grazing on a hillside. He made the flute sing simple and cool. I listened and didn't say a word.

When John stopped playing he looked up at the sky. There was one white cloud floating just above us, blinding in the sun.

"Clouds remind us how everything is changing even as we look," he said. The cloud was fat and perfect in the empty sky. I watched it without saying anything.

"Clouds are our friends when we have no one else," John said. "Clouds remind us how little and fleeting we are."

I waited for him to go on, but he put the flute to his lips and started playing again. The notes seemed to come out of the ground, or out of the sky. I couldn't tell which.

ONE EVENING, WHEN his cold was gone, I said, "Don't you think it's time I left? I'll go away in the morning."

John looked at me and for the first time reached out to me. He took my hand and pulled me closer. He looked into my eyes, and I thought: Everything will be different now. Whatever happens it will be different. I pressed myself closer to him.

He touched his lips to my lips and rubbed slowly back and forth. When our lips met I could feel his touch go all over me. I closed my eyes and felt I was rising and beginning to float. So this is what a kiss is, I thought as he put his tongue between my lips.

Suddenly John pulled away. He stepped back and I opened my eyes. The look on his face was confused, and I thought he might cry. "No," he said, and shook his head. "No, we can't do this."

I reached out to take his hand but he turned away.

"Do you want me to leave?" I said.

"No!" John shouted and turned back to the fire.

I tried to think what to say to him. I thought about telling him everything that had happened to me, about Mr. Griffin and Mama, about Mr. Griffin locking me in the corncrib and the patriots coming to beat Mr. Griffin, about Mama's helplessness and confusion, about the spiders, and about Mr. Griffin chasing me through the woods and attacking me behind the hogpen. But I couldn't tell John about my shame, about Mama clawing my face and accusing me, about waiting for Mr. Griffin in the dark with the ax and chopping his head open, then stealing his clothes and running away into the night.

"I do not know why you deceived me," John said.

I told him the patriots had come to our house and beaten my step-father. I told him my mama's mind was afflicted and that I had to leave home. Dressing as a man was my only chance of escape. My only safety and my only hope had been finding him in the lighted church at Zion Hill.

John said the Lord had tried me and the devil had had his chance with me. I reached out again to take his hand by the fire but he pulled away. I saw the struggle in him, in the way he looked at me and then back at the fire. He was angry with himself, and wrestling with his doubts and his affection. There was nothing for me to do but wait. I saw you could not make a man love you when he was not ready to.

It was three days later, after we had been to services at Briar Fork and Solomon's Branch. We had eaten supper and John played his flute by the fireplace. As I washed the dishes I saw the look on his face. It seemed to me he'd made a decision, but I had to wait to find out what it was. He kept staring at me as I finished drying the dishes and placed them on the shelf. His eyes were on me as I stepped closer to the fire and hung the towel on a nail.

"Come to me, Josie," he said, and took my hand. He drew me to his lap and put his arms around me. It was the best thing, to be held that way.

John's hand was around my back. I moved his hand so it was on my breast. I expected him to pull his hand away, but he didn't. He kept his hand on my breast like he didn't know it was there. It was the best feeling. I pressed his hand harder and he didn't take it away.

My breath got close and short. He looked away toward the wall and

I looked away toward the fireplace. He moved his hand and rubbed my nipple and the sweetness soaked all through me. When Mr. Griffin had fondled me I had been scared, but when John touched me I wasn't scared at all.

We sat like that a long time, and I was afraid he would take his hand away. I was afraid he would say the Lord was watching us. But he didn't say anything. He reached his other hand and put it on my other breast, and then he hugged me closer to him.

It was the first time I really knew what a touch could mean. A touch connects you and makes you feel a part of everything. A touch makes you feel at the center of something. I leaned back against him, for that was what I wanted to do, to touch him more and deeper. I had to press myself against him and rest myself against him.

He was breathing sharp and hard then. I felt his heart jumping against my back. He moved his hand down my belly and stroked lower, so I felt itches and sparks around my thighs and groin. The itch was so bad the skin stretched sideways and prickled.

"Hold me tighter," I said.

I felt something soft on the back of my neck, something hot and damp and knew it was his lips. He ran his lips from the edge of my hair to the top of my shoulder. And he pressed his lips to the back of my neck. I didn't know what I was going to do next, but I leaned harder against him.

"I don't care," I said.

What happened then is hard for me to say, for it was as if a colored smoke covered everything. There was no light in the cabin but the dying fire. I think he took off my shirt and then took off his shirt and trousers, and we got under the blankets in his bed. I remember how I giggled when he put his hand between my legs. The soreness was all gone there, but the itch and tickle were worse. It was the itch of swelling I felt.

"Where have you come from?" John said before he kissed me. He ran his lips along my upper lip and then along my lower lip. He moved his lips across my cheek. I kissed him back. I kissed the short whiskers on his upper lip and around the ends of his mouth. When he shaved he had missed some whiskers there at the corner. I kissed the dimple of his chin.

John moved his mouth down my chin and neck. His kissed my breast and I felt his tongue on my nipple. Is this what love is all about? I thought. I'd always wondered what it was about. What will happen next? I wondered.

When John got on top of me I could feel his weight. He was slim and tall, so much bigger than me. I remembered Mr. Griffin's weight, and the hog shite smell on the ground, and for an instant I was scared. I almost screamed and started to push John away. But he was too big and strong to push away. And after a second I remembered I didn't want to push him away.

When John pushed me open and put himself inside it hurt a little, but not like it had when Mr. Griffin attacked me. It hurt a little, but mostly it felt numb, hot and itchy and numb at once. And then it was like I was being stretched, and the stretching hurt but felt good too.

"I don't care," I said out of breath.

But John didn't answer. In the dark he moved up like he was crawling over me, and then backed away and crawled again. I closed my eyes because I couldn't see anyway, and felt through my skin. It was as if I could see with my skin where he touched me, where he brushed my shoulder and my breasts. In the dark I could see with every part of me. And what I saw was everything stretched out and swelled up and sparkling. Everything was soft and washing in waves. I was turning to syrup and melting all through me. My legs were trembling and my belly was washing around.

And it felt like my bones were turning into June apple jelly. I saw I had to push myself against John down there. I had to aim myself and push myself. I was soft as jelly and sweet as jelly, but I had to aim myself and press firm.

"Where are you going?" I said out of breath. For it seemed to me John was traveling somewhere. He was about to go somewhere far away.

I smelled the blankets around my head, and they smelled like him. They smelled like the powder he put on his face after he shaved, and they smelled of his breath. The bed smelled of wood smoke and powder and coffee, and a little bit of sweat. And I smelled my own hair and sweat too. I smelled my own breath.

John rose higher above me and fell. This is what I have wanted, I thought. Even when I didn't know it, this is what I always wanted. I aimed myself at him and pushed myself. My skin all over had turned to honey. I was yellow honey and red honey with the sun on it.

And then I saw my skin was light and clean, faint as sourwood honey. I think I hollered out, and there came a buzzing in my ears. The buzzing got louder and I knew something was going to hurt. Something was so sweet it was going to sting.

John spoke to me right in my ear, but it was like he was a long way off too. For he was big as a mountain above me, and he reached out long as the farthest ridge. His shoulders were bigger than the oak trees, bigger than houses. His shoulders reared up like mountaintops.

"You have come to me," he said in a whisper. "You have been sent to me." But the whisper could have been a shout that filled the sky. The buzz I heard rose, like wind on a mountainside, or a waterfall during a flood. And it sounded like heavy rain was falling. And I thought water would rub away the sweetness from my skin and from my belly.

But it was too late to stop, for John was pushing. He was driving something that reached a secret place, and when he hollered out it felt like something touched my heart and licked my heart with a hot tongue.

We lay breathing in the blankets as if we were frozen in our sweat. We lay in the dark too weak to move a finger. I didn't want to say anything because there was nothing to say. Whatever there was to say had already been said.

NEXT MORNING JOHN was already up when I woke. He had started a fire and was boiling water for coffee, and he was crushing coffee beans between two rocks. I got up and put my hands on his shoulders, but he didn't look at me. He just kept on crushing the beans between the stones.

"Good morning," I said, trying to sound like a wife greeting her husband. I got dressed and combed my hair. I felt sore as something that has been stretched, but I felt wonderful too. John made porridge, and when we sat down to eat hot porridge and drink coffee he finally spoke.

"What we did last night was wrong," he said.

I knew if I said it didn't feel wrong to me, he would just argue and quote Scripture. So I didn't argue.

John looked at the fire and he looked at his mug of coffee. He nodded his head and looked at me. He was the most eloquent preacher I'd ever heard, and yet he found it hard to say what he was feeling.

"The Lord has sent you to me," he finally said.

"And the Lord has sent you to me," I said.

"The Lord has sent me a helpmeet and a partner," he said. "But we must be married."

I was thrilled and scared, for after what Mr. Griffin did to me, and me to him, I was unworthy.

"We can be married," I said.

"We can't be married," John said, and shook his head. I saw he'd thought it through already. During the night he had waked up and studied on it while I was sleeping.

"Why can't you marry me?" I said, and swallowed.

"All my flocks think you're a boy," he said, and looked hard at me.

He'd thought it through and figured it all out. I'd been so excited the night before I'd forgotten that everybody thought I was a boy named Joseph. Everybody thought I was John's assistant.

We talked about John's letter after breakfast. We talked about moving farther west into the mountains, and about moving down to South Carolina. We talked about me leaving to go to South Carolina, and John said he wouldn't let me go. I asked him why not, since we were in such a pickle.

"Because we are married in the sight of God," he said. And then I saw a light in his face like he had gotten an idea.

"We must perform the ceremony ourselves," he said. "Our wedding must be kept secret for a season."

He said he would perform the ceremony now, but that I should continue to wear boy's clothes. There was no other way for us to be together. At some time in the future, it would all have to come out. I didn't argue with him, for it was the best plan I could think of too. I was happier than I ever thought I could be.

John got out the little prayer book that he carried in his coat pocket. He had me stand beside him facing the fireplace as he read from the little book.

"Dearly beloved: We are gathered together here in the sight, and in the face of this community, to join together this Man and this Woman in Holy Matrimony; which is an honorable estate, instituted by God in the time of man's innocency, signifying to us the mystical union that is betwixt Christ and his Church: which holy estate Christ adorned and beautified with his presence and first miracle that he wrought in Cana of Galilee, and is commended of Saint Paul to be honorable among all men."

John read from the book a long time. I'd been to a wedding of a cousin once, but I didn't remember so many words and such a sermon at that ceremony. I looked at John as he read.

"Josie," he said, looking at me, "will you have this man to thy wedded husband; to live together after God's ordinance in the holy estate of Matrimony? Wilt thou obey him and serve him, love, honor and keep him in sickness and in health; and, forsaking all others, keep thee unto him, so long as ye both shall live?"

"I will," I said.

And then John read the same thing to himself and answered himself. He read some more. We didn't have any rings to exchange, but he read that passage too. He read the whole sermon in the little prayer book. It was such a pretty ceremony I had tears in my eyes.

"Send thy blessing upon these thy servants, this man and this woman, whom we bless in thy Name; that, as Isaac and Rebecca lived faithfully together, so these persons may perform and keep the vow and covenant betwixt them made . . . Amen."

John said the words like they were coming from the heart, as if he was thinking of them for the first time. When it was over he leaned down and took my cheeks between his hands. He looked into my eyes and kissed me. As his lips touched mine he closed his eyes and I closed mine too. His lips were firm and soft at the same time. He ran his tongue over my lips.

I was wearing Mr. Griffin's clothes and my old shoes, but I felt happy as a bride wearing white lace and satin. If I had been standing in a great church, at the altar, with perfume and incense and two hundred people watching, I could not have been more thrilled. John's kiss made me feel I was whirling around, that I was dancing, even though I was standing still. His kiss made the air lavender and pink. I was sixteen years old, and I was married to a tall preacher man, and we were standing in our own cabin in the woods of Pine Knot Branch.

There was no wine to drink, no infare party, no fiddle music for dancing. But we did sing a song by the fireplace, that cold morning, as we held hands and looked into each other's eyes. We sang "Joy to the World" because it was the song that came to mind, and it seemed to fit the way we felt and what had happened between us.

THE NEXT FEW DAYS were the happiest I had ever known. In the night we loved, and during the day we worked around the cabin. We cut a supply of firewood for the winter, and we mixed mud and straw for mortar to chink the cabin walls. We took long walks in the woods and sat on a hill to watch the clouds. We lay in an orchard and sang and John played his flute. We gathered chestnuts under a grove on another hill and roasted them by a fire. We had a picnic by a creek.

One day John remembered we had to go over to the meeting house at Briar Fork. Those folks were expecting him in the evening, and I had to go along as his assistant as usual.

"We do not choose to deceive," John said. "And all is plain in the eyes of God."

I dressed up as usual and put on Mr. Griffin's gray coat and a heavy wool cap of John's. But in my heart I knew I was Mrs. John Trethman. That's who I was in the eyes of God.

Though we had no wine, John had a jar of medicine whiskey in the cabin and we had a cup of that to celebrate before we started out. We drank the strong liquor and it burned my throat and brought tears to my eyes. But it warmed my belly and thrilled my blood, like the last few days had thrilled me.

To get to Briar Fork we had to cross Bee Water Mountain. It was a long steep running ridge, and the trail ran along a kind of shelf about halfway up the mountain. It was a long walk and we had got a late start. We would have to hurry. It had been dry that fall and the dirt along the trail was dusty as chalk. The creek we passed was dried up to a thread of water.

I reckon we'd just gotten to the foot of the mountain when we smelled smoke. The wind had been behind us, and we hadn't noticed the smoke before. It was the smell of burning leaves and burning trees, of scorched sap and roots. We saw the smoke and smelled the smoke, but we couldn't tell exactly where the fire was. Smoke drifted through the trees, but we couldn't see just where it came from.

John stopped and looked around. "Where is the wind coming from?" he said.

I licked my finger and held it up. I'd always heard you could tell where the wind was coming from by which side dried first. I looked at my finger, but it was hard to be sure. John said he thought the wind was from the south.

"I don't want to walk right into the fire," he said.

The trail ran west over Bee Water Mountain. I asked if there was any other trail to Briar Fork, but John said he didn't know of any. If the wind was coming from the south then the fire was on our left.

"We'll have to hurry," John said, and we started walking again, faster. The smoke burned my eyes a little and I coughed as I breathed deeper. As we started to climb I hoped we'd get away from the fire. But the farther we went the less we could see, because the smoke got thicker. There were rocks leaning over the trail and big oak trees. But we could have been in a fog on a rainy day for all you could see. There was nothing to do but hurry on to get away from it. I'd never seen so much smoke. It smelled like the whole world was on fire.

"We can turn back if you want to," John said.

"We can't be late," I said.

The trail ran along about halfway up the mountain. The ground fell away so steeply on the left I didn't want to look down, and the ground rose so steeply on the right I didn't want to look up. Looking up at the steepness made me dizzy, made me feel I was falling away. In the thick smoke the mountain seemed like a place in a dream. The ridge above was steep as dread. My chest was sore from breathing the smoke.

Something flushed across the trail in front of us and I saw it was the white tail of a deer. And then I saw a raccoon and a rabbit run up the side of the mountain ahead of us. Another deer bounded past and didn't pay any attention to us.

"They are running away from the fire," John shouted.

But instead of running out the trail to the west, the animals were climbing straight up the mountainside. I wondered if we ought to be following them. But the ridge above had cliffs and thickets. It looked nearly impossible to climb.

We walked along the trail even faster, but the smoke was getting so thick you couldn't see anything. It was a brown dirty smoke that made you cough. My eyes were watering, but my hands were full. I rubbed my eyes with the back of my hands. I bent lower, hoping to get my face out of the worst of the smoke. We came around a bend where the trail ran near the head of a hollow and I heard a roar.

"What is that?" I yelled. John stopped and listened, but I already knew what it was. There was crackling and popping and a whooshing sound. But we still couldn't see anything except the smoke. Smoke was so thick my throat burned.

The roaring sounded behind us, and then it seemed ahead of us. A polecat ran across the path just ahead.

"We must keep going," John shouted.

Just then we saw the flames. I don't know if the smoke cleared a little or the wind changed, or the fire got closer. But we saw a flame here and we saw a flame there in the woods below us. Fire was jumping from limb to limb and from tree to tree. It looked like there was fire behind us and fire ahead of us.

And then I felt the heat. Before that moment the smoke had been cool. But suddenly the air was warm, and then it was hot. It was like the air just in front of a fireplace, or a blacksmith's furnace. The fire was climbing up the ridge below us and sending its heat and smoke ahead. Burning leaves and pieces of ash flew by us. The blaze was throwing rags of fire ahead. The air was hot enough to scorch you.

"Where can we go?" I screamed.

We looked ahead and saw fire already on the trail at the head of the hollow. Flames jumped from bush to bush up there.

I'd never felt anything like the heat coming up the mountainside. It blistered my face just to look that way. The fire was behind us and below us, and the fire was in the treetops. There was a wall of fire crawling and leaping up the mountain. It was a thousand different fires jumping sideways and straight up. Fire shot ahead and fell to the ground. The ground itself seemed to be on fire.

"Lord help us," I hollered.

"We must climb straight up," John said.

We had to drop the lantern and our bundles. John slipped his Bible and songbook inside his shirt. He gave me a push up the mountain which was steep as a road bank. I grabbed hold of trees and saplings and pulled myself up. I clawed the leaves and grabbed fistfuls of dirt. I crawled on my knees and gripped roots and rocks. John reached back and pulled me over a log.

But the fire was getting closer. I felt the heat on my backside and on my feet. The soles of my shoes were hot. Burning leaves and twigs fell around me. A pine bush burst into flame. I reckon the air on the mountainside was so hot things were just kindling all by themselves.

I figured if we could reach the top of the ridge we might get away from the fire. The fire would slow down at the ridge comb and we could drop down to the cool north side. But there didn't seem to be anything but laurel bushes and rocks and oak trees above us. We were a long way from the top of the ridge.

John looked back at me and yelled, "Take your coat off." Mr. Griffin's gray coat had caught fire on my back and I burned my hands a little jerking it off. The tail of the coat was burning and I beat it out on the ground. John grabbed my hand and pulled me up the steep slope.

But the worst thing was when I looked ahead and saw fire up there too. The fire had leaped over us and the mountainside above was already burning. Other fires were starting around us and in the trees above us. And the big wall of fire was just below us. The air was so hot I smothered and coughed and couldn't see anything. This is what hell is like, I thought. This is the devil's torment.

John turned to the left and he turned to the right. He stumbled backward and pulled me with him. I thought he'd gone crazy. The heat was so bad and the smoke was so bad I couldn't tell anything anymore. We ran sideways but the fire stopped us. The fire had us hemmed in.

"We've got to run," John said, but he looked around confused. He looked up in the trees like he thought of climbing them, but fire was already jumping in the limbs above us. He looked back down the slope, and then he looked at me. I saw a change come over his face, like he'd decided what to do. John rushed forward to where the fire had already burned, and he started raking ashes and smoking leaves. He clawed into the dirt and roots with his bare hands, like he was trying to dig a grave.

"What are you doing?" I yelled.

John dug out a kind of hole in the mountainside, and then he grabbed me and pushed me down into the fresh dirt. He fell on top of me so hard my face was pushed down into the ground. My mouth was right in the dirt and my teeth ground in the soil, and I couldn't move, for John was on my back and holding me down. My nose was mashed into the ground so I could hardly breathe and I couldn't yell. John's head lay right on mine so I couldn't raise up.

He is trying to kill me so I won't suffer from burning up, I thought. He is trying to save me from the pain of roasting. Above John's breathing, I could hear the fire. There was snapping and crackling and a rush of wind like a chimney on fire. There was a whoosh of flames on top of flames, and flames inside of flames. It was the awful breathing of fire.

I thought, this is the last thing I will remember. I couldn't get any breath except dirt in my mouth. There was dirt on my tongue, and I couldn't see anything. John was crushing me with his weight on the back of my head.

I must have fainted then, for the next thing I knew John had lifted some of the pressure from my head and back. He got off me and pulled me up. I was dizzy and my eyes were watering so badly I could hardly see. There was dirt in my nose and in my mouth. I blew my nose and tried to spit out the dirt. I spit and spit and coughed.

There was smoke in the air but it wasn't as thick as before. Everything was smoldering and smoking. Everything was black as soot. The fire had gone on up the mountain. I could hear the flames crackling and raging up above us.

John's face was red and his hair was singed. He had taken off his coat and beat the flames out while I was coughing. And I saw his trousers were burned right at the seat. He'd burned his buttocks and his back as he lay over me while the mighty fire raged past us. His face was black and already blistered. I was not burned anywhere because he had shielded me. He had saved us by crawling into the ashes.

I put my arms around him trying not to touch the burns on his back. The mountainside was nothing but smoldering black trees.

FIVE

IT WAS HARD TO tell how bad the burns on John's backside and back were. His boots had partly burned too, but I don't think the flames had touched his feet. His back was such a mess of soot and blood and burned cloth, and he smelled like meat braised in a pan. I was afraid to touch him again. I wondered if I ought to put my coat over his back.

The fire was gnashing and raging in the woods above us, but the smoke was starting to clear lower down the mountain. John moaned and gritted his teeth when he moved.

"I'll have to get somebody to help us," I said.

"No, I can walk," John said, and winced as he twisted around.

"You can't even stand up," I said.

John held on to me and stumbled to his feet, his teeth clenched with the pain. The burns made him stiff and the burns tore on his skin every time he moved. He held on to my shoulder.

"You go on to Briar Fork and lead the service," he said.

"I can't lead any service," I said.

"You must," he said and looked me hard in the eye. The pain made him sweat through the soot on his face.

"I have never preached," I said. "I've never even led in prayer."

"They know you are my assistant," John said. "Even if you only sing one song and say one prayer, and tell them I'm injured, it's better than to leave them waiting." He reached into his shirt and took out the Bible and the songbook. They had not been touched by the fire. They were clean and cool.

"You are my wife," he said. "You must do this for me." He handed me the books.

I didn't know what to say. I looked at the blood and soot on his back. I couldn't just leave him there on the smoking ground. I was only married a few days, and my husband had asked me to do something for him. I had a duty to him.

"If you love me you will go now and take my message to Briar Fork," John said. "You are my wife."

"Because I'm your wife I'm not going to leave you," I said. It came to me that because of the pain John was not at himself. I had to stay with him and look after him. I was only sixteen years old, but I could see that.

"Then you have deceived me," John said. "I thought you loved me."

"You can't walk by yourself," I said.

"Then damn you!" John shouted.

I broke a stick to use as a crutch, and I helped John stumble down the trail. The mountain was burned as far as I could see and smoke rose thick as pillows into the sky. Sooty birds and burned rabbits lay on the trail. The smells of burned meat and scorched bark and sour roots were sickening. Bushes here and there were still burning. John didn't say any more about me going to Briar Fork, but I could tell he was angry. His face was sooty and grim and he was sweating with the pain and heat of the burns.

It was almost dark as we started back on the trail. We were at least an hour from Pine Knot Branch. We didn't have any lantern, and my night eyes were ruined by the glare of the fire farther up the mountain. As it got dark you could see all the little blazes on the side of the mountain where the fire had been. The mountain looked like hell itself tilted up to the sky.

There were fires burning close to the trail and that made it a little easier to see our way. I stumbled over rocks and charred logs, and held John's arm tight. The woods were dark as a cave away from the scattered fires, and poplar trees loomed above, hung with blackened grapevines.

John stopped walking and leaned on his crutch. He trembled so badly I had to hold him up.

I can't say how long it took us to get back to the cabin. It might have been three hours, or it might have been five. I tried to help John as much as I could, but mostly he had to lean on the stick and hobble. I had to lay down the books and help him across branches.

When we finally got back to the cabin it must have been near midnight. Something was wrong there, for we stumbled on things in the doorway and on the floor. Nothing was where it was supposed to be.

"Is anybody here?" John called out.

Finally I found the flint and tinder on the mantel and struck a fire in the fireplace. John's bed was knocked over and the table was knocked over. Pots and pans and dishes were scattered on the floor. A sack of cornmeal had been cut and was spread like lime on the mess.

When I held the candle up to the mantel I saw the writing in charcoal across the logs. DEATH, it said. I held the candle closer. DEATH TO REBELS, it said.

I turned the bench over so John could sit down. But his backside was too sore to sit down. He would have to lie down on his belly. I turned the bed upright and put the quilts on it and helped him lie down. His pants and shirt were so badly burned I just cut them off. And with the candle I looked at the burns. In places there was blood, and in other places the flesh was black. Around the edges there were blisters big as eggs. John was burned deeply on his buttocks. I'd never seen such burns, nor known somebody in that kind of pain, since Mr. Griffin was beaten.

I'd always heard you put grease on a burn. In the spring behind the cabin there was some butter one of John's flock had given us a few days before. I took the candle and ran to see if the butter was still there. What a relief when I lifted the lid of the crock and saw the butter firm and clean as ever. I grabbed the crock and ran back to the cabin.

Pinching off a piece of the butter, I rubbed it between my hands till it was melted and wiped the grease on John's back.

John screamed.

I told him I'd try to be gentle. But there was no easy way to spread butter on the wounds. Melted butter could be dripped on the burns, but then it would be too hot. I rubbed as softly as I could, and melted the butter in a cup to drip it on the worst places. I covered every inch of the burns with glistening butter.

But John needed something for the pain too. There was nothing I could think of but the jug of medicine liquor. I poured some in a cup and gave him a dram. John gulped the whiskey and shook his head. I reckon the liquor burned his throat.

"What you need is laudanum," I said.

He shook his head like he couldn't think what to say. I asked him what was the matter, but he just kept shaking his head. And then he coughed liquor and spit out of his mouth. He threw up over the end of the bed. I ran to get a pan and held it under his chin. I held his forehead that was streaming with sweat.

That was the longest night I'd ever seen. John couldn't sleep because of the pain, and he couldn't move around either. He had to lie on his belly, and he needed sleep and rest. He needed something to stop the pain. But liquor was the only thing we had, and he couldn't hold that in his stomach. I gave him water to drink and he gulped that. The burns made him thirsty and hot. I went out to the spring and got some cold fresh water. But after John drank he heaved up the fresh water too.

John's shoulders shook and I thought he was trying to say something. But then I saw he was crying. He was weeping like a baby he was in such pain. But almost as bad as the pain was the fact that he couldn't sleep and he couldn't move. He had to lie there on his belly helpless. He was not at himself and he sobbed as if his heart was broken. There wasn't anything I could do but sit there and wipe his forehead and neck with a damp cloth. He had burned himself to save me. It was a miracle we were both alive. I didn't sleep any watching him.

"I'm being punished for my failures," he said again and again.

"You saved my life," I said. "You saved both our lives."

Before it had been me that was in need, and John was the grown-up person in charge. I was sixteen and he was twenty-four. He was the preacher and I was the guilty waif. I wasn't any better than an orphan. But with John helpless and in pain, he might as well have been a child. He couldn't do anything for himself. Even to twist a little made him holler. I was the only one there to do for him. John began jerking with the chills. I built up the fire and heated the cabin more, but he was still shivering. His teeth rattled and his shoulders trembled.

"I'm cold," he said. I'd heard of chills and fever, but you got that in the summer, in the hottest weather. I would have put a blanket over him except his back was so bad you couldn't lay anything over the burns. He couldn't stand the pain of a feather, much less a blanket.

After looking at the fireplace and around the room, I moved a bench and some pots out of the way, and I scooted the bed closer to the fire.

But John kept shivering. He had lost so much skin on his back, I figured there was nothing to hold the warmth in him. There was nothing to hold the warmth of his blood. If I didn't find some way to warm him he might freeze to death.

I got more wood from outside and threw it on the fire. The blaze made the room brighter and threw the glare on John's side. But I saw I had to get the heat under him, under the bed. I'd heard that when people rode in carriages in winter they heated bricks and wrapped them in cloth and put them at their feet, so I ran outside in the gray light of early morning and looked for rocks. There was frost on everything, white as a week's growth of beard on an old man. The brush and sticks in the yard, everything, was covered with frost. But there was a pile of rocks beside the chimney, heaped where they'd been left when the chimney was built. The rocks had frost and dirt on them. I rubbed them off and carried them in one at a time. The rocks were so cold they burned my hands, but I lined them up on the hearth in the edge of the fire.

While the rocks were heating in the flames, I looked around for some other way to warm John up. He was still shuddering and jerking. It's hard to get warm when your blood is chilled, when the blood in your heart is cooled.

There were some rawhide strings hanging from a peg beside the fireplace. I cut them into pieces and stretched them in an X from the four posts of the bed. I stretched the strings about three inches above John's back, and then laid a blanket over the strings. I tied the blanket so it didn't touch him.

"I'm freezing," John said, and his teeth chattered. He sounded weaker.

Water was boiling already in the kettle and I hammered some coffee beans to powder and made coffee. The scent filled the cabin.

When the rocks were hot I rolled them into pans and slid them under the bed. The heat came up through the bed like there was a furnace down there. I poured coffee in a mug and held it to John's lips.

"You don't need to wait on me," he said, his lips trembling.

"There's nobody else to do it," I said.

After throwing up, I guess he felt too weak to drink anything. But he was parched inside. The coffee smelled fresh and strong and he took a sip. And then he took another sip. The coffee was so hot it smoked, but he sipped it between his lips. He was shaking and he took a sip and pulled away. He took another sip.

As the heat rose from the rocks, and was held in by the blanket over his back, John stopped jerking so badly. He took longer and longer sips of the coffee. He was so thirsty he needed the coffee. And the more he drank the clearer it was he wasn't going to throw up again. I'd heard that coffee was good for a troubled stomach, and now it seemed to be true. As he drank more coffee in little gulps, I saw John was feeling better and looked a little better.

"Do you want some grits?" I said.

"More coffee," he said.

"Do you want some whiskey in the coffee?" I said.

"Pour in a spoonful," John said. I added a dram of liquor to the mug of coffee and held it to his lips again.

The coffee was the only thing that seemed to help. It warmed him inside so he quit jerking and his chin stopped trembling. I reckon the liquor helped too. As I watched him sip I could almost feel the coffee going out from his belly into his arms and legs. Strong coffee makes the world seem brighter and your thoughts clearer.

After John drank the coffee, I fed him some grits with butter. There is nothing richer in the morning than grits and butter. It was what John needed to get back some strength.

After he ate the grits John dropped off to sleep. It was the first time he'd slept. His head lay sideways on the pillow and he slept with his mouth a little open. He muttered in his sleep like he was remembering something or arguing with somebody.

The rocks under the bed had cooled and I slid the pans out and rolled the rocks back into the edge of the fire. And then I went outside to get more rocks so I would have some to heat while the others were under the bed. It was a clear cold day, the first day that felt like winter. I carried in three dirty rocks, and when I went out to get a fourth I saw men on horses coming up the trail.

A pain stabbed through me, because the man in front wore a uniform. It was not a red uniform, like an officer of the Crown wore. But a man in uniform was always dangerous.

"Have you seen a cavalry?" the officer called out to me.

"No, sir," I said.

"Don't lie to us, lad," the officer said.

"I'm not lying," I said, and shivered in the cold.

"We know the dragoons came through here last night," he said, and swung down from the saddle. The rest of the men stayed on their horses.

"We were away last night," I said.

"You ain't lying?" the officer said. He stepped up close.

"This is the house of Rev. John Trethman," I said. "The preacher got burned last night in the fire on Bee Water Mountain."

"Are you hiding a soldier?" the officer said, and pushed me aside. He took out his sword and opened the cabin door. I followed him in and saw John had waked up.

"Sir, he is badly burned," I said.

The officer marched to the bed and tore the blanket off the strings. "Who done this?" he said.

"He was burned in the woods fire," I said.

The soldier looked around the cabin and pointed to John. "If you are harboring a soldier of the Crown, you will be burned and your house too," he said.

"I'm just a parson," John said, "and Joseph is my assistant."

The officer searched around the cabin. He saw the writing on the mantel. "You wrote that?" he said.

"That was done while we were away," I said.

"So the dragoons were here," he said. He saw a basket with eggs in the corner and ran his sword through the handle and carried it outside. I followed him.

"We will burn you out if you harbor redcoats," he yelled, and climbed into the saddle. I had been meaning to boil the eggs for us. I was hoping to make eggs and hoecakes. But I figured we were lucky to lose only the eggs. As they rode away I hurried back inside and put the blanket over John, and I put more rocks in the fire.

"These are terrible times," I said to John.

John Trethman

It was the second day, when Joseph got up and fixed hoecakes, then helped me dig the graves, that I understood the help might not be just from me to him. For I never saw a more willing assistant. Though slender in his person, he had hands rough from work and his back was strong. As I watched him fill in the graves I saw the Lord might have sent me an assistant. After my years of solitary travel and preaching, the Lord might have sent someone to share my burden, and my joy. The thought made me so happy I dared not think of it, and I felt guilty, for I had assumed I would do my work alone.

Your will be done, I prayed. For I didn't dare ask for such assistance. But I thought of Paul, and how Silas was sent to travel with him and pray with him and sing with him when they were in chains. And Timothy was sent also. And of course Jesus himself had his beloved disciple John.

But I dared not suggest to Joseph that he become my permanent assistant. For I didn't know what burden he carried in his mind. And I didn't know what plans either. I would not hurry him, and I would not make him feel an obligation. He must stay with me and assist me of his own free will.

Being with Joseph made me feel young again. As we walked in the woods and waded streams and raised a hymn in the glade, as we carried potatoes in our pockets to bake over an open fire for supper, and carried wood for our fire, his presence made the work more significant. His presence made the work seem like play. And the hours with Joseph went by so fast they seemed mere minutes. He was like a younger brother I must cheer up. When I knew him better I would ask what terrible secret he carried in his heart. But in the meantime I would befriend him and try not to pry.

I saw that he did not know the Scripture, and he knew only a few hymns. I would not pry, but I would teach him the Gospels and the Prophets. And I would teach him to sing harmonies with me. I would teach him to read Scripture, and to recite the Psalms and Proverbs aloud. His speech was surprisingly proper. I did not have many books, but I would teach him to read those I had. In the wilderness we would study together and memorize verses, and we would sing.

In those violent days I found no greater support and shield than music. Music soothed the hate and fear in the air. Sometimes every valley seemed heavy and torn with anger. Music seemed to calm and heal the air and the passing hours.

"Joseph, you will sing with me," I said.

"I'll be happy to sing," he said, "though my voice is poor."

"You have a fine soprano," I said. "You might have sung in a boy's choir."

Watching Joseph study the Bible and the hymnbook, I saw that I could become a teacher also. I could someday build a larger house and take pupils. I could teach reading and writing and numbers, music and Latin. I could bring letters and history to that troubled wilderness.

Since a boy I had known my greatest weakness was an ugly temper. I had always been too quick to anger. When surprised by a cousin or school fellow I was one to lash out before thinking. I could be calm and attentive, considerate and helpful, until something surprised me, jolted me, and instantly I wanted to hit and hurt. In a second all my humility was gone.

In school a boy once seized my cap and threw it in the mud, and I hit him with my fist. I looked at his pig-blue eyes and wanted to drive his nose behind the eyes into his brain. I pushed him against a fence post and hit him as the other boys watched in astonishment. And later I was ashamed when I saw the blood on his face and dripping from his chin.

When the other boys teased me for being tall and thin, for studying the Bible, for loving song, I kept my own counsel and smiled at them. For I knew my strength was my cheer and goodwill. I would not be teased. I worked hard to stay calm when baited and laughed with my detractors. As long as I was not surprised I could pretend to be calm. I knew anger made me weak, and conquering my anger was not a choice but a necessity.

At college once a bully asked to borrow my Latin book. When I handed him the volume he opened it and spat a huge oyster between the pages. Then with a smirk he handed the book back to me. Before I knew it I shoved the corner of the book into his face. Fury rose like a flame through my bones and chest and I hit him repeatedly in the eye with the sharp corner of the book. I hit him until his cheek was cut and his eye wet. His nose bled and his ear bled. But once the fit had passed I was amazed at myself.

Nothing makes a minister look weaker than anger. Nothing makes a preacher look more foolish than an outburst of ill temper. One rage can destroy a testimony among a congregation. One tantrum can nullify your witness. When the message is of love and praise one lapse of fury can destroy faith and confidence. I had worked all my life to control my frustration, to anticipate adversity, to conceal my sudden anger.

But the pain of my burns on Bee Water Mountain undercut my will, erased my confidence. I saw that I was being punished for deceiving my congregations, for my secret marriage, for my many other failures. I was being tried, and I had been found wanting. And because of my weakness and pain I could not control my anger, even as Josie nursed me. I was ashamed of myself and ashamed for her to see me so churlish.

Before I was ordained I taught a Sunday school in the country outside Williamsburg. It was a group of boys and girls who met in the school house beside the little church. I read from the Bible and told them stories and we sang hymns. There was a redheaded boy in the class named Ethan, bigger than the other boys. Ethan was always teasing and pestering and bullying someone. He could not keep still, and he could not let the others alone.

I always said a short prayer with the class and had them recite the Lord's Prayer. We stood and closed our eyes and repeated the words in unison. One Sunday we were reciting the prayer and the little schoolhouse rang with their young voices. For some reason I opened my eye a squint and saw Ethan sliding the stool from behind a girl named Selma. Selma was good-natured but almost blind, and afflicted in her mind. She could barely speak plain enough to be understood. Without the stool she would fall on her backside when I told the class to sit.

Quick, before I knew what I was doing, I reached out to push Ethan away but hit him with my Bible. I'd only meant to stop him, I told myself. But the Bible was in my hand, and I hit him on the ear and cheek with the holy book. He looked at me with astonishment, and I was astonished at myself also.

I was so shaken and embarrassed I dismissed the class. As they left the schoolhouse I heard one boy say, "I never saw nobody hit with a Bible before."

Another said, "He throwed the Good Book at poor Ethan."

I expected to be dismissed from the Sunday school. I apologized to the minister of the church and all the congregation. And I promised myself I would be on guard against sudden anger.

Whatever virtues I had, my anger showed my human weakness. No matter that Jesus showed his anger in the temple by chasing the money changers and hypocrites away. And Peter had an all-too-human anger.

In the garden of Gethsemane he cut off a man's ear, and Jesus had to put the ear back on the man's head.

Since nothing will damage a testimony and witness as quick as anger, I steeled myself against rage, and worked to calm and soothe myself. If I could cool my blood and quiet my breath enough to sing, then I could conquer the evil heat that rose in my blood and in my marrow. For anger is the devil's fire roaring to consume the work of love and fellowship. I knew the evil in my own pulse and in my own hot words.

WHEN I FOUND JOSEPH had deceived me and was a girl with breasts under the rough shirt and coat I was stunned. For Joseph was my helper, dear to me and a blessing sent to me. In a daze, I was unable to understand what had happened. Anger rose like a shadow inside the light, something raw and bloody. I saw my ministry ruined from the most unexpected source. My witness had been compromised by the very blessing I'd rejoiced in. Joseph had ruined me just when I was most grateful for his help.

I wanted to slap his face and crush his neck between my hands. I wanted to reach out and break his face, blind him and crush his features. I saw why he had never answered a call of nature in my presence, why he had told me so little about his life before he appeared at Zion Hill. He had invaded and contaminated my mission. He had made me look wicked and foolish.

I wished I could erase Joseph from my house and from the past few weeks. I wished I could expunge him from my life and from the memory of my congregations. I reached back to strike him, but something stopped me. Perhaps it was his eyes, except they were *her* eyes, watching me in grief, as if begging me to punish, begging me to repay the deception.

It was the *her*-ness that stopped me. It was the awfulness of the femininity that had been so close, under my roof those several weeks. I stayed my hand and plunged toward the door. I had to get out of her presence and out of the cabin. I had to get beyond reach of her before I did violence to her or to myself.

Anger destroys our wit; fury makes us stupid. I plunged into the cold woods stomping the ground in my rage and surprise. I was blinded by the tide of fury within me. I didn't notice the northern lights above the trees and their display of heavenly glory. The sky did its dance of seven veils, but I stumbled foolishly through the brush and briars.

In a few seconds my ministry and my career had come to a halt. I would have revenge, but what revenge could be found? What relief, what compensation was possible? To hurt Josie, to murder Josie, would bring neither revenge nor comfort. I would have to become calm and cunning. But what could be cunning enough to save me from the scandal that would ensue? How could I be cunning in the face of such humiliation?

I stalked through the swamps and branches hardly noticing the limbs that slashed my face. I shoved my way through canebrakes in the dark, and tangled my feet in wild peavines. I lost all consciousness of direction. The river seemed to circle my head, going first one way and then another. I spat into my hands and rubbed spit on my face.

Wake up from your stupor, I said to myself. Wake up from the idiocy of rage. The times are dangerous and you are in danger. And you are a danger to yourself and to the Lord's work in the wilderness. Wake up you fool. I saw I must not be merely my angry, failing self, but better than myself. I had to become what I should be. Be still and know, I said. Be still and listen.

I had to make my thoughts clear to myself. I was confused and troubled and the times were desperate, about to break open in some awful way. The world was changing and I didn't know in what direction to go.

When studying Hebrew I had learned the word *tohubohu*, at the beginning of Genesis. The word means chaos, wildness, confusion. We were living in times of *tohubohu*. Everything was off kilter, and out of control. And I was off kilter and out of control.

The truth was Josie had startled me and disturbed me. From the moment she appeared at the prayer meeting at Zion Hill, I was struck by her sadness and honesty. And I was pleased when she stayed with me. I who had always worked alone was no longer alone. I was so glad of her company I felt guilty. I had been called to that region to minister and witness. In those harsh times and in that harsh place, my duty was to sing and pray, inspire and exhort. I had not been sent to enjoy myself or indulge myself in friendships and society.

I had always assumed I would work alone. I had been called to the ordinary work of the circuit, to be a wanderer and a pilgrim, and the wilderness was my home. But if I had been sent an assistant, it was my duty to accept and benefit from that blessing.

Besides my anger, I had always had to struggle with doubt and vanity. It was unseemly for a minister to admit such doubts, but as deeply as I felt called, as much as I felt chosen for worship and praise, I had moments of the blackest doubts. And my doubt was caused not only by the sadness and cruelty around me. Faith was challenged every day by the pain and hatefulness in the world. I wanted to know why Jesus permitted such suffering.

But my doubt came just as often from the quietness and coolness of the world. I looked at rocks and mountains and clouds and thought: The world just *is*. No explanation was needed, no plan of salvation. And most blasphemous of all, I thought: Nothing needs redemption. The natural world was just going on about its business by its own laws. It didn't need any divine explanation or human explanation. I thought of the great ages of rocks and rivers, of the vast distances to the stars and between the stars. I thought of the depth of oceans and the sweep of tides, the power of thunderstorms. And I thought those things needed no explanation. They just were, frightening in their majesty. They were sublime.

That was my temptation and a source of my doubt. I loved natural history as much as Mr. Franklin and Governor Jefferson did. I loved the trees and plants, the rocks and streams. I loved clouds over the mountains and the endless chant of waterfalls. I loved the grays and browns of winter afternoons, and the rhythms of the days and nights and seasons.

And then I saw I had made the natural world an idol. I was in danger of becoming a mere pantheist, a worshiper of nature. And I saw the folly of loving something so indifferent to mankind. Nature had no interest in human suffering or in human joy. The natural world had no interest in individuals, in John or Josie, in William or Sarah. It was the Lord who numbered the hairs on our heads and noticed the fall of the sparrow. It was Jesus who loved us in our weakness and in spite of our foolishness and selfishness. It was Jesus who sacrificed himself for us.

People were so troubled and threatened in their hearts every day with violence they needed to be calmed and shown they were loved. They needed the joy and strength of fellowship. They needed to feel joined in a community of believers, inspired and strengthened. I thought I had done some good there west of the Catawba River. While the world was burning and crumbling, I had tried to put some of the pieces back together.

AFTER ANGER MY GREATEST weakness was vanity. Maybe that was why I had Josie read from Ecclesiastes so often. I needed to hear the preacher's warning to myself.

My vanity was not so much of person and appearance, though I could be as vain as anyone in that sense. I wouldn't have minded vestments if I could have afforded them and worn them on my travels through mud and river, briar and canebrake. But living in the wilderness discouraged vanity of appearance.

My vanity was more of talent, more of spoken word and sung note. From the time I attended school, I was the superior student, reading and reciting ahead of my fellow students. I took pride in being first in Latin, in leading, even in mathematics. I was vain of my learning in school, then in college. And I would have been punished by the other students had I not been tall and strong myself.

When I grew mature and knew the call to the ministry, I vowed to be humble and curb my pride and my ambition. I couldn't preach humility while living myself in vanity and visions of superiority to those I served.

But then I found I took pride in my goodness and humility, and that was the most dangerous pride of all. What an arrogance the feeling of humility could be. I urged myself to be humble and compassionate to all people and creatures, and yet I was prideful, puffed up with visions of my own splendor. My vanity remained.

Jesus says in Matthew that some may be as eunuchs in their service to the Lord. But then Paul says in 1 Corinthians 7:9 it is better to marry than to burn. I was a man like any man, and I told myself that some day I might marry. But I knew that for the moment I must remain single while I traveled to my scattered congregations. In those desperate times I must remain alone, for I had no adequate house and no sustenance to begin a family.

Josie seemed at first like my younger brother, willing to help, and then like my wicked and deceptive little sister. I couldn't justify keeping her in my house, however much I wanted her to stay. I could not send her out into the wilderness alone, and I could not bear to be alone again myself. Yet I could not see how we could honorably stay together unless I married her. But if we married it would look as though she had been my mistress. And she would have the shame of having dressed as a boy and pretended to be a boy. Such a marriage could only threaten and weaken my ministry there where worship and piety were only beginning to take root.

I prayed about Josie and I thought about marriage. I considered sending her away for a season, to Charlotte or Gilbert Town, to return later as a girl. Or I could go away later and bring her back as my wife. But who would be fooled, for her dear features would be the same and her voice would be the same?

And I thought of making a public confession and trusting my future and hers to the loyalty and kindness of my flocks. But I doubted my ministry and my churches could survive the scandal. It was unlikely I could continue there as psalmodist and minister. I thought of leaving, of taking her to the mountains farther west where no one knew us, to South Carolina or Georgia. The settlements were spreading and the wilderness giving way even as the war raged. But I would have to leave my congregations. I could not leave the churches I had struggled three years to build. I would not leave those I was called to serve.

As I lay in pain from the burns, helpless in my misery, I worked to curb my anger, and I thought on these things. And I knew I must expiate my guilt and conquer my weakness and my failure for the work I would do.

It was several weeks after the fire, as I was beginning to heal and could limp out into the yard and stoop in the sun a few minutes, when a member of my flock from Zion Hill came to visit. It was Sister Wensley who loved to testify that her baby daughter Rebecca had been sent as a blessing in her old age. I stooped in the yard and watched her climb the hill with her daughter in one arm and a small sack in the other. It was a fine late autumn day and the bright sun picked out gold leaves floating from the hickories.

"I'm plumb out of breath," Sister Wensley said, and handed me the sack which I saw held potatoes. "Rebecca gets heavier every day."

"Come in and sit," I said.

It was dark in the cabin. I asked Josie to put on some water for coffee, and I brought a chair to the fireplace for Sister Wensley, whose first name was Rachel.

"I hated to hear you was burned," she said.

I told her my burns were better, though I still couldn't sit down.

"It's a blessing you have Joseph to help you," Sister Wensley said.

"Couldn't manage without him."

We drank coffee and little Rebecca played on the floor in front of the hearth. The baby found a pinecone and chewed on it, and when her mother took that away she found a spool of thread and pulled off several strands before Josie placed it on the mantel.

"There has been talk," Sister Wensley said, and looked at me sideways, as if she was embarrassed. I thought she was embarrassed because Josie was there.

"What kind of talk?" I said. My pulse quickened and my breath got shorter. Had somebody found out the truth about Josie and was gossiping it around?

"You know how people will talk, minister," Sister Wensley said.

"I do indeed."

Sister Wensley looked at Josie as if she was reluctant to continue.

"Joseph is in our confidence," I said.

Sister Wensley looked at the door as if she expected someone to be eavesdropping. She lowered her voice almost to a whisper. "The redcoats have been asking questions about you," she said.

I asked what kind of questions. Who had they questioned, and who had told her? She expected me to be alarmed, but the truth was I was relieved that the gossip was about redcoats and not about Josie and me. But I tried not to show my relief.

"Why, numbers of people have said the redcoats come to their houses to ask about you," Sister Wensley said. "Everybody says it."

"What do they ask?" I said, glancing at Josie.

"Why, they want to know who your friends are, and where all do you go as you walk from church to church. They ask where you sleep, and where you get your money. I don't know what all they ask."

"I don't have much money," I said.

"I just thought it was best to tell you," Sister Wensley said, "in case there was anything you could do."

"I'm most grateful to you."

Little Rebecca began to cry and her mother picked her up and bounced her on her lap. "There's one officer in particular that has asked about you," she said.

"Who is that?"

"A Lieutenant Withnail people say. I think that is his name."

"They ask questions about everybody," I said. "It's their business to ask questions." I didn't want her to see my relief.

"I just wanted you to know, Reverend," Sister Wensley said. "The lieutenant asks if you get letters and send letters."

"I send letters to my superior," I said.

"The lieutenant asks who you send letters to," Sister Wensley said.

"Thank you for walking all this way to tell me, and for the potatoes," I said.

When Sister Wensley was gone I came back inside the cabin and Josie grabbed my hands. "I'm so afraid," she said.

"It's probably nothing," I said.

"They think you are a rebel, a secret leader or a spy," Josie said. "They could hang you."

"I've done nothing," I said. "I have nothing to hide." I looked at Josie's pale, worried face and realized how wrong I was. I had a great deal to hide, though not what the redcoats imagined. I was hiding what was most precious to me. It was all so mixed up and crazy it was ludicrous. I began to laugh and finally Josie laughed with me. And then I stopped laughing when pain shot through my lower back.

SIX

THE BAD BURNS ON John's back took a long time to heal. Some were so deep I didn't think they could ever get well. You would have thought the fire had cut into him with an ax. You would have thought he had been whipped with a barbed whip.

I HAD TO CARRY in all the water and bring in all the wood. I had to wash everything in a tub on a bench. It was cold, getting up toward Christmastime, and I liked to stand in the sun in front of the cabin to feel its warmth on a bright day. I liked to get away from the sight of pain for a few minutes.

We soon used up the supply of wood John and I had split. There was nothing for me to do but take the ax and go out into the woods to gather limbs and dead pieces light enough to drag, which was easier than trying to chop down a big tree myself. I hacked off limbs and chopped blow-down trees in two. There had been a sleet storm the winter before that broke down trees on the hill behind the cabin. I gathered poles and long skinny logs there. A lot of the wood was white pine that burned up fast. But pine was easy to chop and easy to find, and light enough for me to carry. My hands got thicker and rougher.

WHEN JOHN'S CONGREGATIONS heard he was sick they sent things to him. They brought a peck of potatoes, and a deacon from Zion Hill brought a sack of cornmeal. A woman from Beulah brought a crock of wild honey, and a man from Crowfoot brought half a ham.

"Your flocks are mighty faithful," I said to John.

"They will drift away if I don't return soon," John said. "It's the meetings that keep them together," John said. "It's the gathering and singing together." He said that once the habit was broken it was hard to get a church started again. It had taken him three years to build up his flocks. He said a church had to be part of people's lives, not just a revival meeting, but a steady part of the community.

I said it was hard for people to come to church in winter, but he said that was all the more reason to keep the congregations alive.

Because his back was in such shape, John stayed bent over even when he got out of bed after the first week. He couldn't stand up straight, but he could crawl a little. He crawled to the bench and got a drink of water, and he crawled to the table to eat stooped over. He even crawled outside sometimes on a warm day just to look at the sun. It made him feel better to see the outdoors and the sunshine.

But most of the time he stayed in bed. It was the only place he could rest. He could read if I put the book on a bench at the end of the bed, or if I held the book tilted. But away from the fireplace there wasn't enough light to see by. I could put a candle on the bench beside the book, but when he turned the pages he knocked the candle over.

Much of the time I read to him. I read from Ecclesiastes and I read from Psalms. I read from Matthew and the other Gospels. And I read from the book of Acts and Revelation. Revelation was my favorite to read aloud. "I am Alpha and Omega . . . I am the root and offspring of David. I am the bright and morning star."

But the passage John wanted me to read again and again was from Luke, chapter 2. It was the story of the first Christmas. It was the story of the angels coming to the shepherds by night. And he liked best the words of Simeon when he saw the baby Jesus. He had me read them day after day.

> *Lord, now lettest thou thy servant depart in peace, according to thy word:*
> *For mine eyes have seen thy salvation,*
> *Which thou hast prepared before the face of all people*
> *A light to lighten the Gentiles, and the glory of thy people Israel.*

It was a song of celebration in the dark days before Christmas. John wanted to hear it over and over. I read it so many times I learned it by heart.

John had other books too. Besides *The Pilgrim's Progress* he had a copy of the sermons of John Wesley. Sometimes he had me read from one of them. I enjoyed reading *The Pilgrim's Progress* most. It was a story I could see so clearly as I read the words, the wicket gate, the burden on Christian's back, the Slough of Despond, the sight of the Beulah land, the Shining Men, the city on the horizon.

We sang songs from the songbook too. John taught me song after song. He lay on his belly and sang and I sang with him. He was in pain but he sang.

"You'll strain yourself," I said.

"Song will help me heal," he said.

When we sang, the music did seem to heal the hard moments of worry and fear. The music softened time and put things in order. The music sweetened the hours. Before I met John, I'd never thought music was worth so much. But I saw that music fed us, nourished us the same as grits and bread did. Music was like a cool drink of water on a hot day. The music was warm as a fire on a cold day.

Sometimes we stayed up far into the night to read and sing. I kept the fire going bright and made fresh coffee. We sang all the songs over again. One night John seemed better than he had before. The pain had gone from his face, and he raised himself on his elbows and looked into my eyes.

"I'm not much of a husband since our marriage," he said. He stared at me as he hadn't in a long time. He stared at my neck and at my bosoms under the shirt. "Come closer," he said.

Resting on his right hand, John reached out with his left and pressed my chest. He started to unbutton my shirt.

"You will hurt yourself," I said.

He looked into my eyes and put his hand inside my shirt. He hadn't touched me that way since before the fire. I was going to say he shouldn't stretch his back and break the scabs. I was going to say he might make himself worse. But all I said was, "You be careful."

I had worked so hard to nurse him I'd almost forgotten we were lovers too. I was taken by surprise. It was a good surprise.

I had long ago taken the strings off the bed so John could raise himself up on his elbows and knees. He raised himself like that with the blanket on his back. I stripped away my pants and slid myself under him.

Something I found out about loving that night was that you don't have to be completely free, and you don't have to be completely well. With his back only partly healed, John could move only a little bit. When I was under him and opened myself to him, he eased down on me and lay that way a long time. My heart was galloping away and my pulse was flying, but he didn't move. He was waiting till he couldn't help himself. He was waiting till the perfect moment.

I would not have thought sickness and weakness would have made loving sweeter. I would not have thought waiting and waiting would make the blood burn and the heart tremble. When John moved it was like he was singing with his body. But he was singing so low he made time stretch out. He made the seconds bigger. He made time swell up and ache as one second strained and touched into another.

"I don't care," I said, but I could hardly get my breath.

John could barely move at all, he was so stiff from the burns; but everything he did was magnified in me. Everything he did was right. I could move farther than he could, but I followed him like a dancer dancing around her partner.

"Where are you?" I said, and slid a little sideways and aimed myself at him. I gulped air and said again, "I don't care."

When John was leading me it was like I was skipping. You know how a child likes to skip and skip along the edge of a yard or trail? A skip is a step and a half. A skip has a slide to it. We skipped and skipped and the slides got sweeter.

But I was too easy to think. I was waiting for his next skip. I was holding my breath.

When John started again it was like he was backing away. He backed away a little at a time and I followed. He backed a little this way and he backed a little that way. And every step I followed, and followed again. Where is he taking us? I thought. Each step back got smaller. His steps got so little I could hardly feel him moving. His steps were so little they made me throb and sweat. I thought I was going to burst open. His little steps made me ache. But it was the sweetest pain somewhere down in my belly. I was waiting and I thought I couldn't wait any longer.

"Where are you going?" I said.

But John didn't answer. He was still and then he made a little move. It was just a little step forward. I waited and he made another step forward. And then he made another. There was something dry at the back of my mind, like bright velvet, like somebody was rubbing the back of my brain with velvet. The cloth was pulled right through my thoughts, and it was dry and soft. My head, the back of my head, was cradled in velvet and satin. My mind was caressed and floating.

"Where are you going now?" I whispered. It was all I could think of to whisper.

The land swooped under me and lifted me. The ground swung under me and slid me away and away.

"Where are you going?" I said, but it came out more of a cry than a whisper.

But halfway up the hill John stopped again. He stopped and turned to the left, and he turned to the right. He felt no bigger than a nerve inside me. But where the nerve touched it was like a spark from a flint, and it burned a needle of candle flame. Where were we going up the hill? Was there nowhere else we could go?

And then I felt John touching me. He touched me on the nipple and on the throat. He touched me on the shoulder and on the back of the neck. And he reached down under and touched my behind and streams of sparks and flutter ran all through me.

And I felt myself opening up. I opened deeper and wider than I ever had. I opened wider than I could, stretching myself and flattening myself to him. I opened so wide I thought I was turning inside out, and I thought I was going to fall backward.

If I open wider there will be nothing left of me, I thought. I will disappear into the spread of my legs.

John was reaching into me so far I didn't want him to reach deeper. If he reached any farther it would kill me. Stop, I wanted to whisper. Stop that, I wanted to say. But I was too weak, and too busy, to say anything.

When he took one more step, and then another, I felt a distant roar, like wind on the other side of the mountain. Something had broken loose inside me, but I couldn't tell where it was. Something had broken loose and was on its way.

"Where are you going?" I said under my breath.

John moved sideways, and then he moved sideways again. He couldn't move far, but he moved just enough. He moved to the left and then he moved forward.

What had broken loose in me couldn't be stopped. I couldn't even tell where it was, but something was on its way. Something was veering and ticking and banging inside me, and I thought, I will finish climbing the hill now. I will claw my way up and look over the top.

But what happened was I felt wings under me and in my thighs, and the wings started moving. The wings bore me up. And I felt bright velvet on my back and bright velvet rubbing the back of my thoughts and lifting me up. And the wings opened wider and flapped faster. I'd never felt such a lifting. I lifted John in the cradle of my wings, right up over the top of the hill into the sunset. And we were soaring in the wind so high I could see to the end of the mountains.

And I thought: The fire of love doesn't burn big and red and hot. The fire of love is purple and blue and tiny and burns in the dark. The fire of love is so bright and tiny it seems like something you remember from a long time ago.

IT WAS GETTING UP closer to Christmas and John was growing stronger. Most of the burns on his back were closing up. He could move better and twist around a little more. But the worst burns on his back and backside had not healed up. They were still runny under the scabs and under the corruption. They got inflamed like they were infected all over again. The longer his back went without healing the more discouraged John became.

When we loved, or when we sang hymns and prayed together, he would feel better. And then his confidence would wear away again and a change would come over him.

"If the Lord is in charge of everything and knows all, why would He let me suffer?" John said. There was bitterness and fear in his voice. "I have tried to serve Him in these woods. I have walked through mud and rain and high winds to my services."

It bothered John that members of his flocks came to see him less often. I told him they were all miles away and working hard at their own places. And nobody wanted to travel in these troubled times.

"I have gone to visit the sick," he said. "I have gone to comfort the grieved and afflicted."

I didn't know what to say to John. He was the one who had read the

Bible and studied on it. He was the one who knew the proper thing to say. I told him that people depended on the preacher. They didn't expect the preacher to depend on them.

When he was most discouraged and when the pain was worst, John cursed like anybody else. When I tried to wash the worst of his sores he yelled out, "Damn me if I don't get over this." As he fussed and cursed I saw that under his commitment and talent to preach and sing, he was just like everybody else. The pain and the long sickness stripped away his talent and inspiration. When he got well and strong again he would get them back. But the pain had taken away his strength and purpose. I was ashamed to see it. I was embarrassed to see him naked of what made him special and kind and above the meanness of the world.

"You'll feel different when your back is healed," I said.

John turned to me with anger in his eyes. "Who are you to tell me that?" he said, as if he blamed me for all his trouble. He was like a hurt dog snarling and snapping at the thing closest to him. And he didn't want to give me any authority to comfort him.

I had to get out of the cabin. I had to get away from his glare and accusations. I put on Mr. Griffin's gray coat and wrapped a scarf around my head. It was an overcast December day. As I closed the door behind me I heard John call out, "Are you going to abandon me?" But I didn't answer. Such a question didn't need an answer.

It was still around the cabin, but wind roared on the hill, on the other side of the hill. I figured I would look for Christmas greens. I needed something to cheer me up. I needed to do something that would give me hope. I tried to remember where there might be a little pine or cedar for a Christmas tree. There were cedars back in the gully below the hill. Cedars liked to follow a ditch or stream. I got the ax and started walking toward the hill.

Cedars make better Christmas trees than white pines because they have thicker limbs. And cedars have a perfect flame shape, a tear shape. But their color is not as pretty and blue as a white pine, and their scent is different. A cedar doesn't smell as good in a house as a white pine. A cedar smells a little musty.

I found a cedar tree by a branch before I even got to the bottom of the hill. It was as tall as I was and so dark it was almost black. It had cedar galls on it that looked like little potatoes. They seemed like decorations. I chopped it down with the ax and dragged it behind me.

I looked for a holly tree with berries on it, and turkey's paw moss I could string over the door, and some galax for greenery. The only way to get some mistletoe would be to climb an oak tree to pick it. I didn't have a gun to shoot it down.

I walked along the hill dragging my tree, and I did find a holly with bright berries on it and broke off several limbs. Holly berries are so red they light up the woods. And on the north end of the hill I did find some beds of turkey's paw moss and pulled up half a dozen strands like garlands. But I wanted some mistletoe. Maybe mistletoe would cheer John up. I could hang some over his bed and kiss him.

I looked around in the woods for mistletoe. Staring against the sky, it was hard to tell mistletoe from a squirrel's nest. There were dark little wads in trees here and there. But farther out the ridge I saw a big oak tree with a huge cluster in it. The mistletoe was big as a bushel basket.

When I was a little girl, I loved to climb trees. I'd climbed hickory trees and oak trees and dogwood trees. I'd climbed the tallest pines and sat in their tops. I dragged my cedar and carried the ax and greenery across the hill. I found an oak with mistletoe in the top, but it had no limbs until about ten feet above the ground. The trunk was too big to shinny up. Even if I took off the coat I couldn't put my arms around the tree.

I looked around and saw the shaft of a dead maple lying on the ground. It was partly rotten, but I thought it might bear my weight. I broke it off and leaned the pole against the trunk of the big oak. I took off the coat and laid it on the ground. Gripping the pole with both my hands and elbows and knees, I shinnied up to the first limb. From that perch I was just able to reach the next limb. From there I pulled myself up the big tree. There was only one place about halfway up where I had to shinny between limbs.

The view from the top of the tree took my breath. I could see way across the valley to the birches along the river. I could see smoke from cabins. And I could see west to the mountains, to the black scald on Bee Water Mountain and to the higher peaks beyond. I was so high I felt close to the gray sky. There were white berries on the mistletoe. The leaves were golden green, like they were filled with honey.

I tore off all the bunches I could reach and flung them down. I watched the clusters bounce on limbs below. It was the most mistletoe I'd ever seen.

Then there was a shout and out of the corner of my eye I saw something move. Turning, I saw a line of men on horses on a trail not too far away. They had seen me and were pointing at me. Maybe they thought I was a spy. They were riding toward me. I started down the tree fast as I could and scratched myself on the rough bark, dropping limb to limb. When I got to the lowest limb I jumped to the ground.

Flinging on the coat, I grabbed the tree and holly and turkey's paw, and as much of the mistletoe as I could carry, and started running down the ridge. It was hard to drag the tree, but I hated to give up what I'd come after. I heard the men hollering behind me. They were on horses and if they found me they could ride me down. My only hope was to stay hidden and run through a thicket where horses couldn't follow.

I figured they would expect me to run straight away from them. It was what anybody would do that was scared. But when I came to the branch at the bottom of the hill, I turned right and started running on the rocks and in the sand and mud. The branch splashed between laurels with low overhanging limbs, and I had to duck and twist sideways to get through. The cedar dragged in the mud and sand, and I dropped some of the mistletoe.

It came to me that I would have to hide the tree and greens and come back later for them. There was a place by the branch with lots of briars and vines and I parted a way into the mess and put the greens and tree behind some stalks and canes.

With my hands free I could run faster. But the hollering was getting closer. I saw they had crossed the branch and then come back because they'd lost the trail. And when they came back they saw my tracks in the mud and sand of the branch.

I ran faster, bending low and panting hard. I was worn out from climbing the oak tree, and my feet were sinking in water and mud. There were cushions of mud and tongues of sand the farther down I went. I sank up to my ankles. Even where it looked like leaves on solid ground I sank up to my shins. Under grass there was mud, slick and soft as cream. I couldn't move faster because the mud was sucking at my shoes.

The mud was cold but I didn't even notice it. I fell across a log. It sounded like the men had gotten off their horses to follow me. I heard them splashing and breaking limbs. At least they didn't have any dogs to follow me.

I couldn't outrun them, and if they caught me they would beat me and hang me, the way they did with spies. No matter what I said they wouldn't believe me. If they caught me, John would never see me again. He would be left to wait on himself and heal by himself.

I saw a sinkhole beside the branch. It was a place where a seep spring had undercut the clay and eaten away the bank. Vines and roots hung over the edge in a kind of curtain. I thought about jumping into the hole and pushing myself behind the veil of roots and vines.

Somebody hollered and a horse's hooves clattered on rocks. In the sinkhole I would be just a few feet away when they passed, and if they saw me I would be trapped. I had to keep running. It was hard to pull my legs out of the quick-mud, but I knew it was my last chance to escape. The mud slurped at my feet and sucked as I clawed my way out of the hole. And once I put a foot on the rocks I saw I'd lost my left shoe. My left foot was bare in the cold gritty mud.

I limped ahead on the rocks and sticks and mud as fast as I could. But it seemed they were going to catch me, for the hollering was louder and closer. There was nowhere to hide, and they could follow my tracks in the mud. You have to think like a fox, I said to myself. Even if I climbed out of the branch they could follow my muddy tracks up the bank. I'd made a foolish choice to run along the stream.

Just then I saw a tall white pine on the side of the hill. It was taller than the other trees, but its limbs started almost at the ground. If I could reach the pine tree and climb it I could hide in the thick branches. But how could I get there without leaving muddy tracks? My only chance was to make them keep going down the branch.

I ran through the deepest pools to wash the mud off my feet and legs. And when I'd gone past the pine tree I came to a place with rocks on the bank. There were rocks up the side of the hill, mossy and covered with lichens. I jumped from rock to rock, hoping the moss would soak up the water from my feet. And when I got above the branch I walked as fast as I could without disturbing the leaves back to the big pine tree.

Staying on the side of the pine away from the branch, I climbed the limbs like a ladder, reaching the limbs with lots of needles just as the men came into view. The leader had his pistol pointed ahead, and some of the men carried their swords bare. They were red-faced and out of breath and angry.

Slowly and quietly as I could, I slipped farther up the tree, out of sight of the ground. I could only fool them a few minutes, so I didn't dare climb the tree any higher than I had to, for when they found they'd lost my trail they'd double back. And when they followed my tracks to the tree they would climb it.

Soon as they were out of sight I slipped down the pine tree. And then I walked carefully. I took off the one shoe and hurled it toward the creek, thinking it might confuse them. I walked on tiptoe and tried not to break any sticks. And when I got out of sight of the tree I ran fast as I could, circling way across to get back to the cabin.

"YOU LOOK LIKE you've been drowned," John said when I came into the cabin. I was so tired I stood in front of the fire with my hands on my knees. My pants were covered with mud and my coat was splattered with mud and frayed by briars and sharp brush.

"You have painted your face in mud," John said.

I touched my cheek and dried mud crumbled off the skin. I reckon mud was splashed on my face and I had smeared my face in the sinkhole. My feet were scratched and bleeding, and my ankles and arms were scratched.

I got some water from the spring and heated it on the fire and washed myself. There was nothing to do but take off my clothes by the fire and scrub myself. I wanted to drop into bed but couldn't until I had cleaned myself up. I took a rag and washed my face and neck. I washed my shoulders and arms.

I saw John out of the corner of my eye watching me. I bent over to wash my legs and ankles.

"I was an ungrateful wretch," John said.

I didn't answer him. I wrung the rag out and washed my feet. My arches were scratched and bruised by all the rocks I'd run over.

"I talked like a fool to you," John said. "I have chastised myself and now I ask you to forgive me."

When I was clean I put on Mr. Griffin's long shirt, and I climbed into the loft and wrapped myself in a blanket and fell asleep.

SEVEN

As it got closer to Christmas John felt better. While his backside healed up, he could stand easier than he could sit. He stood by the fireplace, baking his back and the back of his legs. He stood up and read his books in the firelight. He read the Bible and *The Pilgrim's Progress*. Sometimes he read aloud to me. I liked to hear his voice, and I never tired of the story of the pilgrim.

Finally he felt well enough to play his flute. He put the silver pipe to his mouth and touched the stops and the music sounded sweet as a dove calling in the morning, soft as the voice of a little stream. He didn't play for long, but it pleased me to hear him play again.

One day a member of John's congregation at Briar Fork came with a turkey and a bundle of newspapers. It was a man named Waitley, who was known as a hunter. He took off his cap when he stepped into the cabin. He had a long beard and was stooped, like his back had been hurt by a fall or disease. He wore a long gray hunting shirt.

"Every morning that gobbler came out to the cornfield to eat the ears," he said. "And I hid in the bushes to wait for him."

He said some soldiers of the Crown, must have been a scouting party, had marched through the end of the field and scared the turkey, and he had to wait another hour before the gobbler came out again.

"I could have shot the soldiers easier than the turkey," he said, and added, "if I'd had a mind to."

And then Waitley dropped his voice almost to a whisper. "I have heard a rumor, Reverend, that the redcoats are going to arrest you."

"Why would they arrest me?" John said. "I have not taken sides. I only sing and preach the Gospel."

"Just a rumor I heard," Waitley said.

Besides the bird, Waitley brought the newspapers from Charlotte. John would read the news to me that night, but first I had to fix the turkey.

Turkey feathers are so big it's hard to pluck them. And a turkey is so long there's nothing to scald it in but a washtub. I heated water at the fireplace almost to boiling and poured it in the wooden bathtub, and then I dunked the big ugly bird in the smoking water. But after soaking for several minutes the feathers were still hard to pull out. I had to jerk them out and tear them out in fistfuls and handfuls. I did it outside so I wouldn't get feathers on the floor. And you don't want to burn up feathers, for they will stink up a house.

Once the turkey was plucked, I lit a pine knot to singe off the pin feathers, the down around the neck. Then I took the butcher knife and sliced open the belly. The guts inside were cold, and I raked out the slimy coils and the heart and liver. I hate the smell of bird guts. They're not as bad as hog guts, but the stink is still sickening.

After cutting off the feet, I tied the legs of the turkey together before roasting it. I got a piece of wire to do that, and I found a rod to use as a spit. The body turned like a wheel on the stick and I hung it over the fire to start roasting.

As the bird started to cook, grease dripped into the flames and the fire hissed and spat. A drop of grease hit me on the arm and it felt like a needle prick.

"What if the rumor's true?" I said. "What if the redcoats are going to arrest you?"

"Why would they arrest me?" John said.

John said it was foolish to listen to rumors in those crazy times. He said he knew there was a British officer named Withnail who didn't like him. But he'd been careful to give him no cause to arrest him. I shivered when he said the name Withnail.

WHILE I TRIMMED the cabin with greenery, John read to me from the newspapers. They were a month old, from November 1780. He read that Lord Cornwallis was marching with his army up through South Carolina to Charlotte. The newspaper said the vast army of the Crown was marching up the east side of the Broad River on its way to North Carolina. Col. Banastre Tarleton was sweeping with his dragoons through the upcountry west of the Broad River. He had burned a lot of houses and hanged rebels from their own fruit trees. He had fought skirmishes with bands of volunteers and killed every man that tried to surrender or flee. He took provisions from every house he passed. But he had fought at a place called the Blackstocks and lost a lot of his Green Dragoons.

John was so angry he stamped his foot and slammed the paper against his knee. "The devil has the rule of this earth," he said.

"Can't anybody stop Tarleton?" I said.

"Nobody but the Lord himself," John said. His face was chalky with anger. I wondered if he was thinking of joining the militia himself. John often said he would never kill.

I hung strands of turkey's paw moss over the doorway and over the mantel. It brightened up the cabin to have some green there. I hung holly from the mantel too. The red berries seemed to glow and sparkle in the firelight. I put mistletoe on the mantel and kissed John, and I hung mistletoe from a string above John's bed.

John read in the paper that the Continental army in the South was to be commanded by General Nathanael Greene. "General Greene of Rhode Island has been appointed commander of the Southern Department," he read. "He will make his headquarters in Cheraw or Charlotte. He will resist Cornwallis in his progress toward Virginia."

I tried to think what I could use to trim the cedar tree. I'd nailed the tree to a board so it stood up in the corner of the room. I didn't have any glass balls and I didn't have any candles to put in the branches. I didn't even have painted corn to thread on strings. I had one candle to put on top as a kind of Christmas star.

John had a pair of scissors in his sewing kit and I took the scissors and cut a star from the newspaper he'd just read. And then I cut a paper angel and another. I cut angels with their wings spread. And I cut a snowflake and more stars.

As I hung the angels and stars on the cedar, the tree seemed to come alive. I thought of the tree of life in the Bible. The little tree seemed bigger and deeper. The angels appeared to be flying out of the dark inside the boughs. The stars were large and white, like the sky was close and heaven was close. And the snowflakes I cut were a hundred times bigger than actual snowflakes. They made you feel you had shrunk in the falling snow.

I wished I had some colors to put on the tree. I wished I had some red and green, some blue and yellow. I wished I had something gold and something silver.

John looked at the tree as though he hadn't noticed it before. "You have made a little heaven," he said. "Out of the darkness comes shining angels and sparkling snowflakes."

ON CHRISTMAS EVE John was feeling stronger than he had since the fire on Bee Water Mountain. The holiday excited him and his eyes were shining. He looked at me with a long and steady look.

"We will sing some carols," he said. "And then we will read the Christmas story. And then we will go to bed."

I had hung a paper angel right over the fireplace. "What song do you want to sing?" I said.

John said he would like to sing "While Shepherds Watched Their Flocks." I knew that's what he would say. It was a song that fit him, and fit his feeling about Christmas. We stood in front of the fire and held hands. We didn't sit down, for John could hardly sit down.

As we sang it seemed that in spite of the dark and cold the world was lighted up with sweet music and fellowship. Even though there was a war now, we were at peace in our house together. Even though John had been burned and scarred he was almost well. But I didn't want to feel too happy. It was dangerous to be too happy.

I was right to fear being happy that night, for just after we sang carols John looked into my eyes and then looked away. "Josie, I still don't really know how you came to me," he said.

It was the first time he had asked a question like that in several weeks. Surprise shuddered through me, but I tried to laugh. "You know I walked here," I said.

"But where did you walk from?" John said. I don't know why he suddenly got so curious on Christmas Eve. Maybe it was because his back was mostly healed and he was worried about what we were going to do.

I told him I came from the country north of Charlotte, as I had told him before. I asked him did it matter, since the important thing was I'd found him at Zion Hill Church that night in October.

"I have not wanted to pry," John said. "But I know something terrible happened to you, something too sad to talk about."

"How do you know that?" I said, surprised at the irritation in my voice. The last thing I wanted to tell was what Mr. Griffin had done to me, and what I had waited in the dark to do to him. And I didn't want to talk about Mama's sickness either. If a mama could go mad a daughter might also. And nobody wanted to admit their own mother had driven them from their house.

"You say nothing," John said. "You have told me nothing." The sudden anger rising in his voice made me angry too.

"This is Christmas Eve," I said, "a time of peacefulness and joy."

"It is not a time of peace," John said, his eyes burning at me in the firelight. "You deceived me once. Are you continuing to deceive me?" His anger astonished me.

"And you have deceived your congregations," I said. But soon as it came out I knew I'd said the wrong thing. If I'd learned anything it was that you shouldn't accuse a man of what scares him the most.

"Don't tell me about my congregations!" John shouted. He grabbed me by my arms and shook me. I thought he was going to hit me. All the goodwill and peacefulness had gone out of him. He was sharp and hard with fury.

"I don't want to quarrel," I said. I felt weak in my throat and in my arms and all over.

"You have told me nothing," John said, his eyes blazing. "What are you hiding? Are you a thief? Are you running from the loyalists? From the constable?"

"I had to run away from home," I said. "My stepdaddy beat me."

"And your mother let him?"

I told John that Mama always took my stepdaddy's side, and that was why I had run away. I told him they had locked me in the corncrib for the night, and I told him that my stepdaddy was a spy for the British. Everything I told him was the truth, or mostly the truth. I left out that Mr. Griffin had shamed me and that I had waited for him in the dark with the ax. And I left out how Mama wasn't perfect in her mind. I couldn't tell John about those things.

"You have made me feel ashamed and dirty," John said.

"I offered to leave," I said.

"What else are you not telling me?" John said.

"And what are you not telling me?" I said back to him. It was the worst quarrel we had had, and I felt hollowed out and sore inside. I felt like half the blood had been drained out of my veins. The quarrel had come out of nowhere, just as we were happy on Christmas Eve.

"I don't know what to do," John said.

It was awful to see the pain of confusion in his eyes.

LATER, AFTER WE had gone to bed and been asleep, there was a knock at the door. It wasn't only a knock, but a bang and a crash.

"Open up!" somebody yelled.

"Who is there?" John yelled. But the door burst open and somebody carrying a lantern stepped inside. We had forgotten to bolt the door.

John looked at me and he looked at the newspapers on the floor. I saw the dread in his eyes. He jumped out of bed in his nightshirt and reached down to gather the sheets and throw them in the fire. The man that had rushed into the room wore a red tunic with gold epaulets. He ran and grabbed the papers from the fire and stomped the flames out with his boots. John reached for the pages but the officer pulled him backward. I was still wearing my shirt and I pulled on my pants. And I wrapped the blanket around my shoulders.

"In the name of the king," the man bellowed. Three soldiers had followed him into the cabin and they seized John. Cold air from the door swept in and fluttered the fire.

"We are searching for sedition," the officer said. "We are searching for sedition wherever it is hidden." He picked up a sheet of the newspaper and studied it.

"A man brought that newspaper here," John said.

"Who are you?" the officer said.

"I'm the Reverend John Trethman," John said, "psalmodist and minister."

"Are you a dissenter?" the officer said.

"I am licensed to exhort and to raise hymns," John said.

"Then you are a Methodist and a traitor," the officer said.

"I preach the Gospel and sing hymns," John said. I could hear the fear in his voice. Soldiers that came in the night could do as they pleased. They could hang and burn as they chose.

"Only a traitor would have copies of a rebel newspaper," the officer said.

Two other soldiers came inside and the officer told them to search the cabin. They climbed into the loft and threw the blankets down. They looked in the meal bin and under the bed. They knocked down the tree I'd trimmed. But they couldn't find any more newspapers.

"You won't find anything here," John said.

"I have already found what I was looking for," the officer said. He pulled a pistol from his belt and hit John across the face. Blood spurted from John's lips.

"No!" I screamed. "He's been burned."

The officer turned to me with the pistol raised. "Who is this?" he said.

"He's just a traveler staying the night," John said, and wiped his lip. It looked like a tooth had been broken off.

"Did he bring the newspapers?" the officer said.

John patted his lip. "I swear he did not," he said. "This boy is just a pilgrim and an orphan."

"We give no quarter to enemies of the Crown," the officer said.

"This boy is innocent," John said, "and I am a wandering minister of the Gospel."

"What better mask for sedition," the officer snarled. He ordered the soldiers to bind John's hands.

"You can't hang an innocent man!" I shouted. The officer slapped me so hard I staggered back against the table. Tears plumped and blurred in my eyes.

"I'll do whatever is necessary to stop this treason," he said.

I expected him to take John out and hang him from the closest oak tree and set fire to the cabin. I expected they would hang me too. In a minute the world had turned upside down and was cracking to pieces. Everything was rotten and crazy behind a front that seemed real, and the stink and craziness had burst through again. It seemed that everywhere the common idea was to beat or hang people.

But instead they set John upon a horse with his hands tied behind him, then tossed a coat around his shoulders.

"You have information that will be useful to us," the officer said to John.

"I know nothing but the word of God and songs of praise," John said.

"We will persuade you to remember more than that," the officer said.

The soldiers threw the gray coat around my shoulders and wrapped a blanket over that, and they tied me to a tree outside the cabin. I didn't have any shoes, but I couldn't even feel the cold ground. I was going to call out to John, but in the torchlight he was looking straight at me. He shook his head slowly, meaning I was not to say anything or do anything. He was lucky they didn't hang him right there, and as long as he was alive there was hope he might be spared.

They set fire to the cabin, and as it blazed up I could feel the heat on my face. I turned to watch them march away. In the glare from the fire I saw John look back at me one last time. And then they went around a bend in the trail, and the woods were lit up by the burning cabin.

My eyes were so filled with tears I could hardly see the smoke and sparks rising into the sky full of stars. The logs of the cabin crackled and popped. The Christmas night had turned to horror. My face was burning in the glare and my back was freezing. I jerked at the rope that bound my hands and twisted in the scalding glare from the fire. I looked right into the heart of the flames, to where I should be still lying in bed with John, until my eyes burned.

The fire was so hot I could see right into the cabin. The logs got so hot they seemed to turn into a blinding liquid. Everything we had was burned up. John's flute was melted, and the coins I had stolen from Mama. My eyes stung and I had to turn my face away.

THEY HAD TIED my hands to the tree about waist high. It seemed when I pulled the rope up on the tree trunk it loosened a little. I jumped up again and loosened it a little more. The young oak was tapered, smaller the higher it went. I jumped up and felt the knot loosen still more.

After four or five jumps my hands were up to my shoulders. I crunched my fingers together and made my palms as little as I could, but the rope still caught on the backs of my thumbs. I couldn't jump any higher, and I couldn't make my hands any smaller. The rope seared my skin where I twisted hardest.

Then I tried pulling one hand loose. All I needed was to free one hand. I squeezed my right palm together hard as I could, and crushed the bones under the grip of the big rope. It seemed impossible to pull it free, but I yanked and wrenched my arm, scraping knuckles on the rough rope.

My right hand came free, and it took just a minute to work my left hand loose. I jumped back away from the fire just in time, for the wind changed and leaned the flames toward the tree where I'd been. Branches in the oak tree caught fire.

I was so stunned by heat and all that had happened that night, I couldn't recall what direction the soldiers had gone. The cabin roof caved in and sent a shower of sparks into the sky. Trees around the cabin had caught fire, and I was nearly blinded by the heat and brightness.

The only thing that had not been burned was the ax. It was stuck in the chopping block at the side of the cabin. The handle was smoking a little. I ran to the chopping block and grabbed the handle with both hands. It burned me, but I worked the blade loose and carried it into the cold woods.

The ax was the only thing I had that was John's. His books and his flute were gone. I carried the ax and walked on into the woods. I didn't know where I was going, but I knew the ax could be used to cut firewood and maybe fight off bears and wolves if I had to.

I hadn't stumbled far until I saw I needed light. I didn't have a lantern, but a blazing stick would do. I turned and staggered back to the cabin and found a burning stick near the woodpile. Holding the stick in one hand for a torch and carrying the ax in the other, I made my way through the woods. I held the stick pointed down so it would keep burning bright. And when the stick burned down short I used it to light a pine knot I found. As I wandered through the woods I used up four other torches, and my hand got black with the smoke.

In the long night the woods looked stranger than a dream. I passed under vast leaning trees, and open places where the stars seemed so close I thought I could hear them. I passed big rocks that appeared to shove their shoulders against the light. Big birds like owls flapped around in the limbs above me. The eyes of wildcats and deer shone out of the dark.

Nothing looked familiar. I was in the foreign country of night. The ground reared up in front of me and then fell away when I went around a hill. I walked along a trail where the slope seemed to drop away a thousand miles. In places the woods were a wall hemming me in.

I stepped on something soft and, lowering the pine knot, saw it was a bed of moss. That seemed as good a place to lie down as I was apt to find. I put down the ax and gathered some sticks. After lighting the little sticks I gathered bigger sticks. In the light of the blaze I broke several limbs and heaped them in a pile, and then I took the ax and chopped still more dead wood.

When the fire was galloping and soaring I lay down on the moss and tried to think what to do. I had to follow John, if I could find the way they took him. Since he was held by the loyalists I had to find a loyalist militia, or a troop of royal soldiers. I had no place else to go. I had nothing but the ax. It was likely they would kill John.

With the blanket wrapped around me I looked up at the stars beyond the trees. I missed John so badly the back of my throat hurt. I felt awful we had quarreled on what was likely our last night together. Our cabin was nothing but ashes and spots of melted silver. I wouldn't even know if he was still alive.

With my face resting on my elbow I went to sleep and dreamed of the fire. I dreamed I was watching the cabin burn again and all kinds of things walked out of the fire. Bears and panthers stepped out of the blaze, and soldiers with red coats. The king stepped out of the fire wearing a crown of flames. But when I looked again the king didn't have a face. He had only a skull with grinning black teeth, and worms in the eye sockets. And inside the flames were thousands of worms eating everything, eating the fire.

When I woke it was day and my fire had burned down to coals. I could see the sun and knew which way was east. I tried to remember which way I had come last night. The moss bed looked different in daylight. I couldn't recall which side I'd first seen it from. I looked through the trees at some low hills, but none of them seemed familiar. I didn't know how far I'd run from Pine Knot Branch. If I could find my way back there I could go to some of John's congregation at Zion Hill or Briar Fork and ask for help. I could ask if anybody knew where he was. I had to get something to eat.

I thought I would circle around. Since I didn't know in what direction to go I would circle to look for a road or trail, something I knew. If I walked in a straight line I might miss everything. But if I made a great circle I had a better chance of finding help.

But I had to take my fire. The fire was all I had to warm me and light my way at night. I blew on the coals and threw on leaves and dried moss until the flame started again. I built up the fire until a blaze was stretching, and found another pine knot to light.

With the ax in one hand and the burning pine knot in the other, I started off through the woods, planning to curve around in a great ring to see what was out there. Surely I'd recognize a hill or find a trail. I came to a swampy place, and walked through a canebrake. The stalks of cane reached high above my head, and they rasped and whispered against each other. It was hard to push the canes aside and hold both the ax and the torch. The canes whispered like they were mocking me. I hoped I wasn't losing my mind the way Mama had lost hers. I stopped and listened.

It wasn't long before I had to find a new pine knot. I pushed my way through a tangle of wild peavines. A deer bounded away and I just saw the white flame of its tail. I wished I had a gun, though I'd never shot a gun.

Next I came to a creek and saw a shadow dart deep in a pool. A curl of waterfall over the lip of rock churned the head of the pool. The shadow shot across the pool. It had to be a trout hiding in the bottom of the deep water. The trout waited below the waterfall for any worms or bugs washed down the creek.

I didn't have a fish hook, and the pool was too big to corner the fish in. I didn't have any cloth for a seine. But a baked trout would be wonderful to eat in the cold woods. A baked trout was the best thing I could think of. I looked around for some kind of spear or forked stick. I wondered if I could I throw a rock and hit the fish.

What I found was a kind of thornbush. The limbs weren't long, but the thorns were sharp as needles. I broke off a branch and stripped it of twigs and stickers until only two thorns were left near the bigger end. I'd have to hold it by the tip. A thorn wasn't exactly a hook, but it was all I had.

To keep my fire alive I made a blaze of pinecones and dry sticks on the bank. I couldn't let the fire go out.

It took several tries, turning over rocks and digging in the mud below the pool, to find earthworms. But when I found two worms and stuck them on the thorns the worms slid right off. I had to thread the worms on the spikes, almost tying them on.

Quietly as I could I crept up to the edge of the pool just below the little waterfall. I had to be gentle or the worms would fall off the spikes. I reached the branch down into the pool and let it rest. It wasn't but a second until something hit the tip and almost jerked the stick out of my hand. I pulled the stick up and saw the trout, a fat thing thrashing and flashing its spots. But soon as I pulled the fish out of the water it slipped off the thorn and vanished into the frothing water. One of the thorns on the limb had broken off.

There was nothing to do but get another branch off the thornbush and fix it as I had the first. I turned over rocks until I found two more worms. When the bait was wound around the thorns I eased up to the edge of the pool and lowered the stick into the water. I waited a second or two and held my breath. I didn't want to move the stick or the current might pull the worms off the spines.

The stick whipped in my hand and I pulled quick, hoping to stick the thorn deep in the trout's jaw. The fish throbbed and flopped on the end of the stick. I pulled the branch up and the trout thrashed and splashed on the top of the pool. But soon as I lifted him out of the water he slid off the thorn again, and disappeared into the foam.

I thought I might as well give up. The fish was going to slide off every time I tried to raise it out of the pool. But I didn't have anything else to eat. I didn't have a gun and I couldn't catch a rabbit with my bare hands. There was nothing to do but try again. I broke another limb off the thornbush and fixed it like the others. I wished the thorns were hooked like blackberry briars. But a blackberry briar wouldn't be long enough to catch a fish.

I had been so busy trying to catch the trout I'd forgotten the time. When I looked up I saw it was past noon. The sun was as high as it would get that day. It was Christmas Day and instead of feasting I was starving. I felt the dull weight of hunger all over me.

Gently I lowered the branch into the pool again. The trout had been hurt twice. I wondered if it would bite again. Had it darted to another pool? Surely it could see the branch and the thorns holding the worms.

When the trout hit the worm the branch almost slipped out of my grasp. The stick swerved in the water and bent like a witching wand. I thought the limb might break. I pulled hard to set the sticker in the fish's mouth and raised it closer to the top of the pool.

But this time, instead of lifting the fish out of the water, I jumped into the edge of the pool and pulled the trout toward the lower end. I leaned close to the water and dragged the fish toward the shadows. The trout thrashed a little, but I let it swim and led it into the sand at the end of the pool. Then I jerked the fish right out onto the mossy rocks. The trout flashed and jumped and I fell on top of it.

The trout was so fat it filled my hands. It was slimy and squirming and almost jumped out of my grasp. I carried the fish quickly up the bank and, laying it against a rock, hit the head with the ax. When the body was still I cut off the head and slit open the belly. I raked out the guts and scraped off the scales and slime with the ax blade, then washed the fish in the creek and stuck it on a stick over the fire.

After the trout had baked for a few minutes I ate it off the stick. The meat was so hot I took only a tiny bite at a time. The flesh was sweet and juicy. Nothing is sweeter than trout fresh out of water. I picked the pieces off the bones like they were manna.

When I'd eaten and washed my hands in the creek it was time to leave. If I was going to sweep in a circle, I had to get started. For it was already afternoon. I wasn't sure how late it was.

I crossed the creek and started walking. I came to an old field that might have been cleared by the Cherokees, but there was nobody in sight. I passed the remains of a campfire, but rain had washed away all tracks around it. As the sun got low in the trees I walked toward the sunset.

My feet were numb from walking on the cold ground. I stepped into a branch to warm my feet and saw a high bank above me. It looked like the side of a mountain with big rocks scattered at the foot. The rocks were covered with deep moss. Logs had fallen over the rocks blocking the way. I raised the torch and saw a hole between two big rocks. It looked like the door to the cellar of a castle. I climbed over the logs and stooped to look inside.

The smell told me something alive was in the cave. I couldn't have said what the scent was, but it was different from the wet rock and moss smell, the stink of rotten leaves. I took a step and pushed the light ahead of me.

In the corner of the cave something moved, something that looked like a pile of rags, and pieces of leather. There was a dirty blanket. And then I saw a foot.

"Who is there?" I said, taking a step closer.

And then I saw gray hair. It was an old woman. Her hair was tangled and knotted and piled around her head. She'd pushed herself back against the wall of the cave.

"You scared me," I said. "What are you doing here?"

She pulled back farther and pressed herself against the dirty wall. She was shivering and didn't say anything. I reckon my fire on the stick had surprised her. Her eyes were wide and she was trembling.

Reaching the fire around I looked at the cave. It was just a little cave, with only the room where the old woman sat and a little alcove off to the side. An animal had lived there or died there, for there were bones on the floor, white bones and black bones like they had been half burned.

The old woman shivered so badly she was jerking. I reckon she was freezing.

"Haven't you got any fire?" I said.

But she didn't seem to hear me, or if she did hear she couldn't understand. There was something wrong with her legs. From the way she turned I could tell she couldn't move her legs. She had to push herself with her arms. I wondered if she had been carried there and left. I thought she might have crawled to the cave and then gotten too weak to leave.

"Let me make you a fire," I said. I went back outside and broke some twigs and sticks and gathered dry leaves. After I got a little fire started on the floor of the cave I went back out and broke some bigger sticks. In the dark I could hardly see to chop with the ax. I broke a bunch of sticks and carried them back into the cave.

Smoke had filled the cave, but if you hunkered down you were out of the smoke, for the air was clear along the ground. I coughed and fanned the smoke away from the old woman.

The woman had a leather bag clutched up to her belly. I wondered if she had anything to eat in the sack, or whether it was a poke of medicine and charms or something to wear. I was pretty sure she was an Indian. In the fire light I looked at her face and saw how wrinkled it was. Her lips were cracked and peeling like she hadn't had any water in a long time. She was all dried out.

The floor of the cave was damp and a little muddy. There was no water for drinking. But there was a branch just outside. I'd warmed my feet in the branch before climbing the bank to the cave.

I looked around the smoky cave for a cup or bottle, a bowl or bucket. I didn't have anything but the ax. I didn't even have a hat. Taking a burning stick from the fire, I laid it on a rock at the mouth of the cave for a light. With my two hands cupped tight together, I scooped up water from the branch and carried it quickly into the cave. Water leaked through my fingers, but I got some of it to the old woman's lips.

She pulled back at first and then sucked at the water with her cracked lips as if she was dying for even a drop. She swilled the water up till it was gone with a suck and a hiss.

"I'll get you some more," I said, and ran back to the branch. The light was still flickering at the cave entrance, and I scooped up another double handful from the branch and hurried back to the old woman. I must have done it at least five times, and every time she drank like she was still parched.

And then she wouldn't drink any more. I held my cupped hands to her lips and the water dribbled down on her chin, but she wouldn't sip again. And it wasn't just that she had had enough. It was like she'd made up her mind not to drink anymore, to do nothing. The fire had warmed up the cave a little, but she was still shaking.

"What have you got to eat?" I said. I felt the pockets of my coat and remembered I didn't have anything. I reached for the bag she held to her belly and she didn't resist when I pulled it away. I opened the sack and held it to the light, but there wasn't anything inside but two feathers tied with a leather string, and some black stuff that looked at first like burned bread crumbs. But when I held a piece to the light I saw it was something like pemmican, dried meat cut into little pieces.

"Here, eat a piece of this," I said and held it to her lips. "It will bring your strength back."

But the old woman didn't open her mouth. She didn't try to pull away; she acted like she didn't even see me.

"Aren't you hungry?" I said. But she acted like I wasn't even there anymore. Her eyes stared straight ahead into the smoke of the cave.

Just then I heard a growl. I looked around toward the door and saw a head through the smoke. It was a big cat's head and in an instant I knew it was a panther, and we were in its cave. The panther had been out hunting when the old woman crawled into the lair or was carried there.

I dropped the meat and grabbed a burning stick from the fire. I lunged toward the head, thrusting the burning stick like it was a sword. The fire lit up the cat's eyes and it wheeled around and ran. I followed the panther out until it disappeared into the dark. Holding the torch high I looked around in the trees but saw nothing but rocks and the flash of water in the branch.

I found I was trembling. It had all happened so fast I hadn't had time to be scared. But holding the stick now I was shaking, for I knew the beast would be back. It was the cat's lair and it would come back. Cats were afraid of fire, but it would still come back.

I thought of running out of the cave and getting away. I didn't know where the panther had gone, and it might be waiting just outside. But if I left the old woman, it would attack her and kill her. And the old woman wasn't able to move. I'd have to drag her out. It would be all I could do to drag her out into the woods.

I saw I was trapped. Even if I ran away from the old woman, I could still be killed by the panther. There was another growl outside and then a scream like a woman being torn in two. I'd heard panthers scream before, but never that close up. It was the kind of scream that took all the strength out of your legs and made your guts shiver.

I reached for another burning stick, so I'd have two to jab into the cat's face. But I knew when it came back it would be leaping so fast I wouldn't even see it in the smoke until it was on top of me. And then it would be too late to scare the cat with fire.

Then I remembered the ax. I dropped the sticks back into the fire and grabbed the ax handle. I figured if I stood to the side the cat wouldn't see me when it jumped inside, and I might hit it over the head. Maybe the smoke would burn its eyes till it couldn't see anything.

I put myself right at the side of the cave mouth and held the ax with both hands. There was a growl outside and something stirred in the leaves. The growl sounded closer. But I was afraid I wouldn't be able to see anything in the dim light. What if it jumped on me before I even saw it? I would have to hit fast and hard. I listened and gripped the handle tighter. My heart jumped so hard I thought it was going to break out of my chest.

There were padding steps and a whoosh. Before I knew it the panther had leaped through the smoke. I squinted my eyes and saw it had landed right on the old woman and was clawing her face.

The cave wasn't high enough to swing the ax over my head. I had to sling it sideways, out level with my shoulder. With the blunt side of the ax I hit the cat behind the ears. And then I turned the ax around and chopped right through the back of the head. I cut into the spine and split the spine like it was a piece of heartwood inside a rotten log. I chopped again and again, as I had hit Mr. Griffin, and blood poured and splashed on everything.

When I pulled the cat off the old woman there was blood on her face, but it was mostly panther's blood. Her eyes were staring straight ahead like they had before. I put my finger on her throat and listened to her heart. She wasn't breathing, and she must have been dead before the cat ever jumped on her.

EIGHT

I SPENT THE NEXT DAY getting the body of the old woman out of the cave. I had nowhere to stay except in the cave, and I couldn't stay there another night with the dead bodies. As soon as I woke I added wood to the fire to make it brighter, and then I tried to think what to do.

The panther was a big heavy thing, and it was all I could do to roll the cat off the old woman. Blood had splashed on everything and run out on the dirt and rocks. I held the cat's hind legs and pulled but couldn't really move it. I'd have to leave the panther where it was. I looked outside.

It was a cold gray day. The clouds hung just above the bare trees. The low sky made you feel there wasn't any room in the world. The laurel leaves had rolled up like pipes against the cold. It was the kind of day that made you want to hunker by the fire.

I didn't have a shovel or spade or mattock. There wasn't anything to dig with but the ax, and I didn't want to ruin the blade by driving it into the ground. The panther was too big to move, but surely I could drag the old woman. I looked out across the woods and tried to remember what Indians did with their dead.

I shuddered in the cold and hurried back into the cave. A memory hovered just at the edge of my thought. I tried to grab it but the idea slipped away. The old woman's dirty dress was covered with the panther's blood. Her face was smeared with blood too, and blood had splashed into her hair. Blood had run out onto the rocks around her, and there were pools of blood in the dirt.

I looked to see if there was something to wrap her up in. I didn't want to look at her face, and I didn't want to get the blood on my clothes more than I could help. I tried to see what she was lying on. I pushed her over and saw an old blanket in the dirt under her. It had a little blood on it, but mostly the blanket was just damp and dirty. I could wrap her in the blanket to drag her out into the open.

And soon as I thought of wrapping her in the blanket, I remembered what it was I was trying to recall. My schoolteacher, Mr. Pickett, had said Indians wrapped their dead in deerskins and tied them up, knees against their chest, like babies in the womb. They buried them there with beads and pots and tools they might need in heaven. Mr. Pickett had lived with the Cherokees for several months, and he taught us about Indians as well as drilling us in grammar and proper speech.

I pulled the dirty blanket out from under the woman and rolled the body in it. There was a leather string that tied the bag she had held. I took the string and tied the blanket as tight as I could and dragged the blanket out into the open.

There wasn't any way I could dig a grave. I looked around at the rocks and the cold winter woods. Everything was blank and gray. The air had a withering dampness and chill that made you want to huddle against the ground. I left the body and walked among the rocks till I could see the hill above the cave. It was just a little hill, with rocks scattered all around the slope under the trees. Lichens like peeling paint and crumbling seals stuck to the rocks. Halfway around the hill I found a sinkhole above the branch. Maybe if I laid the body in that hole facing west it would be the closest thing to a Cherokee burial. Mr. Pickett had said Indians were supposed to face the sunset, where all their forebears had gone. I dragged the body around the hill through the leaves. An arm slid out of the blanket and I tucked it back in. The old woman's gray hair trailed in the leaves.

The hardest thing was to get the body into the sinkhole, for the old woman was stiff. That took some studying. I finally had to lean the body up against the side of the pit and push it down into the leaves and mud. Once it was all the way down I smoothed the blanket and laid the leather bag on her chest. And then I thought better and pulled the feathers out and laid them on her head, and kept the bag. I carried rocks and piled them on her so animals couldn't reach the body.

Soon as I got to the branch, I washed my hands and dried them on my pants and hurried into the cave. The fire was still burning and I hunkered down under the smoke and warmed my hands. I was shivering and I was tired. I hadn't had much sleep and I was worn out from all the terrible things that had happened. There wasn't anything to eat, but I was too worried to be hungry.

My feet were so cold they were almost numb. With the ax I cut the bag into leather rags and tied them around my feet. The leather bandages would be better than nothing.

After putting more sticks on the fire, I lay down in my coat and the blanket I'd brought from the cabin. I found a place where there wasn't any blood, as far from the panther's body as I could get, and wrapped myself up and closed my eyes. Before I knew it I was dreaming of winding my way through the woods as fire roared behind me, and gunshots sang out. There were shouts as men hollered at me. I knew I was dreaming. I told myself it was just a terrible dream. But the dream kept going, and I kept telling myself that waking was worse than the dream.

I DON'T KNOW HOW long I slept, but when I woke the cave was dark and the fire had gone out. It must have been night, for no light was coming into the cave. The dark was pure as sleep. The dark was a thick syrup drowning everything. The dark was so heavy it crushed my thoughts and made me want to go back to sleep.

I could get up and look for sticks in the dark and try to start another fire. Or I could just lie in the coat and blanket and sleep some more. In the cave I was warm enough to sleep. I didn't have any way of starting a fire, because I didn't have any flint or tinder. I might as well go back to sleep and worry about the fire later. Anyway, I didn't know where to go when I did wake up.

When I woke again gray light was coming into the cave. The place smelled of sour old smoke and rotten leaves and the dead panther. I thought of food and fire. I didn't even know where I was. I'd plunged off into the woods from the burning cabin and had no idea in what direction I'd run. I didn't know where a road was or the nearest house.

I scrunched myself up under the coat and blanket, trying to think what to do. If I stayed in the cave I'd starve. I had to go out looking for something to eat. I had to borrow fire if I was going to keep from freezing.

It occurred to me I had not had my monthly for a while, not since just after I ran away and joined John Trethman. I had worried about concealing the bleeding and rags that had to be washed out, but had done that for only one period. And after that time it had not come again and I had forgotten. I'd been too busy traveling with John and too worried about being found out. Then I'd been too excited about being loved by him, and after the fire I'd been too busy nursing him.

Now I knew there could be a lot of reasons why the monthlies had stopped. But it came to me that my monthlies might have stopped for the most common reason of all. It seemed strange I hadn't thought of that before. It was silly I hadn't thought of it. I'd been too busy trying to nurse John to think of myself.

I had to go where there was something to eat, for I was not just eating for myself. I had to go where there was fire to keep me warm. I had to go where I could get help and medicine when I needed it. With only the ax there wasn't any way I could get much to eat in the woods.

I must have lain in the coat and blanket for another hour trying to think of something hopeful. When I finally got up the sun was coming through the mouth of the cave. I stepped out into the light and the fresh breeze. At least the sun made things look different. The woods looked open, and I could see farther through the bare trees.

That day I wandered in the woods looking for a road. I followed a creek but never came to any clearing. I caught another trout in a pool but had to eat it raw because my fire had gone out. I came back and sat in the sun at the mouth of the cave and thought how it was almost certain John was dead. I was lost in the woods and John was dead. I wondered if my mind was right. Was I really remembering all the bad things that had happened, or was I dreaming them? That night I slept in the cave again, beside the cold body of the panther.

The next morning I stumbled out into the sunlight. Besides the smell of leaves, the breeze carried the scent of something else. I thought it was the faint smell of smoke. I turned to face the breeze and thought I sniffed frying bacon. I wondered if it was an army camp, or a militia camp.

I'd heard soldiers did awful things to women. It was said that Tarleton himself had raped women that he captured. I'd heard that ruined women followed Tarleton's men to sell themselves as whores, and lived in wagons and tents.

I breathed in deep to see if I could smell the scent of frying bacon again. I stepped down to the branch.

In the reflection of the pool I could see my face all smudged and dirty. I washed my forehead and cheeks and neck. I washed around my mouth and chin, and rubbed my teeth with my finger. I didn't want to look like a gypsy or a tramp.

After drying my face and hands on the blanket, I wrapped the blanket around my shoulders like a cape. I was dressed in Mr. Griffin's clothes still, but the pants were dirty and torn in places. I didn't have any shoes but the rags of leather tied around my feet. I did look like a tramp.

I licked the first finger on my left hand and held it up in the wind. The breeze was coming from the southwest, opposite the early sun. Gripping the ax I turned and walked into the breeze, following the bank of the branch.

The smell of smoke in the wind came and went. Sometimes the scent was strong and certain, and other times it just seemed to disappear.

I picked my way through laurel thickets, and walked under tall hemlocks by the water. The spruce pines smelled of mold and must as they always did in winter. I lost the perfume of smoke until I came over a rise. There was a branch ahead, and I looked around for a log or big rock to cross on. Then I heard a holler, and another holler, and there were shouts one after another.

I hunkered there on the ground and listened. There was a banging and rattling that sounded like pots and pans knocked together. Wherever there were pots and pans there would be something to eat. And then there were shouts that sounded like barks. The rattling and banging went on.

On the other side of the branch was a cedar thicket. I couldn't see a thing through it or beyond it. The noise was coming from the other side of the cedars and I had to go through the thicket to see what was there. I jumped across the branch, but the cedars were so close together I had to crawl under them or slip sideways between them. The sharp needles pricked my face and hands.

When I came out of the cedars I was at the edge of a clearing. It was a field way off in the woods. There were campfires around the edge of the field, and little clusters of men all across the field. I thought at first it was some kind of ball game. They had gathered to play football or some other sport.

But then I saw some of the men carried rifles, and they marched in step, or were trying to march in step. And with every group there was a man hollering orders at them. Some men had uniforms or pieces of uniforms. Some had gun belts and others wore buckskin or hunting shirts, or plain carpenter's jumpers. Some had muskets or rifles, and some had pistols in their belts. The men barking at them sounded angry.

I backed into the cedars to sit and think. This was a militia on a muster ground. I should slip away into the woods and look elsewhere for something to eat. It was dangerous to have anything to do with soldiers. I had smelled bacon from their campfires, but I couldn't walk out into the field and ask for something to eat.

I stood up and started walking away, back toward the branch. But I knew there was nothing in that direction. I had come that way. Maybe I should slip around to the other side of the camp. There were wagons and horses there in the trees. Maybe I could steal something to eat.

I worked my way through briars and brush and cedar thickets to the other side of the camp. There was a wagon backed between two pine trees there, but it had a canvas over the top and I couldn't see inside. I figured if I could just crawl to the back of the wagon and look in maybe I would find a pone of bread or a piece of fatback. Holding the ax and stooping low as I could I threaded my way through the brush.

"Throw down that ax!" somebody yelled at me. I turned to see a man holding a rifle pointed at my head. He wore a blue coat with stripes sewn on the sleeves.

"I'm not doing anything," I said.

"Not yet you ain't," he said. He prodded me with the gun barrel and I dropped the ax. "Are you a spy?" he said.

"I'm not a spy," I said. I knew that spies got shot or hanged.

"Then you are a thief," the man said. "We'll see what the captain says." He pushed me with the gun and made me walk in front of him. I saw there were tents in the woods on the other side of the field. Horses were tied to trees and to wagons with covered tops. Rifles stacked in circles leaned against each other.

I figured the man in the blue coat was a sergeant since he had stripes on his sleeves. Only he and a few others in the clearing had uniforms. Most were dressed as rough and dirty as I was.

The sergeant marched me to a tent at the edge of the field. A man in a cleaner blue uniform sat at a table. A fire blazed near his chair and the top of the table was covered with papers weighted down by a pistol and musket balls.

"This is Captain Cox of the North Carolina militia," the sergeant said. He prodded me to stand in front of the table. The man behind the table wore a blue jacket and a black cocked hat. He was a handsome young man.

"Yes, sir," I said, and made the movement of what I thought was a salute.

"And who might you be?" the captain said. He had blue eyes and a scar on his cheek.

"I'm Joseph Summers," I said, and swallowed.

"Say 'sir' when you speak to the captain," the sergeant said, and pushed me with the musket barrel.

"Sir!" I said, and hiccuped.

"Where might you be from?" the captain said.

"From up the river," I said. "From Pine Knot Branch."

"I caught him spying on the camp, sir," the sergeant said.

"I wasn't spying, sir," I said. My belly felt uneasy, like I'd eaten the wrong thing that morning, though I hadn't eaten anything.

The captain sat back in his chair and looked at me. He looked me up and down and studied my face. He looked at the leather rags on my feet and the dirty blanket wrapped around my shoulders. His gaze was so steady he seemed to be looking right through me. "Are you a spy?" the captain said.

"I'm no spy, sir," I said.

Men all around the camp had turned to look at me. I hoped nobody would recognize me, unless they had seen me with John at one of his services.

"Well, Joseph Summers, if you're not here to spy on us then you must be here to join us," Captain Cox said.

"Yes, sir," I said. The sergeant prodded me with the tip of the gun. "I'm here to join," I said. I was afraid if I said anything else they would shoot me or hang me. But once I'd said yes, it came to me that I wanted to join the militia and fight the British. It was the only way I might get revenge for what they had done to John. I hadn't thought of that before.

The captain looked at my hands. "Do you have a rifle, boy?" he said.

"I have an ax," I said.

There were snickers all around and the captain started laughing. The sergeant laughed also.

"Were you thinking of chopping down the redcoats?" Captain Cox said. "Are you a Viking, or do you plan to keep us supplied with firewood?"

"I want to join the fight, sir," I said. The words just came out like somebody else was saying them. My life took a turn in that instant with me hardly knowing it. But I saw I didn't really have a choice. My tongue had thought quicker than my brain. They could do anything they wanted to me. Joining was my only chance to not be hanged or shot for a spy. I had to eat and I had to live. I couldn't live on my own in the woods in the cold winter. And I had to make them think I was a boy. A boy might have a chance to live in this world gone crazy. A girl unprotected would be shamed and killed, or beaten and cast away.

I saw I had to join the militia, and I had to stay with the militia until things changed or something different came up. There was no other way to live until a better time. And I hoped I could pay the Tories back for taking my husband, and killing my husband.

Something in my belly squeezed and turned. The pain was a sick ache that made me feel dizzy. I was going to be sick, and there was no way I could avoid it.

"Then you must take the oath of allegiance," the captain said.

"Yes, sir," I said.

"The sergeant will administer the oath," the captain said. But as he said it something broke loose in my belly. There was a roll and turn in my gut, and brash punched right up into my chest and into my throat. I closed my mouth and put a hand over my lips and just had time to turn aside and stumble to the brush beside the tent.

What rushed out of my mouth was bitter as the worst sadness. I hadn't eaten in a long time and my vomit tasted like gall. I threw up again something yellow, and something bitter and sour at once. I threw up so hard I coughed and it felt like I was going to choke or smother, for all the air was pushed from my chest. It felt like my heart had bursted and the bitterness bursted out of my heart. I felt like I was puking up venom and the marrow out of my bones.

When it stopped I was so weak my knees trembled and my face was covered with sweat. The sergeant led me back to the table.

"Well, Joseph, I hope you haven't brought the flux to us," Captain Cox said.

"No, sir," I said. My mouth tasted like the floor of a chicken house.

The sergeant made me repeat after him the oath of allegiance to the Continental Congress and the North Carolina militia. I swore the oath before God.

"Give this boy a rifle," the captain said. The sergeant took a gun from one of the piles and handed it to me. The rifle was heavier than I expected. The long barrel made it heavier than it looked. He showed me how to load it, pouring in powder and pushing in the patch and bullet, and how to cock it.

I had rarely held a gun before. I was almost afraid to touch the hammer and the long rod that fit in the rings under the barrel. The metal and the wood had been oiled, and the oil rubbed off on my hands. The oil made the gun smell like the inside of a clock, except for the burning smell in the barrel.

I thought the sergeant was going to make me practice shooting the rifle, but he didn't. Instead he called together the men that were standing close to the tent and made us gather in a line. He showed us how to hold our guns at rest at our sides and how to raise them so they tilted over our shoulders. He made us move the rifles from the ground to our shoulders and back, faster and faster.

When Sergeant Gudger let us take a rest I tried to find a dry spot on the grass. The dirt had been torn up and thawed by all our tramping. I found a tuft of broom sedge and sat down on that. Some of the men lay down on the grass like they were going to sleep, and some walked over to the edge of the brush and relieved themselves. Two men spread a coat on the grass and began playing with a soiled deck of cards.

I wrapped Mr. Griffin's coat around my belly and lay back on the broom sedge. I looked right up into the sky to where there were just wisps of cloud. A bird flew by way up high. Men yelled and barked orders around the field, but I just barely heard them. I looked deeper into the sky, and smelled the oil on the gun beside my head. I thought of the panther in the cave. I wondered if I would ever find out what had happened to John. I gripped the stock of the rifle. It seemed impossible that I was in the militia.

And then I felt the headache. My head felt like the sky had come crashing down and was pressing my ears and my brain. I felt my head was going to burst. I lay still hoping to make it go away. It was the kind of headache nothing but sleep could cure.

"Wake up, you slug!" Somebody yelled. It was Sergeant Gudger. He prodded my side with his boot. I'd been dreaming about the cabin on Pine Knot Branch. I rolled over and got to my feet.

"Pick up your rifle," the sergeant said.

Gudger told a boy named T. R. and me to run in place. My headache returned and my head throbbed like it was going to break out of my skull. My head felt like it was balanced on my neck and about to fall off. I didn't know what the sergeant meant, so he showed us how to hold our guns over our heads and step high like we were running, without going anywhere. I held the rifle over my head and starting jogging. My stomach felt loose and rolled around inside me.

I thought if the captain was watching and not saying anything, then he must approve of what the sergeant was doing. And the other men were watching too. I didn't have any choice but to do what Gudger said. For about a minute I jogged all right. But then my arms got tired and my belly felt numb. I started sweating badly under my coat. My brain felt like it was swelling and shrinking.

"Should these girls be wearing dresses?" Gudger said, and everybody laughed again.

I tried to keep jogging and looking straight ahead.

"Halt," Gudger finally said. I was about to drop I was so worn out. The day before I was free in the woods, and now I was straining and being insulted. And I hadn't had anything to eat. Gudger told us to close ranks and to step forward. T. R. and I stepped back into the line. And then we started trotting across the field so close I kept bumping into T. R.'s elbow. A man behind me stepped on my heel and muttered, "Damn shitepoke."

"Feet high," Gudger hollered. "One two three four," he yelled. He walked at the end of the line.

"About face," Gudger shouted. I took another step and whirled around. Somehow I was out in front of the line.

It was past the middle of the morning when it occurred to me who Sergeant Gudger was. I had seen him in church a long time ago. He was a big red-faced boy a lot older than me. I hoped he didn't recognize me. I had seen him play mumblety-peg and hide-and-seek with the older Sunday school class, and here he was acting like a general in his blue coat with the rough stripes sewn on the sleeves.

I tried to recall what I'd heard about Harold Gudger. He had been in trouble with the law. He had hit a constable, or he had been caught smuggling untaxed goods. I couldn't remember the details, but I knew he had been in trouble of some sort. And here he was giving orders like he was the sheriff.

Captain Cox walked out in front of us. All the groups stopped drilling and gathered to our side of the field.

"We are going to drill hard today," the captain shouted. "And we are going to drill hard tomorrow. Tarleton and his legion are on their way here from Fort Ninety Six. General Morgan has arrived in the area and is camped somewhere between the Pacolet and the Broad. He is the only thing between us and Tarleton's sabers. When we are ready we'll march out and join Major McDowell and the rest of the North Carolina militia. And then we will join General Morgan and the Continental regulars."

The captain was not much older than John, but I figured he'd organized the volunteers himself. I reckon when somebody becomes a captain or a major they have to talk like one. I'd noticed that people mostly do what their station calls for.

LATER THAT DAY a horse and wagon pulled to the edge of the clearing. As we marched past I saw the driver was a slave getting baskets and a black washpot out of the bed. We marched around the field again and when we came back next a fire had been lit under the pot, and the next time we came around the pot was steaming and I could smell coffee boiling. I looked at Gudger, but he didn't give us any sign to stop.

The line seemed to speed up, as if we could get around the field faster we might get to stop sooner. I felt like hurrying too but knew it was just wasted effort.

Next time we came around the sergeant almost let us go past. But when we got several steps beyond him Gudger hollered out, "Halt. Fall out."

The washpot was boiling full of coffee. I'd never smelled anything better. The scent was rich as roasted nuts and secret herbs and powders. I had forgotten about my belly in all the marching. It felt better and it was growling. And the headache was gone, though my brain was a little sore where the pain had been.

The baskets by the wagon were full of hard rolls. Some of the men had cups to dip the coffee out with, and some used their canteens. All I had was a pewter bowl the sergeant handed me. I dipped up coffee in that.

We squatted there in the weeds at the field's edge. I don't know which was better, the sweetness of the rest after all the marching or the sweetness of the stale rolls dipped in coffee. The bread was hard, but the hot coffee melted it. The coffee went out through my belly and into my legs and arms where I had dropped to my knees in the stubble.

John Trethman

I DIDN'T KNOW IF I would ever see Josie again, and I had no way of sending her a letter, no way of knowing where she was or if she was still alive. But my heart and my faith told me she was.

I thought of writing to her lines that in the event of my death might reach her. Perhaps one of my flock might find her and give her my words. But I had no pen and paper for such a message.

When I left Josie tied to the tree in front of the burning cabin, I thought my heart would stop, for everything I cared for most was there in the burning forest. I hated that we had quarreled just before we were separated, and I knew it was my fault. I looked into the gulf of emptiness that surrounds us on every side where there is no faith or love. I saw the abyss open around me and above me.

Lord, what is your will? I prayed as they led my horse into the wilderness behind the lanterns and mounted redcoats. And I thought in my heart the Lord was letting the devil try me, as he tried Job, in the spirit of cruelty. And I vowed to myself I would survive, like Job, and return from the wilderness to my congregations and my wife. In the cold Christmas darkness I swore and prayed, and I shuddered.

We stopped at a camp before daylight, and they brought me bound to an officer in a tent. It was not Tarleton but Lieutenant Withnail, the tall man with a saber scar on his cheek I had met before.

"So we meet again," the lieutenant said.

"Not by choice," I answered.

"You have aught to tell us, parson," he said. "You know perfectly well what I mean."

"I am a minister and psalmodist," I said.

"You help recruit militias west of the Catawba," he said.

"I do no such thing," I said.

He slapped me hard across the face and my nose began to bleed. I had nothing to wipe the blood with but my hands.

I will not describe the long hours of my interrogation. He threatened me with hanging and with shooting. He threatened to cut off my fingers one by one, and to cut out my tongue. He had two soldiers hold me and a third whip me with a stick.

"I am just a humble parson," I said.

The lieutenant was so angry his face streamed sweat and he paced back and forth in the tent. "I will find the seed of this rebellion and I will cut it out," he said.

But in the end he found I had nothing of use to tell him. He found I was nothing but a simple preacher and psalmodist, useless to him. I hoped he would release me to return to Josie.

"Can you read Latin?" the lieutenant said. He handed me a little book of Ovid and I read and translated a few lines of the *Amores*.

"Because you have right of clergy I will not hang you," Lieutenant Withnail said.

"Then I am free to go?" I said.

"You are not!" the lieutenant shouted. "Because you are clergy I will not hang you. But I will draft you into the king's service."

"I am not a soldier," I said. "I will not kill."

"You will do your duty as a subject of the Crown," Lieutenant Withnail snapped. He said that Colonel Tarleton needed a chaplain. The regiment had no clergyman to perform funerals or to pray before battles. The men had no spiritual counselor or confessor. I protested that I was not a priest of the Church of England, but he brushed my protest aside.

"I know what you are," the lieutenant said. "In this godforsaken land we must make do with what we have, even Methodists, dissenters, Baptists, though I draw the line at Roman Catholics."

In short, I was impressed to serve as chaplain for the Crown's regiment. And to tell the truth, I wasn't sure any longer where my duty lay. For though unwilling to join the Tory cause, still I had a duty to serve these men as minister and song leader, counselor and comforter. An ordained minister cannot refuse to lead in prayer or raise a song for men who need hope and guidance, men in danger and perhaps on the brink of despair or death.

And I saw that I was being punished for my failures and my deficiencies, for my deception and my anger. I was being forced to pay for what I had done with Josie. It cheered me a little at that desperate time to think there was a larger plan and I was paying my debts.

Though I was drafted against my will, I saw that I must do my duties with a will and dedication. I longed to return to Josie, to escape the war and return to my flocks and my love. But since I could not, I resolved to serve the Lord where I was. And I began to see also the Lord might have called me out to minister to these troubled and desperate men of Tarleton's legion. Perhaps my captivity was part of a larger plan I knew nothing about.

For though we had heard so many terrible things about the king's army and Tarleton's regiment, about depredations and cruelties, and though I witnessed many cruelties myself, I soon came to see that most of the soldiers were heartsick and exhausted, marching day after day through mud and swamps, canebrakes and brush, in cold and rain, in confusing wilderness, crossing raging rivers and creeks, camping in marsh and mire, burning and looting.

I saw these were men who had come to loathe their service and perhaps themselves. They were angry at the rebellion and the rebels, or they were too tired to even be angry. Their clothes and boots were wearing out, and they were far from resupply in Charleston.

Every day we rode farther into the backcountry of South Carolina and seized what pork and cattle, corn and wheat, we could find. I prayed with the men in the morning and led in song in the evening. Soldiers no older than boys came to me and wept, while others spat at my feet and blasphemed. I had never seen men more distraught, or scared, though some pretended nonchalance, irreverence.

One day I was brought to Colonel Tarleton himself. I was led to his tent in the pine grove and stood before him. Though short, the colonel was a strong figure of a man, with an air of authority, confidence, and a face as pretty as a woman's. His uniform was bright and fine, and he wore an expensive sword. As was often reported, he was arrogant of manner. It was said he had squandered a fortune at Oxford and in London before he joined the dragoons. He was known to have a terrible temper. It was reported he had executed his own soldiers with a sword or pistol.

"Reverend Trethman," he said, "I am pleased you were able to join us."

"It is my duty to serve the Lord," I said.

"And to serve His Majesty," the colonel said.

"I will pray and sing where I am needed," I said.

"You are badly needed here," the colonel said. His manner changed as quickly as if a new wind had swept through a forest. His face softened and he looked like the boy he almost was. He and I were about the same age. His eyes were troubled.

"Reverend Trethman," he said in a lower voice, "my men need to be inspired. They are far from home and far from safety. This wilderness has exhausted them. The traitors harry us and burn our supplies. We are far from the main army of Lord Cornwallis. The men wonder if this rebellion will ever end."

He gestured for me to come closer.

"We need you to inspire us," he said. "We need you to give us hope, to fortify us to do our duty."

The colonel spoke as I had not expected. He said that without a sense of blessing, of the rightness of a cause, men would never serve at their best. He said a chaplain could be worth more than an extra piece of artillery if he could encourage men to see the justice of their cause. A chaplain must ease troubled minds and strengthen hope. He said men have to fight with a sense of purpose and pride, and it was my job to spirit up the men and restore their sense of purpose and justice. I told him I was just a plain minister of the Gospel.

Colonel Tarleton patted my shoulder and said he knew I would do my duty, that I would serve his men well. I did not tell him I would do the same for a patriot army, or any army, where men were in need of fellowship and prayer.

My impression of the colonel was different from what I had expected. He was a more considerate man, and a more varied man, than I would have thought. And he was wiser than the rumors had led me to believe.

I felt I was learning something important there, though I couldn't say precisely what it was. I was learning not to be so quick to judge, to be patient and willing to learn, from strangers and enemies, from anyone. I was learning to be humble and compassionate. And I was learning from my love for Josie, which sustained me. And I was learning to love my enemies, as we are told to do, and to see that there were no enemies, only brothers in need and confusion.

WHILE I WAS SERVING with Tarleton's legion and seeing daily the brutality, the boredom, the stupidity of war, I, oddly enough, began to think more about my own deficiencies, my shortcomings and guilt. Day after day I was exposed to floggings and hangings, to rape of captured women, to men wounded in skirmishes, men dying of fever and blood poisoning. But while I observed and mourned the viciousness around me, as we flung across the wilds of South Carolina and back, I thought of my own sins. My own deceptions preyed on my mind.

While we traveled and while we waited in camp, I saw vividly and felt keenly my own guilt. While serving as a minister of the Gospel I had concealed from my flock the nature of my relation with Josie. She had deceived me and the world, it was true, but she was little more than a child and acting perhaps in desperation. I was not only older; I had the responsibility to set an example, to lead.

It was easy to be pure and moral when there was no trial of character, no challenge to the conscience. But when faced with a drastic decision I had chosen the easier path. I had failed Josie and my congregation, I had failed the Lord and I had failed myself. You are not worthy to lead in song and prayer, I said to myself as we traveled to yet another camp. You want to judge others but are reluctant to judge yourself. What is your witness? What is your testimony to these desperate men if you are no better than they are? You are now paying for your sins.

I remembered that my hero, Archbishop Cranmer, had been married secretly, twice, but that was no salve to my conscience. That was a matter for the archbishop's conscience. And besides, Cranmer was at least married presumably by another priest, not in some mongrel ceremony performed by himself on Pine Knot Branch.

If I ever returned to Pine Knot Branch and Josie, I would confess to my congregations what I had done and what I had not told them. And I would confess to Josie my weakness of spirit and the weakness of my flesh. I was deficient in courage, and was perhaps ruled by lust and vanity, as much as any of the rude men I served.

DAY AFTER DAY Colonel Tarleton's vanity was on display. He always wore a fine uniform, even when riding through brush and briars and canebrakes. He held himself erect in the saddle, and he swung his saber like it was a bolt of lightning shot from his right hand. He was not a tall man, but he could leap onto a horse in an instant. He rode as though he had been born in the saddle. He was such a brilliant horseman I found myself watching him and admiring him.

One day the colonel saw me staring as he rode into camp and dismounted. He tossed the reins to an aide and stepped to the campfire. "Were you ever a rider, Reverend Trethman?" he said.

"Not often," I said. "But I need a horse for my circuit."

"Every man should have a mount," the colonel said. "For nothing else, except perhaps one thing, will give him so much pleasure." He looked at me and added, "I beg you pardon, Reverend."

"A horse is a thing of beauty," I said.

"The best beauty is in the riding, in the coordination and harmony with the steed. I love to feel the power of the horse under me, and the spirit of a good horse. A good horse loves to run, loves to race, and loves to win. A good horse has the courage to run down boars. And there is no greater sport than hunting foxes."

The young colonel took a drink from his flask and wiped his mouth. "Are parsons permitted to hunt?" he said.

"I never knew a clergyman who did hunt," I said.

"Everyone should know the thrill of the chase," the colonel said. "It would make you a better parson, to feel the moment a horse breaks into a gallop as you stretch out across a hill in pursuit, and catch sight of a fox disappearing into a copse."

Several men had gathered by the fire to listen to Colonel Tarleton. He spoke with the enthusiasm of a boy, a young athlete.

"Only one other sport surpasses hunting," Tarleton said, "and it is this, what we are doing here, serving the Crown. From the moment I arrived in North America I have enjoyed riding against the rebels. These militias hide behind trees and brush. They shoot from ditches and behind rocks and logs like cowards. But I have yet to see a rebel force that can stand and face a cavalry charge, or a bayonet charge for that matter. They see us riding down on them and they melt away. Our music scares them, and the sight of our uniforms. In their hearts they know they are guilty of treason and they run like rabbits, soiling their ragged pants.

"There is no exhilaration like riding down such rabble, these buckskin farmers. Often with one swing you can chop a man's head off, or chop a shoulder off. If you lean down you can run a saber through his heart. I have cleared many fields of cowardly militias, from New York to Georgia, and it is capital sport. I will clear the Carolinas of traitors also."

ONE DAY LIEUTENANT Withnail brought a captured horse into the camp. It was the tallest, most slender white stallion I had ever seen, taken from a farm near Fort Ninety Six. It was so wild and strong it had to be led by two men who had put a sack over its head. They held the horse with chains stretched from its halter and bridle.

"Is this crazy creature of any use to us?" Lieutenant Withnail said to the colonel. Colonel Tarleton whistled with awe and took one of the chains. He walked up close to the horse's head and said something to the horse too low for the rest of us to hear.

"I didn't expect to see such horseflesh in these woods," Tarleton said. "American stables are usually worse than poor."

He lifted the sack off the horse's head and revealed the stallion's eyes wide with fear. The horse tossed its head around and reared. And when the animal dropped on all fours again it wheeled around and kicked at the colonel. Tarleton dodged but the hoof caught him on the thigh, not the full blow but a glancing lick. His face turned white with pain and then bright red.

"Bring me my spurs," he shouted to his valet.

The colonel strapped on the very long spurs that looked like knife blades and grabbed two thick riding quirts from the orderly. He told the men to hold the white stallion with the chains while he saddled him. And then he fitted a bridle with a Spanish bit in the horse's mouth. Last he tied two sets of reins to the heavy bit.

Colonel Tarleton leapt into the saddle on the tall horse as if he had been thrown there. The stallion must have been seventeen hands high, or more. I never understood how a short man could mount so quickly. "This American horse needs some instruction," the colonel shouted.

As soon as the chains were taken from the halter the stallion broke away. First it reared on its hind legs as though trying to throw the colonel off backward. The colonel held the reins and kept his seat in the cavalry saddle. He drove the long spurs into the horse's sides. The stallion dropped to its front feet and began running. We were in open country with scattered brush and trees. The horse rushed toward an oak tree as if to knock its rider off on a limb.

The colonel jerked the stallion to the left and whipped its flank with the two quirts. The horse leapt forward and ran several hundred yards before it began bucking. I had never seen a horse buck so. The white stallion humped its back like a camel or a cat. It jumped forward and dropped, kicking out its hind legs. It jumped and twisted backward in midair, trying to swing the rider off. The great stallion seemed to be tying knots in itself. The horse ran forward and stopped abruptly.

It leapt over a bush along the creek.

The horse and rider disappeared and we heard the pounding of hooves. The galloping horse was loud as the sound of my heart knocking. The hoofbeats faded and I was sure the colonel had fallen off and the horse had run away into the forest. But then I heard the galloping again, and after a few minutes the colonel and the stallion came into view. The horse still tried to buck, but it was getting tired. It made a twisting jump, as though trying to touch its nose to its tail.

Even at a distance I could hear the stallion panting, as the colonel rode it round and round and back and forth among the brush and bushes. He made the horse run like it was racing. There was blood on both sides of the horse's belly.

Finally the colonel rode the stallion back to the camp, and as they got closer I saw the horse was drenched in sweat. There was a foam of sweat on the hide so the stallion seemed lathered with soap. And mixed with foam at the mouth there was blood on the lips and jaw where the Spanish bit had cut into the skin and into the tongue.

The stallion panted and sweated and trembled, it was so weak. The stallion was tired like it had pulled a wagon or plowed all day. The colonel jumped off the horse and flung the reins to his orderly. "This is the way we will treat all rebels," he said. He was soaked with sweat; he went into his tent and I never saw him again that day.

But Colonel Tarleton surprised me several times. He could act like a brute and then behave like a gentleman. You never knew which side of him was going to be displayed. He intimidated his men with his unpredictability. They were never able to judge how he might respond.

One day a slave was brought into the camp. He had been an orderly for Lieutenant Withnail, and he had run away. The slave's name was Steve, and he had been caught by a patrol hiding in a canebrake. They tied him to a tree near the campfire. Steve was covered with sweat and dust and looked too exhausted to care much what they did to him.

Lieutenant Withnail tore Steve's shirt off and struck him across the back with his riding whip. "So you would steal from the Crown?" he said.

"No, sir," Steve said.

"You are both a runaway and a deserter," the lieutenant said.

Now I had seen men whipped in camp with ropes and sticks and cat-o'-nine-tails. I had seen men tortured with red-hot pokers applied to tender parts of their bodies and mutilated with razors and bayonets. But something about Steve's plight moved me more than usual. I watched him wince and groan as the whip fell on his back.

"Colonel," I yelled. Tarleton was in his tent with one of the camp women. I knew he was there. "Colonel," I shouted, "you must stop this."

"Keep to your prayers and songbook, parson," Lieutenant Withnail snarled at me.

"You have done enough," I said.

Tarleton appeared at the door of his tent with his shirt hanging loose over his pants. His boots were off and his hair uncombed. He looked at the lieutenant and at Steve and he looked at me.

"The padre wants to interfere," Lieutenant Withnail said. Since Tarleton had ordered many men whipped to death I didn't really expect mercy from him. But this time his mood seemed mild. He walked over to the slave and examined his back. He said something to Steve I couldn't hear.

"Cut him loose," the colonel said.

"This slave deserted," the lieutenant said.

The colonel looked me hard in the eye as he spoke to the lieutenant. "He will not desert again," Tarleton said. "The Reverend Trethman guarantees it."

Tarleton's generosity seemed like a threat somehow. I felt I had been given a warning, but I was still relieved that Steve had been spared.

NINE

As THE TASTE of the coffee and bread flushed through me, I sat on the grass and wondered if I could last in the militia. They'd find out about me sooner or later, and then they would learn I'd killed Mr. Griffin. I was almost certain my husband was dead. But I wanted to find some justice for him, and then maybe I could live in peace. And I saw that serving in the militia would be my way of paying for what I had done to Mr. Griffin. At least my stomach was settled. At least I could hold down the coffee and bread. I just hoped my mind would stay clear.

"This bread was took out of a tomb," somebody said.

"We got loaves but we ain't got no fishes," the skinny redheaded boy named T. R. said.

The bread was hard, but it tasted good, soaked in the coffee. Took several dunks to make a roll soft enough to chew, but once it was melted by the coffee the bread tasted like a memory of summer on the tongue.

When I finished the rolls I was ready to lie down in the grass and go to sleep with the sun on my face. I knew I'd better not say much to anybody.

The more I talked the more likely I was to be found out. My best hope was to say nothing. Make them think I was a dull young boy.

Capt. William Cox stood up and walked over to the washpot. He stood by the fire like a preacher at an altar. The fire made our place important in the woods. The thought gave me a chill for it made me think of John.

"While you all were drilling I got a message," the captain shouted. He held his rifle gun in the crook of his arm. "General Morgan wants us to march down the river and meet his army at Grindal Shoals."

A groan went through the company. The captain said Grindal Shoals was about twenty-five miles away. That was a day's walk, carrying our guns and blankets. It would take till midnight if we walked it straight through. There was muttering all around.

"I didn't 'list to go walking all over South Carolina," somebody said.

"Are we in South Carolina?" I said.

"I ain't going to cross the Broad River," T. R. said.

"Tarleton is coming up from Ninety Six to meet Cornwallis at the Broad River," Captain Cox shouted. "We will be joined to Major McDowell's North Carolina patriots."

"Why can't we fight on our own?" somebody yelled.

"We will fight where we are told," the captain said.

Everybody on the field was quiet. It was like they hadn't thought before they'd be part of a big army. They had forgotten why they were there. The day was quiet as only a winter day can be. There were some crows way across the woods, and you could hear the breeze in the broom sedge and in the pines.

"This evening we will march as far as we can," Captain Cox said. "And don't tell anybody where we're going. There are Tory spies everywhere."

"What if we meet Tories?" somebody said.

"And we will not plunder our own people," the captain said. "Of course, if a Tory has a horse or ham he doesn't need we can accept it as a donation." Everybody laughed.

"Anybody caught sending a message to Tarleton will be hanged from the closest tree," the captain added.

I didn't have anything to carry but my blanket and the ax and the rifle gun. Sergeant Gudger gave me a powder horn and bag of shot and patches which I hung over my shoulder. The extra rifles and cooking things and tents were loaded into the wagons. I'd heard that British regiments carried their own blacksmith shops, but there was nothing in Cox's wagons but a few extra blankets and rifles.

Gudger ordered us to form a line two abreast and we started walking. The road away from the field was so muddy and narrow it was nearly impossible to march on it. Only two abreast could walk there, dodging puddles and the mire in low places.

There was lots of good bottom land along the road, and back of every field we passed stood pine woods and oak woods. In the distance you could see the hills, and beyond the hills the mountains so far away they looked like low clouds. I wished I could turn aside and go to the mountains. I wished John and I had gone to the mountains on Christmas Eve before the Tories came. We could have built ourselves a cabin in the woods and be living there free.

We passed a burned house, and then half a mile down the road we passed another. In the yard of the second house a body hung from an oak tree. The body had been stripped naked and a sign tied around the neck, DEATH TO TRAITORS.

"Halt," Cox called out from where he rode at the head of the line. He hollered to Gudger and told him to cut the body down and bury it. The sergeant yelled to two men named Jenkins and Roberts to take shovels from a wagon and dig a grave. And he ordered T. R. and me to cut the body down.

They had not put a sack over the man's head, and I knew I'd have to look at his face. There wasn't any way to cut him down and slip the rope from around his neck without looking at the face.

It was the worst face I'd ever seen. The body must have been hanging there for several days. The skin was black and the tongue stuck out where the man had choked to death. The body smelled rotten and birds had gotten at the eyeballs and half pecked them away. The skin had been cut by birds or rats.

Horrible as the face was to look at, it wasn't my disgust I was worried about. I'd heard of babies being marked in the womb by what their mamas had seen. Mama had told me about babies with snake eyes and babies that were foolish because they had been marked in the womb. I turned away from the terrible face as I slid the noose off the neck and over the head. The body was already stiff and the rope caught on the nose. I had to loosen the knot again, and my fingers touched the rotted skin. When I finally got the rope over the top of the head I wiped my hands on the ground, but they still smelled like tainted meat. I wiped them again on the grass and tried not to touch my clothes.

I hoped the sickening stink of a corpse could not reach a baby inside the womb. The stink was so bad I washed my hands with dirt. I figured Gudger would order T. R. and me to finish digging the hole and bury the body. We were the youngest in the company and everything low and dirty would fall to us. But he hollered to the two other men to keep digging.

Captain Cox rode up on his horse and said he couldn't keep the company waiting while the hanged man was buried. He told Gudger to stay there with us four and see the body had a Christian burial. "Commit the body to the earth as a Christian," the captain said, and turned his horse away.

"Heatherly and Summers will stay behind," Gudger called out, pointing at me.

"Bloody blackguard," T. R. whispered.

I watched the line of men follow the captain down the muddy road until they were out of sight. Gudger took a drink from his canteen and I caught the scent of spirits. The sergeant had a canteen like a short barrel filled with whiskey or brandy. His face was red as a flag.

"Can we have a drink?" T. R. said.

"Every soldier must carry his own water," Gudger said.

The two men were slow digging the grave. I looked around for a spring or branch where I could wash my hands and slake my thirst. There was no water in sight.

"The devil Tarleton has done this," Gudger said, and pointed to the charred ruins of the house. "He catches us he'll do the same to us." The sergeant took another swig from the little cask and bit off a chew of tobacco from a twist he carried in his pocket. I sniffed the scent of spirits and tobacco, hoping they would cover up the smell on my hands.

"The captain said we had to perform a Christian burial," Gudger said. He looked at Roberts and Jenkins digging the grave and he looked at T. R. and me. He asked T. R. if he'd ever conducted a funeral.

"The sergeant is supposed to say the ceremony and read the Scripture," T. R. said.

Gudger spat on the ground and wiped his mouth. "Don't, by god, tell me what a sergeant is supposed to do." I could tell he was getting a little drunk. "I ain't never preached or prayed in my life," he said, and laughed.

When the two men got the hole about a yard deep Gudger told them to stop.

"I thought a grave was supposed to be six feet," Roberts said.

"That's in peacetime. A yard is deep enough in wartime," Gudger said.

I knew the sergeant was going to make T. R. and me carry the body to the hole and drop it in. I was going to have to get my hands on the filth again and smell the rotten flesh again. I would try to hold my breath so the stink wouldn't get into my chest or in my blood.

"Joseph will preach a Christian burial," Gudger said, and started laughing. I looked at T. R. and at the two men holding shovels.

"I don't have any Scripture," I said.

"Then you will have to sing for us and talk from memory," Gudger said with a big grin.

"I have a holy book," Jenkins said. He reached into the pack he'd laid on the ground and took out a small Bible.

"Now we've got a book and we've got a parson," Gudger said. He grabbed the Bible and handed it to me. I held the small faded book in the late afternoon light and watched T. R. and the other two men drag the corpse to the hole and roll it in. I held the book close to my face and smelled the old leather and paper.

Gudger was making fun of the dead man and making light of the captain's order for a Christian burial. He was making light of the Scripture too. Best thing was to say something short and honest and then go on. I would not mock the dead and I would have no part in mocking the Scripture.

"Well, padre, say a few words," Gudger said, and pushed me toward the grave.

I was so tired I was trembling, and sick at heart. I was confused and scared. But the little book in my hands gave me comfort. The little book was like a rock to hold to. I gripped the small book like it was something to keep me from fainting away. And it was not just because the Bible reminded me of John and the way he carried the Scripture and read from the book. And it wasn't just that the words inside the little book were so familiar and so old. But in that awful place and time, with Gudger drunk and laughing at me and at death, with the smell of death on my hands, I felt how alive the little book was, and how it was a link between different times, between now and old times and everlasting things, between now and the future.

Tired as I was, I opened the little book and saw the print was so vivid it seemed to bite the air. The letters were sharp as needle pricks and razor edges. The words seemed to cut the light.

"Go ahead," Gudger said. "Saint Peter is tired of waiting."

I opened the book and saw the page was John 14. It was the very passage John would have read from if he'd been there.

> *Let not your heart be troubled: ye believe in God, believe also in me.*
> *In my Father's house are many mansions: if it were not so, I would*
> *have told you. I go to prepare a place for you.*

And if I go and prepare a place for you, I will come again and receive
   you unto myself;
that where I am, there ye may be also.
And whither I go ye know, and the way ye know.

I read the words in a slow clear voice. And as I read I looked at each of the men in turn. I looked at Gudger and saw the surprise on his face. And I looked toward the body in the grave. The sergeant opened his mouth to say something, and then didn't. I knew he was in a hurry. But I was not in a hurry anymore.

"I'm not a preacher," I said, and looked at T. R. and Jenkins and Roberts and then at Gudger. "I'm just an ordinary pilgrim like you all. This man has died, and we don't know a thing about him except he was a human being and that he died an ugly death in a bad time. We must pray for the Lord to bless him and bring his soul to Him. And we must pray for the comfort of his family."

I bowed my head, then looked around. T. R. took off his cap and the two other men took off their hats. But Gudger didn't take off his hat.

"Lord, we ask your guidance and comfort in these times of sorrow," I said. "Bring your peace to this troubled land." As I spoke I heard John saying the words in the back of my mind. I heard his voice speaking through my tongue. It made me shiver to think we had quarreled just before he was taken on Christmas Eve. As I went on the words took over. The words seemed to come from somewhere in my blood and far back in my head. It felt like the words had always been in my chest waiting to come out.

"Shine a light in this darkness and lead us toward safety," I said. "Shine the light of your words on our lives so we can find the way. And bring us to those we love."

When I said "Amen," Gudger pointed to the shovels beside the grave. But I wasn't finished. He had told me to say a few words and I was going to do it. For speaking, as John would have spoken, made me feel stronger and safer than I had in days. The words lifted me up over the mud and stink and Gudger's anger.

"I guess we people in our pride and foolishness weren't meant to understand everything," I said. "Our minds are not big enough to see the mind of God. The Bible says the fear of God is the beginning of wisdom. I say the love of God is wisdom also. To be humble and love Jesus and our fellow men is maybe all the wisdom we can know."

The words came to me as I talked. I could see T. R. was astonished. I was preaching like a real preacher. He and the two men held their hats in their hands and watched me. But Gudger was in a hurry to go. He looked at me and he looked down the road. I guess he was afraid the redcoats would come back. He stepped from one foot to the other like he had to pee.

"You don't need to preach a whole sermon, Summers," Gudger said.

"We will sing a hymn," I said. I wished I had John's songbook with me. What was a song right for a burial? All I could think of was "Jesus Shall Reign." I started singing and my voice was crackly at first, but got better when I reached the second verse.

WHEN THE GRAVE WAS filled in Gudger ordered us to fall into a line.

"Ain't we got time to piss?" Roberts said.

"We've wasted too much time mumbling already," Gudger said.

The men groaned and I groaned with them. But the fact was I was relieved. For the most dangerous thing was to piss in daylight. Men could just stop and unbutton their pants and pee standing up. They could turn their backs and it didn't matter who was watching them. But while it was daylight and men were standing nearby I had to hold it in. Or pretend I had to shite. Then I could crawl into the brush and do it. As long as they thought I was shiting I was all right, for people will avoid you while you shite.

I thought how strange it was I had read from the Bible and prayed by the grave. They didn't know that I had killed Mr. Griffin, had waited for him in the dark and murdered him, and that I was a girl pretending to be a boy. Every day was stranger than the day before.

WE KEPT MARCHING until we came up with the company several miles down the road. They were camped in the woods and campfires were scattered among the trees. Tents had been strung up between some of the trees. With men spread around many fires, it looked like the company was bigger than it was. It looked as if the woods and thickets were full of soldiers far as you could see.

After dark it got terribly cold, and men wrapped themselves up in blankets and bearskins and quilts. They tied scarves around their heads, and wrapped rags around their hands. All I had was the one blanket and I saw I'd have to stay close to the fire. Gudger and T. R. and I and the two other men joined a group around a bonfire near a laurel thicket.

I was worried about lying in a tent close to so many men. Surely they'd find me out if somebody rubbed against me. I'd have to keep myself wrapped in my coat and blanket.

But I need not have worried, for there weren't enough tents to go around. Unless you had brought your own tent you had to sleep in the open. There were only enough tents for corporals and sergeants; the rest of us would have to lie in the open.

For supper we had grits flavored with a little hog meat and gravy, and there was coffee and stale bread. But the grits tasted like manna to me, and the old bread was sweeter than cake. I warmed myself with the coffee and the little bit of meat glowed in my belly like a piece of hickory wood in a fireplace.

I was so tired I started to get drowsy soon as I'd finished the last bite. I drank the coffee and felt the sweetness in my belly. I just wanted to lie down in my blanket close to the fire.

"You sounded like a real preacher," T. R. said to me.

"Anybody can sound like a preacher," I said.

"But you sounded like you had done it before," Jenkins said.

"Gudger made me do it," I said. I felt the dust of sleep in my blood, making me weak and floaty.

"If you're a real preacher you can't cuss," T. R. said. "And you can't do it with girls neither."

"The hell you can't," I said.

"Preachers can cuss just like anybody else," Roberts said.

"A preacher farts and shites just like anybody else," Gudger said, and spat into the fire.

"But a preacher don't talk like everybody else," T. R. said.

"How would you know?" Gudger said. Gudger turned to me. "Summers here is the parson," he said, and shoved my shoulder. I didn't like the way Gudger looked at my eyes. He acted like he knew something, that he was privy to a secret.

WHEN YOUR BELLY is full and you're warm and tired, nothing is sweeter than sleep. Sleep raises through you and soaks through your thoughts and tastes rich and powerful. Every time sleep comes in a different shade and at a different angle. Every time sleep has a different touch, and comes from behind or beside you. Sleep whispers in your ear and takes you by surprise.

I was so worn out I was asleep even before I was asleep. I was floating like a thin film of bubbles on top of a pond. I was a thin film that stretched out for miles on a lake. And voices whispered in the sky. They were the voices I'd heard all day, of Captain Cox and Sergeant Gudger. They whispered in the dome of sky.

It was the voice of my baby. It was the voice of my baby already talking in my blood, behind a great rose and lavender mountain, talking way at the back of my head.

I awoke in the night and felt a wetness on my nose. Something cold was licking my face and touching my cheek with wet lips. Was it a little animal? I was still asleep but I listened for rain. I listened for drops. But all I heard was the whine of a fire and a dull prickle and hiss.

I licked my lip and tasted grits of ice. I opened my eyes and something lit on my eyebrows. I looked around and saw a thousand moths flying around the campfire. But it wasn't moths and millers. It was snowflakes. The air was filled with falling snow. And snow had covered my blanket and all the other blankets of men sleeping around the fire. The snow was quiet as spiders climbing down webs or dropping into shadows. The snow was falling so steadily I seemed to be rising into the still air. The woods were still and the blankets and tents were covered with snow.

"Joseph, get up," a rough voice whispered. A hand touched my shoulder, and when I turned it touched my breast. I jerked away. It was Gudger, and though I jerked away and couldn't see his face I knew he'd felt my breast. It was what I'd feared most. I wondered if he had known all along. I was awake instantly and waited to see what he would say, to see if he would give me away to the other men.

"Guard duty," Gudger said. "Your watch, Summers."

I sat up and wrapped the blanket around my shoulders. I was afraid to look at the sergeant, and when I did look I saw him staring at my eyes. I turned away and picked up the rifle gun. The stock and barrel were covered with snow, and I wiped them off with the back of my hand.

"Go out and replace Jenkins," Gudger said, and pointed toward the laurel thicket behind the camp. I reckon there was one sentinel by the road and one behind the encampment.

When I stood up in the falling snow the sergeant stood up too. I turned to step among the sleeping bodies and he followed me to the edge of the thicket.

"What do I do if somebody shows up?" I said.

"Holler 'Halt, who goes there?' If they don't know the password, shoot them," the sergeant said.

"What is the password?" I said.

Gudger said the password was "Liberty." He stood close to me in the falling snow and looked into my face. His body was touching my body. "We should get to know each other better if we're going to serve together," he said.

I jerked away from him and didn't answer. I wanted to get away from Gudger.

"Your secret's safe with me, Private Summers," Gudger said, "as long as you do your duty." He said "duty" so I would understand it had a special meaning.

"I will do my duty," I said, and stepped farther into the woods. The snow was coming down heavier than ever. Flakes brushed my face and touched my eyes like little fingers. The snow lit up the dark woods a little.

"Damn right you will," Gudger said.

When I found Jenkins he was sitting on a log at the edge of the laurel thicket. I reckon he was cold and lonesome, for he was mighty glad to see me. He was all scrunched down and his hat and coat were covered with snow.

"The password is 'liberty,'" Jenkins said.

"Have you seen anything?" I said.

"Ain't nothing in this swamp but ghosts," Jenkins said.

"Ghosts won't hurt us," I said, trying to sound jovial and confident.

When Jenkins was gone I sat on the log and laid the gun across my lap. I pulled the blanket tight around my shoulders. I shivered, but it was as much from worry as from cold. If Gudger had found me out—and I was certain he had—then he could tell on me any time he wanted to. As the sergeant he had power over me anyway. But now he could force me to do whatever he wanted.

I wondered what the penalty for pretending to be a man and a soldier was. It seemed like an army could do anything it wanted to. An army could make its own laws. An army could shoot you for falling asleep on guard duty. An army could hang you for a traitor if you sassed an officer or even a sergeant. A woman had no business in an army.

The snow was so heavy it whispered and clicked as flakes touched each other and settled on the leaves of laurels and on the ground. There was the hiss of the tiny bones of snowflakes breaking when they hit the ground. It sounded like the snowflakes were talking, but in such a low voice you couldn't understand what they were saying. But it seemed they were trying to say something to me. Was the snow telling me what I should do or where I should go? Was John's ghost sending a message on the night air? Was the snow whispering of sorrow and suffering? The snow was muttering of cold and danger, and the promise of peace and rest beyond it all.

You are a pilgrim, the snowflakes said. You are a pilgrim like the man in the book John read. You are the pilgrim's wife following him through the woods and thickets and swamps, looking for love and peace, for the path toward the holy city. You are a pilgrim without any home and without any friends. You are a sinner that has killed Mr. Griffin and deceived John and the world. You quarreled with John and you are paying for your mistakes.

It was strangely comforting to think the snow was telling me that. The message was hard, but I saw it was true. And the firmness of truth is comforting. I felt I was touching solid bedrock. Truth was something you could put your feet on. I was a killer and a liar, and I was paying for my sins.

The air was faintly lit with all the falling snow. But you still couldn't see the trees and ground. I saw this light far off in the thicket, where there hadn't been a light before. It looked like the glow of a lantern or little campfire. Had I got mixed up in directions? Was I facing the camp instead of the thicket? Falling snow made the light dance and lean.

I brushed the snow off the rifle gun and held it out in front of me. As the light got closer I saw it wasn't just a yellow light. It was a green and blue light too. It was a light the color of apple wood burning. It was a light with purple and lavender in it.

Who is playing a trick on me? I thought. Who is trying to fool me and scare me in the snow? I thought it might be redcoats trying to trick me. And I thought it might be outlaws or even Indians. They must have special powder to burn to make such a strange light.

As the glow got closer it grew bigger. It wasn't just a flame but something tall as a man gliding through the trees and through the brush. It was an aura like light from a halo. It was a globe of light. Is this a ghost?

I thought. Is this the ghost of a dead Indian? Or the ghost of a dead soldier? Is this the ghost of John come to tell me something?

I aimed the gun as the light got closer. I wondered if I should call out or fire the rifle gun as a warning. What if it was just somebody trying to find their way? What if it was a patriot soldier trying to find his way back to camp in the snow?

As it got closer the light was not as bright as I'd thought. The light was tall as a man but its purples and greens and blues had faded. The glow was weakening, just beyond some laurel bushes, close enough to speak to.

"Halt," I said. "Who goes there?"

But nobody answered. There was only the swish and crackle of falling snow.

"What is the password?" I said, and raised the rifle. I expected somebody to say "Liberty," but there was no answer except the whisper and scratch of the heavy snowflakes touching each other and piling up.

I thought I was going to have to shoot. I raised the rifle and put my finger on the cold trigger. But just as I was about to pull the trigger the light melted away. It got dimmer and dimmer and just faded until I couldn't tell when it disappeared. Even as I aimed the barrel I saw the light had gone.

"Who is there?" I said, expecting to hear snickering. But the only noise was the snow sweeping into the trees.

I sat back on the log and studied on the mystery. Jenkins had said there were ghosts there. Was the light what he'd meant? Had he been visited by such a light? All my life I'd heard about ball lightning and chain lightning. I'd heard about swamp gas and wills of the wisp. I'd heard about lights coming out of hills and sinkholes. I'd heard about ghosts that searched all night for their lost loves.

Just then I saw another light way off in the woods. It was to the left of where the other light had started. It was a faint light that got bigger, like a wick was being turned up. The light floated like a lantern on a tide. The light moved steadily through the trees and brush.

These woods are haunted by devils, I said under my breath. These woods are possessed by bad spirits. The glow of this light was redder than the other one. This light was red as a devil light from hell. I knew that somehow the snow had stirred up the spirits in the woods or in the ground. Whether it was swamp gas that was burning or the ghosts of Cherokees, it was the snow that had riled them out of their lairs to wander in the night.

After the red light faded there was another one that came from the left. This one was yellow and lavender and almost flat as a tabletop. The light was so thin it could have been glow worms and lightning bugs floating on the surface of a lake. The light was thin as a razor's edge and cut its way through the dark, so flat you could hardly see it.

When the slice of light faded away I didn't see any more. The woods were dark again and scratching with falling snow like there were tiny beetles and mice all around me. The snow itched and drooled on my face. I pulled the blanket over my head as a kind of hood.

Sitting still in the woods will make you cold no matter how much clothes you're wearing. Sitting still without a fire will chill you to the bone and to the middle of your guts. You could freeze to death just sitting still and never know it, getting numb and weak. I jerked myself and shook myself. As long as you're shivering you won't freeze, I'd heard. Shivering and shaking are a way of staying warm.

There didn't seem to be much need for a sentry out in the snowy woods. No redcoats were likely to be stirring in the snow and in the dark, not even outlaws and deserters would be stirring in the cold woods. Only ghosts and wills-o'-the-wisp were about.

Just then I heard steps, the faint sound of boots crunching in the snow. I reckon the snow was two or three inches deep. I listened and strained my eyes to see into the snow and dark. It was hard to see anything. Somebody was coming and I couldn't see a thing. Maybe if they didn't see me they would walk on by. I wouldn't call out halt unless they got really close.

What cause do you have to be out here in danger? I said to myself. You should be protecting yourself and the baby. A woman expecting has no right to put herself in danger. You have no business out here freezing and holding a gun. Your duty is to protect yourself.

I turned my head and listened hard. I saw the steps were coming from behind me and not in front. Somebody was coming from the camp. Could it be somebody to relieve me?

"Halt," I said, "Who goes there?"

Whoever it was kept coming.

"Halt or I will shoot," I said.

"Liberty," a man said, and laughed. It was Gudger.

"Can I go back to the fire?" I said. I was going to pretend Gudger hadn't found out anything, that I was just a volunteer and he was the sergeant.

"I brung you a dry blanket and a mug of coffee," Gudger said. He didn't snarl like he usually did. He sounded like he wanted to be friendly.

"Don't need any coffee," I said, my teeth chattering.

"You are freezing," the sergeant said. I could barely see him, but I could smell the coffee. It was hot and rich like coffee that has just been boiled.

"Put this blanket around you, honey," Gudger said. He took my hand and put it on the warm mug. And then I felt the rifle being slid out of my lap.

"I have to hold the gun," I said.

"You can't hold coffee and the rifle at the same time," the sergeant said.

I saw what a fix I was in. Gudger had found out my secret and was going to use it against me. Gudger could always claim I was a spy, that he'd caught me spying. It was known that women had served as spies for the redcoats. If the sergeant told on me I was dead any way you figured it. I would have to use my wits.

A sip of the coffee warmed my lips, and warmed my throat and belly as it went down. I sipped again and the coffee was like a light on my tongue that found its way down to my belly.

"I saw lights out in the woods," I said to Gudger.

"You seen lanterns?" he said.

I described the glowing things, the blue and green and lavender, the red devil light, and the razor edge of light that slit through the dark.

"You must have been asleep and dreaming," Gudger said.

"I was not asleep," I said. As I sipped the coffee I quit shaking, but my teeth didn't stop chattering. It wasn't just the cold that made me shudder. I was afraid of Gudger, of what he might do or say.

The sergeant leaned up against me in the dark, smelling of tobacco and the whiskey he kept in his canteen. I tried to pull away. "I can help you," he said.

"How can you help?" I said.

"I know you're expecting," Gudger said.

"You don't know anything," I said, and took a big swallow of the coffee.

"When I seen you sick this morning, I knowed what it was," Gudger said. " My mama was a midwife and I know the signs. And when I seen you march and handle a rifle I knowed you wasn't no boy."

"What do you want?" I said.

"I want you to be nice to me, " he said, and pressed closer. He put a hand on my breast and I pulled back. His breath was getting shorter and he was getting excited. I reckon a man can get excited in a second. A man can get all worked up by a touch or maybe just a smell of perfume.

I pushed Gudger's hand away and he put his hand down in my lap. His fingers fumbled at the straddle of my breeches. I saw why he'd taken the rifle away. I saw I was in grave danger. If I hollered out and soldiers came from the camp, he would not only tell my secret but accuse me of spying or going to sleep on guard duty. If I didn't holler out he would have his way, for he was bigger and stronger than me. I didn't even have a knife, and the ax was back in the camp. All I had was the mug of coffee. I could try to hit him with the mug, but that wouldn't do much good.

Sometimes a woman has to be smart and swallow her pride. A woman has to think how to live and protect her children. A woman has to think sometimes in complicated ways. I decided I would resist the sergeant, but I would not holler out. If he overpowered me I would have to let him have his way. I would not give in, but I would not let him kill me either. The Lord would forgive me. Maybe I was being punished for my sins, for killing Mr. Griffin and quarreling with John. It wouldn't be the first time I was taken against my will.

I gulped the coffee like I was pretending his hand wasn't on my groin. His rough paw felt its way under the cloth and I winced when he touched me there. "No," I said, and flung down the mug into the snow. I tried to push his hand away, but he was a lot stronger than me. He pushed himself against me and opened the trousers with his left hand.

"You know you want me," Gudger said. "I'm the most man you'll ever have." His breath was shorter and his words were like hisses.

"You get away," I said.

Gudger was trembling as he held me and pushed me down in the snow. He was shaking from either excitement or cold. "You ain't never had a real man," the sergeant said.

"Get off me," I said.

"You can take it fore or you can take it aft," Gudger said.

The snow was coming down harder than ever. The flakes hit my face like little paws fumbling. Flakes hit my eyes and melted in my eyes. Gudger was pressing me down and opening my legs and I saw there was no way to stop him. I wasn't going to holler out. I wasn't going to give myself away. I'd done all I could.

But then Gudger just stopped, like the will had gone out of him all of a sudden. He lay back like the wind had drained out of him and the meanness had left him. I felt his weight and smelled his breath, but the pushing had stopped. I had felt his member hard and now it seemed to be gone.

"You damn whore," the sergeant muttered. He rolled back a little bit. Something had happened to him. Something had taken the will out of him. The snowflakes scratched my face like spiders and little birds' feet. The air was damp and cold and the new blanket already wet. I thought it must be the cold and wet that had cooled Gudger off.

I opened my mouth and sucked in flakes like they were sugar.

Gudger smacked me hard across the face. "I will finish with you later," he said.

TEN

I EXPECTED THE SERGEANT to give me away the next morning. I figured he'd go back to the camp and accuse me of falling asleep on sentry duty, or say he'd proved I was a spy for Tarleton. After Gudger left me, I sat in the falling snow trying to decide what to do. If I ran off into the woods they would track me in the snow and shoot me or hang me. Running away would be like admitting I was guilty. Running away from guard duty was asking to be shot.

Besides, if I ran off into the winter woods I'd be lost and cold. I didn't have any fire and I didn't know where I was. I didn't know where they had taken John and I didn't have anything to eat. I had the rifle gun but hardly knew how to shoot it. And I had a baby growing in my belly that would starve if I starved. I'd have to stay in the militia as long as I could, until I found what to do.

I sat there shivering and thinking as I wrapped myself up in the two blankets that were already white with snow. My cheek burned where Gudger had slapped me. My skin stung like he'd had poison oak on his hand.

It came to me that Gudger might not tell anybody what he'd found out. I saw he might not tell, for he would have to explain why he hadn't told Cox sooner, as soon as he knew I wasn't a boy. And if he accused me he might also have to explain why he came to me on guard duty out in the woods. Whatever had happened to him there to stop him, he wouldn't want me to tell anybody.

If nobody else knew I was a girl, it would be his secret, and he might be able to use it, and me, in some way in the future. I tried to think the way the sergeant would think. You really can't know how another body thinks, but I had a pretty good guess about how Gudger would think. He reminded me of Mr. Griffin and the boys I'd gone to school with.

I was still pondering what to do when T. R. came out of the dark and told me it was his turn to stand watch. The snow was still falling and it was still dark. But you could tell daylight wasn't too far off by the misty look in the trees. The treetops looked deep underwater.

"The sergeant said I could have the extra blanket," T. R. said.

I peeled the second blanket off my shoulders, shook the snow off, and handed it to T. R.

"This cold makes your thing get littler and littler," T. R. said.

"I'm too cold to care," I said. But I was relieved, for it seemed the sergeant hadn't gone back to the camp and told on me.

I was stiff from cold and from fighting Gudger. I hit a laurel bush and shook snow down the back of my neck. That woke me up and made me scream a little. I saw how hard it was to walk in the snow. I stumbled from tree to tree back into camp, determined to face Gudger and not let him get the better of me.

Fires were blazing all over the woods, and men were boiling coffee and grits. I could smell hoecakes frying and bacon frying.

I went right to the fire where the sergeant and the other boys of our squadron were. Gudger was stirring a pot of grits with a wooden spoon.

"Stir this hominy, private," the sergeant said to me. He stared at me hard, like he was warning me not to say anything. I looked him straight in the eye and took the spoon. I wanted him to feel my scorn for him. I didn't want him to see how relieved I was he hadn't told anybody.

I stirred the grits and turned the bacon in the big pan. I was cold and hungry and the heat of the fire was sweet as maple sugar. I wanted to stand by the fire and drink up the warmth. I wanted to drink the light. The warmth of the fire and smell of coffee and bacon made me feel alive again. But I felt Gudger's eyes on me. Every time I turned his way I found him studying me. I turned away and poured coffee into my bowl.

"Summers, you will make somebody a good wife," he said, and laughed.

The captain came to the fire and put two pieces of bacon and some grits on his plate. I didn't have a plate and I was wondering how I would eat some grits. I couldn't eat hot grits out of my hand. I had only the pewter bowl.

"Too bad we don't have some butter," Captain Cox said. "When you joined you should have brought us some butter, Private Summers."

The warm fire, and relief that Gudger hadn't told, made me feel good. The coffee was rich and hot and I was hungry for some grits and bacon. I wanted to eat and rest. I figured that because of the snow we wouldn't be marching or drilling that day, and I could sit by the fire and maybe even sleep some more.

But when the captain mentioned butter for the grits, and then mentioned it again, something turned deep in my belly. And instead of warmth I felt raw and hot down in my guts. My bones were still cold but my belly was hot.

Sometimes when you're sick at your stomach you can stand still and swallow, act like you're frozen, and the sickness will go away. For sickness is partly in your head. If you feel sick you'll be sick. If you think about throwing up you will throw up. I stood still and looked off at the snowy woods and tried not to think about butter. But what came to mind was a pool of melted butter in grits. The butter was clear, with yellow flecks floating in it.

I swallowed again and took a sip of the coffee, but that didn't do any good. The rawness and harshness in my belly got worse. The soreness down there turned into a pain. And before I could stop it a fist came punching up through my stomach and into my throat. I ran among the men to the edge of the woods, holding my hand over my mouth. And then I held on to a tree while I leaned over and puked in the snow.

After I was sick I felt weak and new. I'd vomited away the poison and worry and now it was time to start again, if I could start again. I'd emptied myself and was so weak I dropped to my knees and rubbed snow on my forehead and cheeks. I put snow in my mouth to soothe my lips and tongue, and clean away the bitter taste.

When I stood up and stumbled back to the fire, Captain Cox watched me and shook his head. "Private Summers, you must take something for the flux," he said.

"It's just a touch," I said.

The captain told Sergeant Gudger to go to the medicine chest and bring back the blue bottle. When Gudger came back from the tent he was carrying a little bottle so dark it looked almost black. The captain poured a spoonful and handed it to me.

"When you have bile on the stomach, take laudanum," the captain said.

I didn't have any choice but to swallow the spoonful of laudanum. It tasted like liquor mixed with some secret salt from deep in the earth. Though the tincture was light brown it tasted blue as the sky before dawn.

"You must take a spoonful of this every morning until the bilious flux is cured," the captain said. He handed me the bottle.

I sat down on a log not too far from the fire and wrapped the blanket around my shoulders. At first I didn't feel anything but the strange liquid in my throat and belly. And then a soothing softness began to spread from my belly. The raw pain in my gut cooled. My belly was empty and clean and full at once.

"Eat quickly," the captain shouted. "We are going to march."

"In the snow?" somebody said.

"Snow will not stop the enemy," Captain Cox said.

AS SOON AS THE MEN ate the hog meat and hominy and hoe-cakes, and drank the scalding coffee, Captain Cox hollered it was time to break camp and march. There were groans around the fires. I reckon we had all hoped we could rest because of the snow.

"Where are we going, sir?" the man called Jenkins yelled.

The captain said again we were going to Grindal Shoals to join Major McDowell's North Carolina militia and General Morgan's army.

"Pack your things," Gudger yelled. His face was red from the cold and heating by the hot fire. As we lined up, with blankets over our shoulders and our guns in the cradle of our arms, the sergeant stopped beside me and said, "Joseph, if you have to puke, don't puke on the man in front of you."

"No, sir," I said, and smiled. The laudanum made the world feel mellow and easy.

Cox mounted his horse and rode out in front of us, and just as we started the snow stopped. The flakes quit falling all at once, like somebody had given an order. The sky was so dark it was almost black, but the air was clear. Everything was covered with snow, the pine trees, the bushes, the road. The world was clean as linen.

The snow on the road made it hard to march, and the uneven ruts and mud under the snow made it even harder. As we trampled the snow the mud stained through and by the time the end of the line came along the ruts were nothing but mud, red mud. The road looked like a bloody wound opened between the snowy woods. The carts and wagons lurched and banged on rocks and puddles behind us. Even where the ground had frozen it thawed under the hundreds of stamping feet. Soon my pants and overcoat and blanket were splashed with mud.

If it hadn't been for the laudanum I don't think I could have kept going. The laudanum gave me strength and made my belly quiet. As we kept walking the sun came out almost ahead of us. We were marching into South Carolina. The sun got bright and the snow started to melt. Hunks of snow fell off trees beside the road.

It was so strange to be marching with the men, I wondered if I was dreaming it all. I wondered if I would wake up and find I was back in the cave or back in the cabin on Pine Knot Branch.

"We got mud up to our arse," a man in front said.

"We're walking through red shite," a man behind me said.

"Shut up," Gudger said.

We crossed the Broad River around noon on rough log rafts. It must have taken an hour for all of us and the wagons to get across. I counted thirty-four in the company besides myself. "I never thought I would cross the Broad River," T. R. said.

"Nobody cares what you thought," Gudger said.

As we kept marching I began to feel numb. It was like my feet were walking but I had no control over them. I was so tired I think I nodded off while marching. My feet were sore but they felt like somebody else's feet, wrapped in the leather strips. A man in front of me did go to sleep while walking and stumbled into a pine tree, and then I stumbled over him.

Gen. Daniel Morgan's camp at Grindal Shoals was spread out along the Pacolet River like a hunting camp. There must have been five hundred or six hundred men there. I figured I was the only woman in miles. I looked everywhere to see if I could catch sight of John, which was a strange thing to do, since I was almost certain he was dead. Yet when I looked at a gathering of men my eyes searched for him. It made me sick that his last memory of me would be of our quarrel.

There must have been a score of cooking fires in the woods mixing smoke with morning fog along the river. Little bands of volunteers like ours kept arriving and joining up until it didn't look like there was room for more. And it didn't seem like anybody that came had brought their rations, any more than we had.

General Morgan sent out parties to gather hog and hominy. They bought rations and they traded for rations and they just plain stole rations. Gudger took me and a man named Gaither out to gather supplies. We opened people's smokehouses and potato holes and took apples out of cellar holes and barn lofts. We got soup beans and cornmeal. But mostly what we found was grits. It was after hog-killing time and a few places had fresh meat. I stayed close to Gaither. When we took hams and shoulder meat we would feast until we ran out again and had to think of finding more.

ONE RAINY MORNING, after we had been at the shoals about a week, we were low on grits and coffee, and out of any meat. Gudger looked me in the eye and said, "Come with me, Summers."

"I have a chill on my stomach," I said. I'd just taken some laudanum and my belly was quiet.

"Come with me, private," Gudger said. With Captain Cox listening, and everybody else listening, I didn't have any choice. Being alone with Gudger was what I had dreaded most. I looked around at the captain and then took a step toward the sergeant.

"Bring your rifle," Gudger said, and handed me a tow sack.

Following Gudger, I took short steps, as if I could slow him down, or slow time down. But Gudger cradled his rifle on his arm and strode into the pine woods.

"We're not following the road?" I said. I thought I'd be safer on a public road.

"You want to be caught by a Tory patrol and tortured?" Gudger said. "Besides, the road ain't nothing but mud."

As I followed Gudger I thought how easy it would be to shoot him in the back. I'd already killed one man that shamed me. I might have to kill another. If I shot Gudger I'd have to run away into the woods where nobody would ever find me. We crossed a field of gray cornstalks and briars and then entered the oak woods.

"Don't shoot me in the back," Gudger said, and laughed.

A deer bounded out of the brush, and ran for a ways into the woods and stopped. I could see its head through the limbs. It didn't have any horns. Gudger raised his rifle and fired. The deer reeled back into the leaves and lay still.

"We'll have venison tonight," he said.

Now while Gudger's gun was unloaded was my best chance to shoot him. I raised my rifle and almost aimed it at him. But I couldn't do it. I couldn't shoot anybody in the back, even Gudger.

I thought we would stop and skin the deer and cut it up in pieces, but Gudger said we would come back for it later. We had other things to gather. He slit the deer's throat to bleed it, and we stumbled on.

We came to a pasture and hid in the sumac bushes at the edge. There were no cattle or horses in the pasture, and no sheep. But a curl of blue smoke lifted from the chimney of the house beyond the pasture. There was a log barn and well sweep in the yard.

"Where there are people there is hominy," Gudger said.

"Will we buy it from them?" I said.

"With a lead coin," he said.

Gudger said we'd stay out of the pasture and approach the barn from the woods. If we were quiet we could fill our sacks and they would never know it.

The rain made everything feel close, and the wet air made every sound loud. I heard a woodpecker knocking, and two trees rubbing together, and thunder crumbled in the distance. Winter thunder meant the weather was changing. Every drop on the leaves looked fat and tall.

"I figured out what you are," Gudger said, as he looked across the pasture. I didn't answer him, and I dreaded what he would say.

"I'm from Pine Knot Branch," I said.

"You don't need to be afraid of me," Gudger said. "It will be our secret." He put his arm on my shoulder and I didn't pull away.

Gudger made me walk ahead of him as we skirted the edge of the pasture. I stooped under limbs and slid between bushes. My pants got soaked like I'd been wading a creek.

"I can be your friend," Gudger said. "You'll need a friend."

We stopped while he reloaded his rifle. He kept looking me in the eye and I avoided his stare.

"The other night in the snow didn't mean nothing," Gudger said as he drove the ramrod into the barrel. "I was just a-teasing you."

I was more afraid of Gudger than ever. But he was trying to act like my friend, and I had to play along.

We kept the barn between us and the house as we came out of the woods. We climbed up to the loft, and found nothing but hay and some old harness. I looked through a crack and saw the corn crib between the barn and the well sweep. Gudger said I would fill my sack at the crib and he would stand guard.

"What if they see me?" I said.

"I'll cover you, sugar," Gudger said.

The crib was just like the one at home where Mr. Griffin had locked me in. I slipped as quietly as I could down the ladder from the loft and around the side of the crib and opened the creaky door. There was a pile of shucked ears on the floor, but no shelled corn. I began to fill my sack with the naked ears. The sharp kernels scratched my hands.

When the sack was about half full I heard a voice. Through the slats of the crib I saw a boy come out of the house. He looked about twelve years old and he carried an old musket. "Get out of there!" he yelled.

I didn't know whether to take my rifle and run or just stand still. The boy came closer and pointed the gun at the crib. "Get out of there," he yelled again.

"Don't shoot," I said.

"You get out of there!" he hollered.

Gudger stepped around the corner of the barn, walking so slow and quiet the boy didn't hear him until it was too late. Gudger knocked the boy down with his gun butt and took the musket away from him.

"He's just a boy," I cried.

Gudger dragged the boy to the porch, and as the boy cried and pleaded Gudger took a pocket knife and a shilling from his pocket.

"I ain't no Tory," the boy said.

Gudger shoved the boy aside and entered the house, and I followed. There was a fire stroking in the fireplace, but nothing to eat except a little cornmeal and a slab of fatback. A jug sat by the hearth and Gudger pulled out the stopper and sniffed, then took a drink.

"Don't you take Pa's drinking liquor," the boy said, and followed Gudger out to the porch.

"This liquor is your Pa's contribution to the war," Gudger said.

"Pa will hide me with a whip," the boy said.

Gudger made me finish filling the sack with corn, and we took the cornmeal and the fatback. We left the boy crying on the porch. His shirt and pants were patched all over, and snot mixed with dirt and tears on his chin.

"You ought not to have taken his knife," I said.

Gudger made me carry the cornmeal and fatback and the boy's musket. He took a long drink from the jug and carried the jug in his left hand after he slung the sack of corn over his right shoulder. I followed him back into the rainy woods and he took two more drinks before we reached the deer. The liquor made him cheerful and friendly.

"I won't tell nobody about you," Gudger said. He made me take one hind leg of the deer and he took the other. We dragged the deer through the dripping woods.

"You women are all whores," Gudger laughed. He stopped and took another drink from the jug. "My wife ran off with a sergeant of the Tories. I reckon she liked the size of his bayonet."

"You are married?" I said.

"Not anymore," the sergeant said. Gudger laughed, and he kept laughing while we dragged the deer over the wet leaves.

. . .

I COULDN'T HAVE MADE it through those days without the bottle of laudanum the captain had given me. Every morning I took a spoonful, and it kept me from getting sick and puking. Gudger watched me and poked me. I had noticed that men like to push things at you. They like to prod and shove with guns and bayonets or fists, or their members. They like to shove things out and drive them into things. Gudger scared me. I was sure he'd do me dirt when he got a chance. I tried not to give him a chance. I kept my eye on him and obeyed orders.

One problem at the camp was a lot of the volunteers had brought their horses and kept them tied in the woods, and the horses had to be fed same as the men. It took almost as much time to gather corn and fodder for the horses as to forage for the men. We hadn't brought any horses except for the one Captain Cox rode himself and the ones that pulled the wagons, and that turned out to be a blessing. It was a hardship to have to walk, but in camp we only had to feed ourselves. The woods were full of horses and the mornings smelled like a stable.

There was a smell the camp had, of horses and the latrine, of mud that's been chewed up and spit on, of burnt wood and sweaty men. But the worst smell was the wet boots and dirty socks. It smelled like everybody's feet were rotting. My own feet stayed wet and raw in the leather bindings. I took them off at night to dry by the fire.

WE CAMPED ON the Pacolet for about two weeks. Captain Cox joined us up to Major McDowell's North Carolina militia. We drilled every day, on frozen frosty ground in the morning and on thawed mud in the evening. We practiced loading and shooting our rifle guns only twice. I learned to pour in the powder and push down the bullet and patch and pack them with the ramrod. I learned to fire by sighting along the bead. Those with muskets just had to take a paper cartridge from their box and bite off the top, then stuff it in the barrel. But we who had rifles had to pack the powder and patch and bullet in separately. My shoulder got sore from the kick of the rifle.

There was trading going on at the camp all the time. Boys would swap knives for bearskins, a powder horn for a pair of socks. There was always somebody playing cards and losing their rifle gun or winning a jug of liquor. Major McDowell tried to stop the men from gambling, but it didn't do any good.

While we were camped on the river, peddlers came by with wagons and you could trade for anything. They sold knives and cloth, harness and gunpowder. A bootmaker came out and set up his shop in a wagon. He would make a pair of boots for a few shillings. But I didn't have any money. The coins I had stolen from Mama had burned up in the cabin. There was a peddler that had two girls in a wagon that sold themselves for a shilling. I only saw them a few times when they came out of the wagon to go to the river. They were fat girls with lots of black hair; everybody who could afford it went to them.

Rumors ran back and forth through the camp about where Tarleton and his dragoons were. Cornwallis was marching his big army down the east side of the Broad River on his way from Charlotte. They were foraging and looting and burning the countryside. But nobody knew exactly where Tarleton and his Green Dragoons and legion were. They said General Morgan had sent out scouts and learned Tarleton had crossed the Tyger River to the south, and the Enoree. But his dragoons moved too fast to track for long. Col. William Washington's cavalry had fought them in skirmishes near Fort Ninety Six and at Hammond's Store and then broken away and come back to the Pacolet.

Every day there were more stories in camp. We heard that Colonel Pickens and the South Carolina militia would join us from the west. One time it was said Colonel Sevier and the Overmountain men that fought at Kings Mountain would be arriving from the northwest. But they never did come. They said Gen. Thomas Sumter and his patriots were camped just a few miles to the east of the Broad River, but we never saw any sign of them. After we'd camped in the damp woods by the river for two weeks, the most common rumor was that we were going to retreat.

Cornwallis's army was on the way and there wasn't anything we could do to face that many redcoats. It was said Cornwallis had twenty cannons. You could hear anything in a camp.

"If Morgan crosses the Broad again I'm going home," Gaither said.

It felt like the woods were full of Tarleton's Green Dragoons, but we couldn't see them. Every pine bush and cedar seemed like a dragoon. Every shadow seemed to hide a saber. It's what you make up in your own mind that scares you the most. And when you don't know where the enemy is you think he might spring out of the trees any second. It wears you out to be scared every day. In the January cold it was like the thickets were haunted. I looked across the river and expected to see horsemen appear. You couldn't go out in the woods to do your business without fearing to see a green uniform like they said Tarleton's dragoons wore. Every tree seemed to be hiding somebody.

Early one morning I slipped out into the pinewoods to relieve myself. I liked to go just as the camp was waking up so nobody would notice me. If I went before anybody else was up I might be shot by a sentry. But just as they were building up fires and grinding coffee and rolling up blankets was the best time.

I pushed my way into the thicket and hung the gray coat on a limb. Untying my pants I squatted and felt the pleasure of released pee. My water steamed on the cold ground. I must have grunted with the satisfaction. Only when I was almost finished did I see somebody watching me from the other side of a holly bush. They must have been watching me all the time.

I thought it must be a soldier that had followed me. My pulse froze, for if they had seen me piss I was lost. I would be shot or shamed and sent off into the woods.

But the feet beyond the holly were not in heavy boots. They were tiny black shoes, women's shoes. I looked up through a break in the limbs and saw it was a woman watching me. It was one of the women from the wagon where they sold themselves for a shilling. Her eyes were wide with wonder, for she was just as surprised as I was. I thought she was going to scream out.

"Hush," I said. "Please don't say anything." I shook my head and stood to pull up my pants.

"You ain't a soldier?" she said.

"I am a soldier," I said, "as far as anybody knows."

I saw she wasn't much older than me. Her hair was black and straight and tied back with a ribbon, and her skin was dark like she was Cherokee or Spanish. She wore a pink gown with lace on it and a blanket thrown around her shoulders.

"Who are you?" she said, looking around to see if anybody else was coming. I figured she had gone out into the pines to relieve herself same as I had.

I told her to be quiet and I stepped around the bush to get closer. She smelled of perfume or toilet water, and her bosoms were heavy and pushed out through the gown. I told her I'd joined the militia so they wouldn't shoot me for a spy, and that I hoped to avenge my husband John who had been taken by the Tories.

"Last year we worked for the Tories," she said. "But then they marched away."

I told her my name was Josie and she said she was called Delores. We spoke in low voices, looking around to make sure nobody had seen us. It was good to talk to another girl.

"What are you going to do?" she said. We moved deeper into the pine woods so nobody would see us. I told her I didn't know what I was going to do. I had to stay with the militia until the war was over.

"You ain't got a husband?" she said, and grinned like she was teasing me. I told her I hadn't seen another woman in weeks.

"You come by the wagon sometime if you want company," she said and grinned again. "Except you'd have to pay a shilling like everybody else. Clancy makes everybody pay."

"Who is Clancy?" I said.

"He's the man I work for," Delores said. She pushed her hair back and tied it again with the ribbon.

"Don't you want to run away?" I said.

"Where would I run to?" she said, and laughed. She said Mr. Clancy had bought her from her mama and daddy when she was fourteen. He made her stay in the wagon and they moved from one camp to another.

"He gives me all the clothes I want," she said.

I asked her who the other girl was, for I'd seen two girls get out of the wagon.

"That's Sylvia," Delores said. "Sylvia is his wife. He got her in Florida."

"You mean he sells his wife?" I said. A shiver ran through me. I felt I was seeing the world in a wild new way. I wondered if being a whore was any worse than being in the militia.

"Clancy would sell his own—" Delores stopped, for someone was coming. We stood still and waited. I was afraid the smell of her perfume would give us away even if we didn't make a sound.

"Joseph," a voice called. It was Gudger. I put my finger to my lips. "I saw you go out into the pines," Gudger yelled.

I looked at the girl and shook my head. We stood very still.

"Bring some damn wood back to the fire," Gudger called, and then we heard him walking away, kicking leaves as he went.

"I could run away if I had somebody to go with me," I said.

"Honey, I would like to run away, but I don't know nothing but whoring," Delores said. "Besides, Clancy would catch me and cut my face."

"You could run far into the mountains where he couldn't find you," I said.

"Sugar, I come from the mountains. I don't want to go back there. Ain't nothing where I come from but rocks and rattlesnakes."

I had to get back to the camp or Gudger would come looking for me again. I asked Delores not to tell on me.

"You could join Sylvia and me," she said. "When we move to another camp you could go with us."

"The sergeant would hang me for a spy," I said.

"No man will hang you if his peter is hard and he wants you to be good to it," Delores said, and laughed.

"I like talking to you," I said.

Delores patted me on the shoulder. "Come to the wagon sometime if you need some loving," she said, and winked.

I hurried back to the camp, but felt the world had changed, or seemed to have changed, just because I'd talked to another woman. The world had tilted in a new way. I gathered up some dead limbs to carry back to the fire, and the camp looked different when I stepped into the open, dirtier and messier than ever, but also smaller, like it had shrunk in the night. I meant to talk to Delores again if I got a chance.

SOMETIMES I THOUGHT I saw John by a campfire, but when I got close it was always somebody else that was tall and skinny. One evening I heard a soldier playing a flute, but when I went to look I found a bald-headed stranger with spectacles playing beside a campfire.

Then came the evening of January 15. General Morgan had taken the main army and retreated to Burr's Mill on Thicketty Creek, several miles to the north. He had companies guarding each of the fords on the Pacolet River, and he had left Captain Cox's company at Grindal Shoals to see that Tarleton didn't cross there. We were just standing around cursing and spitting and cooking grits and mush. We were low on rations and after another day or two we'd have to go foraging again. Everybody said the land between the Pacolet and the Broad River had been stripped bare. The barns were empty and the cellars and smokehouses were empty. Too many armies had gone back and forth across them. The people themselves were near starving.

"IS IT MUSH OR IS IT SAND?" T. R. said as I stirred meal into boiling water.

"You don't have to eat any," I said. We'd had several days of rain and the ground was muck and the river in spate. All our bags and blankets were wet, and we had to rub grease on our muskets and rifles to keep them from rusting. Boots were hung on sticks by the fire to dry. I tied new rags under the leather bindings on my feet. Everybody was tired of waiting, of slipping and sliding through the mud. The ground of our camp looked like a hogpen.

"We get to the Broad River I'm going home," T. R. said for the fiftieth time.

"Me too," Gaither said. "I'm tired of this foot-rot, gut-rot kind of living."

"This ain't living," T. R. said.

"Shut up, you heifers," Gudger said. "Afraid you'll get your petticoats wet." He gave me a quick glance.

I saw Gaither grip the stock of his rifle like he was ready to brain Gudger. I figured it was just a matter of days, whether we fought Tarleton or not, before somebody killed the sergeant. I hoped somebody killed Gudger, and I was ashamed for hoping it. For I felt different about Gudger, after what he had told me about his wife. I wondered if he would do anything more to me. The fact that Gudger knew I was a girl made my days in the militia seem even stranger. I hadn't found out what the penalty for pretending to be a man was, but it was probably death. I planned to leave the militia, soon as I got a chance. But now wasn't the time, with everyone scared and angry. Besides, I still had a duty to pay the redcoats back for what they'd done to John.

"Hey-yoo!" somebody hollered. I looked around and saw they were pointing at the river. Everybody stood up at once, and I stood up too. We were almost on the bank of the Pacolet, and everybody was looking across. The river slopped by flushed full and its banks were mud. On the other side were men in green coats on horses. They looked straight at us. I reckon they were surprised to see us. I dropped the wooden spoon and my bones felt sore with surprise. It was like you looked at the ground and saw a rattlesnake coiled at your feet.

"The Lord a mercy," T. R. said.

"It's the devil himself," said Captain Cox, who was standing a few feet behind us.

We all knew it was Tarleton. And we now knew why we'd been so troubled and so scared. He was the officer who sat erect upon his horse and his hat and black cape made him look even taller. He watched us across the river like we were a band of filthy beggars in our muddy pants and rotting rags, cooking mush in the smoke. Tarleton and his men looked at us like they were counting hogs.

Now the strangest thing, looking back, is that not one of us picked up a rifle and shot at Tarleton. He could have been picked off twice as far away by some of our men. But no one thought to shoot him, not even the captain. I reckon it was the surprise. It's hard to up and shoot somebody unless you're planning to, unless you've been ordered to. We just stood there addled and awed, but somebody could have finished off Bloody Tarleton right there if they had thought of it.

Behind the green horsemen stood a troop of soldiers. Their green coats and red coats looked clean, but their pants were almost as dirty as ours.

Next thing I knew the officer I thought was Tarleton pointed up the river and they turned and started riding that way on the far bank.

"Who is that?" T. R. said.

"That's Tarleton, you idiot," Gudger said.

"That son of a dog," Captain Cox said.

Men stood around without their boots on, with pots of half-cooked grits and mush steaming over the fire. Tarleton seemed to fit what we'd heard about him, that he was bold enough to ride anywhere, that he moved fast and hated volunteers as rebels and traitors. Not a one among us wasn't shaken by seeing the king's colonel appear in all his glory out of the pine woods that way.

"Follow him," Cox yelled, "and don't let him out of your sight."

Those that had boots got them, and we grabbed our rifles and blankets and pots of hominy and started walking up the river. Some ate mush as they walked, drinking it from pots like soup. Mush and grits were all we'd had for several days. I carried the pot I'd been stirring, too scared to think of eating from it. The bushes were wet but we knocked them aside and jumped over puddles and soggy places. Where there was a branch or little creek we splashed right through it. We were soon wet all over again.

But some of us kept the dragoons in sight. High on their horses they looked clean and dignified. The soldiers behind them walked more orderly than we did. The red coats and white pants shined in the late sun. Their brass buckles sparkled in the light. I reckon we looked like a band of convicts and beggars compared to them.

ELEVEN

CAPTAIN COX RODE OUT in front of us. From time to time he turned and hollered back, "Don't let them cross the river." He'd been teaching himself to act like an officer, watching Major McDowell and General Morgan.

We followed the captain through thickets and maple swamps. It was one swamp and bog hole and sinkhole after another. We knocked down fences or just stepped across them. We walked into a deeryard and flushed out half a dozen does. A polecat got scared and threw its stink on some boys in the front. The stink drifted for miles.

But Tarleton and his legion kept going. They rode toward the sunset like they didn't know we were behind them. A marksman could have picked them off one by one. The sun was going down, but we could see them green as cedar trees marching on the far shore.

"We're nigh to Wofford's Iron Works," the captain called back. "Don't let them cross."

"The ford is at Wofford's," Gudger yelled.

I saw buildings up ahead and smoke coming from two or three chimneys in the sunset. I could smell bread baking.

"Take command of the ford," the captain called out. We all hurried to the place where the road slipped down into the sandy river. Cox gathered us around it and we took our places along the bank and beside the road, all out of breath and sweaty. I hoped my gun hadn't gotten water in the barrel. The stopper was still in my powder horn. My hands were jerking and I hadn't noticed it. I couldn't hold the rifle steady if I had to.

A chill went through me when I thought of my bottle of laudanum. Had I left it in camp? I felt of my coat and found the bottle in the left pocket.

Across the river we could see the dragoons making camp. Tarleton and his men put up tents in the pine woods and started fires. We stood beside the muddy river and watched them. Only thing you could hear were their horses shaking their bridles and whickering. Soon all you could see in the pine woods across the river were their fires.

I'd thought Tarleton would make some kind of fight at the ford, maybe try to dash across the river. We'd heard he never paused but plunged headlong into a fight. I thought we would exchange shots across the river. I watched the shadows in the pines and broom sedge on the far bank and felt this awful confusion. I wanted to fight and I didn't want to fight. But my spirits were low anyway.

After it was dark we moved into a field upriver and made camp. The ground was wet and already beginning to freeze. T. R. and Gaither and I made us a fire of poplar sticks and pretty soon there were dozens of fires all up and down our side of the river.

Some had eaten their grits or mush on the way up the river. But I'd carried the pot all the way without touching the grits. The grits now had set into a kind of jelly as they cooled and a crust had dried on the top. I put the pot over the new fire, and pretty soon you could smell the grits frying at the edges and starting to parch. I ate them with a knife like they were some kind of bread. When the wind changed I could smell the soldiers that had run into the polecat. It was a stink like burned paint, and I feared it would turn my stomach. But then the wind changed again.

I WAS HARDLY AWAKE the next morning. I was still dreaming about marching up the river and catching a glimpse of John. It seemed we'd been marching for days, following trees that moved like soldiers. The cedar trees and swamp pines moved, and I thought I saw John in the distance. I tried to call out but couldn't say anything. I wanted to say I was sorry we had fussed. We weren't ever going to catch up with the evergreens. Thorns on the holly bushes stuck out like little bayonets, and briars thrust out their points in my face.

"Wake up, you lazy rascals!" It was Gudger. I pulled the blanket from my head. It wasn't even daylight and the fires had died down to coals. The stars had gone but there wasn't any light yet.

"Get up, slugs," the sergeant said.

"Tarleton has crossed the river," Captain Cox shouted. "He has crossed downstream."

Everybody in the camp stirred and stood up.

"Not five miles down the river," Captain Cox hollered. "They left their campfires burning to fool us."

I grabbed my rifle and blanket and mush pot and was already marching before I knew it. One second we were sleeping and dreaming and the next we were on our way. Tarleton was on our side of the river and he was after us. We must have left half our things on the ground. We left a few tents and stockings drying on sticks. But I don't reckon anybody left their rifles or their boots.

My belly felt awful. With the blanket over my shoulders and the rifle under my arm, I reached into the coat pocket with my left hand and got the little bottle. I had to pull the cork with my teeth, and, holding the stopper between my fingers, I took a sip. The laudanum trickled into my belly while we marched.

"Give me a sip of that," T. R. said.

"Ain't for younguns," I said.

Cox led us away from the river, up this road through the pine woods. It ran north toward Thicketty Creek where Morgan and the rest of the army were camped.

There is nothing as confusing as a march before daylight. You can't see where you're going, and your legs are walking while you're still dreaming. Everything swirls around, trees and clouds, the ground rising and falling. We were rushing and I couldn't see anything, like we were marching in an endless tunnel.

I thought Tarleton's Greens might jump out of the pines any instant and cut us down with their sabers.

"Goddamn Cox," T. R. muttered behind me.

"Cox is going to get us butchered," Gaither said.

"Shut up, you pups," Gudger snarled.

The mud of the road was frozen, like a crust of leather that cracked here and there. The frost on the grass was clean, but where we walked the ruts soon got muddy.

"Halt!" the captain called.

I saw we had come to a field where the big army was camped. There were the rest of McDowell's North Carolina volunteers and Col. John Howard's Delaware and Maryland regulars. It was a sight to see, all the blue uniforms on the officers and the sparkling bayonets. They had already assembled, and when they started marching up the Green River Road we fell in behind McDowell's men. General Morgan rode out ahead on his big white horse, his face red in the morning air. He had a bad scar on his cheek that twisted his face sideways. It was daylight by now and we could see him riding way out ahead. We seemed to get faster with each step.

"Anybody runs away gets shot in the back," Gudger said, and wiped his nose on his sleeve.

I had a catch in my side that the laudanum hadn't cured, and my feet were so cold and wet they were nearly numb. I'd wrapped more rags on my feet the night before, but they were soaked with the red mud. My leather rags were worn out, and I'd tied pieces of canvas on the bottoms, pieces of an old tent and strips of rawhide. I would have given anything for a pair of boots and dry stockings. Didn't seem like I'd ever have warm feet again. The rags on my feet were red as blood.

Cox made us walk on the road four abreast, and Gaither on the left side was stepping through broom sedge and briars, sometimes running into limbs of pines and post oaks. By the time we were joined by another militia company past Burr's Mill we were worn out. There was cursing and muttering all up and down the line. Words and strings of words ran backward and forward along the column. I belched up the taste of laudanum.

"Tarleton is following us" was passed up the line. It was spoken across the ranks as we tramped along. Our feet sucked in the mud and swished in the stubble of weeds and brush.

"Tarleton is behind us," I heard muttered farther and farther up the line toward General Morgan. I reckon the general's scouts were telling him from time to time where the dragoons were. A member of Colonel Washington's cavalry rode by us in his white-and-blue jacket and we stood aside to let him pass. We walked a little faster every time we heard mention of Tarleton.

The general was one of the strongest-looking men you've ever seen. His shoulders were wide in his blue coat and his hands looked powerful enough to grip the reins of ten horses. General Morgan had a voice like a mule driver's. I'd heard he was once a teamster for Gen. George Washington. His voice was loud as a preacher's and twice as rough. And he spoke out of the side of his mouth because of the big scar on his cheek.

"We'll not be caught by Benny Tarleton," the general yelled back at us.

The men in the column cheered. Old Morgan's gray hair fell over his collar. From time to time he looked back and yelled, "I won't be outfoxed by Benny Tarleton!"

There was a man in fine clothes riding beside the general. He wore a light blue coat with lace at the wrists. And he had on a white wig tied with ribbon.

"Who is that old fop?" Gaither said.

"That's Baron de Glaubeck, from somewhere over the water," Gudger said.

"Looks like an actor dressed up in powder and rouge," T. R. said.

"Don't mock your betters," Gudger said.

"He gives the general advice," Cox said.

"How does he keep from getting mud on his fine silk pants?" T. R. said.

"Why are we going to Kings Mountain?" somebody hollered way behind us. Captain Cox didn't say anything. He rode about ten feet ahead of us.

I figured if there had been one fight at Kings Mountain there might as well be another. Marching is like any other awful job. I kept telling myself that a little bit farther and the worst would be over. It would warm up and we would rest. That's the way you get through a hard day. I kept thinking, just a little more and a little more. When we get to that tall pine tree, or the next creek, or the top of the rise, we will halt and rest. You have to break the hardest jobs into little pieces and finish them one piece at a time. You have to feel that the worst is over or you couldn't get through the next few minutes, or hours.

We marched for so many hours I thought I might be dreaming the march. My legs moved on their own, and my back hurt. As my legs got numb it seemed the trees were marching past us, not us marching past them. The ground seemed far away beneath me. I can't go on much longer, I thought. You are a murderer, I said to myself. You killed Mr. Griffin. You deceived John and his congregations. That thought gave me a little extra strength, for I saw I was paying for what I had done.

EVERY TIME WE PASSED a tavern there was a little company of militia waiting. We would halt and the general would talk to the militia captain. Silly as it may sound, I kept on the lookout for John. I thought he might be with one of the ragged bands. I knew it was impossible, but I still hoped to see him. Once I saw a tall skinny fellow in black and my heart thumped up into my throat. But when we got closer I saw it wasn't John. I knew John had been taken to punish me. Everywhere I looked I hoped to see John, but didn't.

The new companies would stand at attention as we marched past, and then they would fall in behind the column and make it even longer. There were men in pieces of uniforms of the regulars, men who had enlisted before and then come home when their time was up. We even saw a man wearing a dirty red coat with the stripes torn off. I guess he had taken it off a dead soldier, or maybe he'd been a Tory himself and deserted.

But mostly the new companies were dressed same as us, some in fur hats and some in felt hats, some in hunting coats and some in buckskin. Some had long mountain rifles and some had Brown Bess muskets and boxes of paper cartridges. A few had pistols in their belts. Not many had bayonets on their belts, but a few did. Some had bags of rations slung over their backs, and some had nothing but shot and powder. One carried a plucked chicken to roast for dinner.

We stopped in front of a tavern somewhere near Hancockville around dinnertime. I could smell bread cooking and chicken baking. A little company was formed in front of the tavern, a poor-looking bunch, and not all of them had guns. Their clothing was rumpled and some didn't have hats. Old Morgan talked to their captain and they drew themselves up to attention and saluted the general. Just then this old man came out the door of the tavern and hurried to the company. His shirt was unbuttoned and he looked like he'd been asleep.

"You ain't coming, Jarvis," the captain said to the old man.

Jarvis could hardly stand up, but he tried to hold himself at attention. His gray hair went every which way. He stretched up to the captain of the company. "Who's giving orders here?" he said.

"I'm giving orders," the captain bellowed.

"No you ain't," the old man said.

"Go back inside and have another drink," the captain said, and flipped him a coin.

The general sat on his horse and watched Jarvis pull himself up and salute him. "The king can kiss my arse," Jarvis said.

"Go back inside or we'll kick *your* arse," the captain said.

"Ain't nobody giving me orders but the general," Jarvis said. He squinted, staring up at the Old Wagoner, who used to be a teamster in Virginia.

It looked like they were going to have to tie Jarvis up to get rid of him. He had gotten it in his mind to be a soldier. Just then a woman came from behind the tavern carrying a bucket. She wore an apron like a maid or a cook.

"Who is giving me orders?" Jarvis said, and raised his fist.

"Martin Jarvis," the woman said sharply.

Jarvis spun around and as he faced her the woman slung the bucket of water right in his face. The water stretched out like a tongue and slapped him backward. He stumbled as if he'd been hit by a horse or a bolt of lightning, then fell flat in the muddy yard. A boy came out of the tavern and helped the woman drag the old man back inside.

The whole column laughed out loud and cheered. We didn't know what else to do, having watched it all. The general pointed ahead and yelled "Forward!" and we started marching again.

Some houses we passed looked empty. There were no younguns in the yards, and no woman with a troubling stick out by the washpot. No smoke rose out of the chimneys, and there were no signs of pigs or chickens. We passed one burned house, and then another. You would have thought everybody had up and left the country. Folks had packed up and moved on, those that had not been shot or hung.

But people must have been hiding too. They heard the army coming and hid in cellars and lofts, in potato holes and in the woods. They took their daughters and put them way back in thickets and swamps, or under fodder in the barn. They had carried their ham meat and cornmeal to holes beyond the pasture and covered them with leaves.

A few people had stayed in their houses. They stood on porches and watched us march by. One pretty girl with long black hair watched from a second-story window. Dogs ran out from under porches and barked and backed away. A spaniel snapped and wagged its tail at the same time. By one cabin an old woman was boiling soap.

The friendliest person we saw that day was a woman way up the road just before we got to Thicketty Mountain. She had a house on a little hill, and I guess we slowed down walking up that hill. Her head was tied up in a wool rag against the wind, and she brought a big bucket of water with a dipper and set it on a stump by the road. She gave a drink to every soldier that came by and wanted one. She ran forward up the line and gave a boy a dipper and he drank and handed it back to her. We never did stop marching, though we slowed down a little and the men behind hollered at us. She ran forward and gave Gaither the dipper and he swallowed quick. Then she filled the dipper and gave it to me. It was the sweetest water I'd ever drunk. It was so cold it seemed to come from the heart of rock or melting snow. It was so sweet it seemed to have honey and silver lights in it. I won't ever forget that woman.

Wasn't till I put my lips to that cold dipper that I found out how dried they were. My lips had chapped in the wind and cold air. They were tight and cracked, with rough pieces of skin peeling off like paint. I pulled one of the pieces and it tore off to the quick. The place started bleeding and I tried to stop the blood with the back of my hand. I tasted salty blood as I walked along.

I must have closed my eyes while I was walking, for I was dreaming of Mama. She was sitting on the porch in a rocking chair looking down the road. She was watching to see if I would come down the road. I wanted to call out to her and tell her I was coming. But just as I tried to speak something slammed into me. I opened my eyes and saw I'd marched into the musket of the man in front of me.

"Wake up, Summers," Gudger snarled. I skipped to keep in step and strained to hold my eyes open.

"'TENTION!" GUDGER CALLED OUT. We all stepped aside while a horseman galloped by kicking up medals of dirt. All the way up the line men stepped aside while the horse cantered past. Once the rider reached the general at the front of the line we stopped, though it took a while for the order to run all the way back to the end of the line, and men behind kept walking, pushing the ranks ahead closer together.

I reckon the rider told Old Morgan some news, for he hollered back to Major McDowell and the senior officers to come forward. The majors and colonels went up to powwow. I guess it was something important, for they took a long time. We had to stand in the road leaning on our muskets and rifles.

"Old Morgan will march until our feet ain't nothing but stubs," Gaither said. He dropped into the broom sedge at the side of the road. It looked so inviting to sit there in the grass.

"I never said you could fall out," the sergeant said.

"You never said not to," Gaither said.

"Get on your damn feet," Gudger said.

But it was as if everybody thought of the same thing at the same time. We all stepped over into the stubble and broom sedge and flopped down as if an order had been given. All up and down the line you could hear sergeants bellowing and cursing.

"You think you are gentlemen and ladies of leisure," Gudger roared.

Cox sat on his horse and didn't say anything. He let the sergeant fuss and curse as much as he wanted to. I reckon that was the agreement between them, that Gudger would do the fussing and shoving and Captain Cox would just give orders when it was necessary and proper.

"You all want to go home to your mamas," Gudger said. "I've seen pussy that would make better soldiers."

"I've seen heifers that would make a better sergeant," T. R. muttered under his breath.

"I'll settle with you later, piss-britches," Gudger said.

"March!" the general hollered at the front of the line.

It was painful to put weight on my feet. It felt like the soles of my feet, while I was sitting, had plumped up with blood that had to be pressed out. And my feet were blistered and sore in the rags.

"Old Morgan is running toward the Broad River," Gaither said. "He's running away from Tarleton."

"You don't know what the general's doing," Gudger said. "Of course, he may ask for your advice, General Revis and General Heatherly."

The soldiers around us laughed.

Gudger stared hard at me. Cold wires went through the middle of my bones down to my feet. I knew the sergeant wasn't finished with me. I'd still have to watch out for him. I had come to feel different about Gudger, after he told me about his wife, but I knew he wasn't finished with me yet.

My hair was all tangled up by sweat and the wind. I wished I could take another drop of laudanum. Gudger shoved my hat straight, so hard my ears rang. I was so tired I felt silly. Wherever I looked I saw black spots.

"'Tention!" was called up and down the column. The line started stepping aside, and we moved to the edge of the trace and looked back. A company of horsemen galloped toward us, and I thought for an instant it must be Tarleton, for some riders were wearing green coats with black fur hats. And then I saw that most wore white and blue coats. Their leader was a heavyset man with a square jaw and a regular cocked hat.

"'Tention!" Gudger shouted.

The riders carried sabers long as muskets, and some held lances and some wore pistols on their belts. They had gold patches on their shoulders and they rode easily, like they lived on their horses. Some had sheepskin capes thrown over their shoulders. I saw there wasn't any way foot soldiers could stand up to dragoons.

"Them's Washington's cavalry," Gudger said.

"General Washington?" T. R. said.

"No, you blockhead, Col. William Washington, that killed so many Tories at Hammond's Store."

We watched the dragoons gallop past like they were lords. I felt scareder than ever. On foot we didn't have an idiot's chance. My guts were sore and sick. I was glad Colonel Washington was on our side.

I didn't count the cavalry as it went by, but I guess there were nearly a hundred horses. How clean the dragoons looked in their white britches and white-and-blue coats. Those with green coats were mounted militia riding with the cavalry, led by Major James McCall. They rode up there above the mud, while we were all covered with clay from the knees down. As the horses dashed by they splashed puddles on us and kicked up twists and pats of mud. Spots of mud stuck to my blanket and even my hands, and to the barrel of the rifle.

I told myself if I ever got out of this I would never go near an army or war again. I would climb into the mountains and live there in peace forever and forever. A woman had no business in such a place with so many men. And yet I felt a little pride too, that I had marched with them and camped with them. I had kept up with all of them.

WE REACHED A LONG open place in the woods called the Cowpens and went on a little ways and then stopped. We could see a low running ridge to the east. "That's Thicketty Mountain," Gudger said. The long column came to a halt.

Somebody had ridden to the Broad River and returned and they said you could see from a distance it was in flood. The brown water had spread out over fields and swamps. The middle of the river swirled like an angry animal cut loose. The flood had washed all the rafts away. They said waves leaped up like stampeding cows. The general sat on his horse

and we all stood on the road and watched him. I reckon it had been rain-
ing or snowing in the mountains to the west and the river was in terrible flood.

"Now what?" T. R. said. T. R. had been planning on running away
once we crossed the Broad River. Now he saw he was in the same pickle
as the rest of us.

"Be quiet," Gudger said. But he didn't need to say it for we were all
quiet, knowing that Tarleton was chasing us.

The general called his officers up to the front to talk again. I could see
them pointing this way and that way and arguing. Then the officers came
back down the line, and the order was given to make camp here.

"Why would we make camp at the Cowpens?" T. R. said.

All my life I'd heard of Hannah's Cowpens. It was the big open place
close to Thicketty Mountain. The Green River Road ran right through
it. It was a half-open meadow used for pasturing cattle. There were post
oaks and hickory trees, with brush and wild peavines and undergrowth
eaten back by cattle. It looked like it must at one time have been an old
field cleared by Indians.

The Cowpens was a kind of meeting place too. The Hannah family
had owned it, I guess, and then the Saunders family owned it after them.
Parties met there to go on long hunting trips into the mountains, and
coon hunters built their fires there and got drunk while their dogs bellowed in the woods. It had been a muster ground for the militias as long
as anybody could remember. And there had been camp meetings held
there too.

"Cowpens is where they gathered to march to Kings Mountain last
October," Gaither said.

The sun had just about sunk into the trees as we marched around the
edge of the Cowpens. As we left the road to cross the open field there
was a low hill ahead. Not a hill, just a rise, more like. And then there
were open woods going out on either side of the road. Off to the left was
Thicketty Mountain, a long-running ridge.

A few patches of snow were left on the north side of cedar bushes like white shadows. Back at the edge of the woods you could see snow in the thickets. But the grazing ground was gray grass with little clumps of broom sedge. Thawing had left the ground soft. We went right back down the road squishing and slipping in the mud. The road was red as the sky in the west.

Old Morgan led us off the road and right across the open meadow. We marched to the top of a rise that leveled out and then went higher. I didn't see any cows in the open places. I guess people had gotten their stock when they heard we were coming, or the cows had already been taken by the armies. I didn't see a beast in all the grazing land except a deer at the far end of an opening in the woods.

We came across another rise, and there was a company already setting up camp. They had fires going and a few tents up and horses tied in the trees. Somebody said they were the Georgia militia.

The Georgians had taken the higher, drier ground. The general halted the line and pointed to the rolling pasture going down to the woods and across the little branch. We were near the back of the column, and would have to take whatever ground the others didn't want. The cavalry was in front and claimed the ground by the Georgia volunteers. Colonel Howard's Continental regulars were next, and they claimed the rest of the high ground.

Captain Cox led us right down to the branch and it looked like we were going to have to sleep in the little swampy valley, but we went on across, through a line of willows and filberts, and came out in a little field all by ourselves. The North Carolina companies spread out on that ground and started to make camp. The grass was deeper there, like it hadn't been grazed on as much as the rest of the Cowpens. And there were dead peavines tangling the edge of the woods.

The whole field by then looked red in the late sun. The sky was red all across the west, with just a few light clouds stretching over. The glow from the sky made the trees coppery, both the pines and the post oaks.

The grass was red as the light from a fireplace, and we all looked bronze as Indians as we gathered sticks for fires and pine limbs to put on the ground for beds.

As I was cutting pine brush for a dry bed, I wished I was far away from there. I wished I didn't have to pretend anymore. Tears came to my eyes as I thought of the baby. I wished I was far away from Gudger. I wished I was in a warm house to protect the baby inside me. The most ordinary life seemed wonderful, compared to the army. Nothing seemed as good as just living your life in the quiet, away from the mud and noise and cursing. Ordinary life seemed almost too good to believe, with Gudger cursing and Tarleton threatening.

Most people had lived their lives in the country before the war, free to come and go and work or rest when they felt like it, with good bread to eat and a warm fire. They could sit by the fire at night in peace and rest on Sundays. Women could sew and play music on spinets. Boys and girls could flirt and write love letters and sing at Christmas. It was hard to believe we'd ever lived that way, with clean stockings and clean leather shoes. We'd slept safe in clean beds.

"What are you studying on?" Gudger said when he came up behind me.

I nearly jumped out of my coat. "Nothing, sir," I said.

He got up close to me and whispered, "You and me has some unfinished business, girl."

I turned away from him with the armload of pine boughs.

"You wouldn't be thinking of deserting," Gudger hollered after me, but I ignored him and carried the pine limbs back to the campfire.

"Gudger may not live long after the battle starts," T. R. said.

"Don't talk that way," I said.

"I would hate for something to happen to our sergeant," Gaither said.

"Go fetch some water," Jenkins said to me.

The spring was in the cedars not too far away. I took the wooden bucket and got some water to wash my hands and to boil grits. I listened to the wind in the pines above for a minute before I returned to the camp. As we sat by the fire to eat and drink coffee, more companies kept arriving. There were lanterns in the woods and people yelling all around. I was glad it was dark for I needed to piss. The sky was clear and stars came out over Thicketty Mountain. It was going to be a cold night.

General Morgan had ordered that some captured cows be butchered, and even as we ate, great pieces of fresh beef were distributed among the groups. Everyone was given a piece of beef, and we roasted the slabs on sticks above the fires or fried them in pans with the grits. The fresh meat was so sweet it burned my tongue. We ate it all quickly. The rich meat made me feel a little drunk.

As soon as the beef and hominy were finished I slipped out of the circle and headed for the woods where I peed long and hard. It was a wonderful relief. The freedom to make water was one of the things I missed most. I squatted in the woods a long time, listening to the clangs and yells from the field.

I'd just gotten back to the fire when somebody else stepped into the firelight. It was a big man with stout shoulders and thick neck, and I saw it was the general himself.

"You boys better cook enough for breakfast," he said, "for you won't have time to cook in the morning."

We stood up and saluted him. I found I was short of breath.

"Keep your seats, boys," the general said. His face was red in the firelight, but the scar on his cheek was almost white. He looked around the campfire and stepped closer to the flames. "Benny Tarleton is on his way and we need all of you to whip him," he said.

In the firelight Old Morgan looked even bigger than he had on horseback. His boots were the biggest I'd ever seen, and his shoulders were wider than anybody else's. I'd heard how he used to be a teamster in the mountains of Virginia and how he was called the Old Wagoner because he drove a team for George Washington. His hands looked big enough to grip the reins of a dozen horses. It was said that when he was young he'd been a champion wrestler.

The general wore a blue coat with white buttons. He stepped closer to the fire and took the coat off.

"Look what these British blackguards did to me," he said, and jerked his shirt out of his pants and raised it up to the back of his neck. We all stepped closer and gasped at what we saw, for his back was a mess of scars and whelks. The scars were raised like ropes and lips over the red hollowed-out places. Didn't seem to be an inch of normal skin.

"They gave me 499 lashes," the general said. "I had slapped a strutting English officer." He turned so all could see his back. "I was supposed to get 500, but I was counting, and they forgot one," he said. "I was not supposed to live."

He dropped his shirt and put on his blue coat again. His silver hair fell down on his shoulders. He walked to the other side of the fire and swung his arms like a revival preacher, and his eyes shone in the firelight as he talked.

"Tarleton is expecting you to scatter before his Green Horse," the general said. "But you boys will fool him. Tarleton thinks he can't be beaten by patriots."

The general squatted by the fire like a horse trader talking about a swap. He looked around in the firelight at each of us. With his big hands he outlined his plan. "All I want from you is two shots," he said. "You don't have to stand up to a cavalry charge or a bayonet charge. Shoot twice and retreat to the next line. Fire at the epaulets and stripes. Don't waste your powder on privates. Two shots and pull back."

That was the best news we'd heard.

"Two shots and you can go home," Old Morgan said. "But make those shots count. Hit the epaulets and stripes, boys."

Morgan talked just like the rest of us did. He was a mountain man from Virginia. Though he was a general and friend of George Washington, he talked just like the rest of us.

"We're going to beat Benny Tarleton," the general said. "And we're going to beat him right here, on this very ground. Your old folks are going to be proud of you, and your sweethearts are going to kiss you. We're go-

ing to beat Tarleton so your folks can keep their houses and you can go
back to your sweethearts."

The general stood up and walked to the other side of the fire. The
gold stars on his shoulders sparkled in the firelight. The real stars blinked
way over his head, and over the top of Thicketty Mountain.

"Old Morgan was never beaten," the general said. "You go out and
shoot twice for me, just like we were hunting turkeys, and we'll teach the
fine young butcher the lesson of his life, or of his death."

There was laughter all around.

"They call me the Old Wagoner," the general said. "And it's true, I
drove many a team over the mountains. I drove wagons all the way to
Fort Duquesne for Braddock's men, and I saw him die. I'll drive Tarleton
out of the upcountry back to his mammy Cornwallis's lap."

It seemed like we should cheer and clap, but the general wasn't finished. He walked around the campfire again. "I'm going to beat Benny
Tarleton on this ground or I'm going to lay down my bones here," he
said. "Our country has been ravaged long enough. Our houses have been
plundered and our mothers and sisters have been raped. Some have had
their tongues scraped and some have been shamed in other ways. Our
fields and stores have been wasted and our brothers have died on English
bayonets and sabers, even while trying to surrender. We have to fight and
we have to win. If we lose we will all be hanged."

The general paused and looked around the campfire. He looked at
Cox and at Gudger. He looked at Jenkins and T. R. and Gaither, and he
looked at me and all the others. He seemed to look into our very hearts.
I couldn't take my eyes off his scarred face. "Your grandchildren, and
their grandchildren, will remember this place and what you did here," he
said. "All I ask is two shots and then you can pull back."

It seemed so odd for me to be there listening to the general talk. I
wondered if any other woman had ever been in a battle before. Was I just
dreaming I was there? Was the Lord punishing me for all my sins? A
woman carrying a baby had no business in an army. I was scared, and I

was scared of being scared. All the boys around me were so thrilled. I was not thrilled like they were, but I was proud I had kept up with them so far. I was scared but I was proud to be listening to the general.

After he talked to us the general talked to Cox. He drew a plan in the dirt and pointed to places out in the dark. All we could see were campfires scattered along the branch and out along the crest of the hill. There were more patriots arriving and new fires had been started in the woods. It looked like there were as many campfires as stars. There were lights everywhere you looked. I reckon Tarleton wouldn't have had any trouble finding us if he had come looking in the dark.

It surprised me that Old Morgan was willing to talk about his plans right in front of the rest of us. He talked the same way to Cox he had to the company. We were all intended to know his schemes and plans. It gave us confidence to see him working out his plans in plain sight. The general appeared sure of himself and of us, there in the firelight telling everybody what he wanted them to do.

I looked at the faces around the campfires. I'd never seen men so carried away, so thrilled. It was so strange to be there with them. I was excited and proud to be there, but mostly I was scared. It still didn't seem possible I could be in the militia. I didn't want to hurt anybody. I just wanted to live. But I wanted T. R. and Captain Cox and the others to be proud of me too.

Before he left the clearing the general addressed us one more time. "Cook your grits tonight," he said, "and eat them cold in the morning. You won't have time to make fires and cook then. Benny Tarleton will be here at daylight for some downright fighting, and we'll be ready for him."

The general strode off into the dark and as I watched him go I thought he was more of a man than anybody I'd ever seen. He looked like he could beat an army with his fists.

We built up the fire again and started heating water for more grits and mush. Cold grits would be slimy as fish, but they would be better than nothing in the morning.

As I stirred the boiling water I heard General Morgan talking at another campfire. I reckon he was giving them the same talk he had given us. The general's voice carried across the branch and the cold night. "Give me two shots, boys" echoed off the pine woods. Another company arrived and set up camp beside us. Captain Cox said it was Colonel Pickens's men.

There was noise all over, of men hollering and horses snorting and fires popping. Fires made from wet wood crackled and sent sparks up into the sky.

"Turn in," Gudger said. "Get your beauty sleep."

"Can't we sleep late like we're used to doing?" Gaither said.

After the grits were cooked, I set the pot off to the side and covered it with another pot. We were out of bacon, but there was still beef grease in a pan.

It was a freezing night. I had forgotten about the cold while the general was talking. It always gets colder in winter when the sky is clear. I looked up at the stars and shivered. It felt like icy air was falling all the way from the stars. I unrolled the blanket and wrapped it around my coat, and lay down on the pine boughs close to the fire.

I was so scared I couldn't even think about anything. The stars looked so close they crackled and whispered. People say stars talk if you know how to listen. But you have to be by yourself to hear them.

When I closed my eyes all I heard was Old Morgan talking across the camp. "Give me two shots, boys, and then you're free," he roared.

It came to me how every day has its own angle and pitch and smell. It's like every feeling has its own stink, its own size, different and surprising each time. There is a texture to the touch of every terrible thing.

The touch of the night at Cowpens was like leather bitter from tanning. It was hard leather that hadn't been oiled or washed. Mr. Griffin had tanned some cowhides in a trough of acid the spring before and I kept recalling the bitter stench of rawhide and bark juice yellow as jaundice. It was a stink so harsh you could taste it in the back of your mouth and it wouldn't go away.

I didn't sleep much that night, and neither did T. R. and Gaither and Jenkins. They kept talking to each other. I rolled myself tight in the blanket and looked at smoke from the campfire melting into the stars. The general was still going through the camps and showing the scars on his back and yelling, "Look what those Tories did to me."

TWELVE

I DON'T THINK I slept at all that night. If I did, I kept dreaming of General Morgan's voice as he roved from fire to fire showing them his back and telling them he was never beaten. It was so cold I jerked when I breathed. I was afraid I'd be sick in the morning. I was afraid that I'd be killed before ever finding out what had happened to John. I felt the bottle of laudanum in my pocket. I had at least enough of the tincture for one more dose.

"Get up! Get up! Benny is coming!" It was the general shouting and I thought at first I was still dreaming. But a horse galloped through the camp and when I pushed back the blanket I saw it was Old Morgan on his horse. I threw aside the blanket and stood up. Everybody else staggered to their feet too. I don't reckon any of us had gotten much sleep. Everybody who had boots put them on in a hurry. There was heavy frost on the grass and the ground was spewed up with ice under our feet.

The general rode back to our camp and shouted from his horse, "Boys, you will be out front with the company from Georgia, with Hammond's men. There has been a lot of talk about who are the better shots, the men from Georgia or Carolina. Today we'll find out the truth of it."

Before he rode off to another company he shouted, "Shoot epaulets and stripes, boys. Two shots and you pull back."

We didn't have any wood to build up the fire. All we had was glowing coals and half-burned sticks. The grits in the pot had a skim of ice. I handed the pot to T. R. for I didn't want any cold grits. I swallowed and stood still and let the laudanum spread in my belly.

"Are your guns loaded?" Gudger yelled.

I held my breath to help my stomach settle.

"Look to your rifle, Summers," the sergeant said.

"I know it's loaded," I said. I hadn't fired the gun since the practice at Grindal Shoals.

"Then check it again," Gudger roared right in my face. I picked up the rifle. My hands were shaking so I could hardly get the ramrod out of its rings and in the barrel, but I finally ran it down to the shot and powder. A little mud had gotten in the barrel somehow. I wiped the red dirt off the ramrod.

"Have your shot and powder ready," Gudger said.

T. R. and Gaither and Jenkins and I filled our powder horns from the cask Cox had taken from the general's commissary. We got extra shot and greased patches. Cox opened another keg the general had given us and everybody got a dram for their flask, if they had a flask.

We had to leave our blankets and cooking pots in one of the wagons Cox had brought.

"Fall in," the captain shouted. He stood in front of us and he looked like a boy compared to Old Morgan. He told us Col. Andrew Pickens and his men would be 150 yards behind us. And the Maryland and Delaware Continentals would be another 150 yards behind them. And Colonel Washington's cavalry would be behind us all.

Captain Cox looked like a young schoolteacher addressing his class. "We're all from North Carolina," he said. "And when this is over we'll go back to North Carolina. Bloody Tarleton has invaded our country and killed our kinfolks. We've got to whip him and run him out of the Carolinas."

It was still dark, but while Cox was talking I could see Thicketty Mountain black against the sky. There was a lot of banging of pots and ringing of buckles and bridles. But nobody said much except the officers. In the dim light I saw boys pissing in the branch. I wished I had peed before anybody woke up. Men led horses to the woods to tie them up, and the train of wagons was starting to groan and grind up to the road. Teamsters yelled and cracked their whips.

The field was a mess of blankets and tents. Men were dressing and companies forming, and the general rode among them talking in his loud voice. "The Old Wagoner was never beaten," he shouted again and again.

The little boy was playing his drum beside the camp of the Continentals. He played the drum like it was a heartbeat that made you step faster. He wore a blue jacket with gold braids, and he beat the drum like he was going to burst it.

"For-ward!" Gudger hollered.

We marched around the other gathering companies and across the branch. There was a wagon stuck in the mud by the stream and some men were trying to push it out. Gaither started to help them, but the sergeant yelled, "Stay in line!"

We stepped right through the mud and bushes and up the other hill. A man tied to a poplar tree farther down the branch had his shirt torn off and a sergeant was flogging him with a hickory. I guess he'd tried to run away or had sassed an officer.

"For-ward!" Gudger yelled.

Cox had not brought his horse. He walked along ahead of us. It was just light enough to see the piles of horse manure in the grass. We walked past an officer of the Maryland regulars who was shaving while a slave boy held a pan and mirror for him. I saw a man emptying his bowels behind a bush.

We marched up to the top of the low hill where Major McDowell was waiting with the rest of the North Carolina volunteer companies. It looked like there was a hundred men, maybe more, and we joined our thirty-five to them.

"We will take the right side of the road," the major said. He sat on his horse and talked calm as a judge. I reckon Major McDowell had been at Kings Mountain and in a lot of other battles too. He seemed sure as the boss of a plantation giving orders.

"We are the skirmishers and marksmen," he said. "We will pick off British officers and then fall back. Give me two shots and retreat to Pickens's line."

The major rode up closer to us, like he didn't want to be overheard. "I know you boys can hit a squirrel in the arse at a hundred yards," he said. "Just kill an officer and you will serve your country well."

We stood shivering in the early dawn. The east was turning faintly yellow. The sky was partly cloudy. The air was damp and cold.

"Get behind a tree or behind a cedar bush or log," the major said. "Or just lie in the grass and hold your rifle steady." In the gold light I could see him clearly.

"Be sure you reload while you're running back," the major said. "The enemy is not expecting that."

I looked around and saw most of the men had long rifles. They held them like they were used to using them. My rifle felt awkward in my hands. I didn't know if I could shoot it or not. It didn't seem possible I was out here holding a rifle to shoot somebody. I wanted to do my part, but I didn't want to kill anybody.

"After you fire twice you will not start running," the major said. "You will move back orderly, then turn and fire from Pickens's line."

I looked over to the right. It was a long way to the thick woods. Oaks and black gum trees were scattered down the gentle slope. I banged my hands together to warm them and my breath smoked like a beekeeper's pot. I blew on my red fingertips and held the gun in the crook of my arm. Everybody else was blowing and stomping in the grass too.

"Find a tree to steady your rifle on," Major McDowell said. "And spread out so you can hardly be seen."

There were chestnut oaks and hickories and post oaks scattered around. Each of us looked for a tree to get behind. Most trees were too slim to hide a man. My teeth chattered and I couldn't keep my knees from shaking. I had to piss something terrible. This is your punishment for pretending to be a boy, I said to myself.

"The redcoats fire in volleys," Gudger said. "They all shoot at once and then rush up and run a bayonet through your guts."

I tried to find a tree for myself. I didn't want to stand out in the open if there was a bush to get behind. I felt cold and naked. I picked a little oak that wasn't bigger around than my leg. It didn't give much cover, but I could rest my gun on a limb. Gaither and T. R. got behind trees a few yards away. The major rode off to the side and Captain Cox took a stand near the Green River Road in the middle of the pasture. The road ran like a red vein to the south. The sun had not come over the ridge yet, but the east was turning red as a carbuncle.

The air got awfully quiet around us. I heard the general hollering at the lines behind us, but all I understood was "This day you must play your part for honor and liberty's cause." His voice flung across the field and faded.

We were on the lowest slope looking way down the road. It was a long way to where the road came out of the woods to the south. Pickens's men were behind us, and the Maryland and Delaware regulars were behind them, alongside the Virginia militia. There were trees scattered all through the pasture, but the pasture was so open you could see a good way. The slope behind us leveled off where Pickens's men stood, and then rose up again to where the Continentals were ranked. Washington and his cavalry were way back to the left, milling around near a clump of pines. I wondered how they were going to help us from so far away.

Beyond the clump of pine trees were the mountains to the north, looking blue and coppery in the early light. I told myself if I ever got out of the army I'd go to the mountains and never leave them. I'd live in a cabin beside a spring and I would have my baby. I would get far away from this place. I would sew and spin wool and knit. The mountains looked so peaceful up there, like the edge of heaven.

I had to pee so badly my belly felt swelled up and sore. My bladder ached and scalded right through my middle. I stood on one foot and leaned on the oak tree, then I stood on the other foot, shivering. Hundreds of men behind me watched for the British to appear any second in front of us. I throbbed something awful. I was scared and I was aching. And then I saw Gaither beside his own blackjack bush pissing in the broom sedge. He made a loud noise like a horse, and his water shone in the red light. Good old Gaither, I thought. Boys have it so easy.

I let off a squirt in my pants. I couldn't bring myself to pull down my pants and squat in front of all those men. I let out another squirt and the pee ran hot on my leg. The wetness ran down my leg under the coat and nobody could see it. I kept pissing and it felt wonderful.

I stood by the oak tree and looked at the frost on the ground. There were sticks and leaves in the stubble, and rocks here and there. It was just ordinary ground, with a cow pile here and a briar there. I hoped Tarleton and his Green Dragoons wouldn't show up at all. I looked at the few brown leaves still hanging on the oak tree. They fluttered a little in the dawn breeze.

"Look to your right," Gudger said. "You ain't got nothing to protect you. And on your left you ain't got nothing but cowards from Georgia. Ain't no swamps close by for you heifers to crawl into. The river's nigh six miles behind us. You got no choice but to fight, like the major says."

Gudger talked just loud enough for T. R. and Gaither and Jenkins and me to hear him.

"First son of a bitch that runs without firing his two shots I will shoot myself," Gudger said, and spat in the grass. "And I can tell if you're aiming or not."

Gudger's face was red like he'd been sitting by a fire, or it was a hot summer day. He took a drink from his canteen. "This rifle will get you before you run twenty yards," he said.

For the first time I saw how scared Gudger was. He'd been scared all along. He was scared to tell on me, afraid people would laugh at him. He was afraid I would tell on him. He was hollering at us, but he was saying too much. He was saying things over and over again. He was trying to keep himself from getting scareder.

"Their muskets won't shoot far as our rifles," Gudger said. "That's why they fire in volleys."

My hands were so cold I put them in my coat and then drew them up into my sleeves. I wondered if it was too cold for powder to burn. It was harder to light kindling when it was real cold. But if our guns wouldn't fire maybe the British muskets wouldn't fire either.

The ground under the broom sedge and wild peavines was hard as an anvil. You could stomp it and it was like kicking a rock. Gudger banged his hands together. His pistol was stuck in his belt and his rifle rested in the crook of his arm. He blew on his knuckles.

The field was brighter now. There was only one flag raised that I could see, held above the Maryland regulars, a red flag. But that was so far away I couldn't see any design on it.

"Who's that?" T. R. said, and raised his rifle.

We jerked to the right and saw a rider gallop out of the trees, swinging across the field in front of us.

"Don't shoot!" Captain Cox hollered from his position near the road. When the rider got out in the open we saw he was one of General Morgan's scouts. He was riding fast and I guess he hadn't seen where the skirmish line was. He swerved in front of us and galloped up the road behind us. Other men hollered back there, saying not to shoot, same as Cox had.

After the rider was gone it was awfully quiet. It was like the moment at a meeting when the preacher stands up but hasn't spoken yet. The whole field was waiting. There was just a little breeze in the trees, a morning breeze. It was going to be a cold day, and the sun was about to come up through the clouds across Thicketty Mountain. Some crows were fussing way over where the tall pine trees stood. I saw this hawk way up in the air and heard a whistle. The hawk circled like it was looking for a little chicken to grab. I guess it had spotted us and wanted to see what we were doing.

"Hey!" somebody yelled over on the Georgia side of the line. They could see farther down the road than we could. We all raised our rifles and aimed down the Green River Road, to where the red track disappeared through a gap in the trees.

Something was coming up the road, but it was so far away and so little you could hardly see it. Was it somebody crawling? Was it a short man? It was moving fast. Was it some kind of trick? Every barrel was trained on it.

"Don't shoot!" Cox hollered.

Captain Cox must have had sharper eyes than the rest of us, but soon as he gave the order we saw it was a deer, a buck, running with his head high and steady. A doe moves her head up and down when she runs. The buck loped almost up to us, and when he saw the line of men he swung aside and jumped high into the brush. His tail throbbed like a white flame until he was out of sight.

Somebody else hollered and pointed down the road. Two more deer came running up the red track. But they saw us sooner, or maybe they saw the first buck turn aside, for they followed him and leaped into the trees.

I strained my eyes and put my hands to my brow to block out the first sun. Something black lumbered out of the woods and lurched across the broom sedge and dead peavines. It was a bear running into the open, and then it turned to the left toward Thicketty Mountain and the low swamp between the pasture and the ridge.

"Don't fire," Cox said.

I reckon a lot of the men would have liked to shoot a bear. Bears were getting scarce. As we looked across the field little things came running out of the woods, rabbits and possums, squirrels and raccoons. A wild turkey hopped along taking jumps and trotting in the tall grass. Crows way off to the left still made a racket.

This thing the color of a Jersey cow stepped out of the woods. Its tail curved up over the broom sedge.

"Looky there," I said to Gaither and T. R. It was a panther.

"Shut up and look for Tories," Gudger said.

The panther never did come right out in the open. It walked along the edge of the woods, pacing fast and low. Its tail reared up over the broom sedge like it was floating. And then I couldn't see it anymore. I wondered if it had lain down in the grass and was waiting for its prey, the way a cat will.

When I looked back at the road all the animals were gone. I didn't even see a possum or rabbit any more. The pasture was empty and still. The shadows behind trees were getting shorter, and the field was streaked with sun sparkling on grass.

And then I saw the horse and rider. He rode straight in the saddle and wore a tall black cap. He came right up the road and out into the open. All at once I saw his coat was green, and I saw the men behind him wearing green. It was Tarleton.

"Hold your fire," Cox said.

Tarleton and his dragoons were a good ways off. The men on horses didn't see us until they had come farther along the road. Suddenly the one in front that sat so straight raised his hand and they all stopped. He pulled something from his saddlebags and put it to his eye. I reckon it was a spyglass, and he was trying to see where we were.

We weren't hidden exactly, but most of us were near trees and our coats and caps were nearly the color of the brush and broom sedge. In the early light everything looked orange anyway, including the frost on the ground that looked like somebody had crushed a mirror into meal.

When Tarleton pulled out his long saber and raised it over his head, my feet turned so cold they ached. I didn't feel like myself at all, but up above myself or out behind myself. I couldn't even watch myself because I was way off to the side. Josie, what are you doing here? I thought.

The saber flashed in the sun like it was a long icicle. The men behind Tarleton raised their sabers too, and they lined their horses up on either side of him. I reckon there must have been more than fifty of them out front. Tarleton raised up in his saddle and hollered to somebody behind him. And then I saw another group of men on horses and they were wearing red. The men in red rode between the dragoons in green and got in front of them. Their horses were prancing and nervous. The men hollered, but we couldn't tell what they said. The men in red pulled out their long sabers. Their faces were in shadow, but the blades flashed in the sun.

"Them blades look sharp as razors," Gaither said from behind his tree.

I looked around and saw the general sitting on his big white horse. He had ridden all over the field and come back to our line. The sunlight made him look like a bronze statue. The scar on his cheek looked silver.

I shivered and scrunched my toes inside the rags. The general rode along maybe twenty feet behind us. "I won't leave this field till I have whipped Benny Tarleton's arse," he shouted.

A yell went up across the field. It was the red dragoons in the front line. A drum started beating and a kind of pipe played. Colorful flags were raised along the British line. With their sabers lifted high the dragoons yelled something like "Huurrraahh!" The drum beat louder and the pipe played faster. It was a fife sparkling a merry tune.

"They have given us the British halloo," Old Morgan bellowed. "Now let's give them the Indian halloo."

I can't say what happened next, for it happened so fast. But I yelled out till my lungs were stretched. I hollered so loud I could hardly hear anybody else. All along the line we screamed like Indians giving a war whoop. It just came out of us when the general said to yell. Didn't anybody have to study on it. The shout went all up and down the line.

Just then the dragoons started galloping toward us and the yell died in my throat, like my breath was just turned off. Didn't seem possible they were galloping right toward us. And it looked as if the one out front was headed straight toward me.

"Cock your guns," Gudger hollered.

"Shoot at the epaulets, men," Old Morgan bellowed. "Hit the epaulets and the stripes."

The dragoons charged like they were on a fox hunt. They galloped like they were going to race for miles. I raised my rifle and leaned it against the little oak tree. I cocked the hammer with a trembling thumb. My arms and knees were shaking. Before I had time to aim at any of the dragoons I saw behind them ranks of soldiers marching out onto the field. It looked like there were hundreds of them, forming a line as soon as they came into the open. Some had red coats and some had blue-and-red coats, and some had bright green coats just like the dragoons. They formed into ranks with flags waving above them while the drum was groaning and the fife was sparkling out a tune.

The red dragoons turned aside off the field and the soldiers behind them reached to their sides and pulled out long knives. They did it all at the same time: they were fixing bayonets. The blades flashed in the sun like sabers.

I don't know which of us fired first. It all happened so fast. Somebody fired at the dragoons as they galloped off to the side, and the British infantry stepped forward in the orange sunlight. All up and down our line men hollered. I think the first shots came from the left, on the Georgia side of the road. Or it might have been some of us, Jenkins and Roberts, or even T. R. There was one shot and then another. A horse stumbled and fell.

My own gun was not even aimed. I couldn't make myself sight down the barrel. I was too scared and I was shaking. I looked over at Gaither and T. R., but they were busy aiming. I looked around to see where Cox was.

"Aim, you fool," Gudger screamed.

"Shoot the epaulet men," the general shouted.

I looked down the barrel of the rifle and it shook even though it leaned against the tree. Guns were firing all around me and the air smelled like smoke. The dragoons were still far enough away so their caps looked like bears' heads. You must shoot for John and for the sake of your baby, I said to myself. Don't let them know you are a girl. And don't let Gaither and T. R. and Captain Cox down.

"Two shots and fall back," the general hollered.

Off to the side three horses fell and the dragoons yelled when they hit the ground. One rider stumbled to his feet and raised his saber. His hat had slid crooked but was held by the strap under his chin. The bead on my rifle trembled as I trained it on the dragoon's head. I couldn't really aim, I was shaking so badly, and I didn't think to squeeze the trigger or steady the barrel by pressing it harder against the tree. I jerked the trigger and the dragoon fell. Whether it was my shot that hit him or somebody else's I couldn't tell.

"Reload, you stupid heifer!" Gudger shouted.

"Give them one more shot," Captain Cox yelled.

Major McDowell was riding behind us. "Hit the epaulets," he barked.

I lifted my powder horn, but my hand was trembling so I couldn't touch the point to the end of the barrel. The soldiers were coming on and hollering like they'd been stung by hornets and bitten by mad dogs. I didn't think I could reload before they were at me. My fingers fumbled on the cold shot in the pouch. I pulled out a ball and it squirted right out of my hand into the grass. I pinched another one tight in a patch till it squeezed into the end of the barrel.

By the time I got the bullet and patch in, the dragoons had gone into the woods on the right. But through the smoke I saw the ranks of soldiers coming closer out of the sun. Light flashed on their shoulders and caps. Old Morgan had said we didn't have to stand up to the bayonets.

"Fire, you fools," Gudger hollered.

"Eeiieehh!" I yelled, trying to give the Indian war whoop again. But it didn't come out right. I just sounded scared.

I crammed the bullet and patch into the barrel and pushed them down with the ramrod. My hands shook and I wasn't even sure they were pushed in all the way. I pulled the rod out of the barrel, but couldn't guide it back into its rings.

The redcoats were getting closer. Their buckles and badges flashed in the sun, and their bayonets reached out toward us. Their gorgets sparkled around the officers' necks. I raised the rifle and leaned it against the oak again, and tried to stop my hand from jerking. I had to fire one more shot before I could run back to the second line. And I had to aim too.

I pointed the barrel at the man in front with the bayonet reaching out toward me. I brought the bead right on him.

At the instant I touched the trigger and the rifle kicked and smoke boiled out of the barrel, the man wearing epaulets raised his head and stopped. A man behind him fell. I'd missed the officer and hit the other man. They all stopped and the row in front knelt down.

The man that had fallen was screaming with pain, but nobody paid him any mind. He crawled a little way and stopped. He put his hands to his chest and it looked like worms of blood squeezed through his fingers. The man searched through his clothes. I didn't know what he was looking for. The other soldiers were busy kneeling and aiming, and they didn't pay him any mind.

From the right I heard one of the officers yell, "No quarter!" It must have been Tarleton himself. "No quarter for traitors," he said.

The man on the grass raised himself so he was sitting. His coat was covered with wetness. His cap had fallen off and he didn't look any bigger than us on the ground.

"Tarleton's quarter," Gudger shouted, and shot the wounded man.

I paused for an instant, watching the wounded man fall back into the grass and jerk. Then I grabbed up my ramrod and bag and rifle and started running back. But I looked back in time to see the whole line of redcoats fire a volley. All their ranks belched smoke and the air above my head and around my ears screamed with bullets. There was a terrible roar, like awful thunder. The sound of the volley scared me more than anything else had. The sky went crashing behind me and over me. The air broke apart and it sounded like a swarm of hornets dropped on my head. And then the drum started playing again.

The whole field was covered with smoke, but when I looked back I saw the redcoats walking steady out of the fog. Their bayonets stuck out in front of them like they were pushing against the air. And out of the corner of my eye I saw something else. Between two companies of the redcoats I saw two little groups of men in blue-and-red coats carrying two cannons forward. They lifted them on rods and brought them ahead, then set them up to fire.

The brass barrels shined like they were gold. First one blew out smoke and jumped back and then the other. They jumped in the air like they were on springs.

"Watch out for the grasshoppers," Captain Cox yelled, and I saw that he meant the little cannons. The shots hissed, going over my head.

The men in blue and red worked fast around the right cannon like they were pieces of a clock. One poured in powder, one pushed in the wadding and ball, and one rammed it down with a pole. Another man stood there with a sparking match on a stick to touch it to the vent. But first he stuck a pin in the vent to make sure it wasn't clogged up. As soon as the cannon jumped back they went through it all again. The shots went way over our heads.

But even as I glanced back, I was running and stumbling. I was driven toward Pickens's line like I'd been carried by a flash flood. The ground was tilted away and I was running up a hill toward the South Carolina volunteers. I was half falling and half climbing. I couldn't believe I was there, and yet I was there, and I had fired at the enemy. I'd tried to kill a man.

As I ran I put the ramrod in the same hand that held the rifle and reached for the powder horn. It was clumsy to try to run and pour powder into the barrel. I expected to be shot from behind. I tried to swerve and zigzag, the way Cox had told us to do, but it was all I could do to keep from falling.

Pickens's men were partly hidden by trees. But there weren't enough trees for all of us to take cover behind. Some men knelt on the ground, and where there was a hickory log, ten men lay behind it with their rifles aimed straight ahead. They were older men than Cox's company. Some were dressed like gentlemen and some were barefoot and wore linsey or buckskin.

I got to their line and wheeled around. There was no cover, for every tree and bush was taken. I stood beside two big redheaded fellows that looked like twins. Gaither was already in the line, but I didn't see T. R. I was so out of breath I could hardly stand up.

A man on a white horse rode out in front of the line. He wore a light blue coat and he had the thinnest, longest face you ever saw, the saddest face in creation, and his eyes seemed to burn at you from under heavy brows. I thought it must be Col. Andrew Pickens whom we had heard so much about.

"Hold your fire until they're in killing distance," the colonel shouted. His face was so thin it looked like it had been stretched. His whole body appeared to have been pulled out long. He sat tall on the white horse. It was a long-legged horse and he towered above us. The sun was behind the colonel and threw his shadow on us as he rode to and fro.

The sun was above Thicketty Mountain now and in my left eye, when I turned toward the colonel. He spoke calmer than the general. "Fire twice and pull back around the Maryland line," he said.

He sounded so calm and dignified. He pointed at the advancing British and then rode behind our line.

I looked around to see where the Old Wagoner was. Our line stretched way across the field to the woods on the other side of the Green River Road. There were officers on horses riding along behind us talking to the men. But I didn't see the general. Way behind us stretched the line of the Maryland and Delaware regulars and the Virginia militia. They had a flag and the little boy was playing his drum. Their uniforms looked bright in the sun. Their officers held long sticks that looked like spears, called spontoons I'd heard. The sticks had blades at the end shaped like fish that sparkled in the sun. Old Morgan was talking to the leaders back there. I guess he was talking to Colonel Howard. He waved his arms and pointed to us, and swung around and pointed to the left.

I followed where the general was pointing and saw the cavalry of Colonel Washington. There were dozens of men on horses hidden mostly by the hill and the clump of pine trees. I wondered if they'd let us take the brunt of the fighting and come out when it was all over. The general pointed toward the horsemen and he pointed toward us. I couldn't tell a thing from the way he was pointing.

I cocked my rifle and turned back toward the front. My hands weren't shaking so much like they had been. The enemy drums beat fast as my heart. It was hard to see their fancy uniforms through all the smoke. Way off to the right I saw the Highlanders with their plaid capes and their white pants coming down to their boots.

"Steady on," a voice among the Tories kept hollering. "Steady on."

The little cannons between the legions fired, and after every puff of smoke you could hear the shot go over like a flock of pigeons. They must have fired grapeshot or buckshot. But they shot way over us, and I looked back and saw dirt kick up and a man fall in the Maryland line. Maybe the grasshoppers were just aimed at the Continentals. The artillerymen didn't think the volunteers were worth bothering with. Or maybe they thought the bayonets would take care of us.

As the Tories came closer, I saw something move in the grass ahead of them. Was it some animal trapped between the lines? The broom sedge shook and then a head raised up. It was a soldier that was wounded and crawling back to Pickens's line. He was hurt so he couldn't use his legs, but pulled himself by his elbows. He looked at the British getting closer and then heaved himself toward us. I thought it was a man from our company.

"Come on," several hollered to him from our line. I yelled too.

He held his rifle and worked himself forward on his elbows. His face looked white as a lace handkerchief, but his hunting shirt was covered with blood and dirt. The redcoats stepped forward like they didn't even see him. They were coming up behind him. Their bayonets pointed right at us. There were so many it was like a row of corn.

"Come on, Roberts," somebody yelled.

Roberts pulled himself forward like a worm inching itself through the grass. He strained and heaved. I saw he wasn't going to make it and there was nothing we could do.

The British drums beat like the rattle of doom. "Steady on, steady on," the officer called out.

"Take aim," Colonel Pickens called, "but let them get in killing distance."

My hands were shaking again so I could hardly hold the rifle. There wasn't any tree to lean on. Only thing to steady the barrel was my left hand. The redcoats kept moving and the end of my rifle jerked back and forth. It didn't seem like I could get it aimed.

Roberts dug his elbows into the grass and peavines like he was swimming. I could see the sweat streaming down his face, or maybe it was tears.

"Don't shoot till they're closer," Colonel Pickens yelled.

It looked as if the British were going to step right over Roberts. They walked all together to the drumbeat, and didn't seem to notice him. When the redcoats were right over him Roberts rolled around and tried to point his rifle at the closest soldier. But before he could raise the long barrel a redcoat lowered his own gun and drove the bayonet through Roberts's chest. It all happened in a second, but I saw the look on Roberts's face as the blade went in. It was like he was surprised, and then blood leapt from his mouth in a red tongue.

I lowered my gun to the left and shot the redcoat that had killed Roberts. Several others fired at the same time.

"Wait!" Colonel Pickens snapped. But it was too late. Boys all along the line started firing. "Pop pop pop," went the guns. It sounded like the top of the sky was blowing off.

"Reload!" Colonel Pickens shouted. I saw the ramrod was gone from my rifle. The rings under the barrel were empty. I'd lost it after reloading while running back. And then I saw the Tory line had stopped in front of us. Smoke from our guns made it hard to see them. They threw shadows on the drifting smoke, like an army of dark ghosts reaching toward us.

"Fire!" a voice barked.

And from the line in front of us, all the way across the field, white smoke puffed from the muskets. It looked like smoke was coming from their bayonets. The field itself, and the air too, turned to fire. And soon as I saw the smoke whoosh out, a terrible noise came at us. It was the worst racket I'd ever heard. All the thunder in the world put together wouldn't equal the roar of muskets in our faces. I was hit in the eyes by the roar and felt like crying. The bullets were so close on every side I didn't know which way to run. The musket smoke rose in a wall of white and rolled across the field blotting the sun. It was a storm covering us.

"Reload!" Colonel Pickens shouted.

I looked around and saw Captain Cox running up and down the line behind us. "Give them one more shot!" he yelled. "Damn it, fire again!"

But I couldn't find my ramrod. The big redheaded twin on my right had been shot and his brother had thrown down his rifle and was bent over him. "Jamie, are you hurt?" he cried.

Jamie's rifle lay on the ground with a ramrod tossed beside it. I guess he'd been trying to reload when he was shot. I grabbed the rod and started to reload my rifle.

"Wake up, Jamie," the brother said, "and we'll go home and have some grits and butter."

I poured in a charge of powder and tried to get a shot out of my bag. But it was like reaching into a bag of jelly. The balls slipped through my fingers, and when I finally did get hold of one it dropped in the grass before I could put it in the barrel. Wasn't any hope of finding it in the broom sedge. That's why some soldiers carried bullets in their mouths, so they'd have one ready. Of course they had to wipe the spit off so it wouldn't wet the powder.

When I reached to get another shot I looked up and saw the British coming out of the smoke. They looked like a legion of ten thousand. Their bayonets stuck out like horns and fangs. They came out of the smoke like demon shadows pointing their blades at us.

Through the smoke I saw the artillerymen loading their cannons and pointing them. They worked all together like the legs of a spider, pouring in powder, ramming in a cannister of shot, touching the vent on the barrel with the match called a linstock. The cannon jumped in the air and spurted out smoke, and the shot went overhead like forty hawks swooping.

I would just have time to reload before the British line reached us. I might shoot one man just as they stuck me with their bayonets. I'd lost too much time looking for the ramrod.

"Give them another shot," Colonel Pickens yelled, running down the line.

But all around me men started dropping back. They saw just as I did there wasn't time to reload before the bayonets reached us. A few did fire again, and I saw a British officer go down clutching his sword. But our line began to crumble and melt back. Wasn't anything could hold it firm before the coming bayonets.

I backed away a few feet and tried to get another shot in the barrel. The big redheaded brother tried to pull Jamie back in the smoke. But Jamie just stared up straight at the sky.

It was like I was in the middle of a brushfire, and there was smoke and popping trees and bursting roots all around me. I couldn't see where to go.

"Fire again, you bastards," somebody shouted. It was Major McDowell riding by.

But our line was broken and backing away and starting to run. I looked around and didn't see anybody I knew. A boy with half his face shot off lay on the ground. And somebody with his legs broken was trying to crawl backward. Splinters of bone came through his blood-soaked pants. Blood was so thick on his boots it looked like jelly. Snot ran out of his nose and mixed with tears and spit on his chin.

I was all confused. I couldn't think of anything and I didn't know anything. Smoke burned my eyes and nose. There wasn't anybody between me and the Tories, and their blades were coming at me. The drums kept thumping and the pipes whistling. You have no business being here, I said to myself.

"Steady on, now steady on," the British officer said.

I finally did get the ball and patch in the barrel of the rifle. But I was walking backward from the advancing line. I wasn't going to run, but kept walking as I raised the ramrod and stuck it in the barrel.

"One more shot!" the colonel yelled. "Give them one more shot!"

There were rifles lying on the ground, and hats and shot bags. Somebody had lost a boot as he ran away. Coats were scattered in the broom sedge. An arm lay on the ground in a bloody sleeve. I didn't see Captain Cox or any of his men.

I kept walking after the others, and when I got the bullet packed down I turned to see the redcoats right where I'd stood before. Two Tories stabbed their bayonets into Jamie's body. Driving the blades into the chest, they made sideways twists, like they were cutting out the heart.

"Steady on," the British officer yelled.

In the smoke I couldn't tell who had epaulets and who didn't. I raised my gun and somebody ran in front of me. It was Gudger. "Don't shoot at me, you idiot," he yelled. His face was bloody and swollen. I didn't see T. R. or Gaither.

"Fire one more time," somebody called. It was Major McDowell, turning his horse this way and that way among the running boys. In the smoke I couldn't see anything clearly. People ran sideways all around me. Crows called somewhere up in the air, like they were riled by all the battle noise.

I raised the rifle in the smoke, trying to see epaulets. But all I could tell in the fog was the British were getting close. They all looked alike in their big hats, holding bayonets out in front of them. The drums kept throbbing and it sounded like somebody beating their own belly. It was such a scary sound, of somebody thumping on their stomach, and it was getting louder.

I squeezed the trigger, but couldn't see if anybody went down, for even more smoke blew across the field. Please, Lord, I prayed, let me live through this. Guns popped all around, but the redcoats didn't fire. They just kept coming on with their bayonets stuck out in front like ghosts marching through a wall. I saw they never did fire when they were moving. And they all fired at the same time. It was only when they started sticking in their bayonets that everyone went for their own target.

I started backing away again, and was going to run to the right as we had been told to do. But my feet caught on something and I fell right on a body lying in the broom sedge. When I tried to get up my face mashed right against the face of the dead man. His eyes stared straight up, but his skin wasn't cold. He must have just been hit. Something was running out of his mouth, and at first I thought it was blood, but then smelled tobacco juice. I was looking right into his eyes, and then I rolled away.

When I staggered to my feet, still holding the gun in one hand and the ramrod in the other, there was blood all down the front of my coat. It looked like I'd been stabbed by a bayonet, but I didn't feel any wound. I stepped over a body with the guts blown out by a cannonball. There was a boy with his leg shot off dragging himself back toward the Maryland line. "Oh Jesus," he yelled.

There was the smell of blood in the air, like where you're butchering hogs.

I was swirling in a flood of human bodies. Was I going to be drowned, or trampled and left behind? I started running. But ahead there were bayonets pointing through the smoke. Had I gotten turned around and was running back toward the redcoats? They stood in perfect ranks with their bayonets thrust out. I was lost in the thick smoke and couldn't think.

"Fall back to the left, to the left," somebody yelled. Everybody started running to the right, and I saw I'd gotten turned around toward the Maryland line. I had gotten separated from McDowell's North Carolina men. I started running as hard as I could. The Continental regulars had blue uniforms with red stripes, but except for the colors they looked just like the British line. Their drummer boy was making his box thump and rattle.

Bullets whined and sang all around me. Tufts of broom sedge kicked up in front of me. It was the cannons firing. A soldier in the Maryland line was hit in the chest and fell.

Dodging zigzag, I dashed to the side like everybody else did. I ran like I was trying to miss the bullets, past a hickory tree and then a sassafras bush. I didn't see anybody I knew. I thought maybe there was cover ahead.

Just then I heard another sound, like shots fired one after another, or a drum beating louder and louder. The sound of a bugle tore the air like a scarf ripped in two. I turned and saw horses bearing down on us out of the smoke. It was the Green Dragoons. With their sabers raised high, they looked like giants on horses. With the sun bright on smoke behind them, they seemed to come out of the sky shooting shadows at us. Ba-ba-ba-boom, ba-ba-ba-boom, ba-ba-ba-boom, they sounded as they galloped closer.

Men ran in front of me and on each side of me. I jumped over bodies and hit others with my rifle and the ramrod. I looked back over my shoulder at the dragoons bearing down.

"Hie, hie!" the horsemen shouted, as if we were foxes they were riding after. They raised their sabers to chop off arms and heads. A bugle splashed out its sound. I had not reloaded the rifle and there was nothing to do but run as hard as I could.

A horse raced up beside me and the dragoon slashed the neck of the man in front of me. The head went rolling like a ball and the neck spurted blood as the body kept running before it fell. Horses dashed on both sides of me so close I could smell them. I figured I was next. I held the rifle up to protect my neck. The taste in my mouth was bad as the smell in my pants.

But suddenly as they came, the dragoons ripped away. The bugle played again and they fell back. I ran harder than ever, thinking this was my chance. The shot pouch banged against my side. I jumped over a tuft of bushes and dashed between two black gum trees. We were past the Maryland line now, heading off toward the north, toward the pine trees.

I couldn't tell where we were going, but everybody seemed to be running in the same direction. Men jumped over each other and shoved each other. They cursed and dodged each other. I didn't see anybody I knew. It looked like we were running back to where we'd camped the night before.

Just then I saw why the dragoons had turned back. Out of a little dip behind the hill came Colonel Washington's cavalry galloping toward us and past us. They had a bugle too, and their hooves rumbled loud as the Greens' horses had. Their white-and-blue coats shone in the sun, and they had their sabers out and flashing as they rode past us. "Whoo-ee!" they yelled, and galloped around us flinging up dirt and grass.

But we didn't slow down, for we didn't know what else might be coming after us. I just wanted to get away, from the bullets and smoke, and the bayonet blades. I wanted to get away where the air was cool enough to breathe. As I ran the air got cleaner and I breathed deeper, but then I saw an officer ahead pointing back toward the redcoats. And there was a boom behind us like the sky had cracked open. It sounded like everybody on the field was shooting their muskets at once. The air itself burst open, and it felt like my ears broke, or my head. There was a sick feeling behind my eyes, and all over me. Flocks of bullets groaned around me and above me, like passenger pigeons whistling through the air. Somebody in front of me stumbled and I jumped right over him.

A big tall man ran out in front of us and yelled, "Turn back and re-load!" He pointed back toward the field, but we ran right past him. If I stopped or even slowed down the men behind me would trample me. The tall man screamed and waved his arms. I couldn't look back.

Something hit me from behind. I reckon it was the barrel of a mus-ket that struck me in the middle of the back. The lick almost knocked me down. I dodged around an oak tree and ducked under the limbs of another.

Behind us the firing went on, pop pop pop, and one cannon roared and then another. I heard screams of men that got hit, and shouts of of-ficers and soldiers. I couldn't see where I was going and just followed those in front of me. We ran through scattered trees and around a farther ridge. Lt. Joseph Hughes of the South Carolina militia jumped out in front of us waving his hat. He had blood on his face.

"You damn cowards!" he yelled. "Stop and fight or we'll all be lost." His face glowed with fury. All I could think of was how sweet it would be to reach the quiet woods where nobody was shooting at me and no bayonets were pointing at me. I wanted to reach the swamp and thicket and hide there. It was hard to remember meadows and quiet streams where people weren't shooting and stabbing each other.

Lieutenant Hughes darted around us and in front of us. "Tarleton will ride you down and chop you to pieces," he shouted. "Your only hope is to turn and fight. Remember the Waxhaws."

Beyond the foot of the hill was a little gully, and beyond that stood a clump of pine trees. The pines grew in a kind of island in the field. The trees were thicker at the north end of the Cowpens, but this little stand of pines stood out from the other woods.

Lieutenant Hughes caught up with us again. He ran out in front and stopped by the pine trees. "Don't be fools," he shouted. "You've got to re-load and make a stand."

But even as he yelled a few boys broke away and dashed into the trees.

I guess some of them had their horses tied in the thickets. Others must have kept running till they reached the swamps.

"The Tories will come after us and kill us and burn our houses," the lieutenant shouted. "We've got to reload and stand by the Continentals up there on the hill."

As we rounded the clump of pines we all stopped. I don't know what came over us. It was a mystery, like everything else that day. Lieutenant Hughes hollered at us and pointed back toward the line. As soon as we got behind the pines the terrible panic went out of us. It all happened at once. We saw there was no use to run.

"Though we haven't got bayonets, we'll ram our rifles up their arses," the officer shouted.

The lieutenant came staggering up all out of breath, and Colonel Pickens rode up too. But we'd already stopped. There must have been several hundred of us, all out of breath and some of us were bleeding. Everybody was dirty and had powder and soot on their faces.

"Reload and go back to the line," Hughes said.

"Our brothers from Maryland and Virginia are taking all the fire," Colonel Pickens said. "We must go back and do our part."

We could hear the pop pop pop pop of muskets, and from time to time the roar of a volley and the boom boom of the two cannons. Crows in the white pines cursed at us.

"Form into ranks," Colonel Pickens called. "And reload while you march back up the hill." I was surprised to see I was still holding the ramrod in my left hand and the rifle in my right. I hadn't even thought of the gun while I was running.

John Trethman

It had been two weeks and I thought constantly of Josie. As we roved over the wilderness of South Carolina I had no news from Pine Knot Branch or North Carolina. But my thoughts of Josie helped sustain me.

I felt we were tending toward some great battle and the outcome would be terrible. Josie was with me every day and every hour in my thoughts and prayers. I didn't know where she was, or even if she was still alive. For all I knew she was burned on the tree outside our cabin. Yet I was certain in my heart she must be alive and that I would see her again some day.

It was one of the miracles of my life that Josie was sent to me. I had never thought I would have a wife, a companion for my pilgrim ministry and for my person. She was sent to me as such a surprise, and in such a way I could not avoid her. It was inevitable that I should come to love her.

The past two weeks we had swung through much of the backcountry of South Carolina. Often I did not know where we were. We waded

swamps and swam rivers. We fought our way through thickets and briars and tangled vines. We veered from Fort Ninety Six to the Enoree
River, parting endless canebrakes.

Once we passed a little church in the wilderness called Zion Hill, and
tears came to my eyes, seeing a place of worship set there in the pines,
and the name from the Bible, so far from any town. It reminded me that
the Lord is everywhere, and of the debt we owe those who came before
us, and handed the church down to us.

I had come to care for those men and respect them, in spite of their
depredations to the country. I had even come to love them, for they were
tired and scared, confused and disheartened, however much they kept to
discipline and protocol. Even those who swaggered and swore were worn
out and uncertain. Twice we had been attacked by militia hidden in the
woods, and at least a dozen men of the Royal Fusiliers had been killed.

The colonel's dragoons fought at Hammond's Store in December
and many were killed. I conducted the funerals, and sang and read from
the Book of Common Prayer, and I was grieved as if they were my own
people.

More than ever I had come to see the hopelessness and futility of war.
War was repugnant to me, and useless in the end, for violence only leads
to violence. One act of hate only leads to another. We are commanded to
love one another, not to kill one another. We are commanded to turn the
other cheek and to forgive seven times seventy. If a dispute cannot be
settled by love and reason, it cannot be settled.

I began to see I had been sent there to learn that the only true way was
the way of peace. I was not just being punished. I was also learning. My
service with that army had made me rededicate myself to my ministry
and to my love. The cruelty I had seen, and the loss, reminded me of my
choice of the way of prayer and praise. I was more convinced than ever
that I had chosen the right path. In the past I sometimes doubted my
call. And I doubted my worthiness to follow the call. But there in the

wilderness, the brutality of men unredeemed had made my mission clear. Only a message of love and peace could win. Only humility and compassion could see us through to a better life. I was weak and I was an imperfect vessel, but the message was clear.

Sometimes I lay awake at night and looked at the stars, and thought of the silence and cruelty in the world. God seemed far away from those mad skirmishes. But I knew it was we who had pushed Him away, and it was our own cruelty that we witnessed day after day.

On the worst days I was reminded I was being punished for my weaknesses and my deceptions. It was I who had failed my congregations, and failed Josie, by my deception, by my lack of courage. My penance was to lose Josie and to serve with Tarleton.

It was my privilege also to be called to serve. I had known no greater honor than to pray with those men so far from home, and comfort them with Scripture and song. Rough soldiers came to me late at night and early in the morning to weep and confess their sins. Officers asked me to pray with them.

Even our brash young Colonel Tarleton sometimes showed his weaker side. By day he was all confidence and bluster. He never paused but acted on impulse. His forthrightness was admirable in an officer, though he may have put his men at risk too often. He did not swagger so much as plunge ahead from task to task, from order to order, never looking back. By day he had his campaign, and by night he had his wine and the several women who traveled with the regiment.

A number of women followed the army in wagons and carts. They were mostly for the officers, though women in some wagons offered themselves to private soldiers for a shilling, it was said. Colonel Tarleton also had a good supply of wines and spirits, as well as tea and coffee. And one wagon was loaded with barrels of rum for the men's daily ration of grog.

After the cavalry returned from Hammond's Store with many wounded and several dead, Colonel Tarleton called me into his tent. He was drinking from a silver flask and his eyes were swollen, as if he had been weeping. We had just buried several of his dragoons, and I had helped nurse the wounded.

"Tell me, parson," the colonel said. "Tell me why these wretched people are so determined to betray the Crown."

"I don't know, sir," I said.

"They have gone mad," the colonel said, and slammed the table with his fist. "They will be damned for their blasted perversity."

I dared not comment on the patriots and the American cause in his presence. I had come to understand the frustration and fury he and his men felt.

"Why will they not surrender and return to law and order?" Colonel Tarleton said. He glared at me as though he blamed me for the rebellion. I stared at the ground to avoid his eyes.

"I'm just a preacher and a hymnodist, sir," I said.

"If you are so wise, tell me this," the colonel said. His eyes burned at me and his words came out as scalding hisses. "Tell me why your god permits such suffering and slaughter. Who is the author of so much pain in the world?"

The colonel was so grieved by the loss of his men his voice trembled He was shaken by the rebellion that had gone on and on. "Tell me what satisfaction your god can get from this unending calamity," he said.

I told him what I could, that the ways and purposes of the Lord were often a deep mystery, beyond our limited human understanding. Perhaps we were not meant to understand all.

"You parsons always talk that way," he said. There was anger in his voice, but also grief and confusion. I had not seen him so shaken. His face was flushed and his eyes glistened. I wondered if I should leave his presence. Was I embarrassing him in his justified grief? I was about to turn away when he said, "Is that all you have to offer, padre?"

"My only comfort is in humility and prayer," I said.

"Then pray with me," he said.

I sank slowly to my knees, for it didn't seem right to stand there. I dropped to my knees, and much to my surprise the colonel knelt also. He took a drink from the flask and closed his eyes.

"Lord, we do not understand the trials and pains of this journey," I said. "We do not understand the grief and danger, the anger and loss of life."

I prayed as plainly and directly as I knew how. I prayed with the colonel as I would with any other supplicant or mourner. My prayer was one of submission and surrender. I felt inspired to be simple and truthful. When I finished the colonel thanked me and turned away. I left the tent and stood beside a campfire and stared into the flames.

If I ever found Josie again I vowed we would go far away from armies and live in peace and honest work in some hidden valley. I would build a church and invite all to come. And I would raise a subsistence on my own fields.

For I had come to believe there was really no right side or wrong side in war. All killing was wrong and all hatred was wrong. I guess I had come to think as a Quaker in that way. It made no sense to kill and then kill again. Better to avoid the fight. Better to be humble and forgiving.

Those weeks in the wilderness had helped teach me that, and my weakness and my love had helped teach me that. For my love had sustained me, sinner that I was, and would sustain me, as I walked in that dark and lurking world.

I ALWAYS THOUGHT there was something ominous about thunder in winter. After I had been with Tarleton's legion about twenty days it began to rain, not a steady rain but violent cloudbursts that clawed at the canvas tent where I slept with several other men and threw cold water in my face while we were marching. The rain came suddenly, accompanied by thunder. I studied thunder the way I once had studied clouds. Sometimes the thunder grumbled around the edges of the sky and sometimes it barked in the night like a frightened dog.

Winter thunder would rumor on both sides of the sky like a story repeated again and again until it was worn out. But then the thunder blasted and shouted as if the sky was tearing apart. One night I felt the thunder was talking to me, preaching to me. I felt it brought a message about my unworthiness, a warning about my future. I wished I knew how to interpret what the thunder said. I sat in the tent and tried to read a passage from Revelation about a new heaven and a new earth, after the great battle of Armageddon. I wondered what the new earth would look like as rain gnawed at the canvas and thunder barked its threats. The candle flickered as if reluctant to burn in the damp air.

An orderly lifted the flap of the tent and said, "The colonel wants to see you."

The colonel usually disappeared into his tent at night with his whores and senior officers. I knew they played cards and drank fine brandy. Sometimes I heard them sing far into the night. It was odd he would summon me in the middle of a thunderstorm.

I closed the Bible the colonel had given me and looked out into the night. A flash of lightning lit up the forest, turning the trees and sky blue. Rain touched my face like a swarm of little wings. A few campfires were burning but they gave little light. Tucking the Bible under my coat I ran to the colonel's tent through mud and dripping brush. Thunder cracked the sky so loud it seemed time stopped, and the world was breaking apart. Rain fumbled at my eyes and I had to wipe my brow to see as I entered Tarleton's tent. I expected to see several officers there playing cards, but found only the colonel and one of his girls.

"Reverend Trethman," the colonel said, "thank you for joining us on such a beastly night." A chessboard was set on the table before him. He pointed to the pieces and asked if I would honor him with a game.

"I'm not very good," I said, and told him I hadn't played in years.

"Nonsense, parson, I know you are a man of keen intelligence," Colonel Tarleton said. He held a goblet in his right hand and fondled the girl with his left. I couldn't help but look at her. She was a brunette with fair skin, and her shawl was open so her bosoms were exposed.

"I'm a rotten player myself," Colonel Tarleton said, "but Susie here has agreed to help me." He stroked her breast as he spoke and I tried to look away. He offered me a goblet of brandy and I accepted. Rain hammered on the cloth of the tent and thunder shook the air and ground. The girl named Susie yelped with surprise.

"I like a game of chess to sharpen my wits," Colonel Tarleton said. "This war has turned me into a lout. Far from the theater, far from the gaming table, and far from family and his stable of horses, a man becomes a savage. It takes a woman to keep a man civilized."

He drew Susie to him and kissed her neck. She giggled and glanced at me. I could not take my eyes off the soft skin of her bosoms. I sipped the fine brandy and felt it burn across the back of my tongue and warm my throat.

The colonel held out his closed hands and I chose the left, the black pawn. He replaced the pawns on the board and moved a white one. I moved a black pawn and he moved a knight. Our opening moves went like clockwork as he brought a bishop out to the center of the board. I took another sip and began to feel the lift of the brandy. I moved a bishop into my opponent's territory.

"Chess is so clear," the colonel said. "Chess has rules and logic and honor, unlike this savage rebellion."

I had learned to say little about the war to the colonel. I did not want to provoke his anger.

"The militias are the dregs of society," Tarleton said as he studied the board. "Many are thieves and criminals. The colonies are populated by convicts, footpads, the lame, and simpleminded. It is a humiliation to fight such rabble."

He hit the table with his fist, and then apologized for his outburst. He saw me looking at Susie whose bosoms had fallen completely out of her gown. A grin spread across his flushed face. "Do you like women, parson?" he said.

"I am a man," I said, studying the board, "no better than most, and with the help of God no worse."

"At Oxford I knew some parsons who weren't interested in women at all," the colonel said. He moved a castle out to the center of his rear line, beside his queen, putting my knight in check. I moved the knight and took his pawn. The brandy made the lantern light in the tent seem ripe as peaches in August.

"It's a shame to fight rabble who don't know how to fight, who don't want to fight," Tarleton said. "What honor is there in defeating farm boys and rude laborers, tramps and lunatics?"

"Darling, you always win," Susie said, and put her hand on his cheek.

"It's not so much that I win as that they always lose," Colonel Tarleton said. "There's a difference. They would lose no matter who opposed them."

He moved his other castle out to the square beside his king, exposing my bishop. I moved my bishop and he took my knight. "Careful, padre, the night is young," he said.

I was not used to drinking brandy. The brandy thrilled my senses and I could not think ahead the way you must in chess. I looked at Susie's neck and at the earring in her lobe. I looked at her hand on the colonel's knee and could not anticipate his next move. I couldn't visualize the consequences of my moves.

"Have you ever had a woman?" Colonel Tarleton said. He looked at Susie and laughed, and then back at me. "No, that's a rude thing to ask," he added. "Forgive me for saying that."

Thunder banged above us like empty barrels in a bouncing wagon. I moved a castle out to the center of the board. "You should not have done that," the colonel said, and took my castle with his knight. I felt foolish to have made such an obvious mistake. And yet I knew that even if I were at myself I should let the colonel win. It was not a mistake to lose to him.

"I'm married," I said. "Your men took me from my wife."

"Now that's a shame," Tarleton said, and grinned at Susie. "You must be lonely here in this muddy, bloody wilderness."

"I will do my duty," I said.

The colonel poured more brandy in my goblet and I took another sip. I had only had brandy a few times before in my life. The purple and maroon colors of Susie's shawl were vivid. Her eyes were very blue and her skin fair and her hair black as a gypsy's.

The colonel called his orderly and told him to bring the girl called Sharon to his tent. A few moments later she appeared wiping the rain from her face. When she took off her hood I saw her blond curls and pink cheeks.

"Surely you know the Reverend Trethman," he said to Sharon.

"Course I do," the girl said.

"The reverend can teach you to read," the colonel said.

"Aw, go on," the girl said. "I don't need to read nothing."

Colonel Tarleton put his goblet down and drew Sharon to him with his right arm. He sat with an arm around either girl, and when his turn came he told Susie to move his piece on the board. He won in four more moves. The brandy clouded my mind and the girls distracted me, but he would have won in any case.

Sharon's face was prettier than Susie's, but I thought her skin was not so fine. Sharon was slender with freckles on her chest. She sat on the colonel's knee and put her hand inside his jacket. I stood up to leave.

"Thank you, Reverend, for a decent game," Tarleton said. "I fear you let me win."

"Not at all," I said.

"Then I am the beneficiary of good luck," the colonel said.

"And I'm a little out of practice," I said. A gust blew against the tent and made the air press on my ears. The brandy hummed behind my ears.

"Reverend, there's something I want you to do for me," the colonel said. He looked at Susie and he looked at me. "I want you to pray with Susie. Her brother has been killed and she is grieving."

I knew I was being mocked, but I could not say to the colonel I would not pray with her. Susie looked at Tarleton as if confused.

"Take Susie to your tent and pray with her," the colonel said.

"I cannot refuse to pray with anyone," I said.

"Then go," Tarleton said.

Susie took my hand and led me out into the rain. Lightning flickered, showing tents scattered in the dripping woods. Susie put her arm around my waist as we splashed through wet leaves and mud to the tent where I slept.

To my brandy-befuddled mind it did not seem strange that the other men who slept in the tent were gone. There was only the candle burning where I had read earlier, and several empty cots with blankets over them.

"I'm all soaked," Susie laughed, and took off her shawl and unbuttoned her dress. "Would you dry me off, sir, before I catch my death?" She handed me a linen towel from one of the cots and I rubbed her neck and shoulders. I rubbed down her back and then I wiped the drops off her chin and off her breasts. I started to say something about the death of her brother and grief, but she put a finger to my lips and with her other hand she loosened the dress somehow so it slid down to her hips.

The buzzing in my ears and behind my ears got louder. Because of the brandy I could not think clearly. The shout in my blood went from the tips of my toes and fingers to deep in my belly. The bigness of Susie's thighs and bosoms enveloped me. I was wrapped in vast contours and nipples, the cushions of womanhood, motherhood, the comfort women are made to give.

I will not say I could not help myself. I didn't want to help myself. The shout in my veins was closer and louder. Susie took off my shirt and dried my skin. She kissed my nipples as she loosened my pants.

"We will pray together," she said, and blew out the candle. As I drew her to me she was swollen and perfect every place I touched. Far behind me thunder shouted and urged and threatened.

"Where is that girl?" someone yelled, and thrust a lantern into the tent. I saw it was Lieutenant Withnail. He stared at our nakedness and laughed as though he had discovered a treasure. "I've looked everywhere for you, Susie. Come with me," he said.

Susie gathered up her clothes, and as she left the tent Lieutenant Withnail winked at me. "Sorry, parson," he said.

I heard laughter outside as I pulled up my breeches, and terrible thunder shook the ground. I saw that Lieutenant Withnail had had his revenge, and perhaps the colonel also. But I saw also the fault was mostly mine, and the author of my embarrassment was my own ordinary frailty. I was made of common clay, and I had much to pray about. I had much to be humble about, and I still had much to learn.

Thirteen

THE GENERAL AND COLONEL PICKENS rode out in front of us as we crossed the mouth of the little dip where Washington and his cavalry had waited before. The horsemen had seen us running and had dashed out to drive Tarleton's dragoons off our heels and necks. I hoped Colonel Washington's men would see us now, calm and stepping in ranks. But the cavalrymen were gone, chasing Tarleton's legion.

By the time we had stepped up out of the dip, everybody had re-loaded. Sweat dried on my forehead, leaving a kind of tight dust. I had gotten separated from the North Carolina militia. I was with Pickens's men. There was still frost on the weeds we tramped through. As we climbed the hill the firing ahead seemed to get worse.

Suddenly the cavalry appeared on our left, riding hard back to the gully. They had blood on their white coats now, and blood shining on their sabers. They rode past us hollering, and one soldier looked like he had taken a bayonet in his kneecap. His pants were cut and blood poured into his boot.

The cavalry had ridden out to save us from Tarleton, and we gave them a cheer. In the cold morning air we screamed our thanks.

"Now it's your turn," one of the riders yelled at us.

"Kill the damn British," another said, and raised his saber.

I felt gratitude so sweet it made my eyes wet. Nothing I'd seen that day stirred me more than the sight of those riders returning cut and bloody. They had charged out and saved us, and now they watched us marching by with our guns loaded. They had done their part and now we had to do ours again. I hollered before I knew it. My pants were wet, but my heart was full and hot.

The cavalry cheered back as they turned into the gully behind us. The horses sank into the shadows of the dip and only their sabers flashed in the sun. Boom boom, went the brass cannons. Men at the back of the Maryland line fell even as we ran behind them.

"To the right," Colonel Pickens shouted and pointed toward the flank of the Virginia volunteers. We ran around the end of the militia and spread out and took our places. Some of us knelt down to aim, and some lay down to steady their barrels on rocks and stumps. All that could find a tree or bush hid behind it. I saw a little hickory and put my rifle across the lowest limb. My hands weren't shaking now. I was scared, but not the same as before. This is something that will always be remembered, I thought. You will never be the same after this day.

The British line stopped a hundred paces away to fire a volley. It took them maybe half a minute to reload and fire again. "Ready, aim, fire," their sergeants yelled out, and smoke puffed out all across their line. It was an awful noise coming out of the smoke. It was like the world was cracking to its doom right in front of your face. I aimed my rifle while the smoke rolled out and parted.

The regulars on our left fired whenever they were ready. Pop pop pop pop, their guns went. They had to reload with their bayonets fixed, but they kept shooting and reloading, calm and businesslike. And the red-coats dropped in their tracks down the line. I aimed at a tall man with gold on his shoulders, and when I pulled the trigger he crumpled into the grass. I never would have thought I could have killed so easily. I was amazed that it seemed so natural. I was aiming and firing just like the men.

"Ready, aim, fire," the redcoats called, and there was another blast from their muskets. Smoke boiled out across the ground between the two armies like a wildfire in the grass. Nobody could see anymore. The pops and cracks on our side paused as the smoke reached us, and I heard the British drums, and the chirping of their fifes.

As the smoke started to clear, both sides began advancing with their bayonets. We volunteers couldn't do anything but watch because we didn't have bayonets. And we didn't have swords either. Most of us didn't even have long hunting knives. I reloaded and waited for another chance to shoot.

But out of the smoke on our right came the strangest sound you ever heard. It was like a scream that rose high in the air. It was like both a woman mourning and a fly whining. Then I remembered the bagpipes. As the smoke thinned I saw the battalion of Highlanders coming toward us on the right. They had swung around the Tory line and were coming at us from an angle.

Now it was the oddest thing. The Highlanders were marching at us from the right and the Virginians hadn't even seen them. They were too busy firing and watching the bayonets advancing in the smoke. I reckon they must have heard the squall of the bagpipes, but they didn't pay it any heed.

The bagpipes were shrill as the sound of madness. I guess they were meant to make you feel you were going crazy. It was the sound of birds and a swarm of awful hornets and giant mosquitoes. The pitch of that noise made you want to start slapping the air and shielding your eyes. I'd heard the Highlanders were the best of the British army and had never been beaten.

I had reloaded and I turned my rifle toward the Highlanders. My hands were steady. By then I must have been scared calm. I drew my bead on a tartan cap. And then another strange thing happened. The Virginians saw the Highlanders on our flank and an officer among them yelled, "About face, left." I thought that's what he said. The Virginians turned away from us. And they kept turning until they faced backward like they'd been ordered to retreat. When they started retreating the rest of us began to back up too. All of us did. We thought an order had been given.

The Maryland and Delaware Continentals must have seen their brother patriots retreating, for they stopped shooting and began to pull back too, just like an order had been shouted. I figured their colonel had given the command, for you could hear their drum. But you couldn't tell what was said, for the cannons were booming and the British muskets and the bagpipes were whining. An awful cheer went up from the British, for they must have thought they'd won. Through the smoke they saw us retreating.

"Death to Whigs and traitors," somebody yelled.

"No quarter," another shouted.

An English officer stepped out of the smoke and pointed his sword at us, and the awful cheer went up again from the red and green coats. I swung my rifle toward the officer that had pointed his sword, and when I squeezed the trigger his head splashed blood like a pumpkin hit by a rock, and he sank into the broom sedge.

With a terrible halloo and cry the redcoats started forward. But they were no longer in a firm line. They charged every which way, firing in the air and stabbing with bayonets. I guess they thought they'd already won.

We retreated with the regulars and the Virginians. We didn't have any choice but to fall back with the others, for the Highlanders were advancing on our right. I stepped fast, trying to catch up with the others. We had dropped back into a little dip and started up the next rise when General Morgan came riding out of the smoke. His hat had fallen off and his gray hair rippled in the wind.

"Are you beaten?" he hollered out to Colonel Howard. "Have you lost the day?"

Colonel Howard rode up close to the general. "Do we look beaten?" he yelled, and pointed to his men retreating in good order.

"Then turn when I say to and give them one more fire," the general yelled. His eyes glittered like an eagle's as he watched the advancing British. "Old Morgan was never beaten!" he shouted.

Our line followed the Old Wagoner up the hill till he pointed to a place and yelled, "Stop!" We all stopped, and all up and down the line you heard the order to turn and fire at the redcoats. We all turned around to face the bayonets. But it happened so fast I hadn't reloaded. All I could do was watch.

The British had broken into a run toward us, with their bayonets lowered. It sounded like every musket and rifle and pistol on the American side fired at once. A sheet of flame stretched from the far left to the far right of the field. The air was full of thunder and smoke. Our volley hit the redcoats right in their faces and chests. They had thought they'd won, and now they were caught in the worst fire they'd ever seen. They went down like clothes on a line that is cut. Bayonets stuck in the dirt and stuck in bodies already down. Men staggered back onto the bayonets of those behind them. Some fell holding their muskets pointed to the sky. The Tory line melted all the way across the field.

The Marylanders stepped forward with their bayonets aimed. It all happened in a few seconds. One minute the redcoats were charging at us, thinking they'd won the day, and the next they sank into the grass. Everything changed in a few seconds. The Continentals stabbed with their bayonets, and redcoats backed away and started to run.

SOMETIMES I DON'T think time means anything. It was just an instant, but it could have been half a lifetime for the way things had turned. The field shifted in that moment, as the regulars and the volunteers turned and fired their barrage. The whole battle, maybe the whole war, turned around in a second. Before, the flood of men had been streaming one way, and the next the tide was washing back the other way. Didn't seem to have a thing to do with anything you could have named. I can still smell the smoke from that moment, and the sweat of fear. There's a smell of gunpowder and blood and cow piles that's not like anything else. And the smell of sweat and shite. I was a girl and I had been a part of it all.

WHILE THE MARYLAND and Delaware regulars and the Virginia volunteers were charging with their bayonets, I reloaded. I didn't have a bayonet, but maybe I could shoot at a redcoat or a dragoon. I belched up brash and spit it out as I drove the ramrod down the barrel, packing the bullet and patch in. My hands were dark with dirt and soot. Here I was a girl, and I had fought and killed just like the men. It didn't seem possible. But then I remembered that I had killed before.

I saw the brass cannon on the left side. But the other one, on the right, I couldn't see. Boom, the grasshopper went, and after a few more seconds, Boom again. I saw it wasn't aimed at the Continentals anymore. It was aimed at Colonel Washington's cavalry riding around the hill and behind the British line. Whoosh! the shots went out over the hill.

The men in blue-and-red coats and white britches worked like they weren't paying attention to anything else. Two rolled the gun forward again and tilted it up, and one stuck a wedge behind it. Another placed a charge in the barrel and one rammed it down with a pole. Another placed a canister and wadding in the barrel and the man with the pole shoved it down. Another stood holding the linstock, and with the sharp pick he made sure the vent was clear. Another poured powder in the vent and the one with the linstock touched his smoking string to the hole. The cannon jumped back two feet in the air, and smoke bloomed from the end as I heard a whizzing above. I don't reckon the whole thing took more than a minute. The men in blue and red carried the cannon forward on poles and started all over again. I aimed at the one with the ram pole and when I squeezed the trigger he sank down like a drunk man into the weeds and peavines. Another man took up the pole and rammed it in.

The line of Continentals was stabbing redcoats with bayonets. They stuck some in the belly and some in the heart. Anybody that ran got stuck in the back. A Marylander lunged forward and thrust his musket. As the Tory jumped back he tripped over a body and the bayonet drove right into his groin. He gave a terrible scream and blood spurted from the straddle of his britches. The Marylander pulled out the bayonet and ran him through the heart. The Tory fell backward over the one already dead.

Some redcoats turned and started running. And some threw down their muskets and raised their hands. I saw men of the Royal Fusiliers drop to their knees with their hands up. And some men lay on the ground with their hands raised.

"Tarleton's quarter," one of the patriots shouted, and drove his bayonet into a man's face. I'd never seen such terror in the eyes of men. The British had never lost before, I reckon. They had thought we were whipped. It was the surprise when we turned around that panicked them. Some of the redcoats were praying and some had wet their pants.

"Taste this rebel steel," a volunteer hollered, and ran his bayonet through a man's mouth.

"Stop that. I say stop that!" somebody yelled. It was Colonel Howard. He was a young man with brown hair and he rode out in the middle of the mess with his sword held high. "Surrender!" he shouted at the British. "Surrender and we'll give you good quarter."

A Marylander lunged at a fusilier with his bayonet after the Tory raised his hands. Colonel Howard tapped the Continental on the cheek with his saber. "We will give good quarter," he said. "We are not Tarleton."

All down the line I saw colonels like Pickens and even Morgan himself ordering their men to give quarter. In a few minutes most of the redcoats had thrown down their guns. Some were running back in the smoke and some crouched on the ground with hands over their eyes as if they didn't want to see what was happening. Grown men and big men cried like babies.

That's when I saw Tarleton and his Green Dragoons gallop onto the field on the far side. His saber was raised and he was shouting something. He rode down on the Virginians like he was clearing brush. He slashed a man on the neck, and blood jumped out as if a keg had been opened. He was coming in our direction and I started to reload.

Tarleton's cavalry trampled men that didn't see them coming. A cannon fired and a bullet sang over my head like a frog call. Out of the corner of my eye I saw Colonel Washington's cavalry sweep around behind the Tories. Their white-and-blue coats still looked bright, compared to everything else on the field. They swung all the way around the running fusiliers. Whenever a man still held a gun they slashed him. Only the Highlanders on the right had stayed together and not run; they kept firing. Here and there a redcoat was still trying to bayonet a patriot.

A Delaware regular and a Virginia militiaman both ran toward a cannon to claim it at the same time. All the artillery soldiers were dead and lying in the weeds. It looked like the Virginian was going to reach the grasshopper first, but suddenly the Delaware man threw out his spontoon spear and used it like a pole to vault right on top of the cannon, claiming it for his company. It was an odd thing to see among all the killing.

Just as I got reloaded, I saw this redcoat looking right at me. I was the only one nearby that wasn't running around. The redcoat threw down his musket and held his hands up, but there was a wild, panicked look in his eye.

FOURTEEN

"Don't cut off my foot," I said. "Please don't."

"You'll have to lie still," the officer said.

It seemed I was sinking back into the warm mud. I was letting go. And I heard Mama's voice, as if she was right behind me where I couldn't see her. "Josie, you never did what you was told," Mama said. "You never did."

As I sank, Mama said I never gathered eggs until it was dark and the fox got them. And I never helped her scrub the floor. I was off playing in the woods when she had to get down on her knees and scour the kitchen and hallway.

Mama said I was never any help, but a burden and a headache, though she loved me anyway. She worked so hard her hands cracked and her back got crooked, and washing clothes every day gave her rheumatism. She had used all her money to send me to school.

I wanted to say I was sorry, but couldn't move my lips. It was like a dream where you are scared but can't scream. I was frozen with disappointment about myself. I was weak as a pile of dust. When you blame yourself and take the blame and admit you've done wrong, you usually feel better. At least you feel stronger, like you have cleared the air and can start again. Chastising yourself makes you feel clean and bare, as if you can see how things fit together.

But as I sank into the mud I felt lost, for if Mama blamed me I couldn't get rid of the blame by just admitting it. Saying I was sorry didn't make any difference, for it was like the world was blaming me and God was blaming me. I needed to sort it all out and strengthen myself, but I felt only weaker.

"Don't cut my foot off," I whispered. "Please don't cut my foot off."

Mama talked behind me, behind my ears. She said I'd teased Mr. Griffin and tried to get his attention. She said I'd played the flirt and the wanton. I had shaken my bosoms at him and sat on his lap.

"I tried to be a daughter," I said.

Sometimes if you have done wrong and you blame yourself and accuse yourself more than others do, you feel better. If you humble yourself into the dirt, and below the dirt, you at least feel you can go on. But now, I scolded myself and condemned myself and I just felt weaker. I had killed Mr. Griffin, and I had killed redcoats. And Mama kept on talking. She wouldn't stop telling about all the things I had done wrong. She didn't know I had quarreled with John, and that I had deceived him.

I saw how much Mama's voice was my own voice accusing me. Mama was in my own mind. As I floated in the mud and began to rise in the swamp water, I heard it wasn't Mama at all. It was me saying awful things about myself and low-rating myself.

THERE WAS THE SOUND of shovels ringing in the dirt, and picks ringing on rocks. And I thought: They are digging my grave. They are shoveling out a hole for me before I'm dead. Unless I'm already dead and don't even know it. Maybe I am in torment, and the punishment is to hear them dig my grave.

But when I opened my eyes I saw maybe a dozen men at the edge of the woods swinging picks and driving shovels into the ground. The red soil they flung up was so bright it hurt my eyes. And the broom sedge was so bright it sparkled like a collie dog.

"Who has died?" I said.

"Over a hundred redcoats," somebody answered.

And I remembered the battle and all the men that had been killed. How could they dig a grave for each of those that had fallen? It would take days, and maybe weeks, to bury all the dead soldiers. I raised my head and tried to lift myself on my elbows to see across the field. The men working stopped and took off their hats. They leaned on their shovels and picks and looked to the right. I pushed myself up to see, and what I saw was a little group of soldiers standing by a grave at the far end of the clearing. A tall man in black stood beside them, holding a book he seemed to be reading from. I caught a few words that drifted across the field and through the hum in my head.

> *Blessed are the dead which die in the Lord:*
> *Even so, saith the Spirit, for they rest from their labors.*

The words were like sweet music. After the weakness and lostness I had felt, it was wonderful to see the sunlight on the field and remember the victory. But I didn't see General Morgan. I strained to look toward the men by the grave and didn't see any soldiers I knew.

"Where is Captain Cox?" I said.

"What you say?" an orderly answered.

"Where is the militia?" I said.

"Army done gone north," the orderly said. "Nobody but the wounded here. And the dead."

> *Man that is born of a woman hath but a short time to live, and is full*
>   *of misery.*
> *He cometh up, and is cut down like a flower;*
>   *he fleeth as it were a shadow, and never continueth in one stay.*

In the midst of life we are in death:
Of whom may we seek for succor, but of thee, O Lord,
who for our sins art justly displeased?

I was thrilled to hear those words. It was like the world had ended but I was still alive. I had slept and then awakened at the bitter end, or after the bitter end. And it was sweet to be there, to listen to the service. Lines from a hymn drifted across the field, as if music was coming out of the ground or from the edge of the sky. The music was coming right through the tall grass and broom sedge. The music seemed to be floating out of time, or beyond time. And then the words of the book came again.

We therefore commit his body to the ground; earth to earth, ashes to
ashes, dust to dust;
In sure and certain hope of the Resurrection to eternal life, through
our Lord Jesus Christ.

I thought it was John's voice. It was a voice so much like John's. But I knew it couldn't be my husband, for he had disappeared with the Tories. I knew he must be dead. I raised myself on my elbows, but my arms shook with the effort. My whole body trembled and I fell back to the ground. Pain and weakness washed over me. A sour taste rushed up into my mouth. My head was washed sideways and I closed my eyes to make the field and sky stay still. I saw the cabin on Pine Knot Branch burning. I felt I was running with the soldiers and the dragoons were chasing us and chopping off heads and arms.

"EARTH TO EARTH, ashes to ashes, dust to dust," floated across the air. "As it was in the beginning, is now and ever shall be, world without end."

I was sure it was John speaking. It had to be his voice, for no one else sounded so musical and so young. No one else made the words so clear and important when he said them.

"John," I said. "I'm here."

"You be quiet," the orderly said. "You have lost a lot of blood."

I tried to raise myself again but couldn't. I didn't have the strength to lift my head. My head swam so badly my thoughts got washed away. You are my husband, I wanted to say. I wanted to shout across the field that I was sorry we had quarreled. But I was too sick to make words come out. The words stayed somewhere in the back of my head and I couldn't hear myself. I could almost think the words, but couldn't say them.

> *O God our help in ages past*
> *Our hope for years to come.*
> *Our shelter from the stormy blast*
> *And our eternal home.*

It was John's voice I heard slipping across the field in bright sunlight. It had to be. But I was helpless to call out or go to him. I was helpless to make my tongue say what I wanted to say. I was weak and I despised my weakness. When I called out it was only a groan that came from my throat. My tongue had melted, like a lump of butter, and had no feeling. My tongue lay in the back of my mouth and was helpless.

"John, you must come to me," I tried to call out.

"You be still now," the orderly said.

I have got to walk across the field or call across the field, I thought. But all I did was sink back into the muck and clabber of the swamp.

"TIE HIM HERE," a voice snarled.

I opened my eyes and saw a bloody man led by two others to a tree.

"This is what we do to deserters," a man in uniform said.

"Ain't a deserter," the bloody man said. I saw he was a boy from the militia. I'd seen him in McDowell's militia that morning.

An officer came up to the men and asked where the boy had been caught.

"We found him in the swamp," one of the captors said. "He was hid inside a holler tree."

"I was answering a call of nature," the boy said. He spoke like some of his teeth had been knocked out. His mouth was bloody and blood ran down on his chin.

"You was answering the call of a coward," said one of the men holding the boy.

The officer stood in front of the boy and asked him questions. He asked him what his name was.

"Hez Carlton," the boy said and spat out blood.

"You have shamed yourself and the militia, Hez," the officer said.

"Ask Luther," the boy said. "Ask Luther if I run away."

"Don't know no Luther," the officer said.

"You say 'sir' when you speak," one of the men said, and slapped the boy across the side of the head.

"Ask Luther, sir," the boy said. He was crying and tears mixed with the blood on his chin. The officer asked him what company he had been in, and what rank he had. The boy cried and wiped his nose on his sleeve. The officer asked him how long he was in the battle.

"I was there till the end," the boy said.

"What was you doing at the end?" the officer said.

"I was running like everybody else, from the horses," the boy said.

"You never even seen the end of the battle," one of the men said.

"I seen all there was," the boy said. You never saw such a look as was in his eyes. He was confused about what had happened to him, and he was scared. He couldn't understand what had gone wrong that day.

"We won in spite of cowards like you," the officer said.

The men that gathered around said the boy ought to be hanged.

"No, no," one of the men who had found Hez said. "You don't hang deserters; you shoot them."

They argued about it for a long time. Some said he wasn't worth the powder and lead it would take to kill him. Others said he wasn't worth the rope it would take to hang him.

"But a rope can be used again," one soldier said.

"You can't use a rope that has hung somebody," another soldier said.

I wanted to tell them to let the boy go. I wanted to say he wasn't any more scared than the rest of us had been. It was just an accident that Pickens and Hughes had been able to stop us and send us back to the line. The boy had run away before the officers stopped us. I wanted to say he was just a boy, and now the battle was over it didn't matter anyway.

But I couldn't move my lips or tongue. I couldn't move my neck. As much as I wanted to speak, I couldn't say a word. My throat was locked and my tongue had melted.

"I didn't go to hurt nobody," the boy said.

"You let everybody in your company down," the officer said.

I wanted to call out to John to come and help the boy. John could talk about mercy and compassion and forgiveness. He could talk about humility and kindness. John could talk better than anybody I knew. But he was over on the far side of the field conducting a funeral, and I couldn't call to him or see him anymore. If it was John.

The men decided they would hang the boy named Hez. They called for a rope and somebody got one from a wagon. The boy tried to jerk away from the men holding him, but they fitted the noose over his head. The boy shook his head like he was trying to shake loose from his body.

"Don't do it to him," I tried to say. But nothing came out of my mouth. Hez Carlton was no older than me. He had run when the rest of us ran from the Green Dragoons. He had hidden in a tree, instead of running until he was a long way from the Cowpens.

They dragged him over to a tree at the edge of the field. The boy's legs kept folding under him and he couldn't walk. They carried him backward to the black gum tree. But there was so much brush and little limbs on the tree they had to hack them away before they could throw the rope over a big limb. They finally got the rope over a branch and jerked it tight.

"You've got to help him, John," I tried to call out. But not a word came from my mouth. I couldn't even get the attention of the orderly because he was looking at the boy with the rope around his neck. Everybody was watching the boy called Hez.

They pulled the rope tight and Hez's head was jerked back. "Mama," he hollered out. He twisted around but they had tied his hands and he couldn't take hold of the rope. They jerked on the rope and he stood on tiptoes.

If John couldn't help him, I had to pray that God would help him. Only the Lord could save Hez. Only Jesus' mercy would keep the boy from hanging. The boy coughed and choked as the rope got tighter. He squealed a little and coughed again as the rope cut into his throat.

Please, Jesus, save the boy, I prayed. He hasn't done anything the rest of us wouldn't do. I know it could be me hanging there, or Gaither or T. R. Show us your mercy, I prayed. Show that you care for the fall of the sparrow. Show that you are listening.

I closed my eyes so tight they hurt. And I strained so hard to say the words my throat hurt. I couldn't hear much. I couldn't hear myself say the words. All I could hear were crows calling across the field.

As they jerked the boy off his feet the coughing stopped, and there was a gasp from his throat, and a grunt. His eyes bulged out and he twisted and wrenched around, and kicked out to reach the ground. He jerked the rope like a trout that was caught.

Lord, you don't hear a thing, I said, suddenly angry. Don't you see this boy suffer? You do nothing. Somebody said the language of God was silence, the big silence of a long time passing. I thought: there is nothing up there in the sky but crows. There is nobody who can hear me.

And then I thought: If God does speak, he speaks the language of cruelty. He speaks the language of pain and torture. Everywhere I looked in the world I saw pain and hurt. I found sickness and brutality. If God talks, he talks with cruelty and silence. The language of the world is hurt and suffering, guilt and hatred.

As the boy was pulled higher his legs danced like he was walking on air. If you couldn't see the rope you would think he was skipping and treading on the air. They pulled him higher and he looked like a body raised in a spell or vision. His eyes stared out like he was startled.

All the men had taken off their hats. They stood respectful, like it was a sacred moment, now that the boy was squirming and dying. They had done it to him, and now they acted reverent out of respect for him. They stood at attention like it was a ceremony to honor him. They watched the body jerk and shudder till it was still.

What does it mean, I thought, that they are all so respectful as he dies? What is the use of that? And what is the use of a God that would let it happen?

Then I was ashamed of myself, for I knew I was out of my head thinking such things. Was I losing my mind the way Mama had lost hers? My anger and my pride had gotten hold of me. Who was I to question the working out of God's will in the world? I was the one who had killed Mr. Griffin and deceived everybody about being a boy. I had killed many redcoats that day. What did I know about the nature and mystery of things? Josie, you be quiet, I said. You should think of your baby. You should think of Mama and of John. I was sorry for my anger, and sad for the young Hez Carlton. I was sad for myself.

THE GROUND WAS SHAKING and jolting under me. The hard ground shoved my shoulders and shook my belly. The jerking was so bad I was afraid my bones would pull apart. I was afraid the shaking would hurt the baby. I wondered if it was an earthquake or thunder.

I was so deep asleep I couldn't open my eyes. I couldn't even turn my head. The ground knocked and rattled. I was afraid it would shake the baby inside me so it tore loose. I strained to put my hand on my belly to hold it still. It took all my strength just to move my wrist.

The jolting rolled me to one side and then to the other. Is the battle still going on? I wondered. Are the cannons firing? Is there thunder and grinding rocks in the ground? Are millstones rubbing together to make this noise?

And then I remembered I'd seen the preacher at the service for the dead soldiers and he looked like John.

"John," I called out, and tried to open my eyes. But my eyelids were heavy as stones. "John," I said again. My eyelids felt glued together, like I had been crying and the lashes stuck. I opened my eyes a little, and the light crashed in and blinded me.

"Oh," I said.

I had to open my eyes. I had to see what made the ground rock and sway. Why was I pushed to one side and then the other? Why did the ground slam against my back and shake my belly?

I opened my eyes a little more and light hit me like a fist driving a spike into my head. "Oh," I said again. It was cloudy overhead, but the light was still bright.

"Now you just lay still," the orderly said.

"Where is John?" I said.

"Don't know no John."

The orderly was moving and trees overhead were moving. Limbs swayed and floated out of sight. I must be in a cart or wagon bouncing on a rocky road, I thought. It wasn't the ground that was quaking, but a wagon bed or cart of some kind. The road jolted me and knocked my belly.

"Where is the general?" I said.

"General done gone north," the orderly said.

I remembered how Old Morgan had winced when he knelt beside me. He had fought the battle while in great pain. Trees washed past in the air above me. As the wagon jolted, trees dipped and swayed. Sycamores and poplars rushed past me.

"Where are we going?" I said.

"Don't know, miss," the orderly said. "Reckon we looking for a place to camp."

The wagon must have hit a rock or log, for I was knocked sideways. And the jolt woke the pain in my leg. Pain washed through me and over me, and I cried out before I knew it. I hollered louder than I expected to.

"When we stop I'll give you some more laudanum," a voice said. I squinted and saw the sergeant walking beside the wagon, the sergeant who had helped the doctor with the wounded.

"My leg hurts," I said.

"We'll stop soon to rest," the sergeant said. "We've got to get away from the field before Cornwallis arrives."

I groaned and reached out to hold the side of the wagon. The pain made me want to crawl away from my leg and out of myself.

"Just hold still," the sergeant said. "We'll leave you at the first house we come to."

"You can't leave me till I find John," I said.

"The major says we can't have no woman in the army," the sergeant said.

"Whoa," somebody called out. The wagon tilted sideways and stopped. I heard horses galloping, getting closer and louder.

"It's not Tarleton?" I said, but nobody heard me, for there was hollering and drumming of hooves. I heard shouts and saw men go by in the sky above me. Horses panted and I smelled sweat and wet horses. Mud and dirt flung into the wagon, and a drop of muddy water splashed on my face.

As quickly as they had appeared the horses were gone. They had passed us and gone on up the road. The hoofbeats faded.

"That was Colonel Washington's men," the sergeant said. "I reckon they chased Tarleton as far as they could." He held a little bottle to my lips and I took a sip of the earthy, musky tincture. I was hurting so badly I needed the sweetness of the laudanum, the saltiness of the tincture. The laudanum soothed like grains of salt on the tongue, making the blood calm and the seconds shiny.

"Don't leave me out in the woods," I said.

"We'll leave you at the first house we come to," the sergeant said.

"I don't want to lose my foot," I said.

The wagon started creaking and jolting again. I slammed from side to side, and the boards smacked against my back. But the laudanum soaked out through me and warmed my legs and toes. I tried to move my toes, but my feet were floating. I was floating and rocked by the wagon. The wagon tilted like a boat in a storm.

I thought how Mama was left alone with nobody to help her. Mama had run me off just when she needed me to stay with her and help her. She was afflicted in her mind. Had the patriots burned her house down? Had they shaved her head and stuck tar and feathers all over her?

If I found John we would go to Mama and help her. The thought of a place in the mountains where we could live in peace brought tears to my eyes. The thought of finding John and going off to the mountains was almost too good to wish for. The thought of being forgiven by Mama in her right mind was too much to hope for. But first I had to find John. I had to ask him to forgive me for deceiving him. I had to tell him about what I had done to Mr. Griffin. But if he was the minister conducting the service on the battlefield we were going away from him.

"You must find my husband John," I said.

"We don't have time to look for nobody," the sergeant said.

If they left me at the first house we came to, I might never find John. If they left me in the woods I would never find my way back to Pine Knot Branch. I could never ask John for his forgiveness. If I died in the woods my baby would die also.

Trees swayed above me and the wagon swung over rocks and banged in mud holes. Would the Lord punish me for my angry thoughts on the battlefield? Would he chastise me because I had questioned his silence and absence? I wondered if I had committed the unpardonable sin.

Don't punish my baby, I prayed. Punish me but don't punish my baby. Don't punish Mama as a way of punishing me. Instead of being prideful and angry I needed to humble myself. Instead of accusing God I should have admitted my own weakness and sadness. I was helpless on my own.

The wagon jolted but I didn't feel the pain anymore. The wagon veered like the ground was having fits. "How far have we come?" I said.

But the sergeant must have gone on ahead, or dropped behind, for nobody answered.

"You just lay still," the orderly said.

WHEN I WOKE AGAIN the wagon bed was tilted so steep I felt I was sliding off. I grabbed the sideboard and raised my head a little. We were on the bank of a wide brown river. I thought it must be the Broad, except water had spread out among the trees and bushes. Water slurped and swerved over the clay banks. Then I remembered that the Broad had been in flood, which was why General Morgan had turned back and fought at Cowpens.

Men were chopping down trees and sawing logs. "Why have we stopped here?" I said. But nobody answered me. All the men except the wounded were chopping and sawing, and sharpening sticks with knives and hatchets.

"Why can't we use the rafts the army used to cross?" I said. Captain Cox's company had crossed here more than two weeks before. And then I remembered those rafts must have washed away in the flood or been used by the army that had crossed earlier that day. The army had left their rafts on the other side, as they hurried away from Cornwallis.

"We don't want to cross over," I yelled to the sergeant when he walked by carrying an ax. But he ignored me, like my words didn't make any sense except to me. If John was behind us helping to bury the dead, I wanted to stay on the south bank of the river. I wanted to wait right there till his party caught up with us. How long had I slept? Maybe I had just dreamed I'd seen John on the battlefield.

The pain in my leg and in my side began to return. As the men chopped and sawed and grunted, the pain woke in my shin and in my thigh. Was the pain going to reach the baby in my belly?

I could feel the baby there in the middle of me. The baby was like a glowing seed. And I thought: It is an eye at the center of me. The eye of the future is watching me and seeing all that is happening. All I do is being seen.

I shuddered with the pain. And I put my hands on my belly to protect the baby from the cold, and to keep it from seeing the mess I was in, the mess the world was in.

"Oh!" I said in spite of myself. The pain licked through my bones and over my side. The pain turned my flesh brown and blue, and pulled my thoughts to one side so I couldn't think clearly.

"Oh!" I said again. But the sergeant and the orderly were too busy to come to me. All the men were chopping logs and joining the logs into rafts with ropes and pegs. Men grunted and heaved. They pulled logs with horses and hollered as more trees started falling. All along the riverbank they hurried as they rolled logs together. They wrapped vines and ropes around logs to make bundles. I tried to look at the river and not think of the pain. But I was too weak to hold my head up for long. The river moved fast and had dimples and pockets and snag scars everywhere. The river was so high it broke in pieces and pulled away in eddies. We can't ever get across, I thought. We will be drowned.

"No," I said, but nobody was listening. The wagon moved, and I watched the orderly drive it up onto a raft. The wagon jerked and tilted. And then I felt the logs beneath grind over mud as they pushed them into the river. I raised my head to see what was going on. The orderly and another man held poles and pushed the raft out into the river. One stood on one side of the wagon and the other stood on the other side. With the poles they held the raft steady and pushed it into the middle of the river.

They leaned on the poles and shoved, and the raft dipped and trembled in the fast water. Water seemed to splash right near my ears and close to the back of my head. I was too weak to move and here I was in the shaky wagon in the middle of the raging river. Lord, you've got to help me, I said. My baby is in your hands.

A duck flew by making an awful noise. The raft jerked and jumped as the men held it steady with the poles. They pushed together and held the raft against the current. I could smell the ugly water. The river smelled of rotten things, earthworms, mud in sinkholes. I figured we were in the middle of the river, where the current was fastest. I figured we were getting closer to the other bank.

"Whoa!" the man poling with the orderly shouted. I couldn't see what happened, but the raft turned like a big hand had spun it around. "Whoa!" the orderly shouted. The raft turned and pulled away, and I felt it sweep sideways.

When I raised my head I saw the bank going by and the furrowed river spinning around. I saw the far bank and the other rafts. We hit a snag and jerked to one side. It felt like the wagon would roll off the raft. The men grabbed the wagon and held its wheels. The mules brayed a cry of terror. The other man took the reins and held the mule's head. "Whoa there," he said.

We veered sideways and turned a little more. It looked like we would be swept away in the flood and washed all the way to the ocean. I held my belly, and hoped I would float. I would hold onto the wagon hoping it would float.

I tried to see what was happening, but fell back and banged my head on the boards. Instead of sinking and turning over, the raft seemed to slow down. I looked out and saw we had come to a bend in the river. The river turned and slowed there. The raft hit a log and almost stopped. The men pushed with poles and we rocked into the still water where leaves and foam and logs circled and backed in the eddy. The men shoved against the poles and we rocked toward the shore.

The men already across the river found us and cut away brush and grapevines and briars so they could drive the mule and wagon up on the bank. I kept my eyes closed and tried not to feel the ache as the wagon lurched and heaved into the woods and we drove back to the road. It was cloudy and darker now.

Before we lined up on the road and started moving again, the sergeant gave me another sip of laudanum. After I drank the medicine I quit shaking and began to calm down. I was helpless to do a thing to protect myself. I was just the fruit around the seed of the baby, like the flesh of an apple or peach to protect the seed and nourish the seed.

As I dropped off to sleep in the jolting wagon I thought I could see another wagon far behind us. It had crossed the river after us. In the wagon were the men who had performed the burial ceremonies. They were ministers riding in the wagon with the men who had dug the graves. As they rode along they sang, and I heard John's voice. I knew it was John's voice. He was tired from the long day and the many burials, but he sang to refresh himself and the others.

As I listened to the voices in my dream it came to me what forgiveness was. I had felt so guilty and angry and disturbed I had forgotten what forgiveness meant. Whatever I had done I would be forgiven. It was that simple. I had heard forgiveness described a hundred times, by John and by others, but had not thought it applied to me. I had forgotten that forgiveness was a gift, and all I had to do was accept it. I would not be forgiven because I was good or because I had earned it. I would be forgiven because I was human and a sinner, and because I was loved. A new world had come into being, and I saw things in a new way. When I saw John I would tell him all, and he would forgive me.

"MAMA," I SAID, and somebody laughed. I opened my eyes and looked around. Tiny raindrops were melting on my face, and a board stuck against my back, jolting and rocking me. I heard a grinding sound, and people talking. I looked around and saw I was still in the wagon, but nobody was driving it.

"Where are we going?" I said, twisting around.

"Lie still, friend," somebody said.

There was a shadow inside the light that I couldn't blink away. The rain falling was so fine it was almost a mist. Trees dripped and my face was damp with a cold sweat. The rain was clean as forgiveness.

"Where are we?" I said.

"Hold on there," a man said.

A blanket was wrapped over my legs and I couldn't see anything down there. "Is my foot gone?" I said.

"Be quiet," the man said. "You're weak; you've lost a lot of blood."

Trees were going by and men were going by. Nobody was driving the wagon, so they must be leading it up front. Crows called in the trees and I saw one flapping across the low sky.

I must have closed my eyes then, for everything got dark and I sank back into the swamp, washed by waves of warm water. But the pool was cooling off and my feet were getting chilled. Rain splashed the pool. I tried to step forward but my feet and hands were stuck under the water. I couldn't do any good.

"We're going north, following the general," somebody said.

The water washed over my face and I rocked deeper and deeper into the silt, the way a crawfish will back its way into the mud by scratching and swaying. The mud was warm at first and then started getting colder.

When I woke again it was evening and the rain had stopped. The wagon rocked along same as before and my back was stiff. My joints were cold and my belly was cold. Was the baby cold? I felt my belly, and trees passed overhead, lurching and tilting away.

"Where are we going?" I said.

"North," was all the man said.

"Whoa," somebody said, and the wagon creaked to a stop. The trees all around looked like apple trees. And I could smell smoke, cooking smoke. It smelled like tenderloin frying.

They spoke in low voices around me, and I couldn't make out what they said. I was so empty and weak the smell of smoke made me sick again. Something rippled and bubbled in my belly, but nothing came up.

"Here you go," a man said and handed me a canteen. My mouth was so dry it felt like flannel. My lips were cracked and peeling. I put the neck of the canteen to my mouth and cold water rushed over my teeth as I swallowed. And then I swallowed again.

I shivered and jerked and could feel my feet, both my feet. The soles of my feet itched and the right foot ached. It started throbbing.

"Have I got both my feet?" I said.

"You've got a busted bone in your right foot," the sergeant said.

The throbbing got worse in my foot, like the medicine had worn off. It was an ugly black and purple kind of pain that licked up the bone in my leg and gnawed like fire on a log. I took another sip of water, hoping the water would soothe the pain.

But knowing they had not cut my foot off soothed the pain more than anything else. I didn't care about the pain so much as long as I knew I could walk, as long as I could carry my baby when it was born. My terror had been that I'd be a cripple and couldn't walk into the blue mountains, away from armies, and find a place to live. I had to be able to walk to take care of the baby.

I raised up on my elbows and looked over the edge of the wagon. We were in a camp and fires blazed all along the edge of the woods. There were wagons and carts and men lying on the ground close to the fires. It was a camp for the wounded, for many of the men had their arms in slings and bloodstains on their shirts, or bandages on their heads. Rain fell in a fine drizzle.

An orderly brought me a plate of grits, but my stomach was too weak to eat, and the pain in my foot made me too sick to eat.

"Got to eat to get your strength back, Josie," the sergeant said.

"How do you know my name?" I said.

"Cause you told us, when you was out of your head," the sergeant said.

I was surprised, and then relieved, for I wouldn't have to pretend anymore. I was tired of acting, of lying. I just wanted to be myself again.

"Oh!" I said as the pain rushed up my leg.

"We'll have to leave you at the first house we come to," the sergeant said. "We can't have no girls in this army."

"Don't leave me out in the cold," I said, and felt my belly.

A man was lying on a blanket by the closest fire. He lay on a kind of stretcher made of sticks. He didn't have any legs. All he had was band-ages above where his knees would have been, and the bandages were bloody and dirty. A jolt went through my heart and chest, for I thought that could have happened to me. I could be the one lying with only bandages where I once had legs.

The man stretched by the fire appeared to be sleeping. But there was a bruise or swelling on his cheek that made me remember something. In the flickering light I couldn't see too well.

"Who is that man there?" I said to the orderly that had brought the grits. There were several men standing around the campfire.

"Which man?" the driver said. I pointed to the man on the stretcher.

"That be Sergeant Gudger," the driver said.

I wondered if it was T. R. who had shot him in the knees.

While everybody was eating grits and drinking coffee around the campfire, I must have dozed off a little. Sleep is the mercy when you're weak and in pain. I drifted off dreaming of Gudger with no legs and a horse with no legs. I saw trees in the woods cut down like soldiers. But as I woke up I heard singing. Was I dreaming music, or was there singing in the camp?

"Jesus shall reign wher-e'er the sun," I heard. It was the sweetest sound. I'd heard that voice at the burial on the battlefield. I turned over under the blanket and listened.

It was the most beautiful sound. I must still be dreaming, I thought. And then I heard a voice pray, and I knew the voice, and I knew it was John Trethman. I had not just dreamed I'd seen him earlier.

I raised up and looked out over the side of the wagon. A tall man was standing by a campfire with a book in his hand. His back was to me, but I was sure it was John. He was speaking to the soldiers and the wounded. Everybody was turned toward him and listening.

"You have fought a terrible battle," John said. "You have walked through the valley of the shadow of death today. The Lord has spared you and now is the time for healing."

I tried to get somebody's attention, but there was nobody close by. They were all listening to John, and I was too weak to yell out. John started singing again.

When the song was over John turned in the firelight so I could see his face. He was slimmer than ever, and paler.

"The moment of victory is the time to be humble," he said. "If a victory has been won it is the Lord's work and the Lord's will. If you have come forward through the troubled times to this night of victory, it is because the Lord was with you and guided you."

John turned away a little so I had to listen harder. He never did have a voice all that loud.

"This is a night of Thanksgiving," he went on. "This is a night of praise and celebration. But it is also a night to remember the cost. I'm sure each of you has paid a great price to be here. I know I have. Some of you have lost friends and some have lost family. Some have lost those dearest to them. Some have lost limbs and some have lost eyes."

John stopped and turned toward the wagon where I lay. I knew he couldn't see me in the dark. I tried to wave, but was too weak to do more than raise my arm before falling back on the blanket.

"This must be a night of mourning also," John said. "This must be our time of remembering those lost in this hard time. This will be our night to honor them and pray for them. This will be our night to be humble and sing of their memory and sacrifice."

I had tears in my eyes, both because of what John was saying and because he didn't know I was there. For all he knew I had burned at the cabin or frozen to death on the tree outside.

"Our only comfort is in the working out of the Lord's will," John said. "Our only comfort is in our dedication. You have won a victory that will benefit your children and your children's children for a hundred generations, but the work of peace has only begun."

After John sang another song and prayed for all the wounded, I was frantic to let him know I was there. I was too weak to holler out, and when I called to the orderly that had brought me the grits he didn't hear me either. I banged on the side of the wagon with my elbow, and then with my fist. I kicked at the boards with my good foot.

A sergeant walking away from the campfire heard me and stopped by the wagon. "Are you having fits?" he said.

"I need to see that man," I said.

He asked if I needed to see a man about a dog, and he laughed and said what man is that. I told him I wanted to talk to the preacher.

I was going to tell him John was my husband. But the man walked away and I waited. It seemed like hours passed. And then I saw John walking toward the wagon.

"John," I called out loud as I could. My throat was scratchy and cracked. I swallowed and tried again. "John," I yelled as loud as I could.

John was walking straight toward me. He looked tall as a tree with the firelight behind him, and when he reached out toward me his arms were long wings of shadow and light stretching far across the camp to touch me. As he came closer I couldn't see his face, but he looked tall as an oak with the lit droplets of rain behind him, tall as a house, as he bent down to see me better.

Acknowledgments

My father, Clyde R. Morgan, first told me the story of the Battle of Cowpens when I was a boy. He was a wonderful storyteller, and his vivid sense of history has inspired many of my stories. At least one of my ancestors, William Capps, fought at Cowpens.

But this is a work of fiction and most of the characters are imagined. In the case of historical figures such as Daniel Morgan and Banastre Tarleton, I have tried to stay as close to the known facts as possible. In instances where the historians disagree I have followed my own sense of the plausible.

For background information and descriptions of the Battle of Cowpens itself I have benefited from reading the following studies and documents: *A History of the Campaigns of 1780–81 in Southern America* by Banastre Tarleton (1787; reprint, Spartanburg, S.C.: Reprint Company, 1967); *Life of General Daniel Morgan* by James Graham (1856; reprint, Bloomingburg, N.Y.: Zebrowski Historical Services, 1993); *Colonial and Revolutionary History of Upper South Carolina* by J.B.O. Landrum (1897; reprint, Spartanburg, S.C.: Reprint Company, 1977); *The Green Dragoon* by Robert D. Bass (1957; reprint, Columbia: University of South Carolina Press, 1973); *Daniel Morgan: Revolutionary Rifleman* by Don Higginbotham (Chapel Hill: University of North Carolina Press, 1961); *The Battle of Cowpens* by Edwin S. Bears (Washington, D.C.: National Park Service, 1967); *From Savannah to Yorktown* by Henry Lumpkin (New York: Paragon House, 1981); *The Battle of Cowpens* by Kenneth Roberts (New York: Eastern Acorn Press, 1981); *With Fire and Sword: The Battle of Kings Mountain* by Wilma Dykeman (Washington, D.C.: National Park Service, 1981); *Battleground: South Carolina in the Revolution* by Warren Ripley (Charleston, S.C.: Post-Courier Books, 1983); *The Patriots at the Cowpens* by Bobby Gilmer Moss (Greenville, S.C.: Scotia Press, 1985); *Cowpens: Downright Fighting* by Thomas J. Fleming (Washington, D.C.: National Park Service, 1988); *Cowpens Battlefield: A Walking Guide* by Lawrence E. Babits (Johnson City, Tenn.: The Overmountain Press, 1993); *A Devil of a Whipping* by Lawrence E. Babits (Chapel Hill: University of North Carolina Press, 1998); *Partisans and Redcoats* by Walter Edgar (New York: William Morrow, 2001).

Finally, I would like to thank Elisabeth Scharlatt and the staff of Algonquin Books for their unfailing help in bringing this story to completion. I am especially grateful to my editors, Duncan Murrell and Shannon Ravenel, for their crucial patience, wisdom, and faith in this book.

BRAVE ENEMIES

A Short Note from the Author

A Reading and Discussion Guide

REACHING ACROSS BOUNDARIES

A Short Note from the Author

Many reviewers and readers have noted that several of my stories and novels are told from the point of view of a woman. They speak as though it is uncommon for men to write from the point of view of women characters. I like to point out that Daniel Defoe published *Moll Flanders* in 1722, one of the earliest English novels, about a woman's life, told in her own voice.

Reynolds Price, who has published several well-known novels narrated by women, says that all men are raised by women and therefore are familiar from infancy with women's voices, women's points of view. One of the models I had in mind when I first wrote from a woman's point of view in my 1992 novella *The Mountains Won't Remember Us* was Thomas Wolfe's story "The Web of Earth," a monologue spoken by his mother.

Modern fiction got started around the time a lot of women in Europe and England learned to read. From the first, novels were written primarily for an audience of women, whether authored by men or women. Fiction is about intimacy, about emotions and relationships, about detail, and often about the powerless and disadvantaged. Prose fiction is almost never heroic, in the older poetic sense. Novels are more often antiheroic; witness *Don Quixote, Crime and Punishment.*

It has been a great surprise to me to find myself drawn again and again to write stories about women, told by women. I always expected to write action stories, stories about warfare, wilderness, the frontier, stories about history and panthers, road-building and hunting. And I have written novels about all those things, but the surprise is that they are often narrated by women who happened to be there.

In the late 1980s I decided to write a novel about the battle of Cowpens in the American Revolution. At least one of my ancestors had fought in the battle, January 17, 1781, just down the mountain near Spartanburg. My dad, who loved history, had told me the story of the battle when I was a boy. I began doing research about the Revolutionary War in the Carolinas and found that Tarleton, the British commander who lost the battle, explained that he had ordered his men to fight after marching all night because he had reports the "Green River rifles" were on their way to join the Americans, and he wanted to fight before they arrived. I had grown up on Green River.

I wrote a version of the novel that became *Brave Enemies* in the early 1990s but knew it wasn't right. I knew the battle scenes were accurate but wasn't sure who the people fighting were. It was only years later, when I imagined Josie Summers, the sixteen-year-old who has been violated and is running away from home with no place to go, that the story really came alive for me. Once I heard her voice and began to feel her fear as she wandered into the wilderness, the story began to shape itself.

A writer's imagination is stimulated most by tasks that are difficult. Yeats talked about putting on an anti-mask, an opposite identity, to stretch the imagination and understanding. I think this may be the case with my fiction writing. Assuming the voice, the consciousness of a woman character in trouble, struggling to survive, is so alien, so difficult for me, it calls forth my best energy and discipline. I demand most of myself, for nothing less will work or bring the story into being.

I often say my best talent is for listening. I was the shy kid who sat in the corner while the women strung beans or peeled peaches. I listened to my mother and my aunts talking while the men were away. I became a fiction writer to get down some of the voices I heard by the fireplace or on the porch back then, and to tell the stories I heard about wars, about panthers and snakes and ghosts, about sickness and childbirth in mountain cabins, about the deaths of children.

I believe I write more about women characters than about men because women fascinate me. I am in awe of women, their toughness and vulnerability. I am drawn to stories of the powerless, people who survive in difficult times. I am drawn to stories where physical danger and hunger are real, and to vulnerable characters who can describe the struggles. I learn from my characters as I go, letting them tell their stories to me. They remind me of things I had forgotten I knew.

A READING AND DISCUSSION GUIDE

1. What lessons does Josie take away from her mother's marriage to Mr. Griffin? In what ways does her mother's marriage affect her relationship later with John?

2. Discuss Josie's actions leading up to her running away. Were they justified? What other choices could she have made?

3. In what ways is the harassment Josie experiences similar or dissimilar to what young women might encounter today?

4. The novel alternates between Josie's and John's points of view. What effect does this narration have on the way the story unfolds? With which character did you most identify and why?

5. Compare the role of faith in the lives of Josie and John. How does it inform who they are and how they behave?

6. Do you think that John has satisfactorily resolved his moral obligation to his church and his love for Josie? Was it ethical for him to support Josie's deception? And why doesn't he reveal Josie's identity to his parishioners? What exactly does he fear from them?

7. "Sometimes a woman has to be smart and swallow her pride," Josie confesses. "I decided I would resist the sergeant, but I would not holler out. If he overpowered me I would have to let him have his way. I would not give in, but I would not let him kill me either. The Lord would forgive me" (page 203). In what ways does Josie succeed at being a woman in man's world? Do you believe women today still need to swallow their pride?

8. In what ways do Josie's and John's journeys parallel each other after they're forced to separate?

9. What drives Josie to not only dress as a boy but also risk her life in battle? How successful do you think Josie is at passing herself off as "one of the boys" in Cox's militia company?

10. After all John has seen, he comes to a realization: "I had come to believe there was really no right side or wrong side in war. All killing was wrong and all hatred was wrong" (page 274). To what extent do you agree or disagree with this statement? How were you affected by the author's vivid depiction of the battle scenes?

11. The book opens with the epigraph from Thomas Jefferson: "Whensoever hostile aggressions . . . require a resort to war, we must meet our duty and convince the world that we are just friends and brave enemies." To what degree does that hold true in the Battle of Cowpens?

12. Who do you believe is the real hero of *Brave Enemies,* and why?

13. It has been said that in the best fiction there is no character who is entirely bad and no hero who is entirely good. Does that apply to the characters in *Brave Enemies*? And if so, in what ways?

Robert Morgan is the author of seven previous books of fiction, including *The Truest Pleasure*, a Southern Book Critics Circle Award winner for fiction, and the award-winning *New York Times* bestseller *Gap Creek*. He has received the 2007 American Academy of Arts and Letters Award for Literature and the North Carolina Award in Literature. He was raised on his family's farm in the North Carolina mountains and now lives in Ithaca, New York, where he teaches at Cornell University.

Other Algonquin Readers Round Table Novels

Saving the World, a novel by Julia Alvarez

While Alma Huebner is researching a new novel, she discovers the true story of Isabel Sendales y Gómez, who embarked on a courageous sea voyage to rescue the New World from smallpox. The author of *How the García Girls Lost Their Accents* and *In the Time of the Butterflies,* Alvarez captures the worlds of two women living two centuries apart but with surprisingly parallel fates.

"Fresh and unusual, and thought-provokingly sensitive." *—The Boston Globe*

"Engrossing, expertly paced." *—People*

AN ALGONQUIN READERS ROUND TABLE EDITION WITH READING GROUP GUIDE AND OTHER SPECIAL FEATURES • FICTION • ISBN-13: 978-1-56512-558-2

Water for Elephants, a novel by Sara Gruen

As a young man, Jacob Jankowski is tossed by fate onto a rickety train, home to the Benzini Brothers Most Spectacular Show on Earth. Amid a world of freaks, grifters, and misfits, Jacob becomes involved with Marlena, the beautiful young equestrian star; her husband, a charismatic but twisted animal trainer; and Rosie, an untrainable elephant who is the great gray hope for this third-rate show. Now in his nineties, Jacob at long last reveals the story of their unlikely yet powerful bonds, ones that nearly shatter them all.

"[An] arresting new novel. . . . With a showman's expert timing, [Gruen] saves a terrific revelation for the final pages, transforming a glimpse of Americana into an enchanting escapist fairy tale." *—The New York Times Book Review*

"Gritty, sensual and charged with dark secrets involving love, murder and a majestic, mute heroine." *—Parade*

AN ALGONQUIN READERS ROUND TABLE EDITION WITH READING GROUP GUIDE AND OTHER SPECIAL FEATURES • FICTION • ISBN-13: 978-1-56512-560-5

On Agate Hill, a novel by Lee Smith

A dusty box in the wreckage of a once prosperous plantation on Agate Hill in North Carolina contains the remnants of an extraordinary life: diaries, letters, poems, songs, newspaper clippings, court records, marbles, rocks, dolls, and bones. It's through these treasured mementos that the irrepressible Molly Petree comes alive. Spanning half a century, *On Agate Hill* follows Molly's journey through love, betrayal, motherhood, a murder trial—and back home to Agate Hill under circumstances she never could have imagined.

"Smith is such a beautiful writer, tough and full of grace, that soon you are lost in the half-light of Molly's haunted landscape, listening to the voices of the ghosts, wishing they'd let you stay longer." *—The Atlanta Journal-Constitution*

"The willful Molly is no hot-house flower, and her determination to live her own life—for better or worse—is the driving force of this powerful novel." *—USA Today*

AN ALGONQUIN READERS ROUND TABLE EDITION WITH READING GROUP GUIDE AND OTHER SPECIAL FEATURES • FICTION • ISBN-13: 978-1-56512-577-3

The Ghost at the Table, a novel by Suzanne Berne

When Frances arranges to host Thanksgiving at her idyllic New England farmhouse, she envisions a happy family reunion, one that will include her sister, Cynthia. But tension mounts between them as each struggles with a different version of the mysterious circumstances surrounding their mother's death twenty-five years earlier.

"Wholly engaging, the perfect spark for launching a rich conversation around your own table." —*The Washington Post Book World*

"A crash course in sibling rivalry." —*O: The Oprah Magazine*

AN ALGONQUIN READERS ROUND TABLE EDITION WITH READING GROUP GUIDE AND OTHER SPECIAL FEATURES • FICTION • ISBN-13: 978-1-56512-579-7

Responsible Men, a novel by Edward Schwarzschild

When a divorced man from a family of mostly upstanding salesmen decides to change his less-than-honorable ways, things do not go exactly as planned. This is the story of three generations of men struggling to be good sons and good fathers in a world of big dreams and bigger temptations.

"Marvelous. . . . It's impossible to avoid falling for Max." —*Entertainment Weekly*

"A compassionately and deftly told story."
—William Kennedy, Pulitzer Prize–winning author of *Ironweed* and *Roscoe*

AN ALGONQUIN READERS ROUND TABLE EDITION WITH READING GROUP GUIDE AND OTHER SPECIAL FEATURES • FICTION • ISBN-13: 978-1-56512-543-8